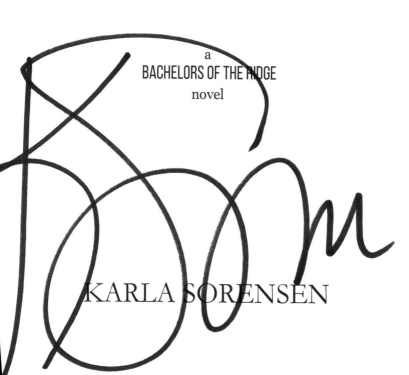

Sometimes we ha...
to h
longest for the
best things...

TRISTAN

a
BACHELORS OF THE RIDGE
novel

KARLA SORENSEN

To the women in my life who love fiercely, no matter what has happened in your past.
You were brave to tell me your stories, to let me pick your brain. But nothing can match the bravery it takes to continually believe in love, and be fearless in the pursuit of it.

I am certain of nothing but the holiness of the heart's affection, and the truth of imagination.

- John Keats

CHAPTER ONE

TRISTAN

I didn't fall in love with Anna Calder the first night I met her. I liked her. Was attracted to her. No, it wasn't the first night. Or the second, though after that I had a hard time pushing her from my thoughts.

It was the third night. Through the years, I did my best not to think about it. Of how she made me feel, the quiet spreading of peace that sitting near her brought me. But I was thinking about it tonight while I sanded down the edges of a bench with smooth, sure strokes. I could've used my electric handheld sander, but I wanted more control, and it took longer.

The sky had fallen dark outside, a product of the shortening days and cooler nights that were slowly introducing fall to Colorado. My workshop was quiet, other than the scratch of the sanding block against wood. Instead of what I was doing, I should've been at home getting ready for my friend Garrett's thirty-sixth birthday party.

Garrett, whose sister I'd been in love with since the third night I met her more than six years ago. That night sealed her into my bones and my blood, and even if I'd been gifted with the ability to reach inside and extract her, I wasn't sure that I would use it.

Without conscious thought, my hand stopped moving and I stared at the variegated wood grain, deeper now that I'd sanded it down further. I'd see her tonight, at his birthday party, and the thought washed me with pain. With longing. And with an ache that I'd never be strong enough to ignore.

After one last pass with the sanding block over the perfectly smooth edge, I took a deep breath and wiped the sawdust off my hands. The window in front of me showed a garish reflection from the bright fluorescent lights behind me. My features were distorted from the way I blocked the light, and that was fine by me.

I'd never wanted to meet my own eyes when I thought of Anna anyway.

That's what happened when you were in love with a married woman. You lost the ability to stare yourself down. Lost the ability to man the hell up and move on. Or maybe that was only me. Maybe I was the weakest person I'd ever known for not being able to move on from Anna. That's why I'd go to my friend's birthday party, with all their eyes on me with varying degrees of pity and sadness. Or maybe they didn't look at me that way, and I only felt like they did. To the credit of my friends, they never judged the sin I committed every time I looked at Anna across the room and felt the burn of her in my heart.

Anna didn't know, of course. And that was the other reason I struggled to meet my own gaze. Because the reflection of me staring back knew as well as the real me that I'd never tell her. I'd simply suffer in the truth of what I felt for her, and she'd stay with him, despite how unhappy she was.

Which is why I turned off all the lights, locked up the shop behind me and walked over the frost-frozen grass to where my truck was parked in the darkened lot. More often than not, I was the last person to leave work, no matter what time of year. My brother and I worked for our uncle's general contracting business, but my preference was to spend my time in the woodworking shop I'd built behind the main building. Any custom work that needed to be done for clients, or side jobs that didn't interfere with our schedule was done there, and I had very few interruptions.

My truck rumbled to life when I turned the key into the ignition, and my hand hesitated before turning on the radio. If I count the number of hours that I spent in silence, it should probably worry me. But useless noise, just to fill the quiet was a waste to me. Words should be spoken because they meant something, music played because it filled a void, or settled a mood.

That quiet was broken with the jarring ring of my cell phone. My jaw tightened, because most days I wanted to bury it in the backyard and never let it see the light of the day again. But I lifted the screen and swiped my thumb across to answer my brother's call.

"What is it?"

His laugh at my curt greeting didn't even grate anymore. Michael was my opposite in every possible way, but he was still the person who knew me best.

"You're coming, right?" he asked, nonplussed as always. My hand tightened on the steering wheel and I squinted against the bright cut of oncoming headlights. I grunted in answer and he chuckled under his breath. "Verbal confirmation, Tristan. Use your words."

I rolled my neck when I stopped for a red light and then sighed. "Yes."

Some people might explain further. If I'd been someone else, I might say that I didn't want to go, I was dreading going, or maybe something mundane like I still needed to grab a shower. Michael knew that about me, and respected it when it mattered most. Anna was something he didn't push me on. No one did, actually. Not even Garrett, who was fully aware of my feelings for his sister. His married sister.

I'd promised him a long time ago that I'd never step over that line, I'd never pursue her while she was with him. Even though we all knew she was miserable with him, even though he was a dick who didn't deserve to trade air with her, I'd always respect her decision to stay.

"Great. Brooke and I are heading over as soon as the babysitter gets here." There was commotion in the background, as there often was when I spoke to my brother. He lived with his fiancée Brooke, and her almost two-year-old twins. His life was the very definition of noise and chaos, laughter and motion. Michael's life with Brooke was bright and alive.

Whereas I lived in a self-imposed space of hushed noises and intentional silence, merely because it fit my mood and my insides. It matched everything for me. How I looked at the world. How I looked at myself.

Michael cleared his throat, and I realized I hadn't responded. "See you soon."

"Don't take too long doing your man bun, bro."

I rolled my eyes and a short laugh escaped me in a puff of reluctant air. When you kept your hair long, the jokes never stopped. Especially when your younger brother was a jackass.

"I won't."

When Michael hung up, I tossed my phone onto the seat next to me and pulled into the driveway of my house. I used to share it with him, until he moved in with Brooke. It was just one more piece of my life, the periphery of it, that had changed in the last couple years.

Within the space of a few streets in our neighborhood, The Ridge at Alta Vista, lived all of my closest friends. Less than three years ago, we were all single, and the proximity wasn't just what introduced us all to each other, but it was convenient, made doing things like hiking on weekends, sharing beer during a football game easier.

Cole still lived across the street, but now he shared his home with his wife Julia and their foster son. Garrett and his wife Rory were across the street, as well.

Dylan, who lived a couple streets over, had been the first to fall down the rabbit hole with his longtime girlfriend Kat. Over the next two years, they all fell like dominoes into a blissfully paired existence. Michael's fall into domestication was the most recent, and watching him move seamlessly into his life with Brooke left me as the lone man standing, as it were.

The only unchanged thing left from a phase in life that felt incredibly far away now that I looked back on it. Unchanged in every way, really.

When I let myself into the house through the garage, I realized that yet again, I'd forgotten to leave any lights on. It was never on purpose, because I usually didn't realize that I'd left the house in complete darkness until I walked back in the door and almost felt swallowed by it.

The glaring symbolism didn't escape me, that I consistently forgot to take action that would make coming home more welcoming, make the space seem less dark and obviously empty.

The shower I took was quick and cold, my movements methodical as I dried myself off and threw the towel onto the bathroom floor when I was finished. The clothes I grabbed were the first I laid my hands on, jeans and a gray Henley. From the stack of hair bands on my nightstand, I snatched one and raked my fingers through my damp hair to pull it back low. Not once did I look at myself in the mirror to see the fruits of my labor. No one would care anyway. I certainly didn't.

Knowing I was ready, knowing that I had zero in the way of excuses before walking across the street to Garrett and Rory's house, made the pit in my stomach yawn uncomfortably. How was I not used to being in the same place as Anna yet?

How had I not steeled myself from knowing that in that home, she'd be smiling and laughing, she'd be kind and talk to me if I approached her. She'd be there alone.

She was always alone.

That's what gave me the pit. That's what made it even harder when I thought about whether I wanted to go or not. If *he* was there, with a hand low on her back, refilling her drink, making her laugh, I'd be able to yank down the steel wall necessary to shut her out.

But he never was.

Which meant I was forced to see her suffer, see the slight pinch of loneliness clear behind her dark eyes, which was as painful as knowing that she still wasn't mine. It was worse, actually.

I let out a slow, heavy breath and stood, snatching my jacket from where I'd tossed it over the back of the chair in my bedroom. While I walked across the street to Garrett's, I didn't even take the time to shrug it over my shoulders, because I liked how the cool air felt.

When I ascended the front porch, there was sound spilling from the house like the walls and windows weren't even there. Like the happiness inside was too big for one space.

Just as I was about to knock, Garrett's wife Rory opened the door with a wide smile on her face. "Hey, Tristan. Come on in."

I nodded and walked past her. Garrett was in the kitchen talking to a couple I didn't recognize, probably someone that he and Rory worked with at the company they ran. Michael and Brooke hadn't arrived yet, but I could see Cole and his wife Julia sitting on the couch. A few other unfamiliar faces filled the room, some that weren't unfamiliar, but not the one I wanted to see.

No Anna.

It was as second nature as breathing, to do a quick scan of the room and look for a glimpse of her inky black hair, a flash of the smile I loved so much.

It was one of the first things I'd noticed about her, actually. Her smile. When you weren't someone who did it often—smiled often—you noticed the people who were generous with theirs. Not just generous, but genuine too. And Anna was.

Never in my life did I fight the impulse to smile back at someone as much as I did when I was watching her, or in the moments speaking to her, sitting next to her, rare that those moments were.

My throat was rough and dry, chalked with disappointment at not seeing her, despite the apprehension I always felt before I did, but I swallowed past it. Rory was talking to me, something about where drinks were, so I nodded absently. Garrett smiled in my direction and I thumped him on the back as I passed, not wanting to interrupt his conversation.

The beer in the fridge was cold, and I opened it as I walked to where Cole and Julia were sitting. She smiled sweetly at me.

"Tristan, can you prove a point for me?"

I froze and Cole laughed.

Julia rolled her eyes but pulled out her phone and flipped it around so that I could see a picture of a wood headboard, some DIY article that would likely make the project seem easier than it really would turn out to be.

"It's a headboard," I said slowly.

Her mouth twitched as she fought a smile. "Yes, it is. And I'm trying to convince my husband here that it would be a piece of cake to make one for the guest room. It wouldn't be that difficult, would it?"

Cole gave me a look. A *don't you dare agree with her right now* look.

To buy myself some time, I took a sip of beer and very much wished I'd sat somewhere else. But she raised her eyebrows and I winced.

"It wouldn't be difficult for me." I tipped the bottle toward Cole. "But I can't say whether it would be easy for him."

"Hey," Cole said.

I lifted an eyebrow. He narrowed his eyes right back.

Julia stifled a laugh at his incensed reaction.

I sighed, resigned myself to the fate of a man who enjoyed projects like that. "Send me the link. I can make one for you in between projects."

She gushed her thanks, Cole smirked like he'd just gotten exactly what he wanted, and I tried to relax in my seat while I took another glance around.

Nothing. But she'd come. Anna was somewhat of a secondary fixture in our group of friends. Her presence wasn't a given when we got together. But for her brother's birthday, she'd come.

"So how's everything in your life, Tristan? We've been so MIA with the baby, I feel like I don't know if there's anything new going on."

"Nothing new with me." I gave her a small smile.

"Oh," she said and flicked her eyes to Cole.

As soon as it left her lips, I questioned my ability to survive the entire night. I liked Julia. She made Cole happy. But that one syllable was so laden with subtext, I was surprised it didn't hit the ground on its way to me. *Poor Tristan. We're all here with our person, and your person is an impossibility.*

"Well," she continued brightly, "It's good to see you. Even if there's nothing new and exciting."

"Yeah. Same."

Cole gave me a concerned look that made me want to dig my eyes out so I wouldn't have to see it. "You sound like you're getting a colonoscopy."

I gave him a dry look when Julia snorted. "Nice." Before they could ask something else that I'd likely read far too much into or really not want to talk about, I tilted my chin at the door. "Are Dylan and Kat coming?"

Cole shrugged. "Not sure."

"They're not," Julia interrupted. "I heard Rory say that Dylan got called into work because one of his assistant managers got sick or something and Kat wasn't feeling well."

I nodded. It was a weird feeling, to miss my friends, miss what we used to have, but also desperately crave my time alone. Someone opened the front door and I fought the urge to look. Instead, I watched Julia's reaction, which was blank. Which meant it wasn't

Anna. Even though she knew Anna the least out of anyone in our group, she'd have a smile, maybe a quick glance in my direction to gauge my reaction.

The volume of the music playing from the speakers mounted in the wall increased in volume, and Julia swayed in her seat a bit. In her lap was a throw pillow that should have looked fussy with the rest of the fabric, but it didn't. It went perfectly.

Because Anna picked it out.

Though Rory had added touches of her personality since she and Garrett got married, Anna had done all the interior design when Garrett bought the place brand new. I pinched my eyes shut, not caring if it made me look crazy. Because of a *throw pillow*.

I stood from my chair, ignoring the curious looks from Cole and Julia. "Just need some air," I muttered and gestured to the slider leading out to the back porch. They'd set up propane heaters in case anyone gathered out on the back porch, but so far the space was blissfully empty.

When I pulled the slider closed, the noise muted and I could breathe more deeply. I sat heavily in the chair closest to me and set my beer down with a hard click.

"Get your shit together," I whispered harshly, annoyance crashing over me as I pinched the bridge of my nose.

Then I snorted, because yeah, like it was that easy.

CHAPTER TWO

ANNA

From where I sat at the vanity in the master bathroom, I could hear my husband on his computer. Marcus had a way of typing that made it sound like he was attacking the keyboard with a two by four. The first year of marriage, I teased him about it. He had rolled his eyes, but nothing else. At the time, I thought that was a sign of indulging me, maybe even slight amusement.

Now I knew better. Beneath my ribs, my heart didn't even blip with disappointment anymore when he ignored me. I'd lost that particular reaction sometime around our fifth anniversary. Apathy was the most comforting and useful talent that I could hone, that I perfected in order to get through every day.

It was harder to be apathetic to the looks I got from my family, who still couldn't understand why I stayed.

Join the club, people. Sometimes you made the same decision over and over so many times that your reasoning got lost in the mundane actions of living every single day. Despite that, the memory of your reasoning felt like enough to hold on tightly, hold on with desperation sometimes. Most days, it was like holding onto smoke.

I stared blankly in the mirror, my brush making slow strokes down the length of my hair until it shone glossy black under the bright lights of the bathroom. The room was beautiful and white. White marble, white floors and white trim, each mirror and light fixture strategically placed when I'd designed it.

Against all of that starkness, the red of my shirt looked violent. Almost garish. When I set the brush down, my eyes caught on my wedding ring that sat heavy on my finger.

My thumb worried the bottom curve of metal, and the diamond caught the light and sparkled. After eight years, it had stayed securely in between the middle and pinky fingers, locked into place by one small knuckle. That didn't seem like enough to hold an anchor in place, did it? One small rounded bone under fragile skin. That was it. But the ring never came off. Another stubborn act on my part, of course.

Me staying in my marriage, this quiet place that I'd learned to accept, was the most stubborn thing I'd ever done in my life. So stubborn in fact, that my father's last wish for me in his will had been that I leave Marcus.

I laughed under my breath, the small puff of sound loosening the tight band around my chest. That had been almost two years earlier. During the reading of his will, Dad had given me the out they all wanted for me.

All I had to do was divorce Marcus, and I'd get my half of Dad's life insurance policy. Across the table, I knew that my mom and my brother Garrett desperately wanted me to take the opening. Marcus hadn't even gone to the funeral with me. Wasn't sitting next to me at that table when we heard my dad's final wishes. The man who raised me, who may not have shared my blood, but gave me every ounce of stubbornness and determination that kept me with Marcus.

My phone dinged with a text from the bedroom and I blinked one last time at my reflection and stood from the small stool. I wiped my hands down my black pants and took a deep breath when I saw that it was from Mom.

Mom: Give your brother a kiss for me, and don't drink too much if you're going to drive home! Love you, sweetheart.

A smile crossed my face, and my chest loosened even more. Even though I'd been out of the house for over ten years, my mom still had the uncanny ability to know when I needed to hear from her. Of her two grown children, I was the one who needed to hear that she loved me with a fierceness that occasionally took me by surprise.

My fingers hovered over her name, and I almost called her, just to hear someone speak my name. Hear someone ask me how my day was. But she'd worry if I did that. She always worried, but if she heard sadness in my voice, it would make it worse.

Me: I love you too.
Me: You know, you could always crash his birthday party and drink with me.

Imagining Garrett's face if our mother walked into his house made me snicker. That would be worth it a million times over.

Mom: Oh goodness, no. I couldn't. But you're sweet to invite an old lady. Call me tomorrow?
Me: I will. <3

I tucked my phone into my purse and headed down the curving stairs of mahogany, my heels clicking quietly as I did. Marcus was on the couch, football muted on the TV screen and his face blue from the light of his laptop. His typing didn't stop, nor did he look at up me, even though I stood waiting for a solid minute

He never did, unless I specifically asked him to.

"I've got Garrett's birthday party tonight."

Marcus jerked his chin up while he continued typing, a brief recognition and probably all I was going to get. I had to suck in a slow breath at that damn typing. Loud, obnoxious pecks at the keys that seemed determined to drown out my very presence.

I turned away, and the sound lessened in intensity. A hot burn of embarrassment clawed its way through my chest, lodged in my throat. *Why are you like this?* I wanted to scream at him, but I swallowed instead. Because if I did that, he wouldn't even care. He'd give me a pitying look and go back to whatever the hell he was always working on.

Always working. Always something else more important. Yes, his job was important. Yes, I knew that a senior research analyst for a major manufacturing firm didn't always work set hours and that his deadlines stressed him out.

But I was his wife. His *wife*.

Instead of walking away, I pivoted to face him, which made him pause. His eyes flicked in my direction, but they didn't actually rest on my face, just somewhere around my hands.

"Are you sure you don't want to come?" I asked, hating myself for it. No longer did I ask him if he *could* come. Because we both know he could if he wanted to. It was never about Marcus's *ability* to do anything. It was the complete and stunning lack of desire. Often, I wondered what he was like at work. If the people around him got the same detachment.

It wasn't lost on me, not in the slightest, that the longer I was with him, the more of his traits I absorbed. Suddenly the apathy that I used as armor felt like a shackle, and I fought not to shudder in an attempt to disrobe it.

"Marcus," I said sharply and he finally lifted his gaze enough that I could see his face. His blue eyes weren't cold, simply detached. Maybe a shade surprised, but even that was deeply hidden. "Will you come with me to my brother's birthday party?"

There was no shame in asking him anymore. I'd lost the shame a long time ago. What I'd lost was the energy to keep doing it. But as he held my eyes—for the first time all week—I felt something crackling through my hands, a restless energy that I didn't know what to do with.

After another prolonged beat of silence, he looked away. "I'm working. But give him my best."

Very slowly, I nodded. Instead of unleashing the million snarky responses bouncing at the tip of my tongue, I swallowed. As I drove to my brother and sister-in-law's home, I couldn't help but feel a pathetic sense of victory that I'd asked him. That I'd forced him to *see* me.

That was the saddest reality of my life. That one small moment feeling like a victory. But I knew why. Long ago, I knew that this was all my marriage to Marcus would be. He refused to speak to a therapist, because he saw nothing wrong with the coexistence that we'd slowly evolved into.

Or if he did, he certainly never showed it to me.

When I pulled onto Garrett and Rory's street, I took a deep breath. No one really gave me pitying looks anymore when I showed up places alone.

Garrett usually gave me the biggest reaction, but his always fell into straight-up brotherly rage. Every single time my husband failed to show up, there was a banked fire in my big brother's eyes that was as comforting as it was painful.

The driveway was packed with cars, and the street as well, so I could only hope that Garrett would be busy enough with his guests that we wouldn't have to have yet another conversation about Marcus. About why he wasn't where he should be. About why I stayed.

Things I didn't have it in me to answer, or to discuss. My week at work had been insane, and not in the good way, with my carpenter backing out on a huge project because of a broken arm, and a client who would not be happy to hear that she might not get the multitude of custom wood furniture that she was expecting.

So yes, all I wanted to do was relax and laugh and have a few drinks in a place where people were happy to see me, happy to be around me.

With Garrett's present tucked under my arm, I walked to the door quickly, as I'd forgotten my coat in my haste to get out of the house. I didn't knock, simply slipped through the door to the warmth inside. Music was playing, people were laughing, and instantly, I felt better.

Rory spied me from across the room, and came straight to me with her arms out for a hug. My sister-in-law was pretty much the exact opposite of me physically. Tall and blonde, with bright blue eyes and sharp features, the type of beauty that was intimidating if you didn't know her.

"I'm not used to you being late. Everything okay?" she asked as she held me tightly. I laughed against the familiar scent of her, even though my eyes stung a bit from the jarring comfort of a hug.

You only noticed things like that when your life had a visceral lack of touch. Of affection.

The subtext of her question was clear, and that warmed me as much as her hug. *Are you okay?*

I nodded. "Took longer than I expected to get ready."

She snorted and gave me a narrow-eyed look. "It *better* take you a long time to get ready. If you told me you rolled out of bed with hair like that, I'd have to punch you."

"Ahh, if only you'd been born with my excellent Korean genes, you could hair have like this too." I snapped my fingers. "Tough break, Blondie."

Rory laughed as I followed her to the kitchen. I knew a lot of people at the party, since it was a mix of Garrett and Rory's friends, and people who worked at our father's company, Calder Financial Services. Well, Garrett and Rory's company now. Since Dad's passing, they ran it together. I'd never felt the need to work there, and fortunately, my parents never pushed me on it.

When I was narrowing my decision between architecture at UC Denver and interior design at The Art Institute of Colorado, my dad had merely hugged me and said that whatever made me happy, made me excited to get out of bed in the morning ... that should be my choice. Interior design it was. And I did love my career, even on weeks like this when it stressed me the hell out.

Often, I thought back on those words, and I knew that's why my father hated my relationship with Marcus so much. It went beyond the fact that Marcus and I didn't make each other happy. It was the fact that it had started draining happiness from the rest of my life too. Ultimately, it's why I couldn't be angry at my dad for including my caveat in his will.

But taking that money, getting paid for leaving my husband made me feel like the cheapest, slimiest kind of person. But I couldn't fault him for doing it. Above all, he loved me. My mom and Garrett and Rory loved me, which is why they cared enough to be hurt on my behalf.

Rory lifted up a bottle of Pinot Grigio with a question in her eyes, and I nodded. She poured a healthy amount into a glass and handed it over to me. Normally I'd sniff it before sipping, but I took a large gulp instead. Amusement might have curled her lips up, but sympathy coated her eyes, and I had to look away briefly.

That's what I hated about coming to these things alone. I didn't feel sympathy or pity for myself, because I made a choice every single day to stay in that house with Marcus. But I couldn't control how others reacted, and I couldn't control how hard it was to glance around the room and see couples laugh and touch and kiss so easily. Did they have any idea how lucky they were?

I saw Cole and Julia in the corner, and he wrapped an arm

around her waist while they spoke to someone I didn't recognize. Did she still warm up on the inside at his simple touch? My guess was that she did. They'd gone through hell after getting divorced years ago, before fighting their way back to each other. But not everyone understood how fortunate they were.

Absently, I rubbed at my chest and realized Rory was still staring at me. I smiled and took a slightly more acceptable drink from my wine. As I swallowed, Garrett walked up with a smile on his face that I roughly equated to more than one beer.

"My beautiful sister!" He wrapped his arms around me and hugged me so tight that my feet lifted off the ground. I was still laughing when he set me back down, relieved at his mood, because I needed that happy around me. He eyed me. "Where's my present?"

"Who said I got you one?" I elbowed him in the stomach when he flicked at my arm. "Ow."

Rory rolled her eyes and pulled him away from me. "Come on, birthday boy. You told Marie we'd go over and meet her new boyfriend."

I smiled when they walked away, content to watch the people around me. Leaning against the kitchen counter, I looked from face to face, only one or two of them unfamiliar. But all couples.

That was pretty typical at these types of gatherings, to be surrounded by couples. Usually the only exception to the evenly paired parties was one of Garrett's friends, who I spotted out on the back patio.

I tilted my head when I realized Tristan was sitting outside by himself. Visible because of the lights mounted on the house, I could see the broad frame of his shoulders as he sat on a patio chair, his head tilted up to the dark sky. He was someone who I never let myself think of too much.

Mainly because *he* was too much.

His hair was too long.

Too many tattoos. Too handsome. Too quiet. Too mysterious.

Too *everything.*

The first few times I was around Tristan, he was someone I liked instantly. Warmed to almost immediately. But that had faded quickly.

We kept a polite relationship over the years, every now and then veering beyond the warm edge of friendship, but I couldn't help but wonder about him sitting out in the dark by himself at a party. Before I allowed myself to indulge the seed of curiosity, I took a fortifying sip of wine and went to speak to someone else.

CHAPTER THREE

TRISTAN

There was always a small ripple of awareness across the surface of my skin when I shared space with Anna. Maybe she wasn't looking at me from inside the house, but she was there all the same. It was just one of the million things that made it impossible to move on from her. How could my body react so instantly if she wasn't someone to me? If she wasn't *meant* to be someone to me?

But every time, every single time, that justification was followed by the swift punch of impotency. Of helplessness. If I respected her less, if I didn't care about possible pain that I might cause her, I could sweep her in my arms, tell her how I feel. Let words of my constancy over the years fill whatever deathly quiet, ripped-open hole he'd left inside of her heart.

No one had come outside to join me, and for that I was thankful. My hesitancy in coming tonight was obvious as I sat in the dark.

Sometimes it was harder to be around her than others, and the jittery sensation caused by her presence told me that tonight would be one of the hard nights.

I'd see her and want her even more. My hands would curl into fists from the desire to reach out to her. My heart would thunder in my chest if she looked my way.

Under my breath, I growled. With shaking hands, I gripped the sides of my head and lowered my elbows to my knees to brace them there.

It was a miracle that the people around me didn't think me insane. Or maybe they did. They probably should have. Hot licks of shame filled me, embarrassment quick on its heels. Then weakness. Because I let the awareness of her pull my head to the side, where my gaze found her unerringly.

Standing in profile to me, she was holding a wine glass and smiling at whoever was speaking. Next to her was my brother's fiancée, Brooke, who said something to make Anna laugh. My lungs squeezed and I turned away. Seeing her laugh frayed the edges of my sanity on nights like this. If seeing her sad was difficult, then her happiness, that light and warmth that first drew me to her, was equally as painful.

I loved seeing Anna happy. Over the years, I saw it less and less, but the punch was the same. The pain came from the knowledge that I couldn't give her that. I'd never be able to give her that.

Desperation made my throat close up, and I pinched my eyes shut against the rising scream in my head that I needed to let this go. Let her go. Move on once and for all.

How? bellowed my heart and my head. *How can I if I haven't already?*

The slider opened quietly behind me, the sounds of the party brief and loud before it closed again. It wasn't Anna. She hadn't sought privacy with me in years, and I knew better than to torture myself that way. Knew better than to put us in that position.

"You gonna puke on my porch?" Garrett asked as he took the

seat next to me. "Or just feeling moodier than usual?"

A reluctant smile pulled at the edge of my lips, but it didn't soothe the raw edge to my feelings. Normally I had no problem keeping them to myself, but tonight for some reason, I wanted to talk to someone about it.

That should have worried me, but it didn't. I'd been friends with Garrett long enough to know that I could trust him with how I felt. He'd been aware of my feelings for Anna for a couple years, and he was no more rushed to tell her about them than I was.

I briefly glanced at him over my shoulder. "You allow moodiness on your birthday? I figured you'd be more demanding than that."

He shrugged and took a sip of his beer. "I'm feeling generous tonight."

"Why's that?"

"You go first." Garrett briefly looked back into the house, and I had a feeling he was looking at his sister. "Unless I can guess what it's about?"

I sighed heavily and leaned back in my chair. More than anything, I wanted to shove all my words back down my throat, even if it hurt and I'd never be able to let them back out again. But even after swallowing a couple times, I couldn't.

"I wish I knew how to let go of this," I said in a low voice. The words came out so quietly that I wondered if he even heard me at first.

"You've tried?" Garrett asked lightly.

Under my breath, I snorted. "Yeah."

That I wouldn't explain to him. Besides Michael, Garrett was probably the only person I felt even remotely comfortable discussing Anna with, but as her brother, there were still limits. They knew I wasn't someone to indiscriminately sleep around, but it still wasn't something I needed to share with him.

"See, I should've known better than to come out here. You're gonna depress me on my birthday, aren't you?"

"It's very possible."

He laughed. Garrett was always laughing. That's why having this conversation with him more than anyone was odd. But he'd also shoot straight with me, because Anna was his little sister.

Slowly, Garrett shifted in his chair so that he faced me more fully. "Can I ask you something?"

"Like I could stop you."

He tipped his beer bottle at me. "True." With his free hand, he scratched the side of his face. "How did this happen, man? I mean, objectively, I know Anna is pretty. I know she's nice and funny and smart. But you've got this hippie Jesus thing going and I know you don't have to work very hard to get female attention. You might need to explain to me the whole long-suffering, unrequited love bullshit you've held onto for so long. No offense or anything."

Now it was my turn to laugh. Or laugh as much as I was capable of, because it sounded hoarse, rusty and painful coming up my throat. To say that Anna was *pretty* was such a gross understatement, it was almost tragic.

I wanted to turn and look at her just to remind myself of just exactly how perfectly beautiful she was. And even though Garrett wouldn't believe me if I said it, that wasn't the thing that stuck her into my mind like a burr.

It was as simple and as complex as I'd never met anyone who made me feel the way she did. It could have been one interaction. It could have been ten, but the fact was that I couldn't shake it. Couldn't shake her.

"No offense taken," I told him truthfully.

While Garrett knew how I felt, we'd only had one conversation about it. No history, no specific questions, just a brother reminding me that his little sister was married, and therefore off-limits.

What I wanted to start with was that the night I met her, I didn't even realize she was his sister. Anna had been adopted from South Korea when she was only an infant, so Garrett's light coloring obviously was nothing like the woman who'd sat across the coffee table from me.

24

Anna was all darkness, a fitting description for the way she bled like an ink stain through my heart so quickly. Like the color of her hair, her eyes. Not her smile though. That was the brightest, most painfully lovely smile I'd ever seen in my life. It covered her face in a way that no part wasn't transformed instantly. I'd never met anyone who smiled with every part of their face like that.

Waxing poetic about her smile wasn't what Garrett wanted or even needed to hear.

"I didn't know she was married the first couple times I talked to her," I started, unable to look at him. My jaw clenched while I thought about the night we met. Now I knew she was just being friendly, but at the time, I thought she was flirting. "I think you and I had been friends for … I don't know, a year or so at that point. I was sitting on your couch and you had all those awful pillows. I tossed one aside, so it wasn't touching me, and she saw me do it."

Garrett burst out laughing. "Oh man, Anna loved picking out all those pillows for me when she decorated the house."

I nodded and took a deep breath. "She asked if I was too masculine to like decorative pillows, and somehow," I trailed off, remembering it as best I could so many years later, "somehow that turned into a discussion about design principles. She found out I built furniture and I found out she was a designer. We started swapping stories, and she was … fascinating, I guess."

Hearing the words come out of my mouth, I felt like an idiot admitting this to her brother. But no more of an idiot than feeling the way I did about a married woman so many years later.

"So you've been in love with her for years because she was fascinating?" he asked dryly.

My voice had an edge when I answered. "No, of course not." My hands curled in fists on the tops of my legs. It was impossible for Garrett to understand what it was like for me, because he could talk to anyone about anything. That was not a talent I possessed. Meeting new people in social settings usually drained me to the point that I craved solitude for days afterward.

Small talk always felt vaguely like a competition to me, stupid surface level bullshit about the weather and how much we all pretend to love our jobs and one-up each other with how busy we are and how stressed we are like it's a badge of honor.

It's why I avoided it, gravitated to the people who didn't rely on it. Most people thought I was an ass when they met me because of it, but that never happened with Anna.

Putting that into words for Garrett, trying to simplify the way that felt to me, back when I didn't even know the guys all that well, it was hard.

"You know I don't like small talk," I started, and Garrett smiled.

"Uh-huh."

"When I talked to her those first couple times, I never had that uncomfortable feeling. Not once. It was ... easy to talk to her, which is not common for me. She's smart. So damn smart, and driven and kind and funny. And I *didn't* know she was married, I swear."

My voice rose with each word, and by the end, my chest was heaving unnecessarily. Garrett was quiet, but it wasn't judgment. When I glanced over at him, he was processing what I'd said.

"When did you find out she was married?"

I laughed harshly. "The night I decided to ask her out. I don't even know if you remember, but we were all at some charity baseball game that you roped us into. She and I were next to each other in the batting order, and she was yelling at the umpire about a strike zone the size of a pea." I pinched the bridge of my nose remembering it. "I was laughing before I even realized it. I don't ... I've never been someone who laughed easily. Not since I was a boy. We didn't have much to laugh about growing up. At least I didn't."

My friends knew about my and Michael's old man walking out when we were young, so Garrett merely nodded. "How old were you when your dad left again?"

"Five," I said tersely. "He came around for a while, did stuff with us. But not very often. Got less and less until I was in high school, then he just stopped showing up."

"No wonder you're such a moody bastard."

I tilted my chin up to the sky again and let out a heavy breath. "Yeah."

"And Anna made you laugh."

My eyes closed and I was right back to where I was sitting next to her in that dugout. She was wearing ridiculous knee socks and punching into her glove like she was a major leaguer. From the moment I sat next to her, I knew I'd want that game to last all night.

Even years later, if someone asked me to pinpoint what Anna did to make me fall in love with her so quickly, so easily, in a way that had only deepened after years of getting to know her from a distance, I don't think I could make a list.

Because she didn't *do* anything. It was the recognition that she was different. That around her, I felt different.

I'd only known my friends about a year, and they still heckled me about how quiet I was. How they seemingly had to force me into being social.

But sitting next to her in that musty dugout, on a cold metal bench that made my ass go numb, I knew I could've sat and talked to her all night.

"Oh look," some idiot on the team had said, "he does speak occasionally. At least we know it's just us he won't interact with."

He meant it as a joke, some guy whose name I couldn't even remember now. It wasn't a new one for me, and it didn't bother me anymore, but at the time, sitting next to this beautiful woman who made me want to smile and laugh, I felt uncomfortable for the way I was. How I must come off.

And she turned and looked at me, appraising my face with a sweet, unassuming smile on her own. "I think Tristan just likes to talk with people who know how to make their words count."

Like she hadn't just plucked a cord of deep understanding in my heart, she turned back to the guy. "Knowing how not to waste someone's time simply to hear your own voice is a pretty amazing talent, actually."

In the moment, there was no possible way she could have known what those words meant to me. My whole life, I'd felt the need to explain the way I was, but dreaded the actual doing of it. Explain that it wasn't personal when I retreated. Explain that sitting back and observing all the things happening around me was my preference.

As she settled back next to me and blew out a bright pink bubble with the gum in her mouth, I couldn't help but look at her with awe.

Oblivious to what was boiling over inside of me, illogical feelings of bright, coppery love, she tossed up her gloved hand and told the ump that he needed an eye transplant.

My mouth opened to ask her if she'd like to get dinner after the game, or a drink, or if she'd just sit in that dugout and talk to me for a while, when she pulled her glove off.

And there it was. Big and bright and glittering, resting on her small hand, her delicate finger. And the breath whooshed from my body like someone had thrown a boulder at my stomach.

"Are you okay?" she asked, turning with concern in her dark eyes. "I'll leave the ump alone if you want. I'm just kidding about slashing his tires after the game."

The whole time I was remembering, Garrett stayed quiet. Just a small blip of time to anyone else who was there, but I left that baseball game feeling like someone had gutted me, because I'd just lost something that was never mine to begin with.

I nodded to answer Garrett's question. He didn't need to know exactly how pathetic I'd felt in that moment.

"It only got worse the first time I actually met him."

There was no explanation needed as to who he was. Marcus Callahan. Garrett's face tightened in annoyance.

"He's such a dick. She deserves so much better than him." He cut his eyes over to me apologetically. "Sorry, that probably doesn't help."

"It's okay," I mumbled.

That line of thinking was on a constant loop in my head. *If* she'd

28

been happy. *If* he loved her, if he ever showed up for her. If he made her laugh, made her smile, I'd have been able to let her go.

"It's not okay though," Garrett said, shaking his head.

Instead of brushing it aside like I wanted to, I closed my eyes. "I know it's not. And believe me, I know how pathetic it is that I think it too. Every time I look in the mirror, I know what kind of man it makes me that I can't let her go."

Garrett chose his words carefully before speaking. "I can't speak to that, because I think you're one of the best men I know, Tristan. And I can't tell you whether you should force her from your head, no one can answer that for you, or tell you how to do it." He took a long sip of his beer and sighed. "What I know is that I love my sister. I know that I hate that she's married to that douche canoe. I know that I think she should leave him. But I also know that no one can make Anna make that decision, just like no one can force you to let her go. And I'll support and love her regardless of what she does."

I looked over at him. "You realize that you're no help whatsoever, right?"

He shrugged helplessly. "It's kind of a shit situation, man. That's not my fault."

"You were supposed to come out here and say, yes, move on. There's no hope for you."

Until I said it, I hadn't even realized it was what I was waiting for him to say. Often it was hard for me—sometimes physically—to put voice to the way I was feeling. This entire exchange was completely out of the ordinary for me.

The way he looked over at me at my quietly spoken plea made me uncomfortable, and I shifted in my chair.

Garrett pulled in a slow breath before he spoke. "Then act normal tonight. Go in there and say hi. Be nice. Be friendly. Talk to her like you did when she saw you shove the pillow off of you. Like you did in the dugout. And if you walk away tonight and think there's no hope for you, then yes. Move on." His eyes practically glowed with intensity, and it gave me a strange sense of foreshadowing, like Garrett was speaking of something even he didn't understand. "If you leave tonight and still feel like there's nothing there for you except misery and pain and hopelessness, then move on from her. You deserve better than this situation too, Tristan. You realize that, right? As much as Anna does, you deserve better than this situation."

I pushed up out of my chair and paced along the edge of the patio, his words causing a strange, raw panic in my veins. In theory, I knew he was right.

Bottom line. I knew he was right. I didn't look into the house, because I couldn't, until I felt like I had more control of my emotions.

"Okay," I said after a few heavy beats of silence.

Garrett nodded slowly. "Okay."

After I took a few deep breaths, the panic receded into something less visceral. Into determination.

I could do this. I could go inside and say hello, and ask how she'd been. She'd lie and say she was fine, say she was happy, and I'd walk back across the street to my quiet, dark house and figure out how the hell to move on from her. For good, this time.

And that's when Brooke opened the slider with a wide smile on her face. "Here's Tristan." She looked over her shoulder. "Anna, he's out here!"

Garrett and I traded a quick glance. My face was probably stamped with panic, his was blatant amusement. Asshole.

"What's up, Brooke?" My voice sounded like nails were crawling up my throat.

She held open the door, and Anna walked out behind her. My breath stuttered in my lungs when she smiled nervously at me.

"Anna was just telling me about a problem she has, and you are *exactly* the person to save her."

Garrett swiped a hand over his mouth to cover his incredulous smile, and my stomach bottomed out entirely.

Hope was there, terrifying and hot, and suddenly I was in a position I hadn't been in for a very long time, the sole focus of Anna's attention.

CHAPTER FOUR

ANNA

"What Brooke means is that I have a work problem I hope you can help with," I rushed to explain in the vacuum of sound that her dramatic proclamation left. My brother wasn't looking at me, which gave me pause, but Brooke looked like someone had just dropped a million bucks in her lap, so I wasn't about to kill her idea. In truth, it was a really good idea. In fact, I couldn't believe I hadn't thought about it earlier.

Tristan looked up at me and nodded slowly, his eyes thoughtful and his mouth in a straight, serious line. But he didn't say anything. My fingers knit together in front of me, and he noticed, a slight furrow in his dark eyebrows when he did.

"What's the problem?" he asked quietly.

Brooke cleared her throat and tapped Garrett on the shoulder. "Let's let them talk shop, birthday boy. I think Michael said something about making you do shots tonight."

They were gone a moment later, Brooke practically shoving him through the slider and back into the party. This was weird. Why did this feel so weird?

Tristan stood slightly and gestured to the open chair next to him. I laughed a little under my breath at how ... gentlemanly it was. Suddenly, I had the thought that if there was a puddle on the ground in front of where I sat, he'd probably lay his jacket over it.

Next to me, I heard him take a deep breath and let it out. Even though we both looked straight forward into the darkness of Garrett's backyard, I could see his strong profile out of the corner of my eye.

My stomach twisted and knotted at the unexpected wave of nerves that hit me.

"It's a nice night out," I said lamely, then closed my eyes so I didn't groan. The puff of air that left his lips was all amusement, and I turned in my chair, tucking my knee up against my chest. "You're laughing at me?"

The curve of Tristan's mouth was slight, but it was there. "Did you come out here to tell me about the weather?"

My face heated, and I was beyond grateful for the darkness around us. "No."

He nodded again, his eyes never leaving my face.

"So," I started, and my voice came out scratchy and full of nerves. I cleared my throat and smiled at him. "Sorry, I don't know why I'm so nervous." Something in his face dropped at my admission, like I was making a declaration about him. I held up my hand. "Nervous isn't the right word. It's just ... I'm about to ask you a really big favor. And I'm fully aware that you might laugh me off this porch when you hear it."

"I won't do that."

The quiet assurance in his deep voice was so tangible that I nodded slowly. I had the fleeting thought that if I reached out to try and grab the words before they disappeared into the black sky, they'd be iron and steel. Unbreakable.

"I have this client that I booked for a whole house design about six months ago." I smiled. "She's ... well, she's intimidating. And rich. And really, really picky."

"They always are."

I laughed even though he was being completely serious. "They are. Do you think there are rich clients who just say, oh go ahead, do whatever you want?"

Tristan shook his head, eyes only briefly breaking contact with mine. "They probably didn't get rich with that kind of outlook."

"I suppose not." When I didn't continue immediately, he lifted his eyebrows in a gesture so minute that I let out a long breath. "Millie was a big coup for us. She has a big family of rich, intimidating, picky people. And I can't do anything but completely wow her, from start to finish. They've started construction on the house, so we're finalizing most of the design decisions now so I have plenty of time to order the finishes she wants."

He nodded. "Where's the house?"

"Just outside of Boulder."

"Total remodel or starting from scratch?"

I smiled a little at that. Millie never did anything halfway. "From scratch. She bought an eighty-acre plot because then she wouldn't have to look at any other houses in case the neighbors had garish taste."

It was fascinating to watch that sink in. The slight furrow in his brow before he let out a laugh so subtle that it could have been a heavy exhale.

Silence lapsed again while I let him process. My hands slowly rubbed up and down the front of my legs where they were still hugged up to my chest, a pointless attempt to stay warm in the crisp fall air.

A beat later, I realized the silence wasn't him processing. He was waiting patiently, because I was a giant moron who hadn't actually told him what I needed. I pressed my hands to my cheeks and laughed a little, hiding my face in my knees. "I'm so sorry. Normally I'm not so scatterbrained."

"I know that."

My head lifted at his answer, not said in jest or flippancy. Why was he the one trying to make me feel better right now? In truth, I hated the curiosity that swept up inside me. It was strong, a burst of wind that moved me in my seat.

"How can I help?" he asked gently.

I blinked a few times to refocus my thoughts. "Millie and I have been working on the design elements for a long time, she's very specific in what she's looking for, and that's a lot of custom pieces. Mostly custom wood pieces."

Seeing Tristan's eyes light up was magnificent. Not because of what it did to his features, which were already perfectly fine in his constant seriousness, but because I don't think I'd seen him so animated in years.

"Such as?"

The laugh that blew out of me made him smile a little. Well, half-smile a little. "Pretty much anything you can think of. Dining set for twelve, breakfast nook, coffee tables, end tables, headboard, accent walls. It would be a huge job, probably for more than one person, honestly. I had someone set up for it, I've worked with him before on a couple smaller jobs and he did great work. But he broke his arm a couple days ago, so he's completely out now." I shrugged. "And me? I'm screwed if I can't pull through. This job could put us in the black for months, with the possibility of a lot of future jobs if she's happy." I swallowed heavily, feeling the familiar pressure ever since we'd signed Millie as a client. "If she's happy with me."

Now Tristan was processing. He was looking at me, through me, while he rubbed a hand across his stubbled jaw and thought about what I'd said.

A slight breeze swept past us and I shivered. Tristan blinked out of his trance and immediately handed me the jacket that was draped over the table next to him. Very carefully, I laid it over my legs and gave him a grateful smile.

I couldn't place why, but I didn't slip it over my shoulders to warm me thoroughly. My finger worried a small crack in the worn leather. It was soft from use and my skin looked even more pale than usual against the black.

When I looked up, he was watching me, and it made me want to look away. Something funny happened when you lived under the same roof as someone who spared you very little of themselves. The moment someone else—a friend, a family member, a coworker—gave you a stretch of genuine focus, a snippet of time where they were so wholly invested in what you had to say, it was borderline electric to your senses.

I'd experienced that electricity a few times in the last handful of years, and this was rapidly becoming one of them. He wasn't just looking at me. He was studying. In the weak circle of light around us, I couldn't pinpoint what color his eyes were.

Maybe they were as dark as mine. Maybe they were so dark blue that they looked black. It didn't matter, because from them, I felt something so intense that I fought to hold his gaze. Against my frail, breakable ribs, my heart thrashed nervously.

You're not ready for this, a voice whispered in between the thudding beats. I didn't even know what it meant, what I might not be ready for.

But I didn't look away. And he kept his undefinable eyes trained on me, still searching my face. For what, I wasn't sure. But I could see the moment he *saw* what he was looking for, when I lifted my chin and refused to look away.

Don't tell me what I'm ready for, I whispered right back.

"I know I'm asking a lot of you, Tristan. I have no idea what your workload is like right now, or if it's something you're even interested in. But if it's too much, I will completely under—"

"It's not too much," he interrupted.

My breath caught, excitement threatening in an almost embarrassing wave. "Would you actually tell me if it was?"

Finally, he looked away, and the pressure against my rib cage lessened. When he looked back, something comforting showed in his face. It was warmth, humor, albeit slight on both accounts. I shook my head before I realized he didn't answer.

"Would you?" I pushed.

In answer, he lifted an eyebrow and took a sip from the beer that had been untouched since I walked outside. Laughing, I reached out to slap at his hand, but he froze, not yanking away, but clearly shocked by my reaction.

"I'm sorry," I said immediately. Mortification heated my face, even though he apologized at the exact same time.

"Nothing to apologize for." But his voice was gruff, and his eyes didn't come back to my face.

Note to self: keep professional boundaries with the mystery man who really shouldn't be this much of a mystery after knowing him for so many years. That should be easy. Of course, it would. Lots of people made good eye contact, and I needed to shake my own issues off like a snake skin, because if it started affecting my work, I'd have yet another thing to be pissed at Marcus for. And myself.

Tristan had been friends with my brother for years, and even though we didn't talk much after the first few times I'd met him, I knew he was a good guy. I knew that he stood for a woman when she took a seat. I knew that he listened when I spoke, and teased in a quiet, unassuming way. I liked that he didn't use a lot of words.

Words were pointless in excess anyway. Using more of them didn't make you a more proficient communicator, it only made you unable to stomach the quiet. And more important than anything about his personality, over the years, I knew that Tristan did incredible woodworking. I'd seen pictures, and I'd seen it in person a few times. If he had the time, he'd be perfect for this job.

"So, you're in?"

Tristan looked back at my light, teasing tone.

"I'm in."

My eyes flicked over his long hair, haphazardly pulled back into a messy bun. "You know, I should really think twice about working with a guy with hair that much better than mine."

Ooooh, that smile was almost a full one, but he looked away too quickly for me to see if I was right. But one side of his lips pulled up completely. And he lifted his beer up to his mouth too quickly. In the dim light, the colorful tattoos on his arms caught my eye.

Normally I'd ask about them, but he seemed uncomfortable at even a friendly attempt at touch. Instead, I filed it away. We had plenty of time over the next few months, I thought ruefully. Maybe I'd unearth some of the mystery that was Tristan Whitfield.

I looked away.

I'd unearth some of the mystery in a *friendly* way. That was non-negotiable. Always had been.

"My hair isn't better."

With a broad smile, I handed his jacket back to him. "You don't think so?"

Of course, he didn't answer. But his gaze briefly landed on my hair before moving back to my eyes. My hands fairly itched to smooth it down, but I sat still until he looked away.

"Can you meet next week?" I asked.

Tristan swallowed. "Shouldn't be a problem."

Maybe I wasn't the only one who was nervous. Oddly enough, it made me feel better.

I pulled my cell phone from my pocket and asked for his number. Slowly and deliberately, he said the numbers before I repeated it back to him. He didn't say anything, only nodded.

It was such a solemn movement that I burst out laughing. He glanced up in surprise at my reaction.

"Don't look so sad, Tristan. Otherwise you'll give me a complex."

Whatever it had been, he shook it off and gave me another one of those small, not-quite-full smiles. "I'm not sad. I promise."

I stood from my chair and he mirrored me. Then I hooked a thumb back at the party. "I should go back in. Knowing Garrett, he's probably sniffed out my present by now, and I need to see his face when he opens it. Are you coming back in?"

Tristan glanced briefly into the house. "I'll be in in a minute."

I smiled at him before going back in.

Not the way I thought this night would go, but I felt the faint flutterings of hope for the first time in a solid week. And they felt good.

CHAPTER FIVE

ANNA

The party wound down faster than I anticipated, maybe because we were all old and no fun anymore. Except when I looked over at my brother standing on the couch and proclaiming himself the winner because he drank longer than anyone else, I knew that wasn't the problem.

If thirty was the new twenty, then we all still could've shut down a few bars, no problem. I was nursing a single glass of wine, since I wanted to be able to drive home. Apparently sooner than I'd thought.

"Well look at that," Rory said from next to me. "A genuine smile."

It took me a second to realize that she was talking about me. She might be half a foot taller than me, and have the ability to take me down with her pinky, but I turned to her like I actually had the capacity to kick her ass. "I smile a lot, thank you very much."

"I said genuine smile." The slight lift in one pale eyebrow dared me to disagree. Her *eyebrow* dared me. That's how ineffectual my glare was to my sister-in-law. "What on earth did you and Tristan talk about out there?"

If the relief he'd given me at agreeing to the job had been heady, and the anticipation at getting started was dangerous, then the defensiveness I felt at her tone was positively radioactive.

"Work." Color me impressed with myself, because I wanted to hiss the word at her, but it came out all even and perfectly kind.

Rory pursed her lips. "I guess it's a good thing that *work* has the ability to make you that happy."

Now it was my time to have a bitchy eyebrow, because I turned and gave her the same lift. Like, *'scuse me, do you want to repeat that?*

"I love my job. I've always loved my job. You know that. So if you've got something to say, Aurora, then just say it."

Her eyes scanned the remaining people in the room, which wasn't many. Michael and Brooke had left about an hour ago. Same with Cole and Julia. Tristan hadn't stayed terribly long.

I'd seen him come in and talk with Garrett and Rory for a while, then his brother and Brooke, and he was out the door shortly after, giving me a polite nod when I waved.

"Nothing to say," she said with a light shrug which I didn't believe at all. "Just making an observation that it's nice to see you smile and know that you mean it."

Shame had me dropping my chin to my chest. Rory loved me, and I knew that. It was always like this when I felt like people were making digs at my marriage, at the fact that I stayed with Marcus when I was clearly miserable.

If I was smiling differently tonight, it's probably because for the last couple hours, I wasn't focusing on anything other than enjoying my time with friends, and the overwhelming relief of having Tristan agree to help with Millie's house.

"I'm sorry." I set my wine glass down and grabbed her for an impulsive hug. Thankfully, she returned it, smiling at me when I released her. "Just in a weird mood. I uhh, I think I'm going to head out."

"Drive safe, okay?"

"I will."

There was no judgment in her eyes while she watched me hook my purse over my shoulder, just speculation and worry. Everyone always looked at me with the slight tinge of worry. It was nothing new. But nothing I was capable of ignoring, either.

Garrett was still playing king of the mountain on the couch, so I snuck out quietly, not wanting to stop his fun.

That was a lie though, I thought as I drove through the quiet streets of their neighborhood. I didn't interrupt him because it was easier than seeing the worry in his eyes too. Being Garrett's younger sister was always fun. Sometimes serious. Rarely contentious. We'd always been close, and there were only a handful of times in adulthood that he'd played the protective big brother card, but it was always about Marcus when he did.

Since my parents adopted me when I was still an infant, I never had any memories of life without him as my brother. Of them not being my parents. Their love was a constant, unwavering thing. An iron core of support that I never questioned.

Maybe that was the reason that staying with Marcus was even remotely palatable. Why it hadn't broken me yet. Because I still had them. Always had them. Rory was part of that now, and she was as fierce of a family member as my mom and Garrett. As my dad had been.

Tears burned heavy at the back of my eyes while I drove home. I'd give anything, trade anything, to have just one more conversation with my dad. To let him hold me tight, to see that stupid worry in his eyes. To ask him how he must have felt when he wrote me that letter that was in his will.

He knew me well enough, or should have, to know that I'd never leave my husband simply for the sake of money. With my palm, I swiped at the dampness on my face. Then again, I thought I knew my dad well enough that I'd never imagine him laying something like that out in front of me. If it wasn't his scratchy, sideways handwriting on the paper that I'd read a thousand times, I'd wonder if I made it all up in my head.

It was very real, though. And all it had done was light a fire underneath me that stoked with every quiet day, every moment that I felt like another piece of furniture in the beautiful house that we shared.

But the thing about that fire was that it wasn't pushing me into action, not toward Marcus, at least.

It was embarrassing to admit how long it had been since I'd approached Marcus on the idea of counseling, because his brush-offs got increasingly gruff, increasingly annoyed. It was even worse when I tried to ask him if he felt the same way I did. Because that garnered me nothing. Only more silence. More aggravated sighs.

It was easier to just accept the way it was than try and fight against it. But maybe I could try again. As I neared our house—still lit up brightly on the inside—I decided I would simply try and talk to him.

The idea that Marcus was any happier in our situation than I was seemed impossible. But I would be doing myself a disservice if I didn't prepare for that. Sometimes, I wanted to grab his face, handsome and cleanly-featured and impassive, and scream at him until he showed me something. *Anything*.

A song came on the radio that reminded me of him, of our earlier years, and I had to punch the button to turn it off. Marcus had always been stoic and steady. I'd loved that about him. That there was something unflappable about this man. Or I thought I'd loved that about him.

As years passed, as nothing changed, as each day was measured in random punctuations of dialogue versus hours spent in silence, I'd had to come to the realization that there was no way that Marcus and I had ever been in love.

For a moment, I sat in my car, the engine still ticking as it cooled off, and I thought about what I wanted to say to him.

Please, talk to me. Look at me.

Say anything that lets me know I'm not alone in feeling like this.

I shook my head. No, he wouldn't respond well if he thought I was begging. And I didn't want to beg anyway. I was long past that point.

"Marcus," I said to myself, my voice firm and my chin level. "I'm not going to bed until you sit down with me, until you look me in the eye and we actually have a conversation with weight behind it. I deserve that much from you."

Yes. That was good. With a trembling hand, I adjusted my rear-view mirror and wiped at some smudged mascara under my eyes. There were no tear tracks on my face, and I pinched my cheeks to make sure I didn't look too pale and drawn.

As I walked to the front door and pulled my keys from my purse, I heard my dad's voice from some cobwebbed part of my memory. *Anna girl, even the smallest step forward is the most important step you can take.* While I blew out a chilly breath that left my mouth in a puff of white, I couldn't remember why he said that to me. Probably something small, something that should have been easy for me to do.

Just like this, I thought as I slowly eased the key in the door. It should be easy to start a conversation with my husband. Of all things I could start on a daily basis, that should be the easiest. I should be able to open my mouth and not feel defeat before the first sound leaves my lips.

But all the *shoulds* in the world didn't count for shit. Not really.

That was the thought in my head when I heard the sound of Marcus's laughter before I'd even cleared the front door. I paused.

When was the last time I'd heard him laugh?

For a moment, I closed my eyes against the cold, aching wave of sadness that crashed over me that I even had to think about it. How had we gotten here? That that was even a question I had to ask myself. Marcus would probably have to question the same for me.

He spoke again, and I knew he was on the phone. He took a lot of work calls at home, but they were normally dry and as fast as possible. But then he laughed again. Differently this time. Low and amused. Genuine.

Something about it raised the hairs on the back of my neck. Silently, I closed the door behind me and walked across the shining wood floors. When I reached the edge of the soft gray rug on the family room floor, I walked more normally, allowed it to absorb the sound of my steps. At the back of the couch, I paused and braced my hands on the soft leather while I listened.

My eyes were trained on his laptop, sitting innocuously on the end table, under a perfect circle of light from the lamps I'd just added last week.

"Well," Marcus said softly, a smile clear in his voice, "I wouldn't exactly say that."

In the silence after, I strained to hear any sort of response, but he was around the corner, probably sitting at the desk in his office.

"Last week, you told me that if I dared try it, you'd owe me something good." That laugh again.

At best, my husband was flirting on the phone with someone. My fingers were cold as ice and my breath shallow when I thought about the alternative. At worst...

At worst, he was cheating on me. But what I'd heard proved nothing.

His office chair creaked loudly, and I jumped in place, like he'd caught me doing something wrong.

Marcus made a sound of low amusement. "That sounds fair. But only if you wear absolutely nothing while you're doing it. It certainly made things interesting last week, didn't it? Hmm. That sounds perfect, angel."

My mouth was cotton and sand, swallowing all but impossible. My skin flushed cold, but my face was hot. Objectively, I knew that hearing your husband all but admit infidelity should immediately bring tears. To a roar of rage that came from some black pit inside of me that I didn't know existed.

But instead, it was embarrassment. Oh, I wanted to roar all right. At myself.

I wanted to take my bare hands and tear that sound from my throat and fling it at him so that he could take the weight. Take the dissonant sound of something so full of anger and shame and hope it made his ears bleed.

Almost like my hands were part of someone else's body, they slowly reached forward and picked up his laptop. Just a piece of metal and plastic and nothing.

It was inanimate, but for so long, it represented all the things about Marcus that I'd grown to hate. That I'd grown to hate about myself. The heat spread in slow prickles and I clutched his computer to my chest.

This time when I took my first step, it wasn't small, and it wasn't difficult. I stepped right in front of the French doors that closed off his office, one closed as always. One open into the room, perfect for hearing conversations. I guess I could thank him for that, at least. With his cell still pressed to his ear, Marcus's eyes widened when he saw me. If I expected immediate pleading, a lie and fake hang-up with whoever he was talking to, I would've been sorely disappointed.

But I was beyond disappointment. All I could wonder was what I looked like to him. I hoped that I looked fierce, not pathetic. More warrior princess than a stunned, betrayed wife.

"I'll have to call you back," he said into the speaker while I lifted my chin and held his eyes without a single fear of what would happen next.

My heart was hammering when he sighed. For a few agonizing, awkward moments, we stared at each other. But I refused to be the first one to speak. No way would I make this easier on him.

"Aren't you going to say anything?"

I shook my head slowly. My whole body was ice and stone, the heat gone and replaced with something that made my backbone exactly what I needed it to be. What I'd needed it to be for years. Firm, straight and unyielding. And I could see in his eyes, I'd shocked him.

About damn time.

He stood from his chair. Slowly and with intention. "You can't be all that surprised, Anna."

I clenched my teeth together, so he wouldn't have the satisfaction of seeing my jaw drop at his soft, firm response. Maybe I should have thanked him in that moment, for making it really, really easy to walk away. My fingers dug into the edge of his laptop as I stared at his face.

The light of his office was dim, but when he braced his hands on his hips, there was frustration written over every inch of his body. That was clear as day.

I wouldn't scream at him, because he didn't deserve the energy that it would take from me. He didn't deserve a single second more of my time, I realized with stunning clarity. I thought about simply turning around, setting the computer where I found it and walking upstairs to pack a bag.

No, I thought. The least that I could do for my husband was deliver his computer back to him.

Testing the weight, I hefted it in my hands, drew back and threw it as hard as I could through the closed French door. With a grossly satisfying crash, it shattered the glass. Marcus shrank back and covered his face with lifted arms.

"What the hell is wrong with you?" he roared.

I swiped my hands down the front of my shirt and tilted my head to the side while I took in the satisfying sight of broken glass all over his office. I pointed at the door. "What, that?"

His jaw dropped open.

I blinked a few times and gave him a polite smile. "You can't be all that surprised, Marcus." Then I turned on my heel and walked away.

"Anna, wait," he yelled as I ascended the stairs. Hopefully my mom was okay with a sleepover with her thirty-year-old, about-to-be-single daughter.

I paused and held his eyes. "I'm going to pack a bag so that I don't have to sleep in this house for another night. If you're smart, you'll be out of my sight when I walk out the door."

Again, his jaw dropped.

"And Marcus? When I come back tomorrow to get the rest of my things, don't be here."

CHAPTER SIX

TRISTAN

"Tristan, you make sure those hot dogs are cooked all the way through. I won't give those babies salmonella poisoning," my mom called through the slider door that led into her kitchen.

It was on the tip of my tongue to tell her that you can't get salmonella from hot dogs, and that Piper and Jacob would've been perfectly happy with microwaved hot dogs for their mac and cheese, but instead, I pushed my tongue against the inside of my cheek and lifted the grill tongs in answer.

I was the only one outside, as it was always my job to grill lunch when we ate at my mom's. Michael and Brooke were inside with the twins, playing with Lord knows what contraption my mom purchased this week. Something with a lot of lights and even more mind-jarring sounds effects.

She'd taken to her role as grandma with alarming speed, considering neither my brother nor I had given her any inclination that we'd have kids soon. And she wasn't the kind of parent to nag. Well, nag me, at least. Probably because she knew better. Michael was her best bet for kids to spoil, in a way she'd never been able to spoil us.

She spoiled us now, in her own way. Even though we could more than fend for ourselves, her feeding us a nice lunch once a week was her favorite way to do it. Growing up, she learned exactly how to spread the grocery budget given that she had to feed two growing boys and work two jobs in order to keep the same roof over our heads that we'd been born to.

It was the same house she was still in, nestled on the outskirts of Golden in a modest neighborhood, where she could see the mountains from every vantage point in her yard without the cost of living on one. The ranch was updated now, mostly in thanks to me and Michael, who did odd renovation jobs for her whenever we were slow at work.

Last winter, I updated her master bathroom and the winter before that, Michael and I had taken on the kitchen. It was a beneficial thing for all of us. Mom got her updates done with zero labor costs, and my brother and I didn't have to lose our minds during the slow season at work.

I liked to feel useful. Inactivity made me ill-tempered. Of course, Michael would've argued that everything made me ill-tempered, but we both knew he said it tongue-in-cheek, given that I was rarely in a truly bad mood, and he knew that.

True introverts were often mistaken for being anti-social, for being in a bad mood. Coupled with the fact that talking about what was going on in my head was equivalent to jamming wooden splints up the beds of my fingernails, meant that I couldn't blame most people for assuming I was always in a bad mood.

It was more that I'd learned how to protect myself against the way that people often drained my energy, depleted my mental stores. I could be around them, but I'd rather sit back and observe than be the center of attention.

From inside the house, I could hear them laughing. Michael opened the slider and joined me on the back deck, still smiling over whatever had happened.

"Those almost done?" he asked, clapping me on the shoulder and taking the tongs out of my hands. I pulled them out of reach and shoved him away from me. "What? You overcook everything. I'm hungry."

"Yeah, but if someone ends up sick, guess who Mom will blame?"

He winced and glanced back at the house. "Should we tell her they can't get salmonella from hot dogs? No shit, last week, I caught Jacob after he'd pulled one from the package, dropped it on the kitchen floor and shoved that thing right in his mouth." Michael shrugged. "He was fine. Germs are good for them."

I lifted an eyebrow. "Probably shouldn't tell her that if you want to make her feel better. She'll have a coronary."

"She definitely likes having the kids around. Makes her happier than I've seen her in a long time."

"Even happier than you usually make her." I glanced sideways at him. "Do you feel replaced?"

"Hell yeah, I do." He stretched and took a seat at the picnic table. "It's great. My fiancée came with two built-in grandchildren, so now the pressure is off. It'll be a couple years before she starts asking for another one."

I snorted. "Whatever you say."

Michael got a devious smile on his face and instantly, I hated it. "Though, who knows. Now that you're working with Anna, maybe she'll fall madly in love with you, leave her husband, and you two can churn out a few long-haired, half-Korean kids for Mom to spoil."

The warning look I gave him made Michael lift up his hands. "I'm kidding."

"No you're not," I said under my breath.

"You're right. I'm not." He sighed and I very much wanted to punch him. "You two would make such adorable babies, Tristan."

Like we'd summoned her, Mom opened the slider with Jacob perched on her hip. When we were all here, the bigger, louder updated version of our family, there were no stress lines around her mouth. And when the topic was possible grandchildren, she took happy to an entirely new level, because her smile was blinding.

"Who would make adorable babies with Tristan?" she asked, eyes bouncing between us.

My glare turned radioactive in Michael's direction, while he struggled to keep his laughter down.

"No one," I said firmly.

"Well, that's not true, is it?" Michael replied slyly. How many ways could you kill someone with grill tongs? He was about to find out. I'd apologize to Brooke later.

Jacob reached out to Michael and jabbered his name, so my mom handed him over. "Brooke wants to know if you remembered Piper's medicine. She needs to take it before lunch."

Michael blew air through his lips in an incredulous sound. "What does she think I am? An amateur? It's in the fridge, as it should be."

I rolled my eyes. Before Michael walked back into the house, he nudged my mom with his elbow. "Make sure to ask him what we were just talking about."

My mom laughed, and I sighed so deeply that I felt it down into my bones. There was no avoiding this.

For a minute after Michael closed the slider, we waited in silence.

"Beautiful day out," she said on a sigh, tilting her face up to the sun from where she'd sat at the picnic table.

The abundance of sunny days was my favorite thing about living in Colorado, besides the mountains. I wasn't a fan of summer, the heat making the nature of our jobs just that much harder. But in fall and winter, there was never a lack of sunshine. You could get a foot of snow one day, and the next, it was a blue sky and bright sunshine as if the previous day had never happened.

"It is."

Moving her attention from the mountains to me when I didn't say anything else, Mom waited me out, despite the rabid curiosity in her face. Most people didn't do that. Most of them rushed to fill the silence.

Not her.

Not Anna either, I thought with discomfort. I was trying so hard not to dwell on my conversation with her the night before. And now my mother was facing me, about to ask me about the adorable non-existent babies I would probably never have with Anna. I'd say that there was a possibility that she wouldn't push the issue, but that was as likely as my mom feeding the twins some raw chicken for lunch.

"I've never heard your brother tease you about a woman."

There was a reason for that. Carefully, I turned the hot dogs and started moving them to the white plate on the sideboard of the grill.

"It's just Michael being an idiot."

"Hmmm."

Without looking at her, I knew that she was pursing her lips and narrowing her eyes. The worst possible thing I could imagine was explaining to my mother that I was in love with a married woman. Even though my dad hadn't left her for another woman, she was still sensitive to the respecting of vows, something that she'd instilled in us our entire lives. "So there's no basis of truth in what he just said?"

Knowing I couldn't give her the full truth, it also felt wrong to lie about it completely. I set the tongs down and closed the grill lid to let the hamburgers cook longer.

"Maybe a little," I admitted begrudgingly. I glanced at her briefly, and she had on her *I'll be patient, but you're telling me something before we leave this deck* face. I hated that face. "She's ... important to me. But her situation is complicated."

Mom hummed. "Does she know how you feel?"

I spoke quickly. "No. It would only make things..."

"More complicated?" she supplied.

With a nod, I caught her eyes and held them. "Yeah."

She spread her hands out on the table's rough surface. I should re-stain it in the spring.

"You don't want to talk about this with me, do you?" she asked with a small smile.

I blew out a deep breath and laughed a little. "When's the last time we talked about my love life?"

Her eyebrow lifted as she thought about it. "Never."

"It's not personal, I promise."

"Hard for a mother to feel like that's really the truth."

Carefully, I watched her face, but she didn't look hurt. Maybe it had been so long since I'd talked to her about anything going on in my life, she just looked accepting, a little resigned. The words were there in my head, to tell her that often it felt more wearisome to explain things fully, not because it was anything against her.

After a prolonged silence, I nodded. "I promise, it is. I don't ... I don't tell many people what's going on with me."

"You tell your brother," she pointed out.

My answering sigh was heavy. "Most of the time, I regret that almost instantly."

She laughed. "I can't hassle you too much anyway."

"Why's that?"

"Michael didn't tell me about Brooke until after they were together."

I gave her a dry look over my shoulder. "Probably because he knew how you'd react to the kids."

With a look so loaded with happiness, she glanced through the slider. "He was probably right. I love those little monsters."

"Really?"

She glared at me. Her fingers knit together in front of her and she took a deep breath. "Maybe ... just one thing about her? Indulge your mother who just wants to see you happy?"

One thing about Anna. Just one thing that would make my mother happy, that didn't pain me to admit. Something real.

"She makes me smile," I said quietly, staring down at the grill. "She doesn't try to. It's just ... something that feels easy when she's around."

When silence met my answer, I risked a glance back at her, and she looked almost moved to tears.

Shit.

"Mom," I begged. "Please don't cry. I'll never tell you anything for the rest of my life if you do."

Against my back, I could feel the weight of her stare, her consideration. I turned slightly so I could see her face without meeting her eyes.

Mom squinted out toward her backyard and thought about that. "Is she ... is she in another relationship?"

My throat worked on a dry swallow and I couldn't bring myself to answer. Lifting the grill lid, I turned the burgers one more time and then placed each one carefully on the plate by the hot dogs, wrapping foil around the edges once I was done. Knowing she wasn't finished with the conversation, I took a seat across from her at the picnic table.

It would break her heart to know that I'd been in love with a married woman for so long. She'd grieve the years that I could have tried to find someone else, to be happy.

"Something like that," I finally conceded. "We're working together for the next couple months."

Mom nodded, gave me a searching look. If she knew how much I was leaving out of my answers, she didn't push me on it. "And that's a good thing, right?"

"I think so."

"Complicated," she repeated.

I gave her a small smile. "Complicated."

"Son, most things aren't nearly as complicated as we make them in our own minds. Just remember that."

"It's not that simple," I told her. "I'm not creating the complications in my head."

"Maybe you're not." She smiled patiently. "But the best things in life, the most worthwhile, warrant some complications every now and then."

I was about to say something, but Brooke yelled from inside, "I'm starving, guys. You better feed me before I get scary about it."

Mom laughed and patted my hand as she stood.

Before she went into the house, she came around to where I was sitting. She pressed a kiss to the top of my head, and I couldn't remember the last time she'd done that. Maybe because I was a solid foot taller than her. Maybe because I might have avoided it if I knew it was coming.

"If you've got feelings for this woman, then I know she's something special. Complications or not, I'm happy for you."

With a last pat to my shoulder, she was gone. Happy for me. If she only knew.

Dropping my head into my hands, I speared my fingers into my hair and squeezed to the point of discomfort. Everything about my current situation felt like I was stuck in a cyclone. If it suddenly stopped spinning, served me with the opportunity to walk out, would I take it?

Nothing was clear for me, despite what I'd talked about with Garrett. This job I was doing didn't really give me any more hope than I'd had yesterday morning when I woke up.

It simply afforded me the chance to be around her in a way that I hadn't allowed myself in years. Maybe that was hope. Maybe it was a test. That remained to be seen.

My phone buzzed in my pocket, and I laughed under my breath when I saw it was a text from Anna. Uncanny timing, she seemed to have lately.

Anna: Is it okay if we push our meeting back by a few days? I had something come up that I need to take care of first.

With a short laugh, I looked up at the sky and shook my head.

There wasn't a single cloud to interrupt the vivid blue. I wish a skywriter would fly past, give me some sort of direction. But there was nothing. Nothing written in the shapes that I could glean an answer from. But I didn't need it.

Me: That's fine. Just let me know when you're ready.

No, this complication wasn't manufactured in my head. But I was walking straight into it anyway.

CHAPTER SEVEN

ANNA

When I got Tristan's response, I set my phone face down on the white nightstand. I'd just bought myself a few days to breathe. Corryn, our office manager and my closest friend at work, already knew I wouldn't be at work tomorrow, so I was free there too. Maybe work would have been good for me. A distraction.

But I'd distracted myself for years, if I was honest. Anything to avoid spending time in my own head, because then I would've had to really work out why I was still in that house, with Marcus. It was easier to follow the winding paths of those distractions than force myself to answer that single question.

Staring up at the ceiling of my childhood bedroom, residue left behind from the glow in the dark stars that I'd thought were such a great idea in middle school, I felt the slow burn of anger toward myself. It would have been easier to push it in Marcus' direction. But it also would've been unfair.

A tear streaked down my temple, and I did nothing to stop it. I'd cried a lot during the night, turned into my pillow so that my mom didn't hear me from down the hall. Even though the door was shut, and even though she never would've encroached on that kind of moment uninvited, I didn't want her to lay awake worrying.

There was a tentative knock on the door, and I smiled a little.

"Come in." My voice sounded awful. Thick and throaty, tears still lingering behind every word.

She pushed the door open with one hand, a tray balanced in the other. I sat up and ran a hand through my tangled hair. On the tray was a cup of coffee, some toast and bacon, a bowl of strawberries and a beautiful yellow rose in a simple bud vase, probably from the garden in the backyard.

"Ready for some food yet?" she asked, but didn't really ask. As she set the tray on my lap and perched on the edge of my bed, I knew I'd be eating a healthy portion of what she had prepared for me, unless I wanted to incur her motherly wrath.

"Thanks, Mom." I picked up the coffee first, since the throbbing in my head probably required that the most. It was hot, the perfect amount of cream. Just that, her putting in exactly the right amount of cream that I liked made me want to cry all over again. But I didn't. I took a few fortifying sips and set it down for some bacon. There would be no fruit ingested today. Oh no. The first day would be fatty, salty foods, carbs and alcohol and that was it. No exceptions.

Like she could read my mind, she smiled and took the bowl of strawberries for herself.

"Did you get any sleep?"

I shrugged and swallowed the bacon. "Off and on."

She hummed. "Well, that's expected, I suppose."

"I think half of it was being back in this bed." I shifted and the springs squeaked obnoxiously enough that we both laughed.

"We can get a new one."

That prompted another heavy exhale. "Should I be embarrassed about moving back here when I'm thirty? That replacing the twin size mattress in my childhood bedroom is the first thing we worry about this morning?"

After setting the strawberries back down on the tray, she took a long look around the room. My last update had been right before I left for college, and nothing had been changed since. The walls were a pale, buttery yellow, with light purple, dark gray and white accents. A bit whimsical now for my tastes, but still pretty good for an eighteen-year-old who hadn't quite found her design aesthetic yet.

Because I'd felt so serious back then, the only thing on the walls were framed Georgia O'Keefe pictures. I almost scoffed. How unoriginal I was. There were so many ways I could do better now. Do exactly what I wanted with this bright sunny room that overlooked the garden in the backyard. Did I want to redo my childhood room to accommodate the woman I was now?

I didn't know her. If I stared in the mirror all day, I'd see things that I didn't recognize. Some good and some bad, probably. My eyes filled and I tried to blink back the tears.

"Oh, sweetie," my mom said and reached for my hands. "We can worry about whatever you want. If you want to move into the guest room downstairs, you can do that too. If you want to find your own place next week, I'll help you. There's no right or wrong here."

Through the heavy sheen of tears, her face blurred. "Isn't there?"

"What do you mean?"

I sniffed and let a tear fall without attempting to stop it. "I stayed for so long and I don't even know why. What does that say about me that I can't even answer? We didn't have kids. Not even any really blissfully happy years that propped me up when it got bad." I squeezed her hands like a lifeline. "Am I that much of a coward that I couldn't just take one step forward?"

"You did though, sweetie," she said fiercely. "You could've walked upstairs and ignored what you heard. You could've convinced yourself it was just a friend he was talking to. You could've convinced yourself that it was a million other things besides the truth."

I tried to swallow around the brick in my throat, but wasn't able to. In fact, I had to work just to get the words out, my stomach and throat and mouth were so lodged with emotion. "I feel like he took away the choice from me. Like all these years, I was waiting for the one thing that would change my mind, and it never came. And his actions are what did it. It wasn't me standing up for myself. I just *waited*, Mom," I said, feeling a desperate edge of panic crawl up my body. "I waited and nothing changed inside of me. And I can't figure out *why*."

While I attempted to breathe through the panic, Mom moved the tray off my lap and onto the nightstand. Then she grabbed my face in both hands, forced me to look at her. My tears fell even faster at the severity in her blue eyes.

"When I opened that door last night, and you were standing there, I was proud of you. I didn't know what happened, and I didn't care. I still don't. It doesn't mean I don't want to send your brother over there with a shotgun and a shovel, but you *had* a choice, Anna. You had a choice in how you reacted, and you made one. Don't you ever give him that."

When a sob broke from my mouth, she wrapped me in a tight hug, and we both cried. The release of emotion was as cathartic as my mom's arms around me. I pulled back first, when I felt like I could actually speak again.

"I wish Dad was here," I told her through my tears. The weight of that wish was so heavy around me, inside of me. Never in my life had I thought it was possible to wish for something so desperately out of reach that it would make your bones hurt. My soul ached to have just one more conversation with him.

For five more minutes with him. His heart attack had been sudden, and by the time I made it to the hospital, he hadn't regained consciousness. When you don't get to say goodbye, there's no ritual for grief that ever feels complete. No empty human process that we go through that can replace that moment to look someone in the eye and say that you love them, while they have the chance to respond.

Her face pulled into a sad smile and she cupped the side of my face. Her own tears fell now. "I do too, sweetie."

"I know this is what he wanted," I said haltingly. "Dad did. I was so angry at him when we read the will. I couldn't believe he thought I would do something like that for money."

"Oh, Anna," she interrupted immediately. "He didn't think that. He'd never think that about you."

"Did you know he was going to do that?"

She sighed. "I knew it was something to do with Marcus, yes. But not that he'd require a divorce for you to inherit anything." Then she smiled. "Your father loved you so much. The moment the social worker placed you in his arms, that was it. His heart was gone forever. Mine too. And when a piece of your heart is stuck somewhere unhappy, somewhere it does not deserve to be stuck, sweetie, you can't imagine how much that hurts as a parent."

It had taken me a long time to think about my dad's letter—his caveat—from that perspective, mainly because they'd always supported me completely. My marriage to Marcus felt like something that would just fall into that category. If they thought I was happy, even if they didn't love him, then they'd be okay. While my dad was still alive, I'd thought I had done a better job of hiding my unhappiness.

When I didn't say anything, she took my hands again, like she had to be touching me to make sure I was okay. "He knew it wasn't about the money for you. That wasn't his point."

"Then what was?"

Her eyes focused on something past me, but nothing that was in the room. "Your father trusted you, and your brother, to make whatever decision was best. You're both stubborn, and you do things in your own time. That's tough as a parent, too. When you wish you could speed up the process. And I think that's what he was trying to do. Help you get to a decision he always trusted you'd make in the end. Money or no money."

"But what about vows? What about those? Maybe I was stuck somewhere unhappy, somewhere that I didn't deserve to be stuck, but where do all of the things I promised to do in front of my family and friends and God fall into this equation?"

I don't think I really expected her to answer. It was more about wanting to get everything out of me in this safe place where I could ask the things no one could really answer for me. Maybe I wanted her absolution, to tell me that it was okay for me to walk away.

"Anna Lin Calder, don't you ever tell me that you didn't honor your vows."

My eyebrows popped up at her stern tone. And her use of my maiden name.

"I'm serious. I'm well aware that we live in a society that has shifting lines from the one I was raised in, that your father was raised in. I don't know that one generation is right and one is wrong, because at the end of the day, we all have to know within ourselves that we can live with the decisions we make for the rest of our lives." She gripped my chin and held my eyes. "Can you live with the fact that you chose to stick by him for longer than most women would have? Can you live with the fact that when you realized he hadn't honored those vows, that you held your head high and walked out because you know you deserve better than that?"

My heart turned over in my chest and I choked down another ugly sob. I knew what my answer was, so why was it so impossible to just say it?

After a deep breath, I pinched my eyes shut.

"Yes," I whispered thickly. There was a beat of silence, and I realized she was waiting for me to look at her again.

She nodded. "Good. Because I can live with it too. I know that I'm proud of my daughter, that I love my daughter, whether she walked out yesterday or three years ago, no matter what the reason. And that will never change."

I hugged her again. "Thank you."

"You have nothing to feel guilty about, sweetie. *Nothing*."

Plucking a tissue from the nightstand, I blew my nose noisily enough that she laughed. Once I was finished, the wadded-up tissue was added to the rest of the pile in the trash bin next to my bed. "Other than the fact that I'm a coward and need to come to grips with the fact that I short-changed myself out of a life with someone who *could've* been making me happy all these years."

"You know," she mused, "that's where I think your generation needs to work on its phrasing. It's not just about happiness."

My head dropped back to the headboard and I sighed. "Do tell."

She reached forward to play with the ends of my hair. "Happiness is always fleeting from day to day. No one can make you happy all the time. Not a spouse, not your kids, not your friends. But what keeps your head up during the times when you don't make each other sublimely happy is knowing what's underneath it. Respect and understanding, loyalty and a fierce love for exactly who that person is. Not what you'd want them to be, but what they are. That's how you stay married to someone who can weather those unhappy times with you, because you both know unequivocally that those other things will never waver."

Oh, if I thought my tears were done, she'd just proved me wrong.

"That is what you didn't have as a foundation with Marcus, sweetie. Not one of those things to guide you through the unhappy times. That's why Marcus doesn't have the power to take away what you did last night. You walked away when you needed to. When it was right in your soul to walk away."

I sniffled. Again. "You're really good at this."

She laughed and shook her head. "I'm old. We come with a lot of advice after living this many years."

"I just want it to be over quickly." Another tissue. Another loud honk from my nose. "I don't want anything from him, so it should be."

Mom gave me a speculative look. "I'm guessing you've done some research over the years?"

After a second, I nodded. "Just to check out my options. I don't want the house. He owned it before we were married anyway. And I don't need spousal support, not with the money from Dad. And he can't touch that as marital property since it was left to me as an inheritance. Once Marcus is served with divorce papers, there's a minimum of ninety days before the marriage can legally be dissolved." I swallowed roughly. "Maybe you think it's stupid that I'd make it so easy for him, that I wouldn't fight him for anything."

"Nothing you want to do is stupid in this scenario." She cupped my face again and smiled. "I could always ask Judge Connors across the street if there's anything he can do to help. He owes me anyway."

"I don't think I want to know why," I muttered.

She burst out laughing. "Oh goodness. I fed their cat while they were on vacation a couple weeks ago. And that cat is the devil incarnate, which he knows. I'll let you finish your very cold bacon and very cold coffee and go give him a ring. Maybe he can speed things up for you. Or at least make sure it's not held up in a stack of papers somewhere."

"Okay. Thank you." The coffee was indeed not hot, but it was still caffeinated, which was all that mattered.

Before she left the room, she paused and smiled at me, hope clear in her expression. "You know you're welcome here, if you don't mind a roommate for a while. Just until you decide what you want to do next."

I smiled after she shut the door with a quiet click. Until I decided what to do next.

Starting small, I needed a shower first. Then I needed to go to the house and pack some stuff up. Then after that?

I just wanted to start living my life. The one I'd missed out on for the past eight years.

CHAPTER EIGHT

TRISTAN

Anna: Does Thursday morning work? Maybe 10:30? I can text you the address for the studio, if it does.

Did Thursday morning work? Like I hadn't mentally cleared everything off my calendar for the entire week when she told me she'd need some more time before I could meet with her at her offices. Typing in an address for LoDo, just outside of the business district in a trendier area of town, I thought I might pass out.

Even the oxygen in my brain knew that I was about to throw myself straight onto the fire, and was making itself scarce. Maybe it thought that it could save us from fallout if it didn't feed the flames at all.

Well, that was well and good, but I needed my hands to work in order to drive. I needed every shred of consciousness to get through this first meeting with Anna. Would there be other people at the office? How many coworkers did she have? I wasn't even sure what her role was within the design firm she'd worked at since I first met her.

Garrett was the only person I'd really ever talked to about my feelings for Anna, and that was because he'd forced the issue as her brother. But I didn't ask questions. Couldn't for the sake of my sanity.

The more I knew, the harder it was. It made me feel like a recovering alcoholic that way. I couldn't indulge my addiction, even a little. One drop, one bit of information about Anna that I hadn't known before gave me a craving that set my blood on fire all over again.

"Stupid, stupid, stupid," I whispered under my breath as I pulled my truck into an empty parking spot next to the curb.

If small drops of information about Anna were dangerous for me, then what was *this*? Willingly putting myself in her path, with her in my debt for the next few months, with who knows how much time spent with just us?

It meant that I had a death wish. Not a single shred of self-preservation.

I looked up at the white modern space of her offices, large circular windows and black iron work within their frames, with my foot slipping right off the proverbial cliff, and I took the leap with my eyes wide open. Every step from my truck, toward the building that was neatly landscaped with bright green topiaries and clean white rock, I knew that I wouldn't be able to walk away from this without something broken or bruised.

And yet, I only had to take a single deep breath before I pulled open the large glass door. Just one to bring as much oxygen to my body as possible before stepping into this world that I'd never allowed myself before. A world where I could stand next to Anna with the distinct possibility that she'd look at me and see. See everything that I'd so carefully hidden from her.

When she stood up from behind a large white work table, a wide smile on her face directed right at me, I felt the surge of it light me on fire, singe my veins and heat the muscle and bone under my skin until all I felt was a painful, wonderful warmth.

Yes, this might leave me bloody and broken, but I knew that there was nothing I wouldn't do to see her smile like that. If that made me a fool, then I'd wear that label on every inch of what was left of me at the end.

"Right on time." She came around the table and started to lift her hand, then laughed and dropped it back to her side. "I don't know if I'm supposed to shake your hand or hug you, because they both feel a little off, don't they?"

Please don't hug me, I thought, pasting a pleasant expression on my face.

I was such a coward. But if she shook my hand, it *would* feel off. We weren't colleagues, but there was no way she'd normally hug me either. We were *smile at each other from across the room* acquaintances. And here I was standing within touching distance, in a space that was seemingly empty of everyone except us.

"You could always punch me in the shoulder." The words were out before I could ask myself what the hell I was doing. "That's how Michael greets me."

Her delighted smile in answer, that's why I said it. "I think we'll give it a couple weeks before we hit that stage." She turned and gestured to the wide-open space, with plentiful natural light from all the windows, either circular, or long rectangles set high on the light gray walls.

The furniture was mostly white with black or gray accents in the main work area. Shelves lined each long wall of the space, binders and books of samples stacked neatly on them. The large table was really three pushed together, black stools lined up on either side and light fixtures hanging low over the entire length. On the closest table were piles of fabric samples from different books, all in shades of blue. The tile next to them stacked just as high.

In each corner of the building was an office, glass walls for absolutely no privacy, but an aesthetic of complete openness. Those offices held the only splashes of color in the whole place, each with its own obvious personality.

"Is that one yours?" I asked without thinking, lifting my chin to the one in the northwest corner. Behind the large gray driftwood desk, the whole back wall of the office was cork. The giant inspiration board was sectioned off in fourths, each quadrant with a visible theme, probably different projects she was working on.

The large drum lights over the desk were wrapped in a dark blue fabric, and the chairs on either side of the massive desk matched, simple white linen like you might find flanking a dining table. On the large bookshelves were vases of pink peonies and on the bench under the window were pink pillows, so pale they almost looked white from a distance.

"How did—?" Her voice trailed off before I realized how stupid it was for me to say anything. I couldn't exactly say, because that office looks like you. It wasn't stark like the rest of the work space, it wasn't too colorful like two of the other offices, and the last office was far too much like the rest of the building. All whites and black and gold, which I didn't see as matching her design preferences either.

"Just a good guess," I muttered, refusing to meet her curious gaze. What would she see if I did? If I squared my shoulders to her and let her? *I see you, Anna. I see so much about you that I haven't figured out how to look anywhere else.* I cleared my throat when she didn't say anything. "Are we working here?" I gestured at the table.

"Ahh, yeah. Let me clear some of this crap out the way. That's for another project."

With brisk movements belying how often she performed them, she shelved the samples and pulled other binders down from the wall storage. I took a stool and flipped through the blueprints. If the address on the top corner was correct, then this was the project she needed me for.

The harsh lines and angles of the blueprints didn't give a feel for the home, unless you were used to looking at them. First, it was big. The design favored open spaces in the gathering areas, which could be tricky to fill with so much square footage, but it also looked like a farmhouse with the peaked roof line and large wraparound porch with simple beams. That called for comfort and warmth—a home, not just a house. Which was an interesting choice for something that apparently had well over four thousand square feet.

"Big family?" I asked.

Anna laughed, setting two new binders down next to me while she took a stool. "Big extended family."

I lifted an eyebrow, but still couldn't bring myself to look directly at her. My tongue felt thick and sluggish in my mouth, clumsy as I struggled with how to fill the yawning silence in the cavernous space.

"And big rental potential," she continued, handing me some 3-D renderings of the inside. Anna's stamp was all over the design concept, enough that it made me smile. "Millie herself is single, but she's got more money than God and a lot of time on her hands. We've pitched a few jobs to her before, but she's never commissioned us before this one."

"Farmhouse style, huh?"

She groaned, but she didn't sound upset. "Thank you *very* much, Joanna Gaines. It's hard enough to differentiate ourselves, and now everyone wants shiplap and sliding barn doors."

I chuckled under my breath. "It can't be that bad." I pointed to a sketch of the kitchen. "I like the island."

"Good, because you're going to help build it."

Anna smelled like grapefruit and lemongrass when she leaned closer. Close enough to nudge me with her elbow. I licked my lips and chanced a look at her. The long black sweep of her hair fell over the shoulder furthest away from me, and there was a teasing grin on her lips.

When was the last time I was this close to her?

A couple years, at least. Instead of feeding into the playful energy that she emitted, something I ached to do, something that made my heart churn painfully in my chest while I tamped down the desire to give in to it, I looked back at the sketch with fresh eyes.

"You could lay out the wood in a staggered pattern, add some visual interest with how much white is in the kitchen, if you don't think it would be too busy." Then I tapped the page where she'd drawn a long wood dining table in the open space past a beautiful brick arch that separated the kitchen from the dining area. "Same with the table, if I'm still building that. I could do a couple things to make that more interesting to look at. Make sure it looks custom."

"Oh, Millie is going to love you," she laughed. If Anna's smile—any of her smiles that were aimed at me—fed fire through my veins, then her laughter was like she threw light over every dark corner inside of me. It was jarring and fast, something that switched off as quickly as it turned on. A tease that I wasn't allowed to indulge the long-term effects of. "Give me any idea you've got. She loves custom, despite the trend that we're feeding into here. So," she shrugged, "we're switching it up where we can. Most modern farmhouse styles use a lot of white, yes, but we're doing deep navy for accent instead of black, just to soften it up. I'm aiming for variation in the wood tones and the stone finishes for the bulk of our ... visual interest, as you noted."

Things I needed to remember never felt real to me until I put lead to paper, so I pulled out my small notepad from where it was always wedged in my back pocket. There was a mechanical pencil laying in front of me on the table, so I lifted it up and looked at her in question.

"By all means." She was laughing at me. It was in the slight twitch to her pink lips, the barely there narrowing of her eyes.

That's when it hit me. When I stop and stared at her for the first time since I walked through the door. Anna looked happy. Tired, but happy. This close—without quickly averting my gaze because staring at her felt like staring into a spotlight sometimes—I could see the small smudges of dark skin in the flawless skin under her eyes. But what I didn't see was the pinch of her forehead, the sad downturn of her mouth.

"Is there something on my face?" she asked, half teasing, half serious.

"Sorry." I scratched a few notes on the lined paper, a shorthand that no one but me would probably be able to decipher. My eyes focused so carefully on the messy scrawl of my handwriting that I thought maybe it would distract me from the embarrassed heat in my cheeks.

If anyone wondered why I kept the facial hair, it was so I had more to hide behind. While I wrote some more notes and a few ideas bouncing around my head, Anna leaned over so she could see.

"Lordy, that handwriting. If you ever got it analyzed, they'd probably say you were either meant to be a doctor or a serial killer."

That's what was different too. It was her voice, the soft lilt of teasing that I hadn't heard from her in so long. Not since those first few nights. She was teasing me.

This ... this threw me a little. For so long, I knew exactly what to expect from my interactions with Anna. We'd be polite, warmly so. Friendly acquaintances because I had my mask so firmly into place. I'd perfected that mask over the years. And even though we were alone, there was absolutely no reason that she'd suddenly treat me differently. Anna had always taken the way I'd interacted with her and mirrored me perfectly, it's probably the only reason I'd stayed sane for so long.

It was just a good mood. Everyone had days that were better than others, and it showed in how they were with the people around them. The way she was with me right now, it didn't mean anything beyond a day that made her happy.

Which is why I flipped to another sketch and started asking questions. Just like she used to, she took her cues from me, and slid instantly into design mode. Most of what she'd laid out was very straightforward, and when she started pulling some samples from the books to give me an idea of what she wanted from me, an hour passed before I'd even realized it.

"Oh, I love that," she said excitedly when I told her about an idea I had for the dining room chairs. "Are you sure you're not taking on too much though? This is a big job for one person."

I lifted my chin and met her eyes, it was easier now that we'd been talking so comfortably. I forgot that my tongue wanted to trip over letters and words to make sure I was saying the right things, the appropriate things. I forgot that this was foreign for us. I forgot that she was acting differently.

I forgot all those things and just enjoyed myself. Maybe that was the key to being around Anna, not drown myself in the ache of what I couldn't have, but enjoy what I could. If I never touched her skin, never knew what it felt like under the pads of my fingers, I could be grateful for knowing what it was like to make her laugh. I could enjoy the easy passing of ideas, enjoy seeing how she worked, the quick way she thought. I could enjoy the way she made me feel, even if I could never do anything about it.

"Tristan?"

I blinked when I realized I hadn't answered her question. "Sorry, just ... thinking through all of this." With two fingers, I scratched the side of my face. Instead of staring at me, she turned and started tidying the sample binders. A phone rang behind the white reception desk, and she excused herself.

Instead of watching her walk away, because the navy pencil skirt was not what I needed to be paying attention to, I pinched the bridge of my nose. Today was just the beginning, even though our time alone would be sporadic over the course of the project.

And she'd asked me if I was taking on too much. It was almost enough to make me laugh out loud. If I was the sort of person to do that, I would've from the sheer, painful irony of her question.

Of course it was too much. Too hard. Too painful.

Or it would be, if I let it. Be too complicated, if I let it be. It was smart professionally, especially if I wanted to do more custom work and less general contracting. And I'd do it because it gave me this time with her. I simply had to train myself to enjoy the moments I did have.

Anna laughed into the phone, turning my direction and giving an apologetic smile. I waved her off and stood to look at some of the inspiration boards on the wall when she lifted a hand to brush her hair behind her ear.

Her left hand.

There was no ring on it. I'd *never* seen her without her wedding ring on.

My heart thudded to a stop, a cement block in my chest for one prolonged moment before it was racing, roaring and flying into an irregular pattern. Something dangerous that made me feel light-headed. All I could do was stare while she walked back to the table, completely unaware of my body freaking the hell out.

And that? That was nothing compared to what my mind was doing. And my mind was galaxies away from my heart.

"Sorry about that."

"You're not wearing your wedding ring." It was out before I could stop it. I didn't even want to stop it. I wasn't even sure my voice belonged to me. Surely someone else let the words go, some tortured soul who needed them out in the world to free itself from whatever prison it belonged to.

Her face froze in a suspended sort of panic at my question. Wait. Had I asked a question? What had I said? It was enough to drain all the color from her face, her high cheekbones no longer holding whatever flush they'd had just moments earlier.

Bah-bomp, bah-bomp, bah-bomp. All I heard was the uneven thump of my heart behind my ribs. She started to lie, I saw it the moment before she opened her mouth.

"It's..." She shook her head a little and then licked her lips. Her chin dropped down to her chest for just a moment and I regretted saying anything. I could've just asked Garrett. He would've slugged me in the shoulder and said she was probably just getting it cleaned. "It's, uh…"

No. It wasn't at the cleaner. I took a step toward her and then froze when it registered what I was doing.

What *was* I doing? Trying to keep my hands to myself, to not grab her by the shoulders and shake an answer from her.

Anna took a deep breath and stared past my shoulder for another excruciating beat. Then her eyes hit mine, and I saw the determination there.

"It's off because I left Marcus on Saturday night."

And just like that, my world stuttered back to a roaring start.

CHAPTER NINE

ANNA

I'd almost lied. The embarrassment of admitting the truth almost had false words falling easily from my tongue. But something in his eyes, pinning me in place, refused to let me. I didn't even really know Tristan that well, but there was something about him that would not let me lie to him.

Those eyes tracked the movement of my hand when I smoothed down the front of my blouse.

"Why?" he bit out, a short, quiet growl. It was barely civil, definitely not polite, and inexplicably, it made me laugh.

"You sound so grumpy about it." I smiled, and he looked at me like I'd lost my mind. Okay. Maybe smiling wasn't appropriate for this conversation, but honestly, Tristan was my test audience. Someone who knew me—and knew I was married—and I'd just said it. I told him. My poor mother had been keeping it from Garrett and Rory this week at my request, because the thought of telling them and seeing the inevitable celebration felt like too much when I was still sorting out how I felt about everything.

It was hard to fight the deep-seeded truth that I'd stayed longer than I should have. Seeing unfettered happiness and relief at the demise of my marriage was just ... it was too soon.

"I'm not grumpy," he said in a less growly tone. Tristan looked away and ran a hand through the top of his hair, upsetting the part of his ponytail that was pulled back. "Just..." He stopped and stared at me. Then he took a deep breath and readjusted. "Are you okay?"

The kindness of his voice made my eyes burn for the first time that day. My rapid blinking must have given me away, because his face took on this surprisingly panicked expression.

"Don't worry," I told him. "There will be no crying today." I pushed a smile back on my face, even as I tried to figure out how the hell we were in this conversation. Even my coworkers hadn't noticed that my ring was off.

Not even Corryn, who hated Marcus, and was the nosiest person I'd ever met. I'd promised myself that I'd tell them before the end of the week, but we'd all been busy enough, off in a million different directions that I hadn't had the chance.

Correction. I hadn't made the chance take place, because I still felt like I needed to shield myself from people's reactions. Self-preservation at its finest, folks. Maybe that was just another cage, this time of my own making. I couldn't blame it on Marcus, and that burned at the edges of whatever question Tristan could have possibly asked me.

He could have ignored what he saw, and he certainly didn't need to see if I was okay. But he had been friends with my brother for so long, someone that I knew to be trustworthy and steady.

"I'm okay," I told him. He looked up at me in surprise. Then I let out a deep breath and tucked my hair behind my ears. "You didn't need to ask that. A lot of people will, I'm sure," I found myself babbling a bit at his intense stare. "But how often do people ask that kind of stuff; how was your day, how's it going, are you doing okay, and they don't really care about your answer. They expect you to say that you're fine or you're so busy or just wait politely until you turn the question back to them. But I think ... I think you meant that. You seem like someone who would mean it. And I feel like I'm okay. I'll be okay."

It was official. My tongue was off its leash. As each word poured out, Tristan's lips curved up just barely on each side.

I cleared my throat and shifted awkwardly. "Thank you for asking."

His dark brown eyes narrowed just slightly, that almost smile still on his face. "You're welcome."

"You're the first person who knows outside of my mom." Then I laughed. "And Marcus, I suppose. But let's not count him."

Tristan's head tilted. "What about Garrett?"

My hand rubbed at my neck. "Oh, please don't say anything to him if you see him tonight. I just ... I haven't told him yet."

"Why not?"

I lifted an eyebrow. "Do you always ask people this many personal questions?"

He shook his head slowly. "No."

If I was waiting for further explanation, I would not be getting it. Another laugh bubbled in my chest, but I swallowed this one down. Weirdest conversation *ever* at the office. Or with someone that was friends with my brother.

"Okay," I said. "I'm ... I'm not looking forward to the *what took you so long* response."

As soon as I said it, his eyes lit with understanding, and he nodded. Nothing past that. Just quiet understanding.

"And it'll get even worse when he finds out it's because I heard Marcus on the phone with his girlfriend."

Tristan's face of quiet understanding froze. "His what?"

I groaned. "I know. It's so cliché. I was miserable for years, but it took him cheating for me to finally be able to leave."

The wide expanse of his chest expanded on a deep breath, his voice incredulous and dangerously low when he spoke again. "He ... he cheated on you?"

My face was hot when I nodded. "Yup. Don't worry though, I threw his laptop through the doors of his office when I found out."

Tristan's eyes widened, his mouth opening slightly. "You..."

Suddenly, I found myself laughing. He looked at me like I'd lost my mind. "This isn't funny. I'm sorry. I don't know why I'm laughing."

"Aren't you ... aren't you furious with him?" he asked slowly.

I took a deep breath and blew it out through pursed lips. "I am. And I'm mad at myself too." Desperately, I tried not to fidget in place when he tilted his head at my answer. "Does that make sense?"

Tristan braced his hands on his hips and searched my face. After a long, long minute, he nodded. "I think it does. And I think I understand why you haven't told you brother."

"I'm going to tell him tonight," I added quickly. "After work. I'll text him right now to see if he and Rory will be home."

"That's a good plan."

My arms crossed over my chest, ridiculously warmed by his responses. Who knew that they'd be exactly what I needed? "I think so too."

Tristan let out a slow breath, enough that his cheeks puffed out while he did. "Good."

A smile spread over my face. "Good."

Then the most adorable thing I'd ever seen happened. Tristan blushed. This large, quiet man blushed and for the life of me, I couldn't figure out why that made me want to laugh out loud.

I didn't. Because somehow, I knew that would make it worse. He tucked his notepad into the back pocket of his worn jeans and wouldn't meet my eyes. "I'm going to start working on some sketches. Can you shoot me the PDF of these plans to my email? I lose papers too easily. I'd rather have all the room measurements in my phone."

"Of course." I looked around for a piece of paper. "I don't have your email address. Can you text it to me?"

He nodded briskly. The flush was off his cheeks, but he definitely seemed out of sorts.

"So, do you want to work on some sketches first based on just the plans? Or would you like to see the house? Either works for me."

Tristan briefly stared out the front window of the office before looking back at me. "If it's not too much trouble, I think I'd like to see the house. That's normally how I'd do it."

"Of course," I said right away. The favor he was doing me was so massive, this was a tiny accommodation to make. "I'm booked all day tomorrow, but how about Monday? After eleven, my day is wide open."

He blinked a few times and then pulled his phone out to check the calendar. Oh yes, definitely out of sorts. "Monday is fine."

"Awesome. I'll text you the address and a time."

"Right. Good." Then he turned to leave and I smothered a laugh. His hand was on the door when he paused and looked at me over his shoulder. "I hope it goes well with Garrett tonight. If it doesn't, let me know, and I'll punch him. Or something."

"Sounds like a plan," I said around my wide smile. "Have a good day, Tristan."

When he walked past the front window, his eyes were pinched shut like he was embarrassed, and something about it made my heart happy. And that ... that felt good. I walked back to my office, humming as I sat down to get back to work.

Garrett and I stared at each other from across his dining room table. I held chopsticks in my hand, and he calmly chewed his fried rice, not blinking.

"Let it out, brother."

With precise movements, he set his fork down and stood from the table. Rory and I watched him curiously. I expected an immediate burst of obnoxious victorious yelling and jubilation at my news, I expected a roar of anger over what I'd discovered when I came home.

Rory reacted about how I expected, simply reaching over and holding my hand tightly. She whispered, *I'm proud of you,* and left it at that. But Garrett remained silent. So silent that it freaked me out.

Even after he got up from the table, he walked casually back to their master bedroom. Once he was in there, he shut the door.

"What on earth?" Rory said under her breath. "My husband is strange."

"I've dealt with him for thirty years, and he never gets less strange."

Then we heard it, like he'd muffled his face with a pillow.

Hell yes, baby, it's about time. Suck it, Marcus, you douchebag. Well, that's the gist I caught through the filter he'd clearly pressed to his mouth. Rory rolled her eyes and refilled her wine glass.

The bedroom door opened and Garrett had a pleasant smile on his face. He looked so much like our dad that for a moment, it hurt to look at him. Then he opened his mouth and my sadness was gone.

"Little sister of mine, I'm so terribly sorry to hear your news." He sat in his chair and faced me, all earnestness and candor. "What can we do to help? Am I allowed to kick his ass now? Bury him in the backyard?"

"Seriously?" I pointed back to the bedroom.

He didn't so much as blink. "I'm older now. More mature. I don't need childish displays of emotion to appropriately react to news like that. That's something I would've done last year."

Rory sighed, but it was heavy with affection. And I wanted to be pissed, but my laughter was instant, and exactly what I needed.

"I guess the fact that I expected you to do that right in my face and you didn't means you're clearly growing as a person, Garrett." I lifted my half empty wine glass. "Congratulations."

He straightened an imaginary tie. "Thank you."

The mood steadied out now that his little outburst was over. Rory spoke first. "Now what?"

"I filed on Monday, he was served Tuesday morning. I don't want anything from Marcus, so I can't fathom he'd fight me on any aspect of this. Colorado is a no-fault state anyway, so it's not like I can use his affair against him. It's just about splitting the marital assets. And since I don't want any of them, in theory, I'm ninety days away from being officially divorced." At their shocked looks, I smiled a little. "It's amazing what can happen when you've got a judge calling in favors for you to one of the attorneys he knows."

"I guess so," Garrett said under his breath. "Judge Connors?"

I nodded. "Mom called him Sunday night. I forgot how scary she can be when she wants something."

"And you're going to stay with Mom for the time being?" Rory asked.

"That's the plan." I gave Garrett a look. "I think she likes having someone at home with her. She's lonely."

No one around the table could argue that, so they didn't. Then Garrett narrowed his eyes a little.

"You better stay lonely for a while."

"What's *that* supposed to mean?" I snapped at him.

Garrett held his hands up. "Just give yourself some time, okay? I know everything feels all happy and hunky dory right now. Yay, Marcus the asshole is gone. Believe me, I understand. But the last thing you need to do is jump into a serious relationship. Or a casual one."

"Garrett," Rory warned.

"I'm pretty sure that's not up to you, big brother."

"Of course, it's not up to me," he said like I was an idiot. He'd find out who the idiot was when I shoved my chopsticks up his nose. "I'm just looking out for you."

I set said chopsticks down when I started getting creative in my thoughts. They could go so many places. "I appreciate your concern. But guess what? I'm not looking for a serious relationship. I'm staying with Mom, for crying out loud. That's not exactly conducive to romance, if that was even what I wanted."

"Good." He crossed his arms over his chest.

Using my fingers, I popped a bite of chicken into my mouth and peered past him for a second. "I'm not opposed to finding someone to help me let off some steam though. I've been through a *hell* of a dry spell lately."

Garrett slapped his hands over his ears. "*Lalalala*, I'm not hearing this."

Again, Rory rolled her eyes. I laughed at how genuinely tortured he looked. Somewhere in my head, it's not like I thought Garrett was wrong for telling me to step forward with a bit of caution. There was a bit of a honeymoon phase that I was in the midst of without Marcus.

My soul felt a lightness that had been violently absent for the past five or six years, each passing year only made that feeling worse. But there was still grief. There were still the emotions knotted around my heart, my head, from so many years of that relationship, and only time could untangle them.

No, I didn't want to complicate that process by jumping headfirst into anything serious. But damned if I would admit that Garrett was thinking the same thing I was. He needed to think he was being heavy-handed and ridiculous.

"Man, even two years ago, I would have the pick of all your friends. Who's still single again?" I tapped my chin thoughtfully, thinking they'd both laugh, and we'd joke about me blowing off steam for a bit. Just to torture Garrett. Which is why I was so surprised when both of their faces turned serious. Rory gave Garrett a nervous glance and I sat up straighter. "What?"

He leaned forward in his seat. "You want to blow off steam, fine. No one would begrudge you some of that. Not even me. But not with Tristan."

I tilted my head. Because *huh*? "I was joking about your friends, Garrett."

"Good."

"What's that supposed to mean anyway?"

It was clear on his face that he didn't want to answer me, but he'd said too much for that. He sighed and took a drink. "He's just ... he doesn't do casual. Ever. And if you want a fling or a one-night stand or anything, just don't look to him for that. I know you guys are working together, but ... he's not that guy. Okay?"

Rory gave me a tight smile, worry in her blue eyes. "Tristan is the best. You know that, I think."

Defensiveness had my face hot and my eyes painfully dry. "Of course, I do. I'd never use one of your friends."

"I know," she said quickly, darting her eyes to Garrett. "And Garrett does too. There's protectiveness all around, right? No one wants you to get hurt either. It's not just about Tristan."

She was right, and I knew that. I rubbed at my forehead wearily. It wasn't like anything they said surprised me, per se. I'd never known Tristan to sleep around, unless he was the soul of discretion. I thought about how he spoke to me earlier at work, concern clear in everything he said to me. No, Tristan wasn't a casual guy. And he'd never take advantage of a woman.

"Sorry," I said to both of them. "This is all new for me. I don't even know what I want right now. Or what I should want."

"There's no should about any of this," Rory assured me. "Whatever you feel will be right, as long as it's not hurting you. Then your brother will get really annoying again. I will too."

I smiled. "No, you're right. You don't need to worry about me. Work will definitely keep me busy for a while, and that's for the best."

I just had to keep telling myself that. Every day if necessary.

CHAPTER TEN

TRISTAN

Anna is single.

Every punch of the nail gun into a stupid, trash piece of wood, that phrase turned over in my head on a rolling loop.

Thwack.

Anna is single.

Thwack.

Unattached.

Thwack.

Unfettered.

Thwack.

Available.

Thwack, thwack.

Because her husband *cheated on her.*

The wood splintered under the weight of too many nails in too small of a space, but my finger kept squeezing the trigger, my body tensed in preparation for the blast of pressure up my arm. It wasn't enough though. Not even close.

Anna is single.

Thwack, thwack, thwack.

When a chunk broke off the edge from the last nail slicing too close to the edge, I set the gun down and yanked the hose out of the bottom of the gun that connected it to the compressor. All weekend long, this is what I'd been doing to myself. How I'd been punishing myself. I'd lain awake and stared at the ceiling of my dark room, lied to myself that I'd still find sleep.

But it was elusive.

There was something strange about finding yourself in a situation that you'd ached to be in, facing a possibility that you wanted so badly that it made your bones hurt. I always thought I knew exactly how I'd feel if Anna was ever single. If she ever walked out the door from that cage of a marriage.

Of all the possibilities, it never occurred to me that I wouldn't know exactly how to feel once it happened. But I found myself replaying our meeting in her office over and over and over. I couldn't close my eyes without seeing the dark circles under her eyes, even though she seemed happy.

Hadn't she seemed genuinely happy?

Or had I been so desperate for any grain of good coming from her direction that I imagined all of it?

It didn't seem possible to me that she could just, *bam,* feel free and happy and whole. Just like that. But I wasn't Anna. And for all the years that I'd spent with her at some fixed point of my brain, I hadn't thought through what she might feel once she walked away.

I only saw her and me. I only saw some snapshot of a future that was as hazy as it was perfectly branded into my head. The details changed occasionally, but through every year that passed, I could *see* it. I just never imagined what led up to it. Where her head and heart might be stuck in the gray fog after swimming out of the black. How difficult it might be to reconcile what her life was like after. I'd envisioned *later*. Not immediately after. And that was as stupid as having been in love with her for so many years.

I'd sketched Saturday and Sunday, knowing that every page, every stroke of the pencil, every erased line and angle and joint might all be a waste once I got out to the house. But it was something I could do.

But once I got to my shop on Monday morning, that activity was too sedate for all the energy I had shooting through my veins. This was the first time that I would be seeing Anna with the absolute torturous knowledge that she was free.

Uninhibited.

Unchained.

Single.

It almost choked me with anticipation and terror and excitement and dread.

"What the hell is wrong with you?" I muttered under my breath.

"An excellent question," Michael said, and I worked not to jump in surprise. He clapped me on the shoulder as he leaned up against the work bench next to me. When he caught a glimpse of my face, he frowned. "What's wrong?"

I sighed and tossed my safety glasses onto the table next to the nail gun. If he was frowning when he saw my face, he shot past concerned when he saw the mangled wood shot full of useless nails.

"Brother," he said slowly, "I'm not sure how to ask this, so I'll just come out with it." He faced me, squinting at my face obnoxiously. "Are you on something? Having a mental breakdown? Working on abstract art fit for a four-year-old?"

When I rolled my eyes, he relaxed a bit. I rubbed at my forehead. "Anna left Marcus last week. I found out on Thursday."

Michael's eyes widened, and he whistled quietly before sinking back against the table. "Holy shit."

I mirrored his stance. "Yeah."

For a few minutes, we both stared at the far wall of the shop. The only sound in the room was the hum of the air compressor.

"And you're like, working with her now, right?"

"You know I am." I folded my arms across my chest and tipped my chin up to the ceiling, but closed my eyes because of the harsh light from the fluorescent bulbs.

Michael scoffed. "So why do you look like someone just kicked you in the balls? Dude, this is amazing."

"Yeah."

"Okay, if you say that one more time, *I'll* kick you in the balls."

Shifting so that my hip was against the work table, I faced him. "And what do you want me to say?"

He gaped at me. "Seriously? I can't believe you're not excited right now. This changes things, Tristan. For the first time since you've met her, things are finally different."

The slow kindling of excitement sparked in my chest and it took everything in me not to stoke that, nurture it and let it roar through me in a sweep of heat. If I had any intention of surviving this new reality in the way I'd always hoped, there was no way I could do that.

"Different, yes. But Michael, she left her husband of eight years a week ago. Seven days. It doesn't change that much. Not this quickly."

"Oh bullshit."

My eyebrows lifted at his hard tone and hard face. "Excuse me?"

Michael leaned forward. "Don't give me that bullshit. If it doesn't change things for you, then what? You made up everything you've felt for her the last six years?"

"Don't push me on this right now, Michael," I ground out. "It's not the time."

He ignored me, even though my chin lifted and my hands curled into fists. His chin did exactly the same thing. "Did you make up what you've felt for her? Maybe you were only in love with the idea of her."

"Michael," I warned, feeling my skin crawl with the need to defend myself, defend her, defend everything that had been embedded into me for the last six years. He had no idea how real it was.

Had no idea how—so many years ago—she made me feel normal in my quiet reserve, and not only that, she made me want to laugh, want to smile.

Had no idea that when I sat next to her in that dugout and listened to her heckle a man four times her size fearlessly, I understood how a man could be well and truly wrecked over a woman, only to have it ripped away from me just a few moments after I realized that I would've given anything to simply sit and talk to her for the rest of the day.

"How does this not change anything?" he pushed again.

My hand tightened on the mangled wood and I threw it across the room before I knew what I was doing. "Because right now, it fucking doesn't, okay? She walked out on a life that she'd had for eight years, man. You don't just wake up the next morning and not feel some sort of wound from that. And I'll be damned if I am the person to slap a Band-Aid over a bullet hole, just so that I can avoid the bloodshed that she may not want to think about right now."

Understanding softened his facial expression, but oh hell no, I wasn't finished. If he wanted to push, he could deal with me pushing the hell back. He had *no* clue, no one would, how much this news upended everything that I'd built up around me to hide what I felt for her.

Brick by brick, until my hands bled to the bone from the force of stacking them, I had figured out a way to live with what I felt for her and find some semblance of shelter. If I tried to tear that wall down too quickly, Anna would get buried under the weight of it.

"Don't you think she has the right to grieve what she went through?" I asked with a ferocity that clearly took him by surprise, because he took a step back and regarded me warily. "To figure out what she wants to do next without me falling to my knees and making some big declaration that would probably send her running in the opposite direction?"

Michael rubbed the back of his neck and sighed. "Tristan..."

"Don't you dare pity me right now."

"I'm not pitying you, but come on—"

"No," I yelled. "You don't get it. I've loved her so long that I can barely see straight when she's around, but I had to put blindfolds on for that *exact* reason for six years. Because if I looked at her the way I wanted to, it made me want to claw my heart out just for some relief from the pain. I needed blindfolds when I had another woman in my bed that didn't look like or smell like her." I wanted another piece of wood to throw. Something to break with my bare hands. I could barely choke out my words because they hurt so badly coming up. But I couldn't keep them in. Not anymore. "It was even worse when they did look like her, Michael. Those blindfolds were the ones I needed the most, because then I didn't have to look at myself either. And if Anna ever looked at me like I made it worse for her, like I was a stumbling block in her getting past this, I'd hate myself more than I already do for loving her for this long, when she was *never* mine to love."

My chest heaved in the silence that followed, my breaths jagged and violent and loud as they left my body. Michael stared at me like he didn't even know me. Probably because outbursts were not precisely my thing. But damned if I didn't feel a little bit better. My temples throbbed, and my throat was dry and thick, but I felt better. When Michael did speak, I braced myself for a joke, but that wasn't what happened.

"I'm so sorry, brother." He turned and dropped onto the bench facing me, like he couldn't stand under the weight of what I'd flung at him. "I can't even," he shook his head slowly, "I can't even imagine what it must have been like for you."

He'd probably tried, I'm sure. They probably all tried to imagine what it was like for me all these years. And even if they had the most vivid imaginations, there was no way they'd be able to touch what it was like. They'd never be able to comprehend what it did to my insides to be around her and not be able to touch her. Or worse, to not be around her and pretend like I knew what it felt like to be able to do just that.

It wasn't their fault that they didn't know, couldn't know.

"I expected you to make a joke," I said gruffly. Emotional Michael was ... weird. Probably as weird as it was for him to have me completely explode.

He smiled, but it was sad. "I think before Brooke, I would have. Before Piper and Jacob. But ... I see things differently now. And trying to imagine what it would have been like to watch Brooke immediately after the twins' father left, watch her every single day as she worked through it, knowing that I'd loved her through everything leading up to it." Michael swiped a hand down his face and stared at me. "It sounds impossibly painful, bro."

I exhaled heavily. He got it. He really got it. Even if understanding something hypothetically was only a brief touch of true, full understanding, he knew what I was trying to say.

The pressure in my chest eased slightly and I sat next to him, braced my elbows on my legs and let my hands hang uselessly in between. A fitting image of how I felt inside.

My self-imposed cage was gone, the door left wide open, but there I sat, motionless. And I didn't see another way around it. For now.

"It has been impossibly painful," I admitted. "And I'm not sitting here because I'm too afraid to lay it all out there for her, it's because I know this isn't the time. It's too soon."

Too soon.

What I felt was too much.

Inside of me, it was too big.

If I laid it at her feet now, it would overwhelm her. And that wasn't something I could live with.

From the table, my phone alarm went off, reminding me that

I needed to leave to meet with Anna on time. I rubbed at the dull pain in my chest.

"I need to head out."

Michael nodded. "Yeah, Uncle Jim and I need to go check out a new site anyway."

If we worked for anyone else, I wouldn't be able to duck out from my usual responsibilities for the general contracting side of the business and take on this job for Anna. Perks of being nephews to the boss, and I had zero issue taking advantage of that for situations like this one. We had more than enough guys who wanted the hours, anyway.

After he stood from the bench, Michael laid his hand on my shoulder and I glanced up at him.

"Sorry I pushed," he said.

"It's okay."

"It's not," he countered. "But it is from a place of love. It's been hard for all of us to watch you like this. If there's a chance, you know we want you to be able to take it."

I laughed under my breath, but it hurt coming out. All the things that I'd kept shoved down about Anna hurt coming up. "I do too, brother."

Driving out to the house, I had to admit to myself that what I'd unleashed onto an unsuspecting Michael had been a necessary purging. My feelings for Anna had been so tightly entwined inside of me that exorcising them was a painful process. And that wouldn't stop simply because her situation had changed. They were knotted and tangled around my bones and muscles, the very fiber of who I was in an inconceivable and illogical way.

Illogical to everyone, including me. When I tried to separate all of Anna's qualities, the things that made her who she was, I knew in my head that I could piece those back together in a different body of a different woman. It should have been easy. But it wasn't, because for the first couple years, I tried to do just that.

If I could have taken the sweetness of her, the sense of humor, the way she saw the world in shapes and colors and lines—just like me—the surprising bite of snark that she let out when she couldn't help herself, I should have been able to find those traits in someone else. I should've been able to find a beautiful smile that twisted up my insides, that made me want to smile back. I should've been able to find the fierce, almost misguided sense of loyalty that we shared for people who either weren't ours, or didn't deserve to be.

But all those things in a different body still wouldn't have been Anna. And *she* was the one who knitted herself around me so tightly that I couldn't—and didn't want to—cut myself free. It wasn't any single one of her traits, it was all of them combined that couldn't be duplicated anywhere else.

The further I drove, the surer I became that giving her space to breathe was the best thing I could do, especially because I wanted all those traits to flourish and strengthen outside of the shadow of her marriage to Marcus.

The thing I could do, that I'd never really been able to do before, was be Anna's friend. Be there for her. Get to know this version of her, let her get to know me in a way I'd never allowed her to.

When I pulled down the bumpy dirt road, fields and trees and mountains rising up behind the wood frame of the large house, I could see her standing on the sprawling porch in jeans and a white sweater that was comically out of place in the construction zone. On top of her head was a yellow work hat. On her face was a smile that competed fiercely with the sun overhead, and it was all I could do not to relish in the brand new crack in my tired heart knowing that it was aimed at me.

Normally, I'd reach a job site like this and stare at the lines of the house, where the best views would be, the way it was seemingly pulled up from the ground and flanked by majestic mountains that made the entire world seem insignificant in their shadow. Normally, I'd marvel at how this house looked exactly right in exactly that spot, among the trees and rock and grass.

But as usual, when she was near, all I saw was her.

Slowly, I put the truck in park and pretended like I was gathering papers from the bench beside me. But I was steadying my breathing, slowing my heart, and getting my head into sharp focus.

I'd spent years setting aside the notion that I was entitled to whatever it was that might make me happy, and just because her finger was empty now, didn't mean that I'd change that.

For right now, what I could do was be her friend. And that was more of her than I'd had two weeks ago. It was more than I'd had for the past six years.

So through the windshield, her still watching me curiously, I gave her a friendly wave before opening the door.

"Are you coming or what?" Anna asked from the porch.

I took a deep breath and then walked toward where she was waiting for me.

CHAPTER ELEVEN

ANNA

It had rained the night before, and my black rain boots sank into the mud as Tristan and I walked around the corner into what would eventually be the backyard. I sidestepped a pile of two by fours and my shoulder brushed against his heavy work jacket.

"Wow," he said in a hushed tone when we both stopped and looked at the jagged sprawl of the Rockies out in the distance. It was late enough in the year that the caps were all white and gray, the heat and sun of summer completely forgotten at their elevation. The aspen leaves were gold, their bark white, and I tipped my face up to the sun.

"Wow is right. Can you imagine owning all this space?" My voice was as quiet as his. There were no workers here today, they were at another site, which is why I'd requested today for Tristan and I to look around. I glanced over at him when he still hadn't answered.

There was something about him that fit into the land that we were standing on. Fit with the imposing mountains and beautiful trees and sprawling, waving fields. Maybe it was because Tristan had all the makings of a perfect mountain man, I thought with a smothered grin, and turned back to the view so he didn't feel self-conscious.

But it was the truth. His pulled-back hair, the strong edge of his jaw that was always covered in dark scruff, even the dirty work boots and the way he wore a flannel shirt underneath his work jacket. I half-expected him to rest an ax over his shoulder and start splitting wood right in front of me.

"I can."

I looked over, surprised that he finally said something. Tristan wasn't looking at me, still focused intently on the mountains. A small smile touched my face that he'd spent that long thinking over my question, which hadn't been much more than hypothetical.

"Should we go in? I'm sure you've got a schedule to keep."

With his hands tucked into his pockets, Tristan turned my direction and shrugged his shoulders. "Not much of a schedule other than to work on this right now. But yeah, let's go in."

"Your uncle was fine with it?"

"Perks of being favorite nephew to the boss."

I smiled as we climbed the steps of the front porch. "Does Michael know you hold this title?"

"Of course. Uncle Jim tells Michael weekly what a giant loud-mouth pain in the ass he is."

My laugh burst out of me in such an indelicate manner that Tristan stopped to gape. Well, his mouth was partially open, so *his* version of gaping. I smoothed a hand down my hair. "What? It was funny."

His dark brown eyes narrowed ever-so-slightly. Then his mouth relaxed into a half-smile when he gestured to the front door. "Shall we?"

When we passed through the framed-out entryway, brightly colored electrical cords snaking up in between the studs, into the great room that hooked toward the dining area, kitchen and break-fast nook, Tristan propped his hands on his hips and nodded while he looked around.

"It's big."

I swallowed another laugh at his gross over-simplification and made a sound of agreement. "It is."

We wandered through the kitchen and back into the master suite, me babbling about I didn't even know what, him taking the occasional note in his small notepad.

"Who was the architect?" he asked, staring at the wall that would eventually be behind the bed in the master bedroom.

When I gave him the name, he nodded approvingly.

"You've worked with them before?"

Tristan glanced at me, his warm brown eyes touching briefly on my face before he looked back at the room. How on earth were his eyelashes that long? "Only a couple times. We don't usually get jobs of the scale that they do. I like how the rooms connect togeth-er. Normally the master suite would be further from the kitchen, but this corner gives it the best view. And separating it using the storage room and butler's pantry gives it some privacy."

"Exactly what I thought. We've worked with them a lot, which helped us get this job."

"You mean you," he said quietly. "You got this job."

My eyebrows raised slightly at his clarification, and I felt myself blush. "Well, it's technically the whole firm working on it, but yes, I pitched it to Millie, which is why I'm overseeing the job."

Tristan rapped the edge of a support beam, eyes passing over the empty room that smelled like sawdust and wood. "You had neutrals in this room, right?"

"I do. Off-white carpet, really plush, at Millie's insistence, whites and off-whites for the linens. Probably brushed gold or copper ac-cents. Why?"

He tapped his thumb against his thigh, staring at where the bed would be. "I'm just wondering about a finish for the beams in the ceiling. I could do the nightstands the same way, maybe make a bench for the foot of the bed if you think it would work."

"Adding more work for yourself?" I teased.

When he looked over at me, his eyes were lit with excitement, warm and contagious. "Have you heard of Shou Shugi-Ban?"

I had, but I couldn't resist messing with him a little, so I kept my face straight. "Why? Because I'm Asian?"

Tristan, God bless him, didn't miss a beat, and it was delightful. "No, because it's your job to know useless and obscure wood-finishing techniques."

He was not wrong. I held up my hand like I was ticking off imaginary points. "An ancient Japanese practice of treating wood with fire. Typically used for exterior finishes like siding and decks, but modern designers have started including it in interiors because of how dark the wood gets and how much wear it can take. The texture is really interesting too."

"That's the one," he said.

I stared up at where the massive beams would end up, imagining them in the almost-black finish, and my excitement was immediate. "I like it. I really like it. It would be a jarring juxtaposition in both color and texture, but in a good way. Make the neutrals seem really soft and warm in comparison."

"It would."

"I can't wait to tell Millie about it." The idea, how it changed things just enough in the room had me jittery and bouncing in place. "I think she'll love it. I'm so happy you thought about it. It never crossed my mind, but probably because I've never used it on a job."

"You're clearly not Asian enough then."

It was so strange how easily my shocked laughter slid out of my mouth, like it had the ability to make up its mind about being out in the world, like it didn't need my permission.

He was watching me laugh, gaze trained steadily on my face, amusement only showing in his eyes. When I finally gained my composure, I blew out a breath and gave him a dry look. "*That* doesn't even warrant a smile from you? You're a smile Nazi, Tristan."

He hummed and looked away.

I tucked my hair behind my ear and gave him a smile of my own. "Well, I think it's a good thing. Then people know you really mean it when you do smile."

"Exactly."

What Garrett said about him the other night rolled through my head, that he didn't do casual, that if I felt the need to blow off steam, Tristan was strictly *verboten*. Just the small pockets of time I'd now spent with him, I knew Garrett was right about that.

And yet ... I couldn't help but look at him through that lens now that it was brought to my attention. Before, objectively, I knew how handsome he was.

Hot.

Tristan was hot. The kind of hot, with his broad shoulders, muscular chest, trim waist and easy, loose gait, that most females were hardwired to notice.

The hair, the eyes, the jaw ... give me a break. That was the icing on a cake that was almost unfair to have walking around for public consumption.

He wasn't a flirt, even the harmless kind. There was intention behind everything he did and said, no accidental touches or inappropriate behavior in the *slightest* and if my brother felt that strongly about me treating Tristan with respect, then I would honor that.

A memory sparked in the back of my head, like an itch I could barely reach. "You know, I think you smiled the very first night that we met."

"Did I?" he murmured. His eyes never left my face and it flipped something low and warm in my belly. Then he blinked away. "Maybe I did. You might have caught me on one of my three days a year when I smile freely. Or that's what Michael says anyway."

The change in mood was like he'd opened a window and let a

burst of cool air into a hot, stuffy room, and I inhaled deeply at the shift. It was good that he had. My mind was so all over the place lately, and this was the last thing I needed, especially when it came to someone like Tristan.

My phone buzzed in my purse and snapped me from the moment. When I briefly glanced at the text from work, I noticed that it was later than I'd thought, and my stomach rumbled almost instantly.

"Do you have time to grab some lunch?" I asked. "There's a great place just down the road, total dive, but they have amazing food. I've met Millie there before."

His visible hesitation almost made me regret my impulsive offer, but I couldn't take it back now. "Look," I said softly, "just a friendly meal, I promise. I won't unload my troubles on you or start sobbing into my pancakes, which are delicious, by the way. We can talk wood-charring and herringbone patterns only." I made an X over my heart.

One side of his mouth curved up. "Sounds like a boring lunch."

"Oh yeah, right. Those are probably the only topics that would make you contribute equally in the conversation."

We walked out of the room, and he waited while I closed up the door behind me.

"Are you saying I'm not a good conversationalist?"

His voice was so dry that I stopped in the middle of the muddy path to our cars and turned to him. "You know that's exactly what I'm saying."

"My friends would agree with you."

"Does that mean you're saying yes to lunch?"

There was a suspended moment where he didn't answer, just looked beyond me to the house, then briefly at me again. Nerves had me crossing my arms over my chest. When he spoke, he chose his words carefully. "Let's do it. Then maybe you can be another new friend on my side when they all tell me that I have the speaking skills of a rock."

I grinned. "I can do that. Besides, the pancakes really are to die for."

Tristan pulled in a slow breath and held my eyes as he spoke. "I guess you know how to hit me in my weak spots."

My laugh was instant. "So that's a yes?"

He gestured to our parked cars. "Lead the way."

We managed to snag two orange stools at the counter of Village Coffee Shop, the crowd heavier than I expected it to be during a Monday lunch hour.

The interior of the restaurant was completely unpretentious, a true greasy spoon, so the first time Millie told me to meet her there, I almost died on the spot when I walked inside.

The booths were faux wood without any cushion, bright orange formica tables, and the old-fashioned padded stools at the counter looked like they were plucked straight from the sixties. But the food was incredible, and Tristan looked comfortable with my choice as he perused the plastic menu. His elbows were spread out, so I made sure to keep my arms down so I didn't hog any of his counter space.

A smiling waitress stopped in front of us, a number two pencil wedged behind her ear in a mass of orange hair that matched the stools perfectly. "What can I getchu two?"

I smiled and tucked my menu back in between two sugar canisters. "I'll have the short stack of buttermilk pancakes, please."

"Sure thing, sweetie." Her eyes flipped to Tristan. "For you?"

"Pancake combo, please. Eggs over medium. And uhh, some coffee, if you get a chance."

"You've got it, handsome. Be back around with some coffee."

Tristan cleared his throat and I saw a slight tinge of red on his cheekbones.

"Do you really only smile three times a year?"

He had just taken a sip of water, and it caught in his throat on the way down. With a closed fist, Tristan covered his mouth until he successfully got the water down.

"Sorry about that," I said on a laugh.

"It's fine." He shifted and his shoulder brushed against my arm. "I guess I've never really counted before, but you know Michael, he tends toward the dramatic."

"That's something I relate to very well. A dramatic brother."

He nodded. "Yes, you probably do."

The waitress popped back in front of us with a hot pot of coffee and she deftly filled two white mugs and slid them in front of us. I smiled at her when she brought back a small bowl of flavored cream.

Against his thigh, Tristan's thumb started tapping again, something I now knew meant he was working something over in his head, so I let him do so in silence. "Did you talk to Garrett?"

Ahh. Yes. I'd told him I was going to. "I did. It went," I paused and tilted my head, "well, about as expected. Though he was less obnoxious than I was mentally prepared for, which is always good."

"Good." Tristan propped his elbows on the counter again and glanced over at me, his hands folded together on the shining surface. "And you're doing okay?"

He asked it so warmly, so unobtrusively that it almost brought tears to my eyes. Most people asked questions like that and it was obvious that there was a slight edge to their question. They wanted to satisfy their own morbid curiosity, their own rabid fascination with why your marriage ended, why you finally moved out, rather than a genuine desire to know if you were okay.

There was no edge to his question. No indication that he'd be disappointed if I told him that most days, I didn't know what the hell I felt. That I couldn't give people any more of an explanation than I was able to give myself.

Not yet, at least. It was that tangle in my head that was the most confusing. And it was the reason that throwing myself into work was the best and worst kind of distraction. Why staying with my mom helped me escape the kind of silence that would force me to work through that tangle.

But here wasn't the place to get into that. And I wasn't entirely sure that Tristan was the person who I should unload it onto. Not yet.

Even if that were true, he deserved an honest answer. So I gave him what I could. I met his eyes and let out a deep, weighted breath. "I'm not quite sure yet."

He nodded, as if he instantly believed that that was the truth. Like he knew that there was no possible way for me to remain unscathed and unscarred from what I'd experienced with Marcus. He wasn't wrong, but I wasn't in the mood to shove that discovery process to the forefront right now.

I felt the tension that had seeped into my frame release with a few focused breaths, with the reminder that I was sitting with someone who wouldn't judge my strange non-answer.

The reason I knew that is because he didn't pry beyond that.

"Nothing wrong with that," was all he said, in that deep, gruff voice of his.

I exhaled a soft laugh. "Most people wouldn't say that. They want to know everything. It's like social media has made us think we're entitled to every thought that's running through people's heads, you know?"

"And that is why I'm not on social media."

One of my eyebrows lifted. "At all?"

He shrugged, clearly a little uncomfortable with my question. "Doesn't seem like there would be anyone who would care about what I ate for dinner or what hike I went on, because they can look at someone else's dinner, see pictures from someone else's hike. It doesn't make the experiences more real for me by making them available for public consumption."

I turned as much as possible in my stool and set my chin in my hand so I could watch his face when he spoke.

"That's so true. Sometimes I find myself putting a picture on

Instagram and I have to fight the urge to delete it ten minutes later, because I have this moment of, who *really* cares about this? They either don't know me, or they only know this filtered version of me. Would they even notice if I didn't post?"

Tristan lifted his coffee mug up to his mouth and took a careful sip, giving me a slightly dry look that surprised me.

"I'm sure lots of people care what you post."

"Why, because I'm a female?" I teased.

"Something like that," he mumbled, giving a quick glance at my face.

Before I could push what he meant, our food was delivered, and we lapsed into a food-lulled silence, punctuated only by my random exclamations of how good their pancakes were.

Tristan took his time buttering his, cutting them into precise squares before he carefully poured syrup around the edge of his plate.

"Oh my *gosh*," I said around a mouthful of pancake. "That's the craziest pancake prep I've ever seen."

He didn't spare me a glance, only shook his head before finally digging in. "What's crazy about it? Now the syrup won't make it soggy."

I laughed. "You're so weird."

His lips curled. Slightly. And I narrowed my eyes, because now I felt like he was withholding the smile on purpose.

We finished our meal with some more talk about the house, and it was just ... nice. Easy.

Even though I insisted on paying with my company card, Tristan glared at me and threw some cash down on the countertop.

"See?" I asked as he held the door open for me and we walked back out into the bright sunshine. "Not a bad work lunch, huh?"

His hands were jammed into his coat pockets, and we were walking closely enough that I could feel the heat from his big, tall body.

"I wouldn't say so, no."

That was his response, and I couldn't stop the wide grin. The way he spoke, the reserved answers and impossibly small expressions, it would take some getting used to.

I swallowed as I pulled my car keys out of my purse and pressed the button to unlock the doors. The lights flashed, and I stopped to face him.

"Or maybe not a bad friend lunch?"

Tristan squinted into the sun before he looked back at me. "Not a bad one of those either."

He nodded as I smiled my goodbye and slid into my SUV. When I pulled out of the parking spot, he was watching me drive away, and I realized that having a friend like Tristan was probably the best possible thing for me right now. Through my body, I felt a slow roll of contentment for the first time all week. Maybe, just maybe, I would be able to untangle the mess inside of me just fine.

CHAPTER TWELVE

TRISTAN

All I'd felt like doing, all I'd *been* doing for the past three days—save sleeping and eating—was work on sketches for Anna.

For Millie, I thought resolutely. For the client. Since she'd be the one using them. I'd had custom jobs over the years that had easily kept my attention, that wasn't difficult. I enjoyed piecing together what the client had envisioned for themselves, finding creative ways to make it real, something that would fit seamlessly into their homes and their lives.

But this was consuming me. Every morning, I'd woken with my mind racing, my fingers twitching until I could put pencil to paper, I'd lean back and stare, erase and tweak and sketch and shade, and then move to my laptop and make those into concrete plans. Everything would need to be approved by Anna and her coworker, as well as Millie, but I knew that what I'd come up with so far would be perfect.

That wasn't narcissism, I just had a feeling deep in my gut that every line and edge and joint of what I'd build would work for that house.

And only once, a miracle considering how often I'd picked up my phone and thought about texting her, I sent Anna a few pictures of what I had so far, just to open the lines of communication. A test to see how well I could actually pull off this friend thing.

Me: Thoughts? [IMG ATTACHED]

I'd sent that one and cringed, because clearly, I did still have the conversation skills of a rock.

Anna: TRISTAN! For the dining chairs? Those are GORGEOUS. The back matches the archway into the kitchen perfectly.
Anna: Will I be overstepping completely if I ask to see the sketches of the captain's chairs, too?

Me: You're the boss, aren't you? [IMG ATTACHED]

Anna: Ha. Yeah, I guess. But that feels weird. We're working together, you're not working FOR me.
Anna: And GAH, that's so pretty I could cry. I can't imagine being able to build something like that from scratch. You are *very* talented, I hope you know that.

Me: I enjoy the work. Thanks for giving me the opportunity.

Ladies and gentleman, Exhibit A of why I was still single. My texting skills weren't much better than my speaking ability. It didn't seem to bother her though, so I decided not to be so hard on myself. If anything, this new layer to my relationship with Anna was allowing me some much-needed practice in normal Tristan, not tortured, brooding Tristan.

And it felt good.

Coupled with the fact that I'd allowed my friends to get me out of the house after so many days of work, I felt like maybe I could handle this new reality better than I anticipated.

"Earth to Tristan," Cole called from the kitchen.

I rubbed my forehead and stood from the couch.

"Another beer?" he asked when I joined them around the island. Cole's wife Julia had baked us some wicked looking cookies before she took their foster son to hang out with Brooke, who was her younger sister, and the twins.

I shook my head, but snagged a cookie. "No, thanks. Just water for me tonight."

If I decided to sketch more when I got home, I wanted a clear head.

"Boo," Garrett said, chucking a wadded-up napkin at me. "What's your problem? You should be the happiest guy in the greater Denver area for the foreseeable future."

Every muscle in my body tensed as a weighted silence fell over the room. Dylan and Michael glanced at me in tandem, Cole shot a look at Garrett, who ignored it and kept staring at me.

Of course, they all knew. They'd probably all discussed it too. That was the problem with a group of friends like the one I had. We'd known each other for years, been friends since before anyone of us had a significant other to share a roof with. Now, I was the only single one, which surprised no one.

The only surprise situation was Anna's newly minted relationship status, and the fact that we'd never discussed this out loud.

Not once.

They all knew how I felt about her. And while it had been hinted, heavily referenced and slipped into random subtext of various conversations over the years, we'd never had an honest conversation about what I felt for Anna. The weight of that pressed over me like hot bricks, and I wanted nothing more than to shove them to the side, as far away from me as possible.

The lightness I'd felt just before Garrett opened his mouth was gone, well and truly out of the building. All because I thought we'd continue with the status quo; my feelings for Anna remaining firmly out of the spotlight until she was able to move past what happened with Marcus.

Michael met my eyes briefly before I leveled Garrett with a long look and even response. "I'm always happy."

Dylan snickered and Cole choked on his beer.

"You know what I mean," Garrett said. My look did nothing to him, because he met it without blinking. Son of a bitch, this was really going to happen. I could see it in his stupid, beady eyes that he wasn't going to let this drop. "I *mean* you should be happy because my sister is no longer married."

I slicked my tongue over my teeth and just stared at him. Because what did he expect me to say?

"Don't pretend like you don't know," he continued. Speaking of not pretending, Dylan and Cole didn't even pretend like they weren't dying to hear what was going to come next, bouncing their eyes between me and Garrett like someone was about to throw a punch. "She told me that you actually knew before I did."

"Oh shiiiit," Dylan said under his breath.

I rolled my eyes. It was a casual movement that belied that violent beat of satisfaction that she mentioned it to Garrett, that I knew first. That I noticed first.

"Not that I need to defend that," I said dryly, "but we were meeting at her office and I happened to notice that she wasn't wearing her ring."

"Did you do a victory dance before asking her about it?" Garrett asked.

"No."

"Fist-pump? High-five yourself?"

"No."

"Not even a little *Oh hell yes, now is my shot, all you shitheads who thought I was hopeless*?"

I exhaled. "No."

That came later when I left the office and realized I'd made it through the conversation with her without passing out or crying tears of relief. But Garrett the asshole didn't need to know that. I loved Garrett, truly, but he annoyed the hell out of me sometimes.

Michael was shaking his head, and even though Cole had a slight smile on his face, no one was laughing. I guess I could be thankful for small favors, because this was something that I couldn't handle being a joke to them, fodder to make themselves grateful for how uncomplicated and happy their lives were.

"Dude," Garrett laughed incredulously. "She left him. And you're sitting here acting like nothing is different. Like we're just drinking beer on a regular weekend."

"We are." My eyes held a warning though, one he clearly wanted to ignore. "Because I don't need your input on this."

"You guys are working together. Don't tell me that there won't be some romantic late-night design sessions or whatever. You'll be bonded forever over oak dining tables and circular saws and ... I don't know," he sputtered, "tile designs or whatever."

"Garrett," I warned. "I'm already handling it."

"Plus," Dylan interjected, "circular saws are not romantic. At all."

My eyes closed and I pinched the bridge of my nose. I heard Michael exhale slowly.

"As much as I hate admitting this with any sort of regularity, but Garrett's right," Cole said. My eyes stayed closed. "Working together is a great opportunity. Especially since your jobs mesh so well. It's a perfect way for her to see how good you could be for her."

My chin dropped to my chest and I rolled my neck. Before I looked up again, I counted out two deep breaths in, two deep breaths out. They're just trying to help, I reminded myself. It wasn't their fault that talking this stuff out when I didn't feel ready made me feel cornered. Inexplicably defensive because I couldn't label my emotions neatly, put them in clean boxes for dissection and discussion.

They wanted a box labeled *Tristan and Anna: What's he going to do now?* And I wasn't ready to open it up for them just yet.

Garrett sounded like a revival preacher, even mimicking the hand motions of a man who felt like immortal souls were in peril of ending up in the fiery pits and he alone could save them.

"You could ask her out to lunch!" He drummed his hands on the counter like he'd just saved one person. "Make up a wood emergency. And then, bam, be like, are you in need of a good man who won't do you wrong? You're lookin' at him."

Cole shook his head and Dylan shoved at Garrett a little. I kept breathing. In and out. In and out.

"Ignore him," Cole said. "That's a terrible idea."

"I'm well aware," I answered evenly. "I really don't need any of these ideas since I already have my own."

But it was like I hadn't even spoken.

"Garrett might be a terrible planner, but he's right, timing is everything," Dylan added. "Look at the four of us. If the timing was off for any of us, we probably wouldn't have ended up where we are now. The timing of this can't be anything other than fate, man."

He sounded so excited. So hopeful. All the things that I'd felt at some point when I obsessed over every facet of my situation. But with every word out of their mouths, I felt the walls close in around me. More than anything, I didn't want a replay of what I'd spewed to Michael in the wood shop. It hurt to let all of that out after bottling it for so many years, even if it had been a necessary purging, a relief after all was said and done.

"I know all of that," I said, but oh man, they were on a roll now.

"Timing, yes!" Garrett said *way* too loudly. "Look at the timing, man!"

"That's enough," Michael snapped.

My head snapped up right as mouth one, two and then three dropped open.

"Dude," Garrett laughed uncomfortably. "Chill."

"You need to back the hell off of him and maybe I will."

I shifted where I stood, trying to put a name to the foreign feeling that slid through me, warm and quick. It wasn't shock, because I'd seen Michael mad before. I'd seen him sad and stressed and hurt, my normally happy-go-lucky, make-everyone-laugh brother. You couldn't go through what we did as kids and not see those things in each other.

No, what I was feeling was something close to awe.

Because what I'd never seen from my little brother was *him* protecting *me*.

Cole had the decency to look chagrined. "We're just trying to help."

"You're not though," Michael bit out. "You're pushing because you think you know what he should do. None of us know that. Because none of us—no matter what the hell we went through with Kat and Rory and Julia and Brooke to end up with them—have any fucking clue how Tristan feels right now."

Garrett raised his hands, but I saw the defensiveness in his gesture. "Need I remind you that Anna is my sister? I'm not talking about a stranger here."

"Yeah," Michael said. "Your *sister*. It's different. And Cole, yeah you waited a long time to be with Julia again, but she was your wife before. You waited for all those years knowing what it was like to have her love you back. None of us know what it feels like for him right now, and unless you do, I suggest you back off and let him deal with this the way he thinks is best."

I cleared my throat in the awkward pulse of silence when I was sure my voice would work right. Because for a few minutes, it felt like I was trying to swallow a ball of cat hair or something.

"It's okay, Michael," I said when they all looked over at me. But I didn't look anywhere but my little brother. I dipped my chin and he nodded slowly. Baton officially passed, in brother terms. "Look, I'm not going to justify my action or non-action, as you may view it. Mainly because I don't have to. You guys know me well enough to know that I'd never do anything to hurt Anna, and that includes pushing her too far, too fast."

Garrett looked away and sighed. Dylan turned his beer bottle on the counter, while Cole rubbed the back of his neck.

"I appreciate the fact that you're excited for me," I continued in their silence. "I know that you only want me to be happy, especially if it ends up being with..." The cat hair was back in my throat and I willed it away. "With her."

"I'm sorry, man," Garrett said. His face held a slight flush of embarrassment.

"It's okay." I looked at each of them. "My situation *is* different. Which is why I'd appreciate it if you could just respect the fact that I know what I'm doing."

Garrett rubbed at his jaw and regarded me for a while. "Can I ask what that is? You know I'm on your side, right?"

Did I want to lay out my plan? Their faces held varying degrees of curiosity, but every one of them was supportive. They wanted this to work out for me, which is why I braced my hands on the counter and took a deep breath.

"I'm going to be her friend. It's not a role I've ever allowed myself before, because it was too hard. Anna deserves the opportunity to work through this big thing that happened to her, and if the time it takes her to do that is time that we can spend getting to know each other in a new way, then I want to be there for her."

Cole lifted his eyebrows. "I give you credit, Tristan. That takes a level of patience not many guys have."

"Maybe that's true," I said. "But it feels right. Feels healthy, for her and me. I haven't waited this long just to screw it up by pushing her too fast."

Garrett narrowed his eyes, finally cracking a smile when no one spoke. "I approve of this plan."

I rolled my eyes. "Oh goody. Now I can move forward with it."

After a low roll of laughter, Michael clapped his hands. "Excellent. The mute has spoken his piece, used more words than we usually hear out from him in a month, I officially became the group asshole for once, and now we're ready for a subject change." He looked around expectantly. "Preferably something happy."

After taking a deep breath, Dylan raised his hand. "I proposed to Kat last night and she said yes."

For a beat, none of us did anything, but then we all moved at once. Thumping him on the back, cracking open beers, shoving each other like idiots, because Kat and Dylan had been living together for a couple years, and he'd been biding his sweet-ass time before popping the question when he knew she was ready for it.

If anyone could understand the value of being patient, waiting for the right time, it would be Dylan. He knew Kat had been through a lot as a kid, and just wasn't quite ready for the next step, even though he was. And he'd respected that time.

"I'm happy for you," I told him, after a bruising hug.

He smiled. "Thanks. I thought I was going to puke when I got down on my knee, especially when the first thing she said was, '*Oh shit, are you having a heart attack?*'"

Everyone laughed, because that sounded like something Kat would do when faced with a marriage proposal. For the first time all evening, I felt a weight lifted off me. Maybe because the attention was off me, and onto something that we'd been looking forward to for a long time.

Maybe because I knew that the first real conversation about me and Anna was off the table. Finally.

And even though I knew they supported me, supported my decision, I also wasn't stupid enough to think that my plan didn't come with some built-in challenges.

Being Anna's friend would be difficult, have an entirely different set of challenges inherent in that role, but in my gut, I knew it was the right thing to do.

More than that, I was excited—not a word I applied to myself often—to get to know her like this. Form new memories with this person I'd loved for so long, in a framework that allowed me to cherish them without the heavy chains of self-loathing that always accompanied them before.

It was an entire new reality, and one I was looking forward to exploring.

CHAPTER THIRTEEN

ANNA

There was something tricky about hope that no one ever told you. It was an elusive, slippery little bitch. It popped in and out on some unknown whim, and when it was gone, best have some wine on hand, girlfriend. I managed to keep hope around me pretty well after falling apart to my mom. We became tentative friends; hope and I did.

And really, I should have known that it was only a matter of time before she flew the coop, even briefly. Why?

Because Emily Dickinson told us that hope was a bird.

What did birds have? *Wings.*

Wings to fly away whenever the hell they felt like it.

And here's the other thing ... you couldn't put on a fake tough front and pray that it brought hope back. You couldn't sit there and say with all your inner gangster, Oh, I'll *force* you back to my side. Oh no. Hope did whatever it pleased, whenever it pleased.

Which was why I found myself sitting in the front seat of my car in the King Sooper parking lot, crying ugly snot tears into a pint of Half Baked. I hadn't even made it home before seeking the unequaled solace of Ben & Jerry's, for crying out loud.

It seemed impossible that only a few days earlier, I'd stood outside Millie's and felt the warm sweep of hope before Tristan and I grabbed lunch. A nice, easy, fun lunch, one where I felt like my new normal was something that I could finally feel excited about.

That triggered a fresh wave of tears, and when I caught my reflection in the rear-view mirror, I dropped my head back on the head rest and groaned. My mascara was more on my cheeks than on my eyelashes, dirty track marks that I tried to rub off with the heel of my hand, but they only smeared more.

"Pull yourself together, Anna," I whispered, and dug through my console for some tissues. I found some, and poured water from my bottle to attempt to fix my macabre makeup disaster. After a few swipes, I looked like a less scary version of myself and took a deep breath.

The ice cream was capped and put back into the bag on the passenger seat floor. But I kept my car off while I took a deep breath and stared out into the bustling parking lot. I'd parked far enough away from the store, that no one seemed to witness my little breakdown.

The impetus of that breakdown left the store while I watched like a creeper, and I fought against the blurry layer of tears that sprang up again. It was nothing that I hadn't seen a thousand times in the last eight years. Just a family. A young family, with a chubby baby perched in the front of the cart, a smiling husband who pushed the cart for his pregnant wife. They'd passed me in the ice cream aisle, and something about them made me stop. Made me stare.

I should've felt hope when I did. And I waited for it in that moment, cold air blasting me from the door that I held open. But it wasn't there. It didn't come in the way I'd been so sure it would.

You can have that now, was the thought I expected in its wake. You can *finally* have all of that, Anna.

But that wasn't what I felt. It wasn't what I thought.

I hate you, Marcus. It was like a wrecking ball into my brain, unlike the soothing, slow climb of hope that I so desperately wanted. The second blow was worse, it hurt more, because I still hadn't figured out how to move past it.

I hate myself for staying so long, was what came next.

That one was even more damaging.

Over the years, I'd tried to bring up starting a family. Less as the calendar passed, because it was perfectly obvious that it wouldn't fix anything for us. It only would've made things worse. But that didn't stop me from wanting it. And now all I could think, watching that smiling, sweet family load up into their practical SUV, was *What if it's too late for me? What if it takes me years to find the man who will warm all these cold corners inside of me and we're finally ready to try? What if it doesn't happen?*

The tears fell again, fast and hot, and I took a few deep breaths before starting my car and driving back to my mom's house. This situation, whatever healing or grieving or processing I needed to do, was like being strapped into a roller coaster blindfolded. I just needed to trust that I wouldn't fall out before I reached the end. And pray that hope would return, fly its way back sooner rather than later.

Hope that out there was a man who'd smile at me in the way he smiled. Who'd push a baby in a shopping cart and lay his hand on my back before he started unloading the groceries. Who'd kiss me full on the mouth in a crowded parking lot, simply because he wanted to.

That any of those things could be mine someday.

It took seven more days before I felt it again. Five long days of work to distract me, ice cream as my healthier attempt at coping (versus my solid second choice of alcohol, so I was counting that in the good life choice category), and two days of happy chick flicks with my mom on the weekend before I crawled back into my twin bed and started all over again the next day.

"You look nice today," Corryn said as she dropped some files off on my desk.

"This ol' thing?"

She cackled when I did a little spin in place, my black velvet heels squeaking slightly on the floor as I did. The sleekly cut olive green dress with cap sleeves and a little black bow at the waist was my go-to for big client meetings, and Tristan would be at the office shortly to show me and Millie his designs.

Throughout the week, I'd gotten some PDFs via email, along with his texts with random pictures attached and I loved what he'd sent, but the thought of seeing everything laid out together had humming-birds flitting through my belly.

Corryn eyed my hair, which was straightened and down my back. "Did you know that if I looked hard enough, I could probably make out my own reflection in your hair?"

I rolled my eyes. "You've been using that joke for four years now, and man, it just keeps getting funnier."

"No, really." She leaned in. "Hold still, I need to check my eye-liner. The last time Millie was here, she told me I looked like a hooker with that cat-eye thing I was trying." With two hands, she tilted my head toward the light. "Seriously, I think I can see myself if you face the lamp."

I laughed and shoved at her shoulder when she really tried. "Blame my excellent genes."

"Actually, I'm pretty sure you must have sacrificed a baby goat somewhere along the way to get hair that shiny. I kinda hate you for it." She patted her dark brown hair that was always slightly frizzy, no matter the weather. "But I did go on a date last night with a guy who told me he loved how much *personality* my hair had."

"That's sweet."

She snorted. "You would think so. But your judgement can't be trusted, since you went lots'o'years without a single compliment on all that annoying gorgeousness, so a man could probably wink and slap your ass and you'd think he was sweet."

While I thought about that, I tilted my head. "Not the biggest fan of sexual harassment, so probably not. It sounds so genuine though. I like genuine. And kind. There's nothing wrong with that."

Something lit in her eyes, and she shooed me aside so that she could take my desk chair. "You know, it's time you went on a date, missy."

"You think so, huh?" I said dismissively, picking up all of my notebooks for Millie and making sure they were in order. It wasn't the first time she'd brought this up since I told her about leaving Marcus.

She spun in the chair and faced me, her legs crossed primly and her hands folded over her knees. "It's time."

I raised an eyebrow. "It's only been a few weeks."

"And there's some handbook out there that says when you're allowed to let someone take you out for a casual dinner? I don't think so. You're on Anna's timeline. No one else's."

"Corryn," I sighed. I loved her, but her nosiness was something I needed divine protection from sometimes.

She pointed a finger at me. "No, don't give me that. Mentally, you were checked out of that relationship the month after your dad died, and don't you dare lie to me and say that you weren't. That was, what? A year and a half? Two years ago? Packing your bags and walking out, filing the papers and getting the process started was a mere formality."

I rubbed my forehead and stared out my office window. People walked down the sidewalk, some on their phones, some talking and laughing and smiling, living their lives.

"I don't want..." I glanced at her nervously, because after so many years of marriage, even to Marcus, I hadn't had conversations like this with anyone. "I don't want hookups, Corryn. Not that there's anything wrong with that," I rushed to say. I didn't want her to think I was judging her, because I wasn't. I worried my fingers together in front of me. "I'm just ... you know that's not me. I'm not ready for ... that."

Corryn didn't even blink. "Bumble."

"Come again?"

She swiped my phone from the desk and typed in the password that I'd regrettably given her one week when I was sick. "You need Bumble. It's like the classier version of Tindr, and women are totally in control of the communication."

"How do you mean?" I crossed my arms at her smug grin. "I'm clueless about all of this stuff, okay?"

Narrowing her eyes at the screen, her thumbs flew as she typed. "How tall are you?"

"Five-four. Wait, are you signing me up right *now*?"

"Mm-hmm. I'm using your Facebook profile picture because you look smokin'."

I placed a hand on my belly, trying to tame the riot of flutters. "Hang on, Corryn, I don't know if I'm ready for this."

Finally, she looked up at me. "Then don't swipe right or initiate communication. If you want to? Great. He has twenty-four hours to respond before the match disappears."

"Really?"

"Really." She waved me over, and I took a deep breath before I stood behind the chair and looked over her shoulder. She tapped a button and showed me the profile she'd just created. "Anna, you're ready. Look me in the eye right now and tell me that you wouldn't mind wearing this pretty green dress that makes your ass look phenomenal and letting a hot marketing consultant take you out for dinner. Just to feel what it's like to ... I don't know, have the possibility of something good. Someone good. Even if it's only dinner."

The screen swam in front of my eyes as I actually gave her question some weight, let it roll through my head and seep down into my heart. Was I ready for that? Something that would strictly be for the purposes of dipping my toes back into that world?

It had been years—my sophomore year of college, if I thought about it—since I'd gotten ready for a first date. Those possibilities were exciting. When you agonized over what to wear and your makeup and hair and you analyzed where he was taking you or what he'd planned.

Maybe he held the door of your car open, and you knew right away he'd be a gentleman, or you came back to your roommates with a giggle-worthy horror story of what stories he wouldn't shut up about. But the possibilities were always there.

It was hope.

And that was something I desperately wanted to keep by my side. Not in a faked, forced way. But leaving the door open for something more, should the situation present itself. That was something I felt ready to do.

I found myself nodding. "I wouldn't mind."

Corryn slapped the surface of my desk and I jumped. "That's what I'm talkin' about. Okay, now let me show you how you search for connections around you." She snickered under her breath. "Maybe the hot carpenter is on here. I'd swipe right *so hard*."

My head twisted in her direction. "Tristan?"

"Who else would I mean?"

"Mean for what?" His voice came from my office door and both Corryn and I jumped. I snatched my phone out of her hands like he could see it somehow. Not that it mattered. I wasn't doing anything wrong.

Corryn was more relaxed than me, and she gave him a friendly smile. Correction, it was flirty. I elbowed her.

Tristan's eyes moved back and forth between us, like he could see my embarrassment. He was dressed up—for him at least—his hair pulled back more neatly than usual, his facial hair trimmed close to the hard line of his jaw, and for the first time, I noticed that his eyes were the exact color of mahogany.

What a weird thing to notice.

"I just signed Anna up for Bumble. She's trying not to have a panic attack about it," Corryn said like she was discussing the weather.

His brow pulled in as he processed what she was saying. Then he glanced quickly at me. "I don't ... I don't know what that is."

Corryn sighed heavily, and I barely held myself back from elbowing her again. "Of course you don't."

"I'm sure Tristan doesn't care what Bumble is."

Why did I feel so defensive about it? Corryn was giving me a strange look, and Tristan just looked, well, downright uncomfortable.

"It's not that I don't care what it is," he said slowly. "I'm just pretty clueless about most social media stuff, as you know."

I smiled at that, thinking of our conversation at lunch. "I remember."

He was starting to smile back and I found myself holding my breath.

"It's a dating app," Corryn said, because she hated me and wanted to see me embarrassed as thoroughly as possible.

His entire body stilled before he turned his chin in her direction. "Oh. Okay."

There was no burgeoning smile on his face anymore, and I felt a flush of embarrassment heat my face for no apparent reason.

"Not a trashy one," I found myself interjecting. Then I shifted my shoulders. I didn't need to justify this. All I'd done was sign up, for crying out loud. "And I don't have to swipe right if I don't want to."

Corryn coughed behind her hand and I wanted the floor to jump up and swallow me whole.

Tristan blinked twice before meeting my eyes, and his broad chest expanded on a deep breath. Then another. It was like he had this ability to visually reset, right in front of my eyes. I'd seen him do it before.

It's a classier version of Tinder, I wanted to yell, but that probably wouldn't mean anything more to him than the word Bumble had. To this man who apparently didn't do casual, who didn't have social media because he wanted his life experiences to mean more than likes and comments and virtual reactions from strangers.

"Is Millie here yet?" I managed, weirdly desperate to change the subject from my non-existent, not-yet-started hypothetical dating life.

Tristan held my eyes before he shook his head. It was that look in his eyes, a touch of understanding, like he knew I was embarrassed and he wasn't judging me for it that made me relax incrementally.

He answered quietly. "Not yet. If you'll just tell me where we're meeting, I'll get all my stuff ready."

"Oh, umm, right in the main work room," I said.

He nodded and left the doorway. Corryn clicked her tongue. "Doesn't know what Bumble is. Now that's a damn shame."

"Corryn."

"What? Look at his ass. Don't tell me you haven't noticed."

"It's entirely beside the point whether I have or not," I muttered, carefully stacking my files together and then picking them up.

Corryn snickered and walked out in front of me. Tristan was staring down at his designs that were spread out on the white work tables, his hands propped on his hips. I did the same thing before a client came in to see renderings for the first time.

What would they see?

Was my vision for them clear?

Did it match the vision they had for themselves?

Tristan was so engrossed in staring at what was on the table, he startled when I came up next to him. I picked up a 3-D rendering of the coffee table and matching end tables and smiled widely.

"These are perfect, Tristan." My finger traced the herringbone pattern that was inlaid in the top of the square table. "I love that."

"Yeah?"

I glanced at him, and his face was so close that I couldn't ignore what I'd noticed earlier. Definitely mahogany. That was it. Warm tones streaked through the iris, almost yellow around the edges in some places. But so deeply brown in others. He'd laugh if I told him, so I looked back at the papers.

"Yeah. I think Millie will too." Taking a deep breath, I risked nudging him slightly with my shoulder. He didn't back away, so I smiled a bit. "But even if she doesn't, they get my vote."

He was about to say something when the door opened, and Millie's booming voice filled the space.

"Ready to wow me, Anna?" Her silver hair was sharply cut, so was her red dress suit. The wrinkles next to her gray eyes were practically nonexistent, and I lifted my chin confidently even though she still managed to intimidate the hell out of me most days.

"We are." I gestured next to me. "This is Tristan Whitfield. He's doing all the custom woodwork."

He held his hand out. "Pleasure to meet you."

Her eyes were shrewd as she assessed him, but she took his hand. "Your hair is too long."

"My mother has mentioned that to me a time or two," he replied without missing a beat.

Millie barked a laugh. "Excellent. Show me what you've got."

Just like that, my hope was back. And I planned on holding on to that slippery little a-hole with two hands.

CHAPTER FOURTEEN

TRISTAN

"This isn't crazy. I would've invited any of my friends to come see this."

Michael pursed his lips, and I slugged him in the shoulder. Hard.

"Ouch." He rubbed at the spot. "What did your text say? Come check out my burnt wood? I bet she was swooning."

My teeth clenched, and I pointed to the door of my shop. "Out."

He was laughing as he left, and I almost cracked my phone screen when I glanced at our text exchange for the fifteenth time in the last two hours.

Me: I'm going to do some practice runs of the Shou Shugi-Ban if you're interested. Maybe around 4?

Anna: Yes! That would be incredible, thanks! See you then. Text me the address?

I rolled my shoulders and tucked my phone away. Again. It was friendly. We were working together. She was excited about my offer. There was nothing wrong with the fact that I'd done it. So what if I didn't need to do a practice run. I picked up a small sanding block and went to work on a spindle for something in my mom's kitchen.

The fact that it had been a week since I'd seen Anna had nothing to do with it. Or the fact that she'd signed up for some stupid, stupid dating app. I didn't realize how hard I was sanding until the spindle snapped completely in half.

"Shit," I whispered, and turned the crank on the vice that was holding it in place. I tossed the pieces into the trash and tried not to feel like an idiot. That was a pointless endeavor though.

I missed her and wanted to see her.

It was a bizarre sensation, to miss someone that I'd spent so many years away from. Not just away from, but purposely adding separation between us. But now I had the ability to pick up my phone and text with her, not that I'd taken advantage of that in the way I should have. So far I hadn't gone beyond work stuff, but that work stuff was giving me more time with her today, so I couldn't be too hard on myself.

Which is why I was dusting off the blow torch to burn some wood. A very friendly reason to see her. But before any pyrotechnics happened, real or imagined, I needed to get a grip. I cranked up the music on my speaker system and grabbed my notebook. No power tools for me until I felt like I didn't resemble a snarling beast in anticipation of her arrival.

If I allowed myself to think back to the second time I saw her, this was exactly how I felt. Like an animal who prowls next to its confines, knowing that a meal is right around the corner. Maybe that wasn't the best analogy for either me or Anna, but it felt appropriate, both then and now.

I'd thought about her often after the first time we met. The way she spoke. The way she paid attention to what I was saying, not just biding her time until she could hear the sound of her own voice again, as so many people did when they talked to someone for the first time. The way she smiled and laughed so easily, but never at my expense when I stumbled slightly over what I was trying to say, and always in a way that was completely and utterly genuine.

Which is why I approached her that second night, when I normally would've hung back a bit to observe how she acted.

Her smile was wide and teasing, when I hadn't said a word yet. For a moment, we stood shoulder to shoulder in Garrett's kitchen, her sipping her wine and me doing the same from my beer.

"You changed your stance on pillows yet?" she'd said, not looking at me.

"Not on the ugly ones."

And she'd tilted her head back to laugh, even though I hadn't been trying to be funny.

"It's a lucky thing that you have such good taste in your friends. You'd be a lost cause otherwise, Mr. Whitfield."

I remember turning toward her, fighting the smile on my face, and being struck dumb at the sight of her. Lost cause, indeed.

In that beat of time, I remember feeling a vivid spark of interest that she knew my last name, when I hadn't given it to her the week before. It was the first time I remember feeling like I was experiencing something special, something that I'd never felt before. A swell of interest so overwhelming that I felt like I needed to brace myself against the counter.

I wasn't someone who believed in love at first sight. And that wasn't what happened with Anna. But the next time I saw her, bringing with it the realization that she belonged to someone else made me realize what that staggering sensation had been during each moment with her; the unerring knowledge that she fit, in a way that no one ever had before. And hadn't since.

Thankfully the music was low enough that I didn't miss the knock on the door. Before I jumped from my seat to let her in, I closed my eyes to reset, to pull myself from that memory and into the present. And until I opened the door, I thought I was doing okay. But at the way she was smiling at me, I promptly lost my heart all over again, right out onto the cold Colorado dirt.

"Hi! I brought my own safety glasses."

She held up a pair and I swallowed roughly. On her head was a slouchy winter hat in pure white, which matched her sweater. Over her dark jeans were sturdy work boots.

I held the door open. "Come on in."

Her eyes took everything in excitedly. "Oh wow, this is so amazing, Tristan. It's bigger than I thought it would be."

The fact that I didn't trip over my feet was a veritable miracle. "Yeah. I spend a lot of time here. Michael calls it my fortress of solitude."

She laughed. "I can see that. You do like your alone time, don't you?"

Great. Good. Remind her that you're not a people person, Tristan. Because that's a solid strategy when you're alone with the woman who makes it hard for you to breathe normally when she smiles at you.

"Every once in a while," I found myself saying. Inexplicably. Because I liked being away from people about ninety-seven percent of my day. But she was flipping through a few pages of my sketchbook and didn't seem to realize that I just lied through my teeth.

"Just every once in a while?" she asked without looking at me.

I pinched my eyes shut and let out a short puff of air. "Maybe a bit more than that."

"I'm teasing." She stopped on a landscape sketch mixed in with my furniture renderings and she picked up the book for a closer look. When I took a step forward, she must have realized what she was doing, because she quickly handed it over to me. "Oh my gosh, I'm sorry. I had no right to nose through that."

"'Sokay," I mumbled and tucked the book under my arm.

She gave me a shy smile. "That was beautiful. Do you do a lot of landscapes?"

"I've got a few." Hundred.

Mentally, I made a note to make sure that any notebooks at home that may or may not include sketches of her be locked away somewhere. Thankfully, I only had a handful of those. It was too hard to spend time sketching the cupid's bow on the top of her lips or the curve of her cheekbone without wondering what they would feel like under my fingertips, under my mouth.

Anna caught sight of the propane torch leaning against the wall and her eyes widened. "That's what I'm talkin' about. You use that? Can I? Please?"

I smothered a laugh at how excited she seemed. "I don't see why not. We'll have to do it out in the yard though. I hope you brought a coat."

"Yeah, it's out in the car." A trilling sound came from her pocket, and she dug out her cell with an apologetic look. "Sorry. It's Corryn."

I turned slightly to give her some privacy, but she declined the call. "You can take it if you want."

She waved a hand. "Nah. She's just bugging me about something."

Behind me, something caught her attention and she rushed forward with an awe-filled expression on her face.

Then she looked at me with wide eyes. "Tristan."

"What?"

Her finger pointed at the bench I was working on for another project. "What? Are you serious with this? Did you do these engravings?"

I cleared my throat. "Yeah."

"Get outta here." She nudged me with her shoulder and ran her hands over the seat. "This is ridiculous. You should have your own retail store or something."

"That sounds awful," I said immediately.

She froze, and so did I. Her lips twitched, and my face flooded with heat. After a couple seconds, she lost the battle, and peals of laughter left her mouth.

"Yeah, having to deal with retail customers might not be your favorite thing in the world, huh?"

I lifted an eyebrow and she held her stomach, she was laughing so hard.

"Glad that image is so funny to you," I told her, but I couldn't help but love her reaction. She had this uncanny way of laughing without ever making me feel she was laughing at me, even though she kind of was.

She straightened and wiped a hand under her eyes. "I'm sorry. You're just so earnest about it. I love it."

With that bomb dropped, she turned and started inspecting the bench again, like my heart wasn't shooting up my throat at her using 'love' in *any* way, regarding me.

She moved on to a couple chairs and stood back to study them. Watching her look at my work, and knowing what I did from her office, I was already getting a good sense of what she liked.

Slowly, she looked at every single piece I had in the shop, pointing out what she loved and oohing and ahhing over almost everything.

Michael could shove it, making fun of my reason for inviting her over here to watch me burn wood. I knew what worked.

When she got to the last piece, she sighed. "Well, I've nosed around everything. You probably want to get started, huh?"

Not really.

I nodded. "Sure. I've got the planks right behind you."

Without me needing to ask for her help, Anna picked up the ends of the two long cedar planks that I had lining the floor. I grabbed my flamethrower with my free hand, the other ends of the plank with my other, and we walked outside. While she grabbed her coat from her car, I got some fireproof white gloves for both of us.

"Have you ever done this before?"

I burned four boards earlier when I knew she was coming. "You don't trust me?"

Nice evasion, asshole. Anna smiled but didn't say anything. While I laid the boards side by side, I thought about something she

134

said before we came out. I could do this. Be her friend. Ask things that a friend would ask. No sweat.

"You said Corryn is bugging you about something?"

Anna dipped her head, but I saw a flush climb her cheeks anyway. "That stupid dating app she signed me up for."

Honestly, I just hoped my mouth could open wide enough to shove my work boot in there, because it was not often that I experienced moments where I said too much. This was officially at the top of my list.

"Right," I said, and I grimaced when I realized my voice sounded like I was choking on barbed wire. I cleared my throat. "Bumblebee or something?"

Anna laughed. "Bumble." She gave me a sidelong look. "Do you really want to hear about this?"

Nope. Not in a thousand years for a million dollars.

"Of course."

Slowly, she pulled the white gloves over her thin, graceful fingers. I'd always loved watching her hands, and now that I'd seen her work, it was even worse. If I gave her my flamethrower, and she knew what to do with it right away, I might actually lose control of my body.

I crouched and lined up the boards so they were flush against each other, resting on top of two metal rails to keep them off the ground. It was a good thing I wasn't facing her too, because the next thing she said made me want to throw up.

"I went out with someone last night. That's why Corryn is bugging me."

Even though the boards were perfect, I fidgeted with them some more, ignoring the yawning pit in my stomach at how nervous she sounded. I closed my eyes for a moment and centered every scattered, painful thought in my head.

"How..." I cleared my throat. "How did it go?"

It took every ounce of control that I possessed over my own body to be able to stand and face her. What if that's why she was smiling? Because it was good.

Being her friend was undoubtedly the stupidest idea I'd ever had.

"It was," she paused and laughed under breath and I wanted to die before she finished that sentence, "it was so awful that it's not even funny."

Was I smiling? No. Okay, good. Excellent. "That ... sucks. I'm sorry."

"Oh, it's fine. It was kind of a relief to have it be so bad."

Feeling far more confident in my ability to light a torch and wield fire, I turned the valve on the tank and held my igniter in front of the end of the torch and clicked the pin. The hiss of propane lit and I turned the tank down a bit.

The noise wasn't so loud that we couldn't converse, and I felt such a roaring euphoria in my veins, that I needed to burn something just to give me an outlet. For a minute, she watched with unconcealed fascination at the blooming black finish that spread across the boards as I walked with even steps next to the boards, moving the torch at a steady pace.

"You only need to burn about the top eighth of an inch of the board," I told her and she nodded. "It won't take much more than ten minutes to burn all four of these. We can wrap the ceiling beams pretty easily."

"I *love* it," she gushed.

"Why was the date so bad?" I asked before I lost the courage. Flamethrower in my hands made me pretty damn chatty, I guess.

She sighed. "Well, he was about ten years older than his picture, and I'm pretty sure he rolled out of bed wearing his clothes from the day before. I figured I could at least grab a drink to be polite. But, oh no, I was 'worth more than just a drink', so he insisted—with much arm touching—that we split an entree. In the time it took to pick at half a mediocre burger, I learned about why he and his ex-wife got divorced and how awful their sex life was." She smiled down at the boards, and I felt an irrational pang that it wasn't directed at me. "The two hugs he managed to get from me after he insisted he walk me to my car wasn't even the worst part."

My hands tightened on the torch. "What was?"

She shook her head. "When he messaged me this morning about how excited he was to see me again, I politely told him that it was nice to meet him, but I didn't think I was ready to take things any further." Finally, Anna glanced up at me, and her eyes were lit with humor, which did little to soothe the snarling beast that was raging in my head. "He sent me his address so that I could mail him twenty bucks."

"What?" I barked, almost dropping the torch in the process.

"Yup. Apparently, if he'd known that I was only looking for a one-night thing, he wouldn't have paid the check, so he told me to act like an adult and send him my half."

I was going to hunt him down and light him on *fire*.

The last board was fully blackened by now, and I—quite calmly—leaned over and turned the torch off. I picked up the bucket of water I had ready and poured it slowly over the boards. My chest was heaving, and couldn't quite manage to rein that in when I faced her again.

"That is insane," I told her quietly.

"I know, right?" She rolled her eyes. "Trust me, no more dates planned for this week."

"Good."

Anna laughed at my emphatic response. When she crouched down by the boards and pulled off her gloves, I knew the subject was closed. Which was excellent, because I didn't think my heart could take another conversation like that with her, not until I was little bit more mentally prepared for it. Sure, I'd heard Corryn say it was a dating app, but I didn't expect her to go out with someone the next *week*.

"You sound like my mom."

I always loved Anna's mom. "She doesn't think you should date?"

Anna shrugged. "She just worries about me. I think that's why she's not pushing me to move out anytime soon." Then she smiled up at me. "Well, that and now she has someone around the house to try and help her fix things. The other day, I found myself trying to light the pilot in her fireplace and praying I didn't blow up the entire house."

I cut her a look. "That's pretty difficult to do on accident."

She nudged my leg with her shoulder where she was still crouched. "You shouldn't underestimate my abilities. I'm sure I could still find a way."

I didn't answer right away, and after a moment, she glanced back up at me. My mouth curved slightly. "The next time you're worried about explosions, you could always call. I've yet to blow up a house, so I'd be happy to help. Anytime."

Her cheeks pinked at my teasing, and it made me want to beat my chest with a closed fist. "I'll keep that in mind."

"Good."

Anna exhaled slowly, studied the boards again. "Now you clean them?" she asked.

I nodded. "After they're completely cooled off. The dust can be pretty nasty from the charcoal on top. Then they dry fully. You can leave them unfinished, but since it's interior, I'll probably use Penofin oil. That will need to be done yearly, but it's not hard."

"Tristan, this is going to be so amazing. Thank you for the idea." She stood and wobbled slightly. Without thinking, I reached out and grabbed her elbow to steady her. Her hand gripped my forearm, and I felt every single finger press into my skin like ink seeping down, down, down, black and permanent and perfect.

When she let go, I did the same, but the touch was there, simmering beneath the surface. I'd feel it all day. I'd feel it all week. And I'd hate how vividly I remembered a moment that small and insignificant.

But when it came to Anna, nothing was insignificant to me. There wasn't anything about time with her that I took for granted.

And it was the saddest part of the last six years of my life, because I still wouldn't change it. Not if it led us right here, to her hand on my arm.

Again, her phone went off and she grimaced. "It's my boss. I better grab this."

She pressed the phone to her ear and walked away. I heard her sigh deeply. "Yeah, I can be back in twenty. No problem."

I guess I wouldn't see Anna wield the flamethrower today, so I shut it off completely, smiling a little when she gave it a wistful glance after disconnecting the call.

"I guess my fun will have to wait." She smiled at me. "Thanks for inviting me, really. And for listening to my stupid dating story."

"No problem," I managed. She dipped her head and trotted off to her car.

As I watched her drive away, I felt that familiar anger choke me. She was single, yes. But stories like that still made me feel as helpless as I'd been when she was married. My plan was a good one, I knew it. I had faith in that. But these kinds of interactions with her would take some getting used to, to what they did to my insides, how they made my gut churn with fire.

There were men out there stupid enough to take a night with her for granted. To boil it down to dollars and cents and whether they gained something concrete out of their transaction. They didn't realize what they had sitting across the table from them. Reducing her to nothing. Like she wasn't even a person.

A growl made its way out of my mouth, and I realized that my hands were clenched into fists at my sides.

Someone walked out of the main shop, some stupid kid that my uncle hired the year before, and I probably hadn't traded fifteen words with him until what happened next.

"Whoo, who was *that*? Did someone get me a sexy little ninja for my birthday?" He whistled. "That ass."

I moved before I knew what I was doing, my hands fisted in his shirt as I slammed him against the wall of my shop.

"What the—"

His words cut off in a gurgle when I pressed my forearm against his throat. I moved so close to his face that I could feel the panicked bursts of air coming out of his nose.

"If I ever hear you talk about her like that again, you stupid little punk," I growled, "I will shove a circular saw up your ass. You got it?"

When I pressed harder, he started choking, and I vaguely heard Michael shout my name behind me. The kid's eyes were red, but he nodded and I let him go. He slumped into a heap on the cold ground, but tried to glare up at me. I took a step and he lifted his hands over his face.

"What are you *doing*, Tristan?" Michael yelled.

"You keep that asshole out of my way and if he so much as runs his mouth about any woman like that in my presence again, he's gone." A squeak of protest came from the ground, and I glared at him.

My brother lifted his hands and gawked down at the kid, who was rubbing his neck, but wisely saying nothing.

Michael cleared his throat. "Uhh, okay, you got it." Then to the kid, he said, "Dude, just beat it."

The kid disappeared, Michael gave me a worried look before he did the same, and I had to take a solid thirty minutes to calm down before I could even think about leaving for the day. My reaction to the kid probably should have terrified me, it was so far out of the norm for me. But it was the easy objectification that just … pissed me the hell of. She was more than how she looked.

So much more.

And it was so much more difficult than I thought to hear her talk about another man taking her out on a date.

Today had felt like a test, and I still wasn't positive that I'd passed. Everything that I'd mentally prepared for felt clear cut, in theory, at least.

Be Anna's friend. Get to know this side of her.

Be there for her emotionally, for the inevitable fallout that I might witness.

Allow her to get to know me, the sides of me that I've always wanted her to see.

Watch for signs that she's ready for more. For a serious relationship. The finalization of her divorce felt like a natural jumping point for those signs.

The reality I thought I was prepared for was even harder than I ever could have imagined. My course of action still felt very much like the correct one. Dates like that, even if they were awful for her, were clearly something she needed to get out of her system.

Before I even registered what I was doing, I'd pulled my phone out of my pocket and typed into the search bar, *How long does it take for someone to get over a divorce.*

Tristan, you are one stupid son of a bitch, I thought when the headline, in bold, explained to me that the *Wall Street Journal* did a study showing that it took about two years to overcome the emotional trauma of a divorce.

Before I clicked on the link, I snorted. "From two thousand thirteen. That's not even remotely relevant anymore," I muttered. The next headline said something about there being no timeline for grief, and I felt my eyes begin to swim as I scrolled down and down and down. More and more articles, attempting to define something that probably wasn't definable. Not in a way that would help me out of my current situation.

With a huff, I slammed my phone down and pushed my fingers into my eye sockets. Even if it did take Anna two years to recover, it wasn't like I was gearing up to walk away if I didn't get a date with her in the next thirty days or something.

No, that wouldn't happen. But just to be safe, it looked like it might be best for me to avoid Google for the foreseeable future.

CHAPTER FIFTEEN

ANNA

"This is ridiculous," I whispered, jamming my bruised knuckle into my mouth and sucking at the torn skin. "Ouchie."

From where I stood on the step stool, which was on top of the dining room table, I looked down at the hardwood floor and it seemed a million miles away.

"Okay," I said on a shallow, nervous breath, "just take it one step at a time."

With each successful step that my foot landed on, taking me on step closer to the table's surface, and then the blessed, even ground, I breathed a little bit easier. Before my mom left to have lunch with her friends, she mentioned that the ceiling fan above the dining room table was wobbling a little when she turned it on high.

Easy enough, right? I knew how to use a screwdriver. I could tighten it while she was gone, make sure I wasn't just some mooch living under her roof but not contributing at all.

My hands were shaking slightly when I braced them on the table. So close. When my legs swung from the side and I hopped off, the bottom of my chucks squeaked on the floor.

I swept my hair from my face and glanced back up at the ceiling. "Holy shit, that was stupid."

From where I'd left it on the table, my phone taunted me. The entire time I was up on the stool, I kept thinking about what Tristan had said about blowing up the house. How I could call him if I needed help. And my promise to myself was if I made it down from the stool alive, I'd take him up on it, given that I didn't break any limbs or give myself a concussion in the process.

But it felt ... odd. As far as I knew, Tristan had never been to my parents' house before. Why would he? The ability to talk myself out of calling him was just at my fingertips. Most people made offers like that and didn't really mean them. Empty words, not necessarily because they didn't have the desire to help, but because it was likely you wouldn't reach out to take them up on it.

Not him though. That much I already knew. The shiny black screen of my phone flashed the reflection of the sun streaming in the window when I picked it up and stared up it. They weren't empty words to Tristan.

I didn't think he was capable of those at all. If I searched through my memories of meeting him, so many years ago, I had the vague sense that I might have even said something to that effect. But the words were jumbled, the memory foggy.

It made far more sense to call my brother first. Make him fix the shit that was broken. After all, it was his mom's house. Make him risk his neck to tighten that damn screw that was hiding at a weird angle.

I glared at my now-bleeding knuckle while I called Garrett. After only a few rings, it went to voicemail. My thumb tapped on the screen as it went dark.

Instead of calling Tristan, because that felt more intrusive and urgent than necessary, I tapped out a quick text and hit send.

Me: On the scale of 1 to blowing up the house, where does your offer to help fall when it comes to a wobbly ceiling fan that desperately needs tightening?

Almost immediately, there were three bouncing dots.

Tristan: Did you try and fix it yourself?
Tristan: It's the only way I can answer accurately.

Me: Yes. I have the bloody knuckle to prove it. The screw was hiding from me.

Tristan: You turned off the breaker, right?

I found myself wincing while I answered.

Me: ummm.... no?

Tristan: An 8. Please don't touch it again until I get there.

Me: Scout's honor. No rush if you can't come now.

Tristan: Nothing else going. Text me the address and I'll head over.

I did, smiling as I set my phone down. While I waited, I threw in another load of laundry and briefly glanced at myself in the bathroom mirror, frowning when I attempted to fix the messy, high ponytail that had seemed sufficient for a Saturday putzing around the house.

When I wasn't quite such a hot mess, I shrugged and straightened the t-shirt hanging over my black leggings.

There was a knock on the front door, and I skipped down the

steps. Beyond the etched glass, I could see Tristan's tall frame, his shoulders almost as broad as the door itself.

I was smiling as I opened it, and his mouth almost softened to match.

"That was fast," I told him, as I motioned for him to come in.

His dark eyes took in the large entryway, the dark curving staircase leading to the bedrooms on the second floor, and I suddenly wondered what my parent's Wash Park home felt like to him. If it felt pretentious and stuffy, too rich for his blood. How it compared to the place he grew up.

To me, it was home, but that didn't mean I was unaware of how blessed we'd been, to have a financially stable upbringing, parents who worked incredibly hard to provide me and Garrett with a good life.

"Beautiful place," he said, looking down at me from where I still held the door open. One eyebrow lifted slightly. "You gonna let me stay?"

I blushed and close the door. "I was planning on it."

As he followed me into the dining room, I felt the quiet of the house more acutely than I had before he showed up. The space was smaller with him in it, and when he set a handful of tools down on the table, he sighed heavily.

"What?"

He gestured to the step stool on top of the table.

I scrunched up my nose and shrugged. "It made a lot of sense at the time."

The look he gave me was one of patent disbelief, and for some reason, it made me laugh.

"Unbelievable," he muttered and shook his head. At no time did I sense that he was being patronizing, or making fun of me. There was a warm easiness to being around Tristan that was slowly becoming something that buoyed my mood, even when I didn't know it needed buoying.

With another shake of his head, he pulled the step stool off the table and set it on the floor.

"If you want to show me where the breaker box is, I'll go find the right one."

"No need," I told him. "I can do that. My dad was OCD about labeling that stuff correctly."

Before he could argue, I went out into the garage and flipped the gray metal door open, dragging my finger down the line of heavy black switches until I found the right one.

I pressed it to the off position.

"Got it," Tristan called. "It's off."

When I walked back into the dining room, he was standing on the table, his long, denim clad legs spread wide and his heavy work boots braced firmly on the surface. Given his height, which had to be six three, and the table underneath him, he was eye level with the ceiling fan blades.

"My mom would have a coronary seeing your boots on the table," I told him.

"You falling and breaking your neck seems like a good alternative to avoiding it."

"Har har."

His lips hooked up to one side in a half-smile and I found myself mirroring it.

"Your mom a germaphobe?"

I tilted my head and watched him wield the screwdriver deftly, no bloody knuckles in sight. "She's not so bad, actually. But shoes are one of her things. We had to take our shoes off immediately after walking in the house, even as kids. My dad always forgot, and I remember her yelling at him about all the places he'd walked and whether he was okay with tracking it all over the place where we lived. If you wouldn't eat your dinner off the bottom of your shoes, then you shouldn't be bringing it into the house," I mimicked in her voice.

He gave me a quick look before going back to what he was doing. "And what would he say?"

I smiled, feeling the pinch in my heart that still accompanied bittersweet memories. "That some day he'd prove to her it wasn't that big of deal, make us use our shoes as our dinner plates."

Tristan coughed, like he was hiding a laugh, and my smile widened. My dad had said it so many times, always to make my mom laugh. My eyes burned and I blinked rapidly, looking down at my lap until I didn't have to worry about getting to maudlin. But of course, Tristan caught it.

"I wish I'd known him," he said quietly. "He sounds like he was a good man, from what Garrett's said."

I exhaled slowly and watched Tristan test all the screws, finally satisfied when the disk of the ceiling fan was flush against the ceiling.

"He was," I agreed. "Garrett is so much like him, it's eerie sometimes. The way he walks, how he laughs when something funny happens that he wasn't expecting. It's like hearing my dad."

Slowly, Tristan crouched, coming down from the table with graceful movements despite his size. "Well, then you'll never forget what his laugh sounded like."

I gave him a surprised look. "No, I guess I won't."

"How are you like him?" Tristan asked.

His words had me closing my eyes. Most people wouldn't have asked, knowing I didn't share a drop of blood with my parents, who couldn't conceive after having Garrett. Who saved to be able to adopt me five years later. Who absolutely shaped me into the person I was, who celebrated my background and loved me beyond all comprehension.

I opened my eyes again, even though they burned with the press of tears, and gave Tristan a small smile. "I'm stubborn like him. And I'd like to think I listen to things people *don't* say. He was really good at that."

"You are too," he said quietly.

Don't cry, don't cry, don't cry. When I felt like my voice would come out steady, I swallowed. "Thank you."

He nodded, but didn't say anything else. Suddenly, I wished I had something else for him to do. Another reason for him to stay.

"Are you like your dad?" I heard myself asking.

When his face went carefully blank, I wished I hadn't asked, even though he hadn't answered yet. Tristan's thumb tapped on his thigh. His eyes met mine and when he spoke, it was measured and quiet.

"I hope not."

Questions sprang up on the tip of my tongue, but I swallowed them down, simply nodding instead. It was so cryptic, so loaded with meaning, with a sadness that I couldn't explain, but I had the sudden urge to hug him.

But behind that, was the knowledge that this probably wasn't something he'd want dug up for dissection. Empty words, I thought again. Something he wouldn't offer up. And in that three-word answer, it was enough.

I gave him an encouraging smile and nudged him with my shoulder. "Well whoever you're like, they must be proud."

He shifted, clearly uncomfortable with my praise, which I could see in the now tell-tale flush on his cheekbones.

"Thank you for helping me," I said when he didn't respond.

"You're welcome." The embarrassment cleared at the topic change, and his dark eyes were lit with dry humor. "Let's add possible electrocution and unstable climbing techniques to the list of reasons to ask me for help."

I laughed. "Deal."

"Anything else I can do while I'm here?"

"Like change some light bulbs?" I teased.

"Yeah," he said, watching my face. "Like that."

I rolled my eyes. "I managed those okay without injury. But you'll be the first I call if I can't."

"Deal," he said back to me.

Tristan gathered up his tools and I followed him to the front door. He gave me a brief nod when I thanked him again, but nothing else.

While he walked to his truck, I watched him with my shoulder propped against the door frame. After he got in, my phone buzzed.

I was grinning when I saw it was a text from him.

Tristan: If your mom comes home and sees boot prints on the table, don't tell her it was me.

Me: I promise.

When I glanced up, he was watching me through the windshield and I waved. If I expected him to actually smile in return, I was sorely mistaken.

Someday, I thought ruefully, shaking my head as he drove away. Someday, I'd see him smile.

CHAPTER SIXTEEN

ANNA

Redemption came to me in the form of my sister-in-law, opening the front door of their home with a welcoming smile.

"Hey, I wasn't expecting you tonight." Then, God bless her soul, she looked me up and down. "Oh, you look so pretty!"

I sighed. "At least you thought so."

Rory waved me in, and thankfully my brother was absent, because he didn't need to witness this. "Come in, come in. I was just trying to convince myself that I didn't need to watch another episode of *Project Runway*."

"Why would you try to convince yourself of that?"

She looked past me at the TV screen and blinked a few times. "No clue. It felt like an important decision at the time."

Without asking permission, I opened their fridge and rooted around until I found an opened bottle of chardonnay. Rory handed me a clean glass, and I dumped the remainder of the bottle in it.

Her eyes widened. "That bad?"

I sank onto the couch and stretched my legs out once my nude heels were off my feet. The hem of my burgundy skirt edged up my thighs, and Rory gave me a curious look, but come on, if no boys were present, I was not about to care.

"Just ... underwhelming."

The chardonnay was cold and had a nice buttery aftertaste when I swallowed and I could feel the tension seep from my shoulders the longer I sat there.

"How so?"

"Maybe it was my fault for having higher expectations for this one than the first one." She snickered, because I'd told her about the first date. Or *the bill-splitter* as I now referred to him. "He looked cute in his picture, and he was cute in person. You know how you almost have to be wary of the ones who are too attractive? Like they're guaranteed to be a-holes."

She nodded sagely. "Absolutely. Cute ones are usually nicer than hot ones."

"Right." I took another sip. "Well, this cute one wasn't. I met him at the restaurant—right on time—and he looked me up and down and didn't say a word, and then he goes, 'I've been waiting for a few minutes, but it's okay you were late.'"

Her jaw dropped.

I raised my glass too quickly and the wine sloshed dangerously close to the edge. "I know!"

"What an *asshole*."

"Unfortunately, I think he was just really clueless. Zero social skills. He spent two hours talking about himself. I know more about the stock market than I ever cared to. Didn't ask me a single question, and then at the end of the night told me he was very much looking forward to our second date." I laughed into my glass. "Probably not, cute clueless psuedo-asshole Grant."

Rory's face was sympathetic, and I drank more so that I didn't have to see it. Here I thought the pitying looks in my direction were over, but now I just got a new kind. Poor Anna, she has to deal with the dating world.

Except I didn't have to, did I?

I was choosing this, and at the moment, I was trying to figure out why.

Like she read my mind, Rory's bright blue eyes narrowed in my direction before she flicked a glance at the slider out into the backyard.

"Everyone has crappy dates, Anna. Unfortunately, that's the nature of the game now. But it's not a necessity. Especially this soon. You've had two winners now." She took a careful sip of her own drink. "Are you going to risk another?"

What I loved about her was that I knew she wouldn't expect me to answer right away. I turned on my hip, set my sadly empty wine glass onto the end table, and then tucked one of the couch pillows into my chest. The knotted edge was soft when I worried it between my fingers and thought about it.

"There's still something exciting about waking up every morning and knowing that each day is truly my own," I started. "That novelty hasn't worn off yet. There will be no one ignoring me while I drink my coffee alone at the table. While we move around each other in the kitchen and then alternate who's using the bathroom to get ready for work so we don't have to be in there at the same time."

Rory didn't answer, just tucked her long legs up under her in the arm chair she was sitting in.

"I had a big, formative chunk of my life feeling like I didn't matter in the slightest to the person who was supposed to place me first. Who was supposed to care about the thoughts in my head, about the things I wanted out of life. And I know that somewhere along the line, I stopped caring about those things for him too. I know that now. It wasn't right, and I'm not defending myself, because I know I gave up on Marcus too." I pressed my nose into the pillow and breathed deeply. "And ... I don't know, Rory ... there's something about getting ready for a date that feels exciting. Feels like it's pumping life into me, into the places that have been atrophied for so long."

"Even if the reality doesn't match up to the expectation?" she asked, then glanced at the slider again, almost nervously. Oh great, maybe Garrett was putting her up to these questions. He probably thought it was completely stupid that I was doing this in the first place.

I sat up and pulled my hair over one shoulder. "I think so, yeah. It's like ... it's like I need to know that I can put myself out there again. Even if all that comes from it is seeing how awful it is out there. There will be dates that aren't awful. Maybe they'll be nice, fun, make me laugh. I believe that can still happen."

"I give you credit," she said quietly. "I don't know if I could be as optimistic as you are, after what you went through. It's pretty badass, Anna."

"*Anyone* can fake optimism."

"You're not though." She lifted an eyebrow, like she was daring me to contradict her. "If you were faking it, you wouldn't be following through on what you're saying. Someone who's faking will spew all manner of things but never really follow it up with action. You're putting yourself out there, and to me, that means you're a badass."

Answering didn't seem possible, not when all I wanted to do was deny what she was saying. There was nothing about how I felt that even remotely felt badass. Even with the heels that made my not-very-long-legs look long and dress that gave me curves where my curves were usually slight, badassery was in short supply laying on my brother's couch and drinking his wife's leftover wine after a date that should be reserved for a magazine article or something.

"I don't feel like one."

Rory leaned forward. "Don't you get it though? That makes it even more true. You're not faking anything right now, Anna. You're not wearing the mask of *Oh isn't my newly single life amazing and wonderful and perfect*. Honesty is hard. It's hard to be honest with people about a lot of things, but it's even harder to be honest with yourself, because that requires a good long look in the mirror.

There's a staggering number of people who can't manage that."

I blinked a few times. I'd never thought about it that way.

"Anna, even if you didn't leave Marcus until recently, you were honest about what it was. You never denied it to us, or tried to defend what your relationship had become. And now, you're still being honest about what your situation is, how you feel about it. So don't come in here and drink my wine and try to tell me that you being hopeful about the future isn't brave. Because it is."

Turning on my side again, I stared at her. My heart soaked up her words like I was shriveled, dried-up sponge. "Did Garrett know you were such a good cheerleader when he married you?"

Rory tilted her head and stared out the slider again. When I looked over my shoulder, I couldn't see anything. "I don't think I'm in cheerleader mode."

I snorted. "'K"

"I'm not," she insisted. "If I was saying something you weren't willing to hear, or something that you weren't ready to hear, you wouldn't feel like you were being cheered on."

"There's a difference?"

"Hell yes there's a difference."

The wine had settled with a pleasant weight in my stomach, and I could feel my tension seep out my body. "Maybe someday I'll ask you about that, but not tonight. I think it would make me think too hard."

Rory laughed. "Fair enough."

"Where's that pain-in-the-ass brother of mine?"

"Outside."

"Ahh, so that's why you keep looking out there."

She looked away, her fingers fidgeting in her lap. "Just want to make sure he's not eavesdropping."

"Much appreciated."

For a moment, Rory stared at that slider again, and she chewed on the inside of her lip before glancing at me. "So let me ask you something."

"Like I could stop you," I said.

She conceded that with a lifted brow. "Hypothetically, say the guy tonight hadn't been a raging narcissist."

"That's a really big hypothetical for me right now considering how big that glass of wine was." I closed my eyes and decided to play along. My hand waved at her in some motion that urged her to continue.

"You know what I mean. You've had two bad dates. What if date number one or date number two had been like, an eight on a scale of one to Ryan Gosling, and he opened doors and asked intelligent questions, laughed at the appropriate times, was kind to the wait-staff and didn't stare at your boobs."

I opened one eye. "Keep talkin'."

"What if he paid the bill and held your hand as you walked out, and kissed you by your car and asked if you wanted to come back to his place. Are you ready for that?"

"Oh geez, this is like, a serious game." With a groan, I sat up and tucked my hair behind my ears. "Am I ready to sleep with someone else? That's your question?"

"Partially."

"You said he's an eight?"

She gave me a long look.

"Sorry. Just making sure." My thumb tapped my kneecap. I pulled in a deep breath, closed my eyes again and imagined the scenario as she had painted it. My head was shaking before I even got to the hypothetical kiss by the car. "No, I'm not."

Rory narrowed her eyes slightly, like she was gauging the truth in my answer. "Do you think there's anything wrong with it, if you did?"

"No," I said right away. "It's not that. It's not a moral issue, or anything that's right or wrong. It's more like ... I want to know that person before it goes to that level." My hand pressed against my breastbone and what I felt behind my thumping heart, I tried to put into words so that she would understand it. "I'm not saying I need to be in love, but I want to look at him and feel that sense of rightness that was completely missing from my life before."

Rory's eyes warmed and her lips curved into a slight smile. "That's tough to define."

"I know," I sighed. My head dropped back onto the arm of the couch. "But it feels, I don't know, Rory, it feels like I'd be cheating myself out of something if I didn't have the emotion to back up the physical desire. Because I craved it so badly. Before."

She mulled that over, I realized how good it felt to answer her question. Like it settled something that I hadn't realized I was wrestling with.

In swiping left and right, and looking at connections on the innocuous app on my phone, I hadn't let my brain jump to that point. Was *that* something I was ready for? Going on these dates almost felt like a rite of passage for me, like it was a way that I could prove that Marcus hadn't turned me into this bitter husk of the woman I was before him.

Maybe I wasn't ready to sleep with someone, but I was not huddled in the corner and allowing him to take any more of me than he'd already taken.

I needed to prove that this wasn't the birth of a failure, where I was left to fit together a jagged, broken puzzle with shaky hands. I wasn't a failure because I'd stayed.

This was the birth of a new me, and I was a person who wanted to look ahead. Not stare behind me and bemoan what led me here.

Lord have mercy, I was ready for these types of conversations to not be the norm anyway.

"Good," Rory said decisively. "Now can Tristan and Garrett come inside?"

I blinked. "Tristan is here?"

"Yeah, they're fixing something out there. I can't remember what. I sent Garrett a text that he wasn't allowed inside until girl talk was over."

That made me laugh. "Well, Tristan has already been subjected to that. He heard all about my first date, poor guy."

Rory froze, but recovered almost instantly, and I wondered if I'd been imagining it. "No kidding."

The slider opened, and Garrett came in first, followed by Tristan.

"Hello, sister of mine," Garrett said, ruffling my hair as he passed the couch.

Discreetly, I pulled my skirt down my legs when Tristan nodded at me in greeting. Of course, he didn't smile. If I hadn't seen it before, I'd wonder if the muscles of his mouth even allowed it to happen. That only made me smile at him more readily.

"Gentleman. Tristan, I was just telling Rory that you've already had to hear some of my date horror stories, so you wouldn't have been phased in the slightest tonight."

Garrett's head snapped over to his friend and he narrowed his eyes. "You did what, huh? When?"

"He was showing me how to burn some wood and I told him about date fail number one." I stared at Garrett. "Why are you acting weird?"

"How to *burn wood*?" he asked, flicking a derisive glance in my general direction. "Don't know how to start a fire, do you?"

I flipped my middle finger at Garrett. Tristan coughed.

Garrett plopped onto the floor in front of Rory's chair and she wove a hand through his hair. From where he was standing, Tristan seemed like he was trying to make a decision about something. It was odd how easily I felt like I was able to read him now.

And I saw the moment he made it, because he sent me a dry look. "You gonna keep hogging the couch, or do I need to sit on the floor too?"

Garrett smothered laugh, and I pretended to consider not moving my feet for him. "I'm so comfortable though."

"She did have a rough night," Rory said sagely. "Date number two was another train wreck."

Tristan's eyes were trained steadily on my face, no visible reaction to what Rory said. "Did this one ask for his half of the bill up front?"

I laughed, and it felt good coming out of my mouth, easing some of the pressure left over in my chest from my heavy conversation with Rory.

Tucking my feet underneath me, I waved a hand out toward the other half of the couch. "Be my guest. My neglected feet can suffer through not having the entire couch."

With a cryptic half-smile, oh what a *tease* he was, Tristan sat down.

Garrett smiled goofily at us. "Well, isn't this a sweet picture? The four of us all cozied up on a Saturday night, watching *Project Runway* together."

I rolled my eyes and Rory pinched the back of his neck.

He swatted at her hand and Tristan shook his head slowly.

When Rory leaned down to whisper something into Garrett ears, Tristan gave me the side-eye.

"What?" I asked.

It took him a second to answer, and it was only after he made sure Garrett and Rory weren't listening.

"You look nice tonight." Against his jean clad leg, he tapped his thumb. "I'm sorry the guy wasn't worthy of it."

"Thank you, Tristan," I told him, unbearably touched.

He dipped his head, which was the only acknowledgement I got to my thanks, and we fell quiet. Rory switched to a different channel, and we all settled in to watch the movie she'd picked. Something with Mel Gibson that we'd all probably seen a hundred times.

Garrett stood to get some beers for him and Tristan, and opened another bottle of wine for me and Rory. By the time I finished my second glass, my eyelids felt heavier and heavier with each blink.

During a scene with explosions and gunfight, Rory asked if Garrett could help her find something, which left Tristan and I in the dark family room.

His arm was stretched along the back of the couch, his long legs propped up on the coffee table in front of us.

I pushed my face into the pillow still clutched to my chest and wished I had some socks or something, because my bare feet were frickin freezing. Even though I tried not to, I shivered.

Tristan leaned closer to me. "Are you cold?" he asked quietly.

My nose wrinkled as I looked at him. "I'm realizing the dress wasn't the most prudent choice given the weather, yes."

He reached over and plucked a blanket out of a large wicker basket on the floor next to his side of the couch. Instead of handing it to me, he stood and draped it over me carefully.

One side of his face was lit up in harsh blue from the TV screen, and I tried not to smile at how serious his features were, even now. The messy ponytail, the harsh line of his jaw, the dark, heavily lashed eyes, Tristan so easily could have been one of the most intimidating looking men I'd ever been around. But as his warm hands laid the soft blanket over my shoulders, I couldn't stop the way my heart melted at his small acts of chivalry.

"Thank you," I whispered.

He stared at me as he straightened to his full height. One nod. That was all I got. And it didn't bother me in the slightest.

When Garrett and Rory came back from the kitchen, Tristan clenched his teeth and gave them a considering look.

"I uhh, I think I'm going to head home," Tristan said.

"Coward," Garrett mumbled under his breath. Or at least, that's what it sounded like. Tristan was too busy glaring at my brother for me to ask.

Tristan gave me a slight smile and turned to go, slugging Garrett's shoulder on his way out.

"Good to see you, Anna. Rory, thank you for the hospitality."

"You don't want to thank me?" Garrett asked.

"Don't think so," was Tristan's response before he walked out the door.

The door shut behind him, and I stared at it for a few beats before speaking. "Anyone want to explain what just happened?"

"Nope," they said in tandem.

I shook my head. "Okay then."

"Back to *Project Runway*?" Rory asked brightly. "I can open more wine."

"Sold."

Garrett rolled his eyes. "And on that note, I'm going to read in bed."

"You know how to read now? Good job, big brother."

It was his turn to flip me off, and I sank into the couch smiling, the fuzzy white blanket pulled up around my shoulders. Maybe date two hadn't been a winner, but I was ending the night with a smile on my face, and that was a good thing.

CHAPTER SEVENTEEN

ANNA

There were so many things *right* about date number four.

Just ... not the guy.

God bless him, Scott McAlister was so sweet that my teeth were aching before we hit the entrees. The delicious entree at the lovely, romantic and appropriately lit restaurant where he pulled out my chair and asked question upon question about me.

The first thing he told me was how beautiful I looked, and it was clear he meant it. He laughed when I said something that was even slightly funny, albeit a bit harder than was probably necessary. His hygiene was good. Clean, straight, white teeth. A hairline that was receding just a touch, but he had kind hazel eyes, and wore his gray suit jacket quite nicely over his tall frame.

Not once did his eyes stray for too long to the V of my pink dress, and he smiled at the server when she delivered our food.

"And how long have your brother and his wife been married? You said they work together, right?"

And he *listened*.

So why did I feel like I was out to dinner with a third cousin that you only see once every ten years?

I finished my last bite of risotto and set my fork down next to my plate before taking a sip of water. "They've been married just about a year, and yeah, they actually run a company together. It was my father's financial firm before he passed away."

Sympathy made his forehead wrinkle and he patted my hand, lingering for a moment over my knuckles with the tips of his fingers. "You mentioned on the phone that it was a heart attack. I'm so sorry."

When he pulled his hand back, I stared at my own, practically willing myself to feel some sort of flicker of excitement over him. Just a spark. Anything, really. Shouldn't I feel *something* on my first date that was a legitimate contender?

Yes, date four was definitely the best I'd experienced, even if the fireworks hadn't quite decided to show up yet.

And what about date number three?

We weren't discussing date number three, because it hadn't actually taken place. Date number three wanted to meet a few nights earlier than we'd planned, and given that I'd just wrapped up a ten-hour work day in four-inch heels, and all I wanted out of that particular evening was leggings, my fuzzy black slippers, and a charcoal mask while I watched *Big Little Lies* with my mom.

Date number three was such a classy guy that when I explained, more than once, that I'd rather stick to our original night, he felt it necessary to send me my first dick pic.

Not that he could've known it was my first one, of course. But with his parting words of "You can suck on this, bitch", he cemented himself as the date that would never, ever happen.

That's why—staring across the dimly lit and perfectly appointed table at Scott—I wished that I felt something. Even getting ready that night, my usual excitement was missing in action.

The server cleared our plates, and he thanked her. Genuinely thanked her, too. What was wrong with me?

"Can I interest you two in dessert?" she asked.

Scott leaned back and patted a hand over his flat stomach. "I don't know if I have it in me right now. But maybe give us a few minutes to talk about it?"

Then he looked at me for approval, and I wilted a little inside. He was a textbook date.

"I'm so full, but thank you. Everything was delicious."

His hopeful expression dropped just slightly, and I felt very much like I'd kicked a puppy. I pulled in a deep breath as the server walked away, determined not to give up on him just yet.

"I know you said you have family that lives nearby, but not who," I said. "Are there a lot of you around here?"

Scott's smile was wide and instant, making the skin by his eyes wrinkle attractively. "Not too many. My parents, my sister, Rachel, and her husband and two kids. Thankfully Rachel's filled the grand-child card, otherwise I'd be getting a whole different kind of pressure than I get now. Don't you think our families are more forgiving of us getting divorced if they've got a grandchild somewhere?"

I laughed, but it was sad-sounding to my ears. Scott must not have noticed.

"I'm afraid that's something I can't answer. My brother and Rory don't have kids yet." I shrugged my shoulders a bit. "And it wasn't something I got around to either. But my mom has been very supportive of me, grandkids or not."

He held up his hands quickly. "Oh of course. I'm sure she's won-derful. I didn't mean anything negative."

"It's fine," I told him. Because it was.

"No, that was rude to assume." Scott sighed and looked away before giving me a sheepish smile. "Subject change?"

I smiled. "If you want, but it really is okay."

"How about them Broncos?"

See? Sweet.

"Well, I can't say much about football. But maybe you could tell

KARLA SORENSEN

me about your sister's kids? Do you see them often?"

That lit him up from the inside out, because he immediately pulled out his phone to show me pictures of two adorable kids. He'd taken them to the zoo the week before, and there was another of the three of them with matching face paint from a carnival at their school.

I could feel myself getting frustrated. Not with him. Everything he was doing was perfectly fine. Perfectly nice. Perfectly polite.

And yet, here I sat, wishing for more.

From him. And from me.

We made small talk for another fifteen minutes or so while we waited for the bill, which he refused to let me contribute to, and when he walked us out of the restaurant, he made sure to hold open the door not just for me, but for the couple coming out behind us.

"I had a wonderful time, Anna," he said quietly when we reached my car. I already had my keys out and clasped in front of me, which he noted quickly before smiling. "I really hope we can do this again."

The hope in his eyes was almost enough to break me. Even wearing my heels, he stood a head taller than me, a perfectly respectful amount of distance in between us. Not so far that I knew he wasn't interested, but not so close that I might feel pressured. His gaze briefly touched on my lips and I made sure not to move them in the slightest.

When he met my eyes again, I gave him a small smile. I could give him another chance, this sweet man who probably would've wowed me a lot more had it not come after the dick pic of date number three. If he'd been date number one, I might have even kissed him, just to see how it would feel.

"Why don't you text me a couple options once you look at your schedule."

His face lit up. "I can do Wednesday, Friday or Saturday next week."

I laughed at his eagerness and he blushed before looking down at his feet.

166

"I think Friday would work for me, but I'll let you know once I look at my calendar."

Scott swiped a hand down his face. "Sorry, I'm still working on my tact when a beautiful woman agrees to go out on a date with me. You'd think I'd have this nailed down by my thirties, but I just really don't yet. Sometimes I feel like I was born into the wrong era."

Now that made me smile genuinely. Tentatively, I touched his forearm. "I like that you don't have it nailed down yet. It's sweet."

Before he could lean in, I unlocked my car and opened the driver's side door. Scott held it while I settled into my seat and laid my purse on the passenger side.

"Goodnight, Anna."

I smiled. "It was nice to meet you, Scott."

Carefully, he closed the door, and then stepped back while I started my car. I waved as I pulled away from the curb, and he did the same. If he was disappointed that I hadn't allowed for a kiss, or even a hug, he did a good job of hiding it.

As I drove home, I knew that's why I was giving him another chance, even though I didn't get any immediate chemistry, because I appreciated a man who knew how to act like a gentleman. Maybe Scott was born into the wrong era, but I liked that there were still men like him left.

How many men did I know like that?

Tristan.

His name was immediate, and I got a flash of his face in my head, the way he always watched me so intently when I spoke. The way he helped me up the other day at the shop, covered me with a blanket when he noticed I was cold. Always respectful, always thoughtful, even if he was the most reserved man I'd ever met.

Yes, maybe Tristan was born into the wrong era, too. Especially if what Garrett had said about him was any indication, that he didn't do casual.

Was that something I was looking for? A man who seemed like

he was from a different generation than the one we currently lived in? Who thought nothing of holding open doors and being chivalrous because it's who they were, not because they were trying to impress me.

Maybe it was what I was looking for.

Even though I was on date four, I wasn't sure how much time I'd spent thinking over what it was that I wanted in a man. Maybe that was a piece that I was underestimating, the kind of man who felt like finding a treasure in a strange place.

Respect and understanding, loyalty and a fierce, passionate love for exactly who that person is. Not what you'd want them to be, but what they are.

That's what my mom had said to me that first night. They weren't just words, carelessly applied labels, not to me. When your most formative romantic relationship had been lacking every single one of those labels, they felt like a gold mine to a pauper. And I when tried to imagine what the person looked like in my mind, the prototype that I should be chasing, it was fuzzy. Indistinct.

More than anything, I wanted to feel safe and protected. I wanted to burrow myself in someone's arms and know that when they were wrapped around me, I was being held by someone who loved me for me. And they'd be a person that I held right back in the same way.

Should that be so hard? It didn't seem like it. But trying to grasp onto the idea of it, to wrap my fingers through it and make it a reality that I could wrap my arms around felt like scaling a wall of hundred-foot tall rock.

I pulled my car into the left side of the garage door after it opened, next to my mom's. Maybe my future dream man was fuzzy and indistinct because I was still living at home with my widowed mother as my TV binging partner in crime.

Whatever. People could judge that all they wanted, because when I let myself into the back door, she greeted me with a smile, a hug, and a new martini recipe that she was trying out.

"Blackberry! Want one?"

I took it with careful hands and hummed after my first sip. "Oh, yum. Is there coconut in this?"

She nodded and motioned for her glass back. "Not much, but yes. Coconut rum. Want one?"

"Let me change first, but yes." I kissed her cheek as I passed.

"This is like when you were in high school all over again. Get home from a date and change into pajamas before you tell me about it."

"Except with martinis, so much better."

As I ascended the stairs, she was laughing. And that was good to hear too, another reason why I wasn't in a huge rush. The time together was as good for my mom as it was for me, so I wasn't in a hurry, as long as we still held some boundaries.

When we were snuggled under blankets with martinis in hand, I told her about Scott McAlister the accountant, and she shook her head while she smiled.

"Poor guy. All the pieces are there, huh?"

"I think so. I just don't think they're assembled in the right way for me."

Her eyes were shrewd, but understanding. "So why go on another date with him? Is that cruel to string him along?"

Ugh. I didn't want to be that woman. Especially given the look in his eye when he rattled off the schedule he'd clearly memorized.

"I don't think I'm stringing him along. I genuinely want to give him another chance, see if maybe he was just nervous tonight." My martini was cold when I drank more, but warmed my belly as I swallowed. "Who knows, if he loosens up a little bit, he could be perfect."

"Okay." Clearly, Mom wasn't buying it.

I lifted my eyebrows at her. "Maybe you should start going on dates, and then you can school me on how to handle these things."

She smiled sweetly, sadly. "Sweetheart, I still think about your father every single day when I wake up, still have to take a few moments to remind myself that *this* is life without him. I'm in no rush. Someday, I'll make it through my coffee in the morning before I think about him, maybe even until lunch that day. And then it might be time. And if that day never comes, then I'll be just fine."

That. *That's* what I was looking for. Someone who made me feel like my mom did about my dad, even after all the time he'd been gone. I wanted someone who bettered my life because they were in it, would leave a bittersweet void if they left the world before I did.

"You'd really be fine with that?"

"Oh goodness, yes." Then she tilted her head. "Well, as long as someone gives me grandchildren before I die."

I couldn't help it, I burst out laughing, the image of Scott's puppy dog eyes the only thing I could imagine.

"We will, Mom." I lifted my glass, and she clinked hers against it. "I truly believe that we will."

There it was again.

Hope.

That night, it sounded like my mom's laughter, and it tasted an awful lot like blackberries with just a hint of coconut.

CHAPTER EIGHTEEN

TRISTAN

Me: Haven't seen you around since last week at your brother's.

Anna: Is there a question buried in there? Or just an observation?

Me: I'm a slow typer, you'll have to forgive me. If you'd waited one more minute, my follow up was, just checking in to see how you're doing.

Anna: Ha. Sorry.
Anna: My mom had martinis waiting for me when I got home the other night. Is it strange that stuff like that makes me never want to move out?

Me: Strange? No.

Anna: ...

Anna: You thoroughly enjoy making people suffer by your truncated reactions, don't you?

Me: Only on Tuesdays.

Anna: LOL. Liar.

That one exchange, which I'd read countless times because I was so damn proud of myself for initiating conversation with no work reason, no manufactured excuse for why, and it was a good exchange. But that was it for another week.

Throughout the days that I didn't see her, didn't text her again, I thought of all sorts of reasons to stop by and see her.

Hey, Anna. I was in the neighborhood. I rented this movie and wasn't sure if you'd seen it yet.

Hey, Anna. I was in the neighborhood. Just checking to make sure you've got your snow tires on your car.

Hey, Anna. I was in the neighborhood. Just making sure you ate today. Oh, you didn't? Great, I was just on my way to grab some food if you want to eat with me.

Each progressive idea made me feel crazier, which is why I would pick up my phone and end up setting it back down again. Part of it might have been the fact that I'd never been friends with females. The rules were different. I could go weeks without any sort of communication from my guy friends and never thought twice about it. Was it the same when guys and girls were friends? Would she notice the difference?

And when the next one came in, I knew that I was a horrible person. Awful. I'd never been so happy to hear about a flood in my life.

Anna: So apparently there was a flood in the distribution warehouse that had our entire batch of flooring and I have to pick something new if we want to stay on schedule. Are you at the shop today if I swing by with some of the samples I have? I want to make sure they work with the dining furniture.

Me: Yeah, I'm here all day.
Me: Sorry to hear about the flood.

I wasn't sorry.

The thought of seeing her overrode everything, even common decency, apparently. But for the next two hours before she stopped by, I was a nervous wreck. We'd crossed a few major hurdles lately, and each successive one made me feel like I was that much closer to my goal.

I jammed my hands into my hair more times than I could count, which meant I had to redo the messy knot enough that I wouldn't have turned down the offer to have someone shave my head. My normally steady fingers didn't seem to work right as I did some finish work on one of the chairs for the dining table.

Anna: Can I grab you a sandwich from Las Tortas on my way? This is doubling as my lunch, so I'll need to be rude and eat in front of you.

Me: That'd be great, thanks. Whatever you're having is fine.

Anna: Two Tortas de Nortena coming up. :)

Like an idiot, I stared at that text and found myself smiling. Just a small smile, but it was enough that I didn't even want to suppress it. For the millionth time, I glanced at the clock on the wall of the shop, and knew she'd be here any minute.

I ran a hand over the seat of the chair and knew it was ready for varnish. The chairs at each end of the table would be high-backed and upholstered, so I didn't need to make those, but Anna did want a matching bench that could be stored away and taken out easily for entertaining purposes, which was next on my list.

The tentative knock on the door, follow by Anna's voice almost had me jumping in place.

"Yeah, come in," I called, not wanting to seem too eager by sprinting over to the door and yanking it open.

She was using her shoulder to push open the heavy metal door, and that did have me moving toward her, since her hands were full of food. I held it open and took one of the white bags.

"Thank you," she said with a grateful smile. Her eyes moved from me to the space I'd cleared at the main work table, complete with two stools that we could sit on. "Someone must be hungry," Anna teased. "How often is that spot wiped down?"

Never.

I shrugged and set down the bag, taking the second one from her while she unloaded some flooring samples from the giant bag slung over her shoulder.

"Figured you'd want a place to sit. I'm used to eating standing up, but I didn't want to be rude."

She laughed. "Isn't that funny? I eat standing up all the time too. Especially over the kitchen sink." While she looked at me, she scrunched up her nose and I wanted to kiss where the skin wrinkled slightly. "I wonder why that feels so different from sitting down and eating alone?"

For a beat, I stared at her, and wished desperately that I had the power to warp time, to make it slow and stretch. There were so many hours and minutes and seconds and days and nights that I'd spent dreaming of small moments just like this one, what it would be like with her. To have the reality be better than what my brain had been able to conjure up was heady and humbling.

She was more beautiful, even in the harsh light of the shop. Not because her features had changed, but because she was free and happy. Her smiles came more quickly, the light she'd always had inside of her shining so much more brightly. Seeing it now, only available for my eyes even if just for a moment, I knew I'd be capable of great violence if someone ever dimmed it again.

Focus. Talk to her.

"I've never really thought about it," I admitted. "But I do frequent the kitchen sink as an eating spot."

"See?" She nudged my shoulder with her own. "Weird, right?"

"Maybe a bit." I hid my smile and turned to pull one of the stools closer to the table. "Work first and then eat?"

"We can do both." She grinned. "I'm very talented that way. Plus, I don't have a ton of time, unfortunately."

Anna unwrapped both tortas and handed me one. The bread was soft and still warm, the beef tender and spicy and I couldn't stop a low moan when I took my first bite. "*Wow.*"

"I know," she answered with a full mouth. She looked so indelicate, so unlike her, that I laughed under my breath. She held up a little fist. "Oooh, that was a close one."

"What was?"

"You almost smiled." Her eyebrow lifted and I couldn't help but stare at the brown in her eyes. Then it registered what she said.

"You're keeping track?" Idiot. Idiot. Idiot. The fact that she was keeping track, the sly smile she gave me as her only response made my heart stutter. This felt dangerous for how far it could carry me.

Anna took a prim bite, used a white napkin to wipe at her mouth but her eyes were smiling when they met mine.

"How was your Thanksgiving?" she asked after she swallowed.

"Good. We usually go to my uncle's. Lots of people, lots of food. Yours?"

"Quieter than that," she said. "Just the four of us at my mom's, but she loves to cook, so there was enough food for eighteen."

I smiled at that, and she slid the wood samples toward me on the surface of the work table.

"Those are my two favorite options, but one is clearly warmer than the other and I want to make sure it still works."

I smoothed my hand over both and held them up to the light. "Do you have a preference?"

"Yeah," she said dryly. "Whatever one allows for little to no change to what we already have."

One side of my mouth tipped up, and I stood to pull the finished chair up off the floor and onto the table where it would have the best light. Anna made a little gasping noise.

"Tristan," she exhaled. "That's so beautiful."

Her hand ran over the seat and almost brushed the tips of my fingers where they held onto the side.

That had me buzzing as much as the thick beat of pride in my work.

"Thank you."

"I'm serious." She glanced at me briefly before she leaned in to look more closely. "You really should be doing this full-time. Most of my clients would pay huge money for this kind of workmanship. I think you undersold yourself a bit on the price you quoted me."

I swallowed, but didn't say anything. Had I cut her a deal to make sure that I got this job?

Hell yes, I had.

"Let me get a damp rag," I told her in lieu of an answer. "I'll wipe some of it down so you'll get a better idea of how it will look once it's finished."

She held the samples up to the chair once I did, and moved her head to the side. "I think the one on the right." Her face tilted up to mine, because of course, I wasn't looking at the chair. She blinked in surprise, probably not expecting me to be looking right at her. "Wh-what do you think?"

I think you're the most beautiful thing I've ever seen.

That's what I wanted to say, but my tongue was a messy tangle and even though I let out a slow breath, I couldn't force the words out. Her eyes searched mine when I didn't respond, and for the first time, I didn't force my mask up, didn't actively work to hide what I might be feeling. Could she see it? Could she recognize it for what it was?

"Which one do you think?" she prodded gently, a confused smile twisting her mouth to the side.

I blinked and gave them a quick look. "I agree. The one on the right."

Anna set the samples aside with a smile and picked up her sandwich again. I had to turn away and close my eyes in frustration. Why was this so hard for me? Why did this feel like such a risk?

"Well that was easier than I thought."

I moved the chair to the side and sat back down. "Everything else going okay?"

She wiped some sauce from the side of her mouth and I took a vicious bite of my sandwich so I didn't do something stupid like use my lips to help her. "Yeah. The builders are actually ahead of schedule by a few days."

"That's great." This was the kind of small talk I hated, and while I didn't hate any sort of conversation with Anna, I felt a flicker of frustration that this wasn't going more smoothly after all the little victories leading up to it.

Conversation skills of a rock was right.

"What kind of martinis did your mom make for you?" I asked, and she visibly startled at my inelegantly blurted out question. Then her lips morphed into a pleased smile.

"You remembered that?"

I shrugged.

Anna set her sandwich down and took a drink from her water bottle. "Some blackberry coconut thing that almost brought a tear to my eye, it was so delicious."

"That's a serious statement."

"It was a serious martini." Her eyes searched my face. "You've got a good memory, you know that?"

I could tell you the very first thing you said to me. Instead, I just tapped two fingers to the side of my head. "Steel trap."

"And so humble about it, too."

When she twisted her lips up in a smile, like she always did right after she said something meant to tease, I felt a heady buzz through my entire body, an aching desire to lean forward and kiss her.

To fit my mouth over hers and sink my hands into her hair until she melted against me. What would happen if I kissed her like I wanted to?

Like I wanted to when I covered her with the blanket on Garrett's couch. Like I wanted to when she asked me about my father, but didn't push after I gave her the only answer I was capable of giving. Like I wanted to when she looked at me. When she tucked her hair behind her ears. When she laughed. When she breathed.

When I didn't respond at all, she shook her head, but she was still smiling. "What day did you say you like to torture people with your non-responses? It must be today."

I was about to respond when the door to shop opened. Annoyance made me glare over my shoulder, when I saw Michael and Brooke walk in.

Anna leapt up with a happy exclamation and went to give Brooke a tight hug. I glared at Michael and he held up his hands in silent apology.

"This is a nice surprise," Brooke said to Anna. "I came to talk Michael into having lunch with me when I saw your car."

She gave me a slight nod and I mentally buried my head in my hands. I wasn't stupid. I knew that Brooke was probably aware of my feelings for Anna, at least to some extent, given that Michael had an unfortunate tendency to run his big mouth all the time.

Anna leaned against her stool, but was facing Michael and Brooke now. "Yeah, we had a flooring emergency, so I decided to make this a working lunch. There's no way I can finish this torta if you want half. There are chips and salsa in the bag too."

Brooke looked tempted, and I gave Michael such a scorching stare that he actually looked afraid.

"Babe," he said to Brooke, laying a hand on her shoulder, "let's let them work."

"Oh, we're done," Anna said. "I knew this would have to be a quick visit anyway. I have to get back to the office shortly."

"No really, it's okay," Michael said quickly. "Besides, I was craving Italian."

Brooke gave him a strange look. "We had Italian last night."

"I'm craving *more* Italian."

I'd underestimated Brooke's stubbornness. *Why* did I like her again? I tried to remind myself that she made my brother blissfully happy and she was my future sister-in-law.

"Slow your roll. I don't get to see her often, and Rory told me that I need to ask her about Scott the accountant. Apparently, someone *finally* got a second date with Miss Anna here."

My heart lurched painfully, and I struggled not to press my hand to my chest to make sure it was still there. Michael closed his eyes and sighed heavily. *Scott the accountant?* Blood was rushing in my ears so loudly that I barely made out what Anna said in answer. She had a second date with someone?

My hands curled into fists and Michael's face was so pale, he looked like he was about to witness a bomb go off.

Anna laughed quietly. "Someone finally did."

"And?" Brooke prompted, folding her arms over her chest and ignoring the frantic looks that Michael was sending her way. I didn't want to hear anything about Scott the accountant. I hated Scott the accountant who probably wore suits and ties and made good money and loved fancy restaurants and knew what kind of wine paired with everything.

"He's nice," Anna said after an agonizing second. "Very sweet."

Asshole.

"You don't sound too excited," Brooke said.

No, no she really didn't, did she? Brooke was right. I liked Brooke. She was very astute.

Anna shrugged and looked sheepishly at Michael and then me. "Sorry, guys, I'm sure this isn't a very exciting topic."

"Err, on the contrary," Michael said graciously, even though he still gave me nervous eyes. "Anything that makes Brooke happy to hear about is very exciting to me."

Brooke rolled her eyes, and so did I.

But in light of her not sounding too excited about Scott the accountant, I found myself turning more fully in Anna's direction.

She sighed and set her sandwich down. "I gave him another try because he was so sweet and nice. Much more so than any of my other sad attempts at dating. But ... I don't know. I think he's just too sweet and nice, if that makes sense."

"It does," Brooke said.

No, no it doesn't, I wanted to yell. That was too ambiguous. Sweet and nice was good, but not *too* sweet and nice. How the hell were men supposed to know how to work with *that*?

"So yes, he got a second date, but he won't get a third, unfortunately."

I took a distracted bite of my sandwich, because even though that was good news for me, I still felt like there was a canyon separating us. Before, it was a mountain, and somehow, that felt less daunting when there was just one asshole of a man to contend with. Now I had limitless possibilities that were too sweet and nice, and I still had to read the signals of whether she was ready for something serious.

Anna glanced at the clock on the wall and jumped up. "Oh goodness, I have to go. I had no idea it was this late." She smiled at me as she wrapped up the rest of her sandwich and tossed it into one of the bags. "Thank you for letting me crash. And for sharing lunch."

I opened my mouth, I'm sure it was to say something witty and funny and not too sweet or nice, but she hugged Brooke and was gone in a flash of long black hair. I sank back on my stool and sighed heavily.

Michael flicked Brooke in the arm.

"*Ouch*, what was that?" She flicked him right back.

"You weren't catchin' what I was throwing down, woman!"

She lifted an eyebrow. "'Scuse me?"

Michael waved an impatient hand in my direction. "Do you think he wants to have us interrupt his time with her so we can hear about Scott the accountant?"

Brooke gave me a sheepish, apologetic smile. "Well, I already knew from Rory that she wouldn't be seeing Scott the accountant again. I asked on purpose."

My head lifted. "You did?"

"You did?" Michael repeated.

Brooke rolled her eyes. "Yes. I knew Tristan wouldn't ask about her date, and I'm sorry, but whatever plan you've got going on isn't working if she's going on second dates with guys that are as exciting as wet cardboard. You need to make something happen, Tristan. Because it won't happen on its own."

"Oh shit," Michael mumbled. "She's got that devious look in her eyes."

"No," I said.

"What are you thinking?" Michael asked Brooke.

"No," I repeated. "And I thought you liked my plan, Michael."

They both ignored me.

"This work bullshit isn't cutting it," Brooke told my idiot brother. "We just need to make some quality time happen, which is easy enough."

"No."

Michael nodded sagely. "I am thoroughly enjoying the way your evil brain works, my love."

She leaned forward and smacked a kiss on his lips. "I know. You tell me that every day."

I pinched the bridge of my nose. It wasn't even worth talking anymore.

"An intervention," Michael said and clapped his hands. "I like it."

"Do I have any say in this?" I asked.

"No," they said in tandem.

"The truth is this," Brooke said in a gentler tone, "it's been like, what? Seven, eight weeks since she moved out? We're not saying you need to profess your love right away. But you *do* need Anna to see you outside of work mode. That's all. Have fun in the same place that she's having fun."

"She's seen me outside of work mode," I mumbled. "Quite a few times."

Brooke shook her head. Michael gave me a slight shrug of his shoulders. "Dude, I was in favor of your plan, and I still am. But Brooke has a point. She's dating. That's a big deal. It might not be stupid to set up something date-like for you two, without it being date-like. Nothing stressful, it just gives you another opportunity."

I dropped my hand and regarded them warily. "That's all?"

"That's all," Brooke said.

From the look in her eyes, I could tell she meant it, so I nodded slowly. "Okay."

Michael raised a fist in the air. "Atta boy. Just show up where I tell you, and we'll take care of the rest."

And that was exactly what I was afraid of.

CHAPTER NINETEEN

TRISTAN

Michael: Ophelia's Electric Soapbox at 8pm. And for shit's sake, trim your beard so you don't look like a homeless person.

Why, why, why was I going along with this? I thought it for the millionth time that day. I thought it while I trimmed my beard so I didn't look homeless, even though it wasn't thick enough to be *that* bad. I thought it while I actually stood in front of my closet and picked what I thought was one of my nice button-down shirts and rolled the sleeves up. I thought it while I pulled my hair back and studied my reflection longer than I ever cared to.

The colors of my tattoos on my forearms seemed brighter when I wondered what Anna thought when she saw them. Her ex-husband was clean-cut. Buttoned-up. He fit the stereotype of whatever stupid research job he'd had.

And I was the exact opposite. I worked with my hands, came home smelling like sawdust and sweat and drywall mud and hard, physical labor.

I was different than what she was used to.

Maybe that's why I was going along with this. Because even though I knew that giving Anna space to work through her divorce without me smothering her was the right thing, I also knew that Michael and Brooke weren't wrong. I'd never admit that to them, but I knew it.

I also knew that despite my plan, some friendly intervention wouldn't hurt. It was uncomfortable for me to imagine ways to manufacture time with Anna, save just asking her out. Which would come.

It would.

"When it's the right time," I told myself as I slid my arms into my coat and walked out to my truck.

It was 8:02 when I walked into the bar, which was packed. Later, there would be a band playing on the stage on the lower level of the bar, where Michael had secured a large booth for our group. I made my way through the crowd, shrugging off my coat as I did.

A group of women turned in my direction as I passed, and someone made a comment I couldn't hear through the din, but it made them all laugh and my face heated regardless. I wasn't blind to the attention that I got from women, I just didn't care about it. I never had.

Garrett stood up from the booth and waved when he saw me. I jerked my chin and walked over. The band was setting up, but the music playing from the sound system was bluesy and southern, heavy on the guitars and bass. I saw Michael and Brooke, Garrett and Rory, Dylan and Kat, but no Anna yet. Cole and Julia weren't there either. There were two spots open right at the end of our booth.

I gave Michael a look and he shrugged innocently.

Someone touched my back and I looked over my shoulder to see Anna.

"Looks like we're both a little late to the party," she said, leaning up so I could hear her. She smelled like warmth and spice and woman, and I tilted my head down unthinkingly, so I could inhale her scent before she moved away.

"I guess so."

"Anna," Rory said. "There's a hook right there for our coats. It's pretty warm back here in the booth."

Anna blinked. "Oh, okay." She turned to take her purse off her shoulder and Rory gave me a meaningful look before staring at Anna's coat. Okay, so tonight was going to be like *that*. Garrett grinned and slung an arm around his wife. I set my jaw and shook my head, but leaned closer to Anna regardless.

"I can take that for you," I said by her ear. She looked over her shoulder and gave me a small smile when I helped slide her coat off her shoulders. I gulped audibly, because her dress was light purple and tight. Tight everywhere. While I stood there holding her coat, she used her hands to gather all her hair and pull it over one shoulder.

"Thank you."

If I was capable of speech, I'm quite sure I would've said *You're welcome.* Or maybe *you are sublimely perfect and I could watch you do that with your hair all day long on a loop.*

Rory waved her to one of the open spots at the back of the booth, which left the last spot right next to her. Of course. Michael smiled and Brooke bounced in her seat a little. Kat took a conspicuous sip from her margarita while I hung Anna's coat and then slid into the booth next to Anna.

Her hip brushed mine and she smiled again. "Tight quarters."

They sure were. And every single freaking eye at our table was on the two of us. I leaned forward and picked up the menu, even though I wasn't sure it was smart for me to add alcohol into the mix with so much outside help already.

"Where are Cole and Julia?" I asked Brooke.

"Ugh, babysitter bailed last minute because she was sick or something."

I nodded. If there was a couple who probably didn't mind staying in because their babysitter canceled, it was probably Cole and Julia.

"Honestly, I think they were excited about it," Brooke said.

I smiled a little. "I bet they were."

A waitress came around, and when Anna leaned in my direction, I had to close my eyes because the ends of her hair were draped across my bare forearm.

"I'll have the Sex Machine," she said loud enough that Garrett shoved his fingers in his ears and started humming loudly. Rory burst out laughing at Garrett's reaction, and I had to grit my teeth at the delighted peals of laughter that Anna let out when the waitress left.

It was a new kind of torture to be seated next to her. Sitting across from her, I would've been able to unabashedly watch that laughter, absorb the sound like it was the only thing I could hear. Watch the way it curved her lips and showed glimpses of her white teeth and pink tongue. But next to her, I could feel it. Feel the way it made her shoulders shake, because her shoulders were pressed against me.

Every time she swayed to a song, with perfect natural rhythm, my skin hummed and I wanted to sweep my hands over her body to know what those movements felt like under my fingers.

Around us, people talked about work and home, family and friends, plans for the holidays. There was laughter and happiness. Anna and I maybe have been the impetus for the get together, but it was clear we were overdue for something like this.

"So, Tristan," Kat said loudly. Too loudly to be natural. "I was trying to convince Dylan that he needs to grow his hair out."

Dylan gave her a weird look until she elbowed him in the side. "Yes. She was."

"Why's that?" I asked against my better judgment.

Kat blinked. "I mean, guys with long hair are hot. Aren't they hot, Anna?"

Oh.dear.sweet.hell. If I crawled under the booth, would it be too obvious? Because I was not going to make it through this night.

Anna shifted so that she could face me, and she gave me a mock appraising look. I held my breath when she grinned, mainly because I was afraid what would come out of my mouth if I didn't.

You're perfect for me.

I adore everything about you.

Stuff like that. So yeah, I held my breath. Especially when she lifted her hand like she was going to touch my hair, but she dropped it after a moment.

My entire body was strung tight, like someone had a rubber band pulled to the point just before it broke.

"I'd have to vote in the hot column, Kat." Then gave me a wink so small, I almost missed it. Like we had a secret. Did we?

Was she ... was she flirting with me?

Absently, I sipped my water, wondering when I'd gotten so bad at this.

Anna's second drink was delivered, not a Sex Machine this time, and she took a tentative sip, then proclaimed it a winner. Garrett reached his arm along the back of the booth and tapped the wall behind us to get my attention. Then he held up his phone. Mine vibrated in my pocket and I cursed the idiocy of the people I'd invited in my life.

I pulled my phone out and tilted the screen so Anna wouldn't be able to read it.

Garrett: Talk to her, you giant hipster Jesus of a man. SHE JUST SAID LONG HAIR WAS HOT. WHAT MORE COULD YOU WANT OUT OF LIFE???

Over Anna and Rory's heads, I gave him a warning look, which he met with one of his own. My phone buzzed again.

Garrett: So help me, dude. If you don't step up soon, I'll take matters into my own hands and you don't want that.

I rolled my eyes and took another sip of my water. *Buzz, buzz, buzz.*

Garrett: DON'T PUSH ME. I'll go up to the bar, find the most unsuitable guy there and PAY HIM to dance with Anna so your chicken-shit ass has to sit here and watch.

Finally, my fingers started flying across the screen, because my annoyance turned to actual anger.

Me: This isn't a game. Don't it treat it like one. I've been sitting here for twenty minutes, can you COOL IT?

"Oooh, who are you texting?" Anna whispered next to me and I slammed my phone down on the table, face down. Her face was so close to mine. I hated that they were all watching us, hated it so much that it made my bones hurt with the desire to be alone with her like this.

It would've been easy for me to slide my arm along the back of the booth, when I realized, why *wouldn't* I do that?

So I did. My arm didn't touch her, but it allowed me to tilt my head closer and pretend like I hadn't heard her.

"What was that?" Oh, I was going to hell.

She lifted her chin at my phone. "You don't strike me as the type who would text while you're out with friends, Mr. No Social Media."

That made me pull back in surprise. She was right. I wasn't that type at all. I hated when people did it.

There was no judgment or annoyance in her face, just genuine curiosity. Her lashes were so long around her eyes, the bright, moving colors in the bar cast her cheekbones in shades of pink and purple, and I hated them. Anything that hid her, that distorted her features suddenly felt garish and wrong.

Garrett coughed loudly, and I shook my head. "Actually, it was your brother."

Her brow furrowed. "What was?"

"Your brother was texting me, and you know how annoying he can be when he feels ignored."

Anna sighed and turned to give Garrett a look that I couldn't see. "You would text someone sitting three people away from you."

"You told her," Garrett accused.

"Yup," I said.

He narrowed his eyes, and I could feel Anna looking between us. Rory was the only other person really paying attention to the exchange. After a moment, Garrett pulled his wallet out and made a dramatic show of pulling out a twenty.

I narrowed my eyes. He wouldn't.

"I'll be right back," he announced, and I glared at his retreating back.

"Man, it's times like this where I love reminding him that I'm only *legally* his sister and my gene pool is not the same as his."

I smothered a grin and took another drink of water, tried desperately to quell my rising sense of panic that Garrett actually *would*. "You say that to him?"

Anna laughed. "I do. Not often, but it's fun to give him shit."

I wasn't familiar with the typical family dynamics when one sibling was adopted and one wasn't, but Garrett and Anna seemed to have such a healthy relationship, so maybe theirs was the norm. Garrett wasn't back at the table yet, but when a man in his mid to late forties approached the table, I stiffened immediately.

Apparently Garrett *would*, and he *did*. That ass.

The man was tall, and if Garrett meant 'inappropriate' in the way that he was completely normal looking, then he hit the nail on the head. Begrudgingly, I had to admit that he was a good-looking guy, and he smiled at Anna like he just won the lottery.

"Excuse me, can I be completely forward and ask if you'd like to dance?"

Brooke's eyes widened comically, and Anna stammered a bit next to me, but it didn't sound like a no. "There's only a couple people dancing."

The man put on a charming smile that had earned him roughly twenty bucks. "Then we'll make it a couple more. If you say yes."

He held out his hand, and I had to clench my fists so as not to knock it away.

Anna gave me a brief questioning look, and I held her eyes, my heart thudding uncomfortably in my chest. Too big and too loud, there was no way she couldn't hear it. It felt like the whole bar could hear it. The choice was mine, it was clear. I didn't have to let this happen, all I had to do was make a choice. Take a chance.

"Do you want to dance?" I asked her instead of moving out of the booth so she could go to him.

She pulled in a deep breath and didn't look away.

"I..." she paused and glanced at the man who was waiting patiently, "I wouldn't mind a dance."

I nodded slowly. There was no tangling of words, no hesitation this time when I spoke. "Do you want to dance with *him*?"

Slowly, so slowly, her lips curved into a smile. "I'd rather dance with someone I know."

I nodded again, and stood from the booth, my back to the stranger who just made the easiest money he'd ever make in his life, because he wasn't getting shit for it. Then I held out my hand to Anna. There was no shake. No tremor visible while I waited for her. "Shall we?"

It seemed like the entire table held its breath until Anna slid her palm against mine. Her fingers were cool and smooth when I wrapped mine around them and pulled her from the table. Garrett took his seat next to Rory, smiling smugly. Anna glanced behind her, and everyone looked away immediately.

The song that played as we walked toward the dance floor was soft and sweet, the singer's voice raising goose bumps along my arms and I recognized the weight of Anna's hand in my own. Now I might have been shaking slightly, or maybe I imagined it.

There were only a handful of other couples swaying to the music, but when we faced each other, I saw a few others stand up and make their way over. Anna's hands slid up my shoulders and she folded her fingers together behind my neck. The curve of her waist was impossibly small under my palm, and my entire being vibrated with the violent desire to pull her flush against my body. But I held her at a respectable distance, my fingers spread across her lower back.

We didn't so much dance as we swayed gently, even though my pulse was hammering dangerously.

Anna's fingers moved against the back of my neck and I looked down into her face, so precious to me that I had no way to keep it off my expression.

Not when I was this close to her, knowing that against me, her face would tuck perfectly underneath my chin, that if I wrapped my arms fully around her back, her nose would hit right at the base of my throat.

Not when I could see the delicate ridge of her collarbone disappear under her dress, or how she took shallow breaths that seemed to match the beat of the song and how it expanded her slender rib cage under my fingers.

"You haven't been working too hard, have you?" she asked, tilting her chin back so that she could study my face.

For a moment, I held my breath, because I wondered how many of my thoughts were stamped, inked, tattooed over me for her to see. But her face only held kind interest.

"I don't think so."

She hummed, her eyes searching my features. "You look tired."

"Gee thanks."

Anna laughed and shook her head as we spun in slow circles. "You know what I mean."

"Do I?" I murmured. Briefly, I glanced back at our booth, and every *single* person was turned in our direction and staring unapologetically. I rolled my eyes and tried to turn us in a way that wasn't obvious to Anna.

I didn't want any of them intruding on this moment, not even from a distance. It was mine, and it was hers. No one else belonged in it with us.

Her fingers traced an absent pattern against my skin and I felt that movement slide hot down my spine, all the way to my toes. "It's just my way of making sure that you're not overdoing it because of me."

My eyes closed briefly, because I had been. Not because I felt any sort of pressure from her, but because of my stupid brain.

"I won't overdo it." My hands itched to tangle in her hair when I felt the ends brush against my knuckles. This was almost too much, but I'd stay. I'd stay as long as my feet could hold me in this perfect moment, and even then, I'd refuse to walk away if she didn't want me to.

Anna gauged the truthfulness of my answer and must have been satisfied, because she smiled, tipping her chin down slightly.

"You're a very respectful dancer, Tristan," she said quietly, so quietly that I almost didn't hear her.

"Am I?" Was that my voice? It sounded like I'd gargled with acid.

My sanity was thready and thin, almost non-existent, and the only thing keeping me in that precarious balance was each breath in and out. My body screamed at me to pull her into me, bury my nose in her hair and make her feel warm and safe and surrounded by all the things that I couldn't find the strength to say.

If I'd ever marveled at my own self-control, it had never been anything compared to this moment. The pain, the perfection, of holding her, even with the smallest distance separating us was so great and heavy that it felt impossible to endure.

But I would.

I'd hold her just like this every single day if that's all she needed of me, until the moment she was ready for more.

She smiled up at me, so sweetly that I lost another ounce of my soul to her. She could have all of it. She already did. "I like it. Not all men are."

I felt heat crawl up the back of my neck and my fingers tightened reflexively against the smooth line of her back. "Gotta keep room for the Holy Spirit in the middle when you dance."

Her smile bloomed immediately, and for a suspended, horrifying moment, I couldn't believe those words had actually come out of my mouth, an embarrassing throwback to something my mom had told us when we were in middle school and heading out to our first dance.

Anna pressed her lips together before speaking. "Is that so?"

I closed my eyes for a beat and sighed before looking at her again. "If you tell Michael I just said that, I'll never, ever live it down."

Her laugh was immediate and loud, her head tipped back from the force of it, and I was so incredibly happy sharing this moment with her, even if I'd said something horribly stupid, I didn't care. She made me so happy, something I always imagined being able to relish in, and now I was. Her eyes widened when she looked at me again.

Before I realized what was happening, one of her hands slid from my neck to lightly cup the side of my face. Her thumb rested next to my mouth. "There it is," she whispered.

"What?"

"Your smile." Affection warmed her eyes, and I struggled to keep breathing. "I knew it was in there."

Her hand returned to my neck, and mercifully, she didn't say anything else. And me? I was incapable of speech without embarrassing myself completely.

I'll never leave you, not if you give me the chance to stay.

You are meant to be in my arms.

I'm so in love with you.

The song ended and for a moment, she didn't move. Neither did I.

"Thank you, Tristan." Anna looked down, and I couldn't place the emotion on her face when she lifted her chin again. "It's been years since anyone has asked me to dance. I'm really glad it was you."

When she pulled away and walked back to the table, I followed, knowing that she couldn't have taken another ounce of my soul with that smile.

She owned every part of it. And even with that knowledge, Anna had the ability to break my heart for her all over again.

CHAPTER TWENTY

ANNA

"I can assure you that this won't happen again, Millie."

She narrowed her eyes at me, and I fought to sit still. To not shrink slightly under the iron weight of her annoyance. It wasn't really aimed at me, but it felt like it was.

"He should be here."

"I agree."

We'd made plans to meet Millie out at the house for an update, since drywall was up and the new flooring had been delivered, though not installed yet. Tristan hadn't shown up.

My first thought had been instant worry for him, but I couldn't say the same for Millie.

"I expect professionalism from all of my subcontractors on a job of this level," she continued, this time staring down the foreman like he'd done something wrong too. Underneath his hard hat, his ruddy cheeks flushed even deeper red, and I tried to give him a comforting smile.

Will and I had worked together on a few jobs, and there was

nothing that made him more uncomfortable than confrontation with the client, given his easy temperament.

"Tristan is incredibly professional, Millie," I said in a soothing, but not patronizing, voice. "I've seen some of your pieces already and they will be stunning once everything is finished. I promise."

One perfect silver eyebrow arched. "Are you a woodworker now that you can promise me that?"

I let out a deep breath. "No, but his reputation precedes him. And I've seen what he's accomplished so far. I love it. On his behalf, I apologize for the miscommunication. It's quite likely I told him the wrong time."

Will cleared his throat, because he could see right through my bluster, but it was either that or snap at her because a clawing defensiveness was making my spine stiff and rigid as she insinuated that Tristan wasn't professional.

Millie let out a slight humph, but accepted my apology with a nod. "It can't happen again."

"It won't," I promised.

Will took pity on me and drew her over into the kitchen now that my portion was over, and my shoulders dropped slightly. Taking a small portion of the blame for Tristan wasn't hard, because there was no way she'd hire someone to replace him at this phase of construction, but I hated the idea that it might cost him future business if she thought he was flighty.

Tristan. Flighty.

It was laughable. Tristan was one of the most steady, reliable men I'd ever met. I didn't need to dig very deep to know that he was almost certainly working himself too hard. I'd seen the circles under his eyes when we danced, saw the faint lines of fatigue on his chiseled face.

That. Dance.

While I walked to my car, I welcomed the cold air against my cheeks, because any time I'd thought about it in the last few days, I felt ... warm. Really, really warm.

There wasn't even one singular moment that I could pinpoint through his complete respectability, his almost painful gentlemanly exterior that could cause me to feel that way. Something about how much bigger he was than me maybe. Or the way his hands, large and hot through the material of my dress, never strayed beyond the small of my back.

Actually, the most surprising moment had been when he'd asked me to dance in the first place. The way he'd looked at me in the booth, goodness. It flipped my belly upside down even remembering it. Those deep brown eyes had been so dialed in on me that it still left me slightly breathless.

I'd *wanted* him to ask me to dance.

Sitting next to him all night, his arm stretched out behind me and the heat of his body up against mine, I very much wanted Tristan to be the one who led me out onto the dance floor. Not some random stranger, no matter how kind he'd seemed.

And even though the dance had only lasted a few short minutes, the span of a single song, I was struggling to not obsess over it. Even days later.

This was the part of single life that I didn't miss, and still felt a little bit unprepared for. The dissection of feelings, of gestures and looks and responses. What did he mean when he said that? Did a vague text response mean he was mad at me? Or was he simply busy at work? When he touched my arm like that, did it mean something? Or *something*?

Because there was a difference, thank you very much.

Placing Tristan within the crosshairs of my emotional analysis felt like I was doing something vaguely wrong, because of what Garrett had said to me. His warning was so clear, this is not a dude you toy with, whether it's intentional or not.

And yet, I couldn't *not* mull over these little snippets of time that I kept experiencing with a man who intrigued me, who I undoubtedly found attractive, who made me feel good, who'd proven to be a surprising friend when I needed one. Those moments with Tristan held weight, even if it was only to me at this point.

If it was one-sided, that side being me, and Tristan was only being kind to his friend's sister, then I'd never want to embarrass him.

And if it wasn't, I wanted to tread carefully, because of what Garrett told me about him.

In my hand, my phone buzzed, a text from the man himself like my thoughts had summoned him.

Michael: Hey, you haven't heard from Tristan at all today, have you? He's not answering his phone.

My brow furrowed instantly, worry making my fingers cold.

Me: I tried to call him a couple times too. He missed a client meeting. I didn't think that was typical.

Michael: He mentioned he wasn't feeling well last night, so maybe he's sick? I'm about to walk into a client meeting, so I can't duck out of work to check on him until tonight, but I can let you know once I do.

I shook my head while I tucked my phone in my purse. "Of *course* you got sick, you stubborn man."

When we danced, I'd seen the tiredness in his eyes. My brother would rather have his teeth pulled sans anesthesia than admit to not feeling well, so maybe Tristan was the same way.

Not to generalize one half of the gender split so widely, but men didn't have the best reputation for admitting when they didn't feel well. And Tristan … was a man. Especially with that hair, and the impossibly broad shoulders, I thought with an unrepentant grin. Another thing I'd tried not to obsess over since Saturday … the way he filled out the shirt he'd been wearing.

It stretched. Nicely. That's all I'm sayin'.

As I started the drive back toward Denver, I thought about him feverish and miserable, alone in his house. Maybe even throwing up. I knew that once Michael moved in with Brooke, Tristan never got a new roommate. He was completely alone.

I hated being sick. One of the ways my mom had spoiled Garrett and I was to unapologetically baby us when we didn't feel well. She loved making us toast and soup and refilling our cup of Sprite, complete with a straw and everything.

It wasn't that I owed Tristan, precisely, but I did feel bad because I knew he'd overworked because of this job. Which was the only reason I could explain why I called Brooke.

Or the only one I'd ever admit out loud.

"Hey!" she answered brightly. "What's up?"

"I think I'm having a stupid idea, and I need you tell me if it is."

"It's what I'm best at."

I laughed. "Okay. Well, Tristan just missed a client update meeting, and Michael just texted me that Tristan wasn't feeling well last night."

"Ugh, that's not good. Is the client pissed?"

Yup. "Millie will be fine." I glanced in the rear-view mirror, squinting slightly at the sun reflecting back at me. "I feel bad because I noticed on Saturday how exhausted he looked, and I know he's working so hard on this job. Is it stupid to stop by his house and bring him a get-well care package?"

"Not stupid at *all*," Brooke said before I'd barely finished my sentence, and I blinked at how enthusiastic she sounded. "I think that's a spectacular idea, in fact. Those Whitfield boys just love having someone fawn over them while they're sick."

"Really?" Tristan didn't strike me as someone who wanted any fawning, but maybe I was wrong.

"Uh-huh. Let me text Michael while we're talking and get some ideas."

"Oh, don't bother him, I know he's working. I can come up with some stuff. I'll just drop it off, I don't want to bug him."

"Nonsense. There's a spare key tucked into a magnetic box underneath the right side of the porch. When Michael doesn't feel well, he always wants chicken noodle soup, so maybe Tristan is the same way. Spoon feed him that shit if necessary."

My eyebrows furrowed. "Do you think that'll be necessary?"

"Who knows? Maybe he's *really* sick. Can you imagine if you drop it off and he barely has the strength to even stay standing when he tries to heat it up?" Brooke clucked her tongue sadly. "I was that sick with the flu when Julia was staying with me, before I had the twins. It was miserable, I'm telling you. Thought I was dying."

"I wouldn't want that," I said slowly, and I scrambled to think through my afternoon at the office. The truth was, I really didn't have anything after my meeting with Millie. "I guess it wouldn't hurt to check on him while I'm there."

"Excellent. Also, I did text Michael and he also thinks it's a great plan. He said no ginger ale because he hates it, and those little oyster crackers piss him off because of how small they are. Saltines only."

"Huh. I thought Michael was walking into a client meeting, which is why he couldn't check on Tristan."

Brooke was quiet on the other end of the line. "Oh! Umm, I'm sure he is. Maybe he stepped away for a minute when he saw it was me." She cleared her throat. "Remember. Only saltines."

I laughed. "Okay, okay. I'll stop at the store over by his house. I'll let you know how it goes."

"No rush," she answered airily. "Have fun!"

Fun? I stared at my phone when she hung up abruptly. "Thanks?"

It was over an hour later, a full grocery bag in one arm, that I stood on Tristan's front porch and hoped this didn't blow up in my face. He didn't answer when I knocked quietly, and through the windows on the side of the door, I couldn't see anything. Inside, there wasn't a single light on.

Briefly, I hesitated, because letting myself in with the hidden spare key might cross over into intrusive territory, but I couldn't shake the image of him miserable and unable to do anything, so I set my bag down on a beautiful Adirondack chair next to me and crouched down on the right side of the porch to where the lip of cement ended. My hand felt under the edge until I felt the cool metal of the key box.

It slid into the lock silently, and I took a deep breath before I turned it.

"Here goes nothing."

CHAPTER TWENTY-ONE

ANNA

The house was dark, quiet and almost eerily still when I let myself in. The sound of the paper bag when I shifted it in my arm was jarring in the silence.

"Tristan?" I said quietly. Still standing by the entrance, I paused and listened, but didn't hear anything. Because I couldn't help myself, I took in his home, the space that he spent all his time in. You could tell so much about a person by the things they chose to surround themselves with, by the colors they chose and the furniture that they picked.

Nothing about Tristan's home surprised me—warm, neutral colors on the wall, dark tones in the furniture, which all looked worn and inviting and comfortable, but not shabby in the slightest. His dining room table almost made me gasp, and I leaned in to run my hand over the surface. He'd inlaid a design into the wood, crisp, sharp edges with a natural edge around the table itself. It could easily seat eight people, maybe ten, and it dominated the space.

He'd chosen nothing that could soften it in the open space, no rug underneath or decor along the top, but my mind spun with possibilities.

Three drum lights hung over the center would look amazing, especially wrapped in linen, maybe a long rectangular box with some succulents for a centerpiece. So many possibilities.

"Holy table envy," I said under my breath. The chairs were all handmade too, slightly mismatched, but somehow, they worked. His kitchen was immaculate, warm cherry cabinets and stainless appliances, only an empty can of soup in the sink and an opened, empty box of crackers on the granite. Quietly, I set the bag down.

My hands ran over the back of the couch while I shamelessly peeked around, and the material was soft and wonderful under my fingertips, almost like a leather bomber jacket that someone had taken years to break in just right. The TV mounted to the wall was as large as I expected in a bachelor's home, but the bookshelves on either side of it were chock full of books of all kinds. Travel, carpentry, philosophy, some poetry, a few crime novels sprinkled throughout.

In the corner was a large leather chair that I imagined he used for reading all these different books, and a matching ottoman that was clearly well-used. Next to it was a small cherry end table with a scarred surface that was simple, but when I ran my hands over the edge, I still saw stamps of his workmanship.

The layout of his house was similar to Garrett's, and I quietly crept down the hallway toward where I imagined I'd find the master bedroom. My foot froze when I finally heard something, like someone shivered, followed by the rustle of blankets.

His bedroom was dark, and again, I questioned the sanity of essentially breaking into someone's home who hadn't invited me and hoped that he was okay with me seeing him sick. Through some heavy curtains, the muted gold light of the afternoon gave me just enough that I could see a massive California King bed with a head-board that had to have been made by him.

Ho-lee *headboard* envy, I thought with no small amount of wonder. He was almost stupid talented, honestly. But my attention snapped from it when I heard Tristan cough. He sounded awful, the hacking sound chesty and wet, the kind that almost made you want to cough in response just in case you could help them feel better.

There was a large lump underneath the simple dark gray bed-spread and I crept around the side that I thought he was facing. My heart lurched when I saw how he was laying, with his arms curled around his pillow and his face buried into it like he was clutching it in a hug. He wasn't wearing a shirt, and I would've had to be dead not to see how his biceps curved up when he tightened his grip. But the riot of color from his tattoos was what held my eyes, more than anything.

The designs were beautiful, and in the dim light of his room, I had a hard time making out exactly what was in the blacks and blues and deep purples that covered the top half of his arm.

I left the room and turned on the hallway light so that I could see him better without waking him, and then perched carefully on the edge of the bed so that I could lay my hand on his forehead.

"Oh my," I whispered, "no wonder you didn't call."

He was *hot*, the skin clammy and almost painfully warm against the back of my fingers.

Tristan made a groaning noise, and I smoothed a hand over his forehead, wiping my thumb along the wrinkles that popped up when he made another pained sound.

"Sshhh," I said a bit louder. "We'll get some medicine in you, okay? You'll feel better soon. I promise."

In his troubled sleep, he settled at the sound of my voice. It was the first time I'd ever seen Tristan's hair down, and briefly, I let my fingers drift over the tangled brown locks over his shoulders. It was darker than I thought, and I almost giggled when I imagined asking him what product he used to make it so soft.

I left the bedroom and unpacked the things I'd bought at the store, glad I got the full array. Cough drops, tissues, Sprite, a box of straws, saltines (*not* oyster crackers), bread, the good kind of chicken noodle soup from the deli, and bottles of both Advil and Tylenol so that he could alternate if necessary. Since I wasn't sure if he had a thermometer, I'd gotten one of those too.

To find a pair of scissors so I could open that asinine, impossible to open, adult-proof packaging that they thought thermometers needed to be in, I had to do some searching through the drawers in his kitchen. As talented as Tristan was making furniture, the culinary arts clearly weren't of importance to him, because at least four of those beautiful, deep drawers were completely empty.

"Unbelievable," I muttered, but couldn't help a smile. Every piece of him that I uncovered felt important, felt like I was learning something valuable that others might not know about him. Tristan was so self-contained, and it made me itchy to dig beneath the surface.

My obsessing over the dance we shared had me asking questions that I'd never really put thought into before.

Namely, *how* was he single?

He was clearly handsome, almost painfully so. Rugged and strong and precisely the kind of masculine that drove women to tittering and hair-tossing in his presence. I'd seen it happen, actually.

He was talented and kind, employed and owned a home. Not even simply *kind*, he was unthinkingly chivalrous. No criminal record that I was aware of. By every standard, he was a catch with a capital C.

But I'd never seen him with a woman. Never seen him bring one home on the odd night the whole group had gone out and I'd been invited. There'd never even been a time where I'd seen him buy someone a drink, go talk to a woman at the bar for a few minutes of shared conversation.

I stopped mid-opening of the first container of soup, my hand suspended in the action. Maybe Tristan was gay. I didn't think so though. Being in interior design, my gaydar was pretty well-honed, and I didn't get a single non-heterosexual vibe from him. And I could tell, even with the straight looking ones.

No, Tristan wasn't gay. And even if he was, I *still* wouldn't understand why he was single.

I poured some Sprite into a plastic cup that I found over the sink and popped in one of the straws from the box. The sight of it made me laugh, especially when I imagined giving it to him. He'd think I'd lost my damn mind, that was for sure.

When I entered his room again, he'd turned to his back and oh my, okay, hello Tristan's chest. I froze, feeling very much like a perv.

The wide expanse of it was ... well, it was perfect. He had a sprinkling of chest hair, dark to match the hair on his head, and the round muscles of his pecs shifted when he tried to get comfortable. Visible above the edge of the blankets were the first couple lines of his abs, the edge of muscle clear as was the line that bisected each side.

He moaned again, one of his large hands came to rest over his heart, and I frowned. He was still feverish, it was clear in his discomfort. I set the soup and Sprite down on the nightstand and went into his bathroom to find a washcloth.

You know, I was having all sort of envy today.

Dinner table envy.

Headboard envy.

A little chest ogling that made me envious that some women got to enjoy those kinds of chests envy.

And now I was adding master bathroom envy to the list.

It was huge and bright without being sterile, wood-framed mirrors over dual sinks and beautiful tile work in an open-air shower that seriously almost made my mouth water. And the tub. Get the eff out with the garden tub. I allowed myself one moment to whimper at the sight of it before I searched out a washcloth in the linen closet next to the shower.

I ran some cool water over it until it was damp, and then sat on the edge of the bed so I could take his temperature. I'd gotten one of those temporal ones, just swipe it over the forehead was what the directions said. So I turned it on and gently hooked his chin so that his head was angled away from me. In a gentle arc, I swiped the scope over his skin and grimaced when the display read one-oh-two point one.

After setting the thermometer aside, I laid the washcloth over his forehead and he jerked slightly.

"Sorry about that," I said, cupping the side of his face to bring it back to the way he was originally facing.

His beard was soft when it tickled my palm. When I let my hand linger, his eyes blinked a few times until he tried to focus on my face.

"Wh-what?" he said, his voice hoarse and confused, slow coming out of his mouth. "Anna?"

"Hi," I said softly. "Do you need something to drink?"

But he didn't answer. Tristan stared. And stared. The slow, deliberate blinks of his eyelids got longer and heavier, like he was fighting sleep. Sluggishly, he clutched my hand to his face and let out a shuddering breath, his eyelids falling shut.

If his face was warm, his hand was even warmer as it trapped mine against his skin. The veins mapping along the top of his hand fascinated me, until he did what he did next.

He turned his head and breathed against my fingers. His nose buried right at the spot where my fingers ended at the joint, I watched slack-jawed as Tristan Whitfield pressed a tender kiss into my palm. His lips were dry and warm, and they lingered.

Lingered!

With one last deep inhale of my skin, he turned his face back into his pillow and his eyes remained closed.

"What the fu—" I whispered, catching myself lest he was able to hear me.

In his sleep, he mumbled something, and I leaned in.

"What did you say?" I asked quietly, my hand still against his face for some reason.

"Stay," he breathed. "Please stay."

His voice was garbled and indistinct, but I heard his words that time, feeling my eyes widen as I realized what he'd said.

Very carefully, I pulled my hand from underneath his and took a few minutes to just ... stare at him. Because umm, what the hell was that?

1- Tristan was feverish. People did weird things when they were feverish.

2- He'd said my name, so he knew it was me.

3- What was *that*?

Before I could dissect it further, even if that would've helped, my phone started vibrating in my pocket. I snuck out of the room before I picked up the call from Michael.

"Hey, what's up?"

"I heard you're playing nurse."

I smiled, peering back into the bedroom, but Tristan wasn't moving in the slightest. "Something like that. He's pretty out of it. I'm not surprised he missed work with that temp."

Michael grunted. "Well, I'll warn you that Tristan is an awful patient. Like trying to wrestle a cat into a bathtub to get him to take any medicine, even if it'll make him feel human."

I couldn't stop my laugh at the image. "Noted. Even if he just lets me heat up some soup before I go, I'll feel useful. Unless you'd rather check on him? I don't want it to be weird that I'm the one here."

"Oh no, no, no," Michael rushed to assure me. "I promise my brother would rather see your pretty face than mine when he wakes up more. He'd probably punch me in the balls if I took his temperature for him."

"We wouldn't want that."

"Nope." He cleared his throat. "But he's not like, dying or anything?"

"No. Just regular ol' flu from what I can see. It doesn't look like he was throwing up at all."

"Blech. Good. I can handle a lot now because of the twins, but vomit is not one of them. I'm a sympathy puker, so it just makes things worse for Brooke if I try to help."

I laughed. "Well, I'll remember that. But I think he'll be fine."

"Thanks, Anna. I appreciate you checking on him. It means a lot."

"No problem." And it wasn't, truly.

But as I sat and waited for Tristan to wake, unsuccessfully, I stared at him from the doorway of his bedroom and thought. What had Winnie the Pooh called it? Puzzling. I puzzled and puzzled and puzzled some more, to no avail.

He'd asked me to stay. Or whoever he thought I was. No, even that didn't explain it—if he thought I was someone else—because he said my name before falling back asleep.

While he slept, I went into the kitchen and cleaned off the counters with disinfecting wipes that I found under the sink. All the things I'd bought at the store were organized neatly up against the backsplash, and I found the recycle bin in the laundry room for the empty soup containers.

By the time I went back into his room, the soup on the nightstand was cold. Tristan shifted slightly, and I pressed the back of my hand to his forehead again.

It felt the same.

Picking up the bowl, I took it back into the kitchen to reheat it in case he was waking up.

As I walked back into the room, he was trying to sit up.

At the sight of me, Tristan froze.

He blinked a few times. "Anna?"

I gave him a cautious smile. "Hey. I'm sorry for being so presumptuous, but when I heard you were sick, I wanted to do something to help."

His eyes were wide as he stared, and the dark circles under

them made my chest tight. He looked miserable. And very, very confused.

"I *knew* you were working yourself too hard," I said in an attempt to tease him.

But he didn't smile. In fact, he frowned, then broke into a deep coughing fit that wracked his large frame. Feeling awkward and out-of-place, I set down the soup, but didn't take my seat on the bed like I did when he was still sleeping.

He was still coughing, and I cautiously handed him the Sprite.

His eyes took in the straw suspiciously, and I smothered a smile when I thought about what Michael had said. Like trying to get a cat into a bath.

"I have Advil too if you want to get some of this soup down."

Grudgingly, he took a sip of the Sprite, though not out of the straw. I didn't smother the smile that time, and he frowned again.

"How did you get in the house?"

My face felt hot. "Brooke told me where the spare key is. And Michael told me what kind of stuff to get. Don't worry, no oyster crackers for you."

"Oh for crying out loud," he mumbled, his cheeks flushing a slight pink, which I knew wasn't fever.

"How are you feeling?"

"Like hell," Tristan answered right away. He laid back and closed his eyes, another shiver making his entire body tremble. "How can one stupid fever make your skin hurt?"

"I don't know." I cracked open the Advil and shook out two. "At least eat some crackers before you take these."

He eyed both options. "The soup doesn't sound bad." Then he glanced up at me. "Thank you."

"You're welcome." I smiled and held it out to him. "I think you can manage feeding yourself, despite what Brooke told me."

Tristan shook his head and took the soup from me, lifting the bowl straight to his mouth and not even bothering with the spoon. With his hair down and around his shoulders, his beard thicker than I normally saw it, something about him reminded me of the Beast, drinking from his bowl at the dinner table, and I swallowed a laugh. After a few healthy sips of the soup, he set the bowl down and let me drop the Advil into his palm.

After he took the pills, his eyes closed again and he sank down onto his pillow. "I'm sorry if I'm not very good company."

I fought the urge to check his forehead again, but with him awake and the full lucid force of his eyes able to focus on me, I didn't dare. "It's okay. I'll get out of your way now that you took something. Text me if you need anything though, okay? I don't have any plans tonight. I could ... I don't know, just watch a movie or something. Go read on the couch, be here in case you need anything."

Against his pillow, he stared at me for a few seconds, like he was doing some puzzling of his own. It was on the tip of my tongue to tell him he kissed me ... or my palm, ask what the capital F that was, but the words stayed lodged in my throat. "I don't want to make you stay, if all I'm doing is sleeping."

"The conversation skills would probably be even less than usual, huh?"

He let out a soft puff of air through his nose that I took as a laugh. "Yeah. Hard to imagine, huh?"

"I think your conversation skills are just fine," I said quietly.

Again, he leveled his eyes at me, and even though they were still slightly glassy from the fever, exhausted from little sleep, I felt the weight of them in my stomach, heavy and pleasant.

"Thank you for the offer," he said finally.

That was my cue. I waved it off. "Anything else before I go?"

"A sledgehammer to stop the throbbing in my head would be great."

Regretfully, I clucked my tongue. "Forgot my sledgehammer at home."

His large body was already starting to relax, and I carefully pulled the sheet up over his shoulder, unable to stop myself. Moving carefully, I used my fingers to smooth his hair away from his forehead. Against my face, I could feel the force of his dark eyes watching me, but I didn't meet them.

Only when my hand dropped back to my side did I manage eye contact. His face was expressionless, almost carefully so. A hot burst of nerves lit my belly. "I left the thermometer in the kitchen, but I can bring it back in here."

He licked his lips and then grimaced. "That's fine. I'll make my way there eventually, maybe after I sleep for a while."

I nodded and stepped backwards, not wanting to outstay my welcome. Especially because it looked like he was falling asleep as I stood there, judging by the heaviness in his eyelids with each blink.

He knew it was me now, what would happen if I stayed as he slept? If I went and curled up in his reading chair with a book from his shelves.

Questions lay heavy on my tongue, and in my heart, as I took another step backward, still staring at him as I did. I froze when Tristan opened his eyes and zeroed in on me, but didn't speak. I returned the look evenly, curious if he could see all the unanswered questions on my face.

I blinked and cleared my throat. "Feel better, okay?"

He gave me a pained half smile and turned onto his side. "Yes, ma'am," came his mumbled reply against his pillow. Quietly, I let myself out of the house, locking the door behind me and placing the spare key back into its place.

Still crouched on his porch, I turned my hand over and stared at my palm.

If I looked hard enough at my skin, would I see where he'd touched me? A vivid outline of his lips against the lines of my hand, or just a fading mark from where his breath warmed me.

How long had it been since a simple display of affection like that had been given to me?

And the most curious of all, I couldn't stop wondering about whether Tristan had been truly thinking about me when he'd done it. More importantly, I recognized as I tried to fall asleep later that night, did I *want* him to have been thinking about me?

Knowing what I did about him, what would that mean for us within the framework of our strangely sweet, burgeoning friendship?

Sleep eventually came, deep and restful, but the answers to every single question eluded me.

CHAPTER TWENTY-TWO

TRISTAN

Twenty-four hours after Anna walked—quite inexplicably—out of my bedroom, I still felt like I wanted to die.

She texted me later that night to check on me.

Anna: How are you feeling? Did you manage to eat anything else?

Me: I had some crackers and soup, thank you. They're helping.

Anna: I am an excellent picker of soup.
Anna: I'm really glad you're feeling better.

They weren't making me feel better. Short of a coma, I didn't think anything would ever help me again.

And yes, I warred with the fact that I could have called her to return. Take her up on her offer of company. But if I spent more than five minutes contemplating it, I knew I wouldn't.

Any scenario I'd imagined where she was within arm's reach of my bed did not include me feverish, in desperate need of a shower and wanting to cry every time I needed to move.

Forty-eight hours later, I felt human again, though weaker than I wanted. But three days of only eating some soup and crackers and Sprite would do that. It took me another day before I went back to work, and the first person I saw was my idiot brother.

His smile, smug and wide, made me want to break his face with a two by four.

"Oh hey, pumpkin, feeling better?"

I walked past him into my shop and let the door slam loudly behind me. He came in, undeterred.

"I had an interesting talk with Anna the other night."

"Yeah, so I heard." I gave him a look. "Next time, how about don't tell her where the spare key is to my house?"

Michael cocked his head to the side. "Why? No time to hide the shrine you have of her?"

That made me pause, because my sketchbook hadn't been out, had it? Anna didn't strike me as the type who would do too much snooping, and it left a brick in my gut imagining how I might explain the few sketches I had of her face. No, it was shoved into my desk.

I let out a deep breath, because the truth was, I'd been unable to rid myself of the disquieting feeling that I'd done something embarrassing. Other than simply be sick in front of her, which was embarrassing enough.

"I'm joking, Tristan. Come on, the worst thing that could've come from it is she realizes how boring your decorating style is." He snapped his fingers. "Actually, that might be great. You could hire her to redo your place. You know, just tell her she can do whatever she wants within those four walls that would make her want to stay there and never, ever leave."

"I'm not trying to imprison her, asshole," I mumbled and flipped through some papers that had stacked up on my desk in my absence. "I'd settle for a first date at this point."

He held up his hands. "We tried. You're the one who hasn't taken it a step further."

With my head hanging down, I braced my hands on the cold surface of the table and sighed. *I was sick*, I wanted to argue immediately. And I had gotten sick soon after our night at the bar, after that dance, but I could've called her once I was feeling better. I could've asked her if she wanted to meet for coffee, and make sure work topics didn't come up once.

And yet, I hadn't.

Michael let out an exasperated sigh. "What are you waiting for?"

"I don't know," I told him truthfully and then shrugged. "I don't know, Michael. Did you know that me asking her to dance was the first time that had happened in years? She said that when we were done."

He grimaced. "What a tool that guy is."

"How do I know that anything she'd be looking for right now wouldn't instantly classify as a rebound? Yeah, she's gone on some dates. That doesn't mean anything about her readiness to move on."

As Michael opened his mouth to answer, my phone vibrated.

Anna: Hope you're feeling human again. :) Millie is going to be out at the house today, floors are installed, and if you've got a couple hours, I thought maybe you could bring out some of your finished pieces.

"Michael, I can't have this conversation right now."

He shook his head, but didn't push.

There was this part of me, raw and unrestrained, that wanted to peel out of my body, turn around and shake myself. *Take a stand*, it would scream at whatever was left of me. Tell her. Make her understand, make her see, make her want and then don't waste whatever opportunity might come next. And then if she walks away, you'll know.

For the next few minutes, Michael helped me load up the larger delivery truck that Uncle Jim had, strapping in the dining room chairs and table, the coffee table and end tables. Everything else would have to come later. The bedroom pieces would be last, except for the burnt wood that would wrap the beams, those were already finished, but wouldn't be needed until Anna gave me the go-ahead.

When I pulled the door shut and turned the latch over, Michael clapped me on the shoulder. "Just ... just don't wait so long for some perfect sign that you miss it."

Instead of dismissing him like I wanted to, instead of telling him that I'd know Anna was ready the minute I looked in her eyes and saw it, saw whatever it was that I was looking for, I just nodded. Because if I didn't recognize that possibility that I might miss it, I'd be doing myself a disservice. Not just myself, but Anna, too.

I pulled myself into the driver's seat of the truck and took a second to send her a text that I was on my way, and then let my head fall back onto the headrest.

After so many years of watching her, absorbing any detail about her that I could glean from our interactions, it certainly felt impossible that I'd miss any signals of that magnitude. Not only that she might be ready to try for a relationship, but that trying for a relationship with me was on her radar.

The drive out to Boulder went quickly, the traffic light since it was midday, and the time that it gave me to think made me face a hard truth.

It wasn't entirely about waiting for the knowledge that Anna was ready for something serious. It meant that I was opening myself up to the horrifying possibility that even if we went out on a date, even if we dated for months, she fell in love with me, it didn't mean that it would last forever.

Not for her, at least.

Anna didn't know me in the way that I knew her. Not yet. And it wasn't impossible that she might not love the imperfect parts of me—my self-contained nature, my struggle in putting my emotions into words when it was convenient and necessary, my desire for silence and solitude to recharge—in the way that I loved the imperfect parts of her.

The parts of her that kept her with a man who clearly didn't love her or respect her or cherish her. Because I didn't think that was a bad trait, not like a lot of people might. That decision reflected her selflessness. Her tenacity. Her loyalty, even if it was misguided.

The kind of misguided loyalty that led her to break into my house uninvited to take care of me, unasked, when I was sick. Even though I could feel the heat of embarrassment hit my face again, I smiled.

For a brief second when I'd opened my eyes and saw her standing in my bedroom, I honestly thought I was hallucinating. But if I'd been doing that while sick, I'm sure the vision of Anna would've been wearing a naughty nurse outfit or something.

I shifted in my seat. Not a good thing to think about when I was five minutes away from seeing her.

For the rest of those five minutes, I blared Led Zeppelin and recited football stats and tried not to think about the fact that the last time I saw Anna, she was serving me soup while I was shirtless in bed.

Which was difficult to put out of my mind.

When I pulled down the long dirt driveway, her SUV was parked next to an Audi, which I assumed was Millie's. The foreman's work truck was at the end, and I carefully threw the truck into reverse and backed up so that I was as close to the front door as possible.

I was lifting the door when Anna stepped outside.

"Hey, thanks for coming out on short notice." She was smiling widely, her black hair shining almost blue underneath the midday sun. Her eyes twinkled, like we had an inside joke, and my ribs squeezed painfully. The fact that I didn't grab her with both hands, clutch her to me so that I could claim her pink lips in the way I wanted to *every single time* I saw her should've earned me some sort of self-control merit badge.

Or a medal.

Or a solid gold trophy.

"No problem."

At my gruff reply, her smile somehow got even bigger.

I set my jaw. "I was sick, okay? Everyone gets sick sometimes."

Anna laughed, a light tinkle of sound, like bells or wind chimes or angels singing. "You were an adorable patient, if that helps."

I was— what now?

Instead of answering, I blinked a few times. Because I was an idiot who took a solid three point four seconds to recognize flirting when it was aimed at me. Anna winked and went back into the house. "Will? Can you help Tristan unload this stuff?"

I hauled myself up into the back of truck and started loosening the straps holding the furniture in place, then pulling off the blankets. The foreman, Will, joined me and we carefully unloaded the table, turning it onto its side and angling it so that it would fit through the front door.

Millie stood back and watched us silently. I'd called her and apologized to her the morning after Anna came by, and she sounded fine when we spoke, but even now, she managed an air of *I will ruin you if you disappoint me.*

Will and I held the table wordlessly, and Anna gave small directions as to where she wanted it. Once it was down, I'd be able to appreciate the open space now that it was drywalled, floors installed, naked light bulbs hanging down from wires.

I let a small exhale of relief when the table was down. Will nodded appreciatively and Anna grinned.

"It's perfect," she whispered, leaning her head toward me.

Millie pursed her lips as she stared, her arms crossed over her chest when she started walking around the length of it. After an agonizing few moments, she snapped her iron gaze at me. "It's beautiful."

I nodded. "Thank you."

"Can I see the chairs?"

"Of course." Will, Anna and I all filed outside to pull them from the truck, assembly line style. It only took a couple minutes before they were placed evenly around the edge. The herringbone inlay in the surface of the table looked incredible underneath the lights, with sunshine streaming through the large windows facing the mountains.

Millie nodded. "I'm impressed. I can't wait to see the rest, Tristan."

Anna nudged me with her shoulder and I let out a breath of heavy relief. "I'm glad to hear it."

"Feel free to bring everything else in, but I have to go." She brushed her hands down the front of her pristine black pants, somehow free of dust or dirt even in an unfinished house. Her eyes bounced briefly between Anna and I before she spoke again. "I had my doubts, as you know, but I think the two of you make a pretty stellar design team. If you can manage to pull it through to the end, I'll recommend you to everyone I know."

And with that, she walked out like a queen.

Anna gripped my bicep and did a little bounce next to me. "Oh my word, did you hear that?"

I smiled down at her, not because of what Millie said, but because her excitement was tangible and warm and contagious. I couldn't not smile at her. "I did. I'm happy for you."

"Be happy for *us*, you crazy man."

For us.

My brain switched into high gear at her innocently spoken words. Will joined in the conversation, pulling Anna away into the laundry to show her something.

For us.

For us.

Excitement made me want to wrap her in my arms, whisper into her ear that all I'd ever wanted was to be an *us* with her. Fear paralyzed me. That and the fact that Will was in the house, and I didn't need an audience.

I dug my fingers into my hair and pulled, like it would somehow draw a firm, decisive thought out of my muddled head.

Something was changing. Correction; something *had* changed.

CHAPTER TWENTY-THREE

ANNA

"And you're a bitch."

I gaped up at date number six when he pushed back from the table and stalked away, not even tossing down any cash to cover the multiple drinks he had.

"Asshole," I muttered under my breath, trying to quell the bitter sting of mortification that made my chest hot, my face cold.

If being a bitch meant I didn't want to sneak off to the bathroom and 'let him make sure that what was under my dress matched my face', then I'd tattoo that word on my forehead. And of course, the glass in front of me was empty, which needed to be rectified immediately.

What made all of this worse is that I'd actually been excited about this date. Checking Bumble after a solid two week break had clearly been a mistake, despite the sudden urge to do it.

Why I'd felt that urge, almost a desperate one, was still muddy.

Part of me wanted to give it one more shot, see if the things I was feeling when I was around Tristan were about him or me. Maybe it was both, but maybe I was simply ready to feel those things with *someone*. Not a specific someone. Especially a specific someone who hadn't given me any clear signals, who I knew would only pursue serious relationships.

So I Bumbled. Yet again.

There was something in John's profile that made me send him a message. He had dimples and broad shoulders, dark brown eyes and a quick sense of humor that had me laughing when we spoke on the phone to set up our date.

A quick sense of humor that hid the fact that he was a raging, misogynistic asshole, apparently.

When I realized I was one step away from sucking any remaining alcohol off the remaining ice in my glass, I wearily pushed back from the table and found an empty spot at the long wooden bar. We'd chosen the location because it was casual but not a dive, far enough outside downtown Denver that it wouldn't be uncomfortably packed on a Saturday night.

The patrons skewed a bit older, as did the music, but I liked the old-fashioned lighting that was strung down the length of the gleaming bar that had been varnished and polished to a shine. The bartender smiled at me while she poured a beer.

"Be right down," she told me, winking at the customer in front of her while she took his cash.

"No rush." I set my chin in my hands and stared blankly at the rows and rows of bottles lining the back of the bar. Suddenly, a sweet, girly drink didn't feel like enough for my mood. Was I whiskey drinker? Ooh, or maybe tequila on ice, so I could try on *Badass Anna* for the evening.

After a minute, she was in front of me, smiling sympathetically at the clearly miserable expression on my face.

"That bad?" she asked.

I exhaled heavily and looked at her. She was beautiful, with deep purple hair and a dainty nose ring that glittered under the low lights of the bar. Why couldn't I pull off black lipstick like that? I'd look like Vampira, and this chick looked incredible.

"He called me a bitch when I wouldn't disrobe in the bathroom with him."

She snorted. "I tell you what, first drink is on me, but I get to pick."

"Deal."

Deftly, she pulled a bottle of tequila out and flipped it upside down, adding a generous amount into a lowball glass. Giving me a quick once over, she took out the soda gun and pushed a white button before adding it to the tequila and ice.

"If I had grapefruit on hand, I'd stick a piece in there." She slid the glass toward me, watching while I took a slow sip.

"It's good."

"A Paloma. You want to ease yourself into something straight, that'll be the drink to do it."

I laughed and shook my head. "Am I that obvious?"

She scrunched up her nose. "Nah. But bad dates have a way of bringing that out in people. I'm Gretchen."

"Anna."

"Nice to meet you." When I extended my hand, she shook it. After a quick glance down the bar to make sure no one needed her, she started drying some glasses. "Usually I get bored old men sitting up here by me on a Saturday night, or bored young ones who think they've got a shot."

"Glad to mix things up a bit."

"So was it a first date and a last date, or just a last date?"

"First date *and* last date." I tipped my glass back and finished it in a few eye-burning swallows. If Gretchen was impressed, she didn't show it. "I'll take another, please."

While she went to work, I thought about all the stories she must have heard across this simple bar. Each patron feeling like theirs was important enough to impart to a stranger. Was mine?

Gretchen set another Paloma in front of me, and I could tell by the color that she'd added even a bit more tequila this time, which didn't bother me in the slightest. I'd sit at this bar all damn night until I sobered up, but I did not feel like I was ready to go sans alcohol.

"So what's the story? You're my best bet at entertainment for the evening, you know. Those three down there will leave sometime in the next thirty minutes, and then it'll be a long couple hours until I close out."

Instinctively, my thumb rubbed at the spot underneath my ring finger, which was empty now. Before, the ridge of metal was a heavy reminder, and now it was just ... gone. And I was out on dates with handsome men who were calling me a bitch after a mere ninety minutes of meeting him for the first time.

I started talking.

About Marcus, my dad's will, how there wasn't a single person who could understand why I'd stayed, and how I found myself here, with absolutely no clue what I even wanted out of a man, second guessing all the things that I was feeling. About everything.

Occasionally, she'd have to serve another customer, or refill my glass, but Gretchen was a phenomenal listener. She hummed in sympathy, cursed under her breath when appropriate, laughed raucously when I told her about chucking his laptop through the doors of his office.

A solid hour later, my throat was hoarse from talking, my head was swimming pleasantly from the tequila and Gretchen gave me a large ice water.

"Look, if you want my unsolicited advice, I think you're looking at this dating thing wrong." She held up her hands. "Trust me, I made my fair share of mistakes after my divorce. You're trying out all different types of men, right? That one was steady but boring, this guy tonight was charming and handsome, and you're trying to find a list of qualities that fit into a box. But at the end of the day, it's about one thing."

I leaned in. "Please tell me what that thing is and don't say it's between his legs."

Gretchen threw her head back and cackled. "No, but knowing how to use that doesn't hurt either."

I blushed and hated how ... non-worldly I felt sometimes.

She reached out and tapped the bar to get my attention. "The most important thing isn't a list of combined features or finding a type, it's being around someone who makes you not want to date around anymore. Where you're not sitting there defining the pieces of him into subtypes. You're simply wondering when you can see him again."

Blinking, I stared at her for a while. "That sounds remarkably simple, doesn't it?"

"It's not easy to find in another person, not the way things are done now. Apps and matches and notifications and forced interaction and algorithms pairing us with strangers."

My shoulders sagged. "It's exhausting."

"It doesn't have to be. And that's not the only way to meet someone who can make you feel that way."

Had I felt that way yet?

Certainly not on any of my dates. Not even close.

And those were the places that I was actively seeking it out, to find someone who made me simply want to be around them.

From the jukebox in the corner, I heard the beautiful strains of a song come on, but I couldn't place it. Because tequila.

I cocked my head and listened more carefully, finally connecting the dates as my body started swaying along to the slow, sweet rhythm. Tristan and I had danced to this song. She sang about tightropes and I rubbed at my chest with the blooming realization yes, of course, I had felt like that.

I'd felt like that with Tristan, even though we'd never actually been out on a date. Besides my mom, and my coworkers, he was the person I'd spent the most time with since leaving Marcus.

We were a good team. Millie had said so, damn it.

And I knew, I knew that he looked at me with at least a small amount of interest. He'd kissed my palm!

Why hadn't he ever asked me out? Even for a friendly coffee.

His lips had been *connected to my skin*. That had to have meant something.

Using a tequila-soaked brain to figure it out wasn't giving me the clarity of thought that was necessary. For much of anything, really.

"Gretchen, I have had that feeling," I said slowly.

"Ooh, do tell."

First, I showed her my empty water glass. "Since I was a good girl and finished this, can I get another Paloma?"

"If you show me when you order your Uber, then sure."

While she started mixing my next drink, lighter on the tequila this time, I tapped my lips.

"He's a friend of my brother's. I've known him for years, actually. And he's polite, quiet, very ... steady." Gretchen all but sneered, and it made me laugh out loud. "No, in a good way. And he's hot," I groaned, covering my blushing cheeks with my hands. "Like sexy mountain man, with tattoos and muscles and hair that is definitely better than mine."

She raised an eyebrow. "That sounds better than steady."

"We're ... friends. Since I left Marcus, he's been a good friend to me. There have been all these little moments that make me wonder whether it's more, or if I'm just trying to make it more because I'm lonely, you know?"

"What kind of moments?"

I blew out a hard breath. "Besides the time with the flamethrower?"

Gretchen's mouth fell open. "Not what I expected to come out of your mouth."

I giggled, felt myself sway in my seat a little. "He put a blanket on me. And he loves pancakes as much as I do. And hates social media. And he blushes when he's embarrassed. *And* we danced about a week ago, and I couldn't even figure out why it was so ... attractive to me that he was so respectful about it. But he was. But when he looked down at me?" I shook my head slowly, everything boiling up in me like a frantic, rolling wave, the moments bleeding into each other like a watercolor. "It was like ... like his eyes were *warm.* Do you know what I mean? I would've kept dancing with him all night if he'd asked."

My new best friend Gretchen smiled at me. "There you go. Has he asked you out?"

"No."

She pursed her lips and then held up her finger when someone called her name. I was still pouting about it when she came back.

He'd been nice to me. Tristan was nice to everyone.

His eyes were warm when we danced.

What the hell did that prove? You could look at a puppy and have the same ooey gooey eyes.

With a whimper, I dropped my forehead onto my folded hands on the bar's surface. "I'm hopeless. I'm probably just a cute little puppy."

"Oh great, she's lost it," Gretchen said.

I propped my chin on my hands. "Just overthinking. Which is not a good combo with tequila, because all my thoughts are fuzzy and too big for my brain and I don't know how to make them smaller."

She stared at me. "Yup. Just water for you for the rest of the night."

"You're no fun."

Her answering smile was enigmatic. Magically, another huge water appeared, along with a bowl of pretzels.

"Can I ask you something?"

I nodded, drinking greedily.

"Why did he stay?"

"Who?"

Apparently we were good enough friends now, Gretchen and I, that she rolled her eyes at me. "The ex. Marcus. Why did *he* stay?"

It felt like she'd swung a chair over my head, the way my body reacted. I sank back in the stool, grateful that it had a high back so that I didn't fall the hell off. "I—"

Gretchen's perfect black eyebrows lifted high on her forehead. "You never asked?"

"No," I whispered, my hand coming up to cover my mouth. "That's awful, isn't it? I never even really thought about it." Suddenly, with my head muffled and my emotions bouncing like a rubber ball, I sat up straighter and felt like I needed to *do* something. "Should I text him and ask?"

"No," she answered firmly. "Definitely not right now. But maybe someday, if it's something you find yourself thinking about."

Nodding absently, I knew she was right. Maybe someday. Someday was good. After I slept and drank a gallon of water and finished four bowls of these pretzels.

"Want something off the menu?" Gretchen asked when I took another large handful of the meager snack she'd offered me. "Kitchen is still open for another thirty minutes."

"No, these are fine. I should think about going home actually. My head will already hate me tomorrow."

"Eh. Drink enough water and you'll be fine."

She walked away to cash out another customer, and I pulled my phone out, carefully scrolling until I saw the Uber app. Did I want some quiet stranger taking me home? Not really. No more than I'd wanted to bare myself to John the Asshole in the bar bathroom.

I just wanted someone who I trusted not to judge me, who'd make sure I was safe and taken care of with a ridiculous amount of tequila working its way through my body.

My thumbs were moving before I could put too much thought into whether it was a good idea or not.

Me: I'm sorry to text you so late, but I find myself in need of a safe ride home. Me + a bad date + tequila = no driving. Could you come and pick me up?

I hit send and gently set my phone down on the bar. Leaning my head in my hand, I let my eyes fall closed. My head was so heavy. All my limbs sagged like they were being set in concrete. Maybe I could just nap here until I heard back. There was a chime from my phone, and my eyelids popped open. That was fast.

Tristan: Already in my truck. Where are you?

"Gretchen? What's the address?"
She looked up from the cash register. "Doesn't Uber automatically recognize the location?"
My face flushed hot. "I asked a friend to come get me."
Her eyes narrowed.
I lifted my chin. "Tristan. I asked Tristan if he could give me a ride home."
Gretchen's lips curved into a small smile. "Hand it to me. We don't want any typos, do we?"
With a shake of my head, I handed it over to her and she did as she said. By the time I had my phone back, he was answering, those three gray bouncing dots taking forever to come through.

Tristan: Sit tight. I'm on my way.

Maybe Tristan thought I was cute like a puppy, maybe he was as nice to me as he was to everyone, maybe I was reading into all these moments between us because I liked him, or maybe it was more than that. Maybe it wasn't. But so help me, this night wasn't ending without me asking.

CHAPTER TWENTY-FOUR

TRISTAN

The roads were dark and dry, and the wheels of my truck flew over the asphalt. Not fast enough though, never fast enough, especially because I knew she was waiting for me. With a careful eye, I watched the needle of my speedometer creep higher than I normally allowed it to on the highway, and I felt the corresponding shake in my steering wheel.

Begrudgingly, I backed my foot off the gas pedal and took it down a few miles per hour. A speeding ticket wouldn't help me at all, but my body was having an almost uncontrollable physical reaction to the fact that she reached out to me on a night where she needed a safe ride home.

Not one of her friends, or Garrett or hell, Uber. Me.

The GPS on my phone told me which exit to take, and I did, cursing the red light at the end of the off ramp. The normally twenty-two minute drive had taken me closer to fifteen, so I had to take a moment of gratitude that I hadn't seen a single cop and that the roads weren't covered in snow. The forecast had called for it, but it seemed that I'd been granted a reprieve.

Winding through the quiet streets, only the occasional car passing in the opposite direction, I forced myself to take a few deep breaths. But my heart still thudded wildly, like it was being powered by a completely different entity than myself.

The bar, small and unassuming, was tucked behind a larger office building, only a few cars left in the well-lit parking lot. I pulled my truck into the open spot closest to the imposing wooden doors and made sure that she hadn't sent anything else, like, 'Oh never mind, I called an Uber'.

That would happen to me, the first time she reached out to me for something like this. She'd change her mind, not knowing how it would gouge through my skin and pierce that jumping, thrashing organ branded with her name. And I'd have to figure out how to get it started again. Just like I always did.

But my phone was blank, and I tried not to smile.

For all I knew, I'd find Anna throwing up, or passed out. Panic had me moving quickly to the door and yanking it open, my eyes scanning the nearly empty room for her. She wasn't seated at the gleaming wooden bar where a dark-haired bartender gave me a polite smile. A few guys were at a table back in the corner, and an older gentleman turned in his stool to give me an openly curious look over his shoulder.

"You Tristan?" The bartender asked.

I gave her a narrow-eyed look. "Yeah."

She jerked her chin at the back corner of the bar, a wry smile on her face. "She's by the jukebox. I cut her off about thirty minutes ago, but I'll warn you, the tequila damage is already done."

"Thank you," I sighed and scratched the side of my face when I spotted her. Back to me, she was leaning against a brightly lit, old-fashioned jukebox. Her slim hips swayed unsteadily to the beat of the oldies song that was playing, and her hair slipped easily over her shoulder when she moved too much. Anna straightened and pushed a couple buttons, and in the light, all I could see of her face was the high curve of one cheekbone.

From the table in the corner, one of the men stood and started approaching her. My fists curled up, and I took a step closer, but I didn't interfere right away. I heard a low chuckle from the bartender, but didn't take my eyes off Anna.

He said something to her, from a respectful distance, but he was standing in a way so that once she faced him, I couldn't see her at all. They exchanged a few words, and Anna swayed slightly before she shook her head.

The guy didn't move right away, and I took another couple steps. Anna gave him her back, and I felt the blood in my veins start to simmer. Luckily for him, he started walking away. I exhaled heavily and kept moving.

Then he paused when his friends started laughing, turning back toward Anna and flipping up both middle fingers. Then he grabbed his crotch and made a motion with his hands that had me seeing red. Bloody red. Maybe he would've done more. Maybe he would've gone back to his seat, but I was stepping up into his face before he could make either decision.

"Walk back to your table right now," I told him through gritted teeth.

He narrowed his eyes. "Why don't you mind your own damn business, *friend.*"

I was taller than him by at least three inches, but he was stocky. And probably drunk. When I glanced over at the bartender, she was watching with keen eyes, but not making a move to interfere. Getting myself kicked out wouldn't help anyone. Then I thought about Anna behind me, swaying adorably to whatever awful music she'd chosen. What if I'd been five minutes later? What if he hadn't taken her polite no for an answer?

I leaned in closer. "If you want to take a swing at me, go right ahead. But I'll tell you right now, if you do something like that again to someone who is my business, you won't need to take a swing." My chest expanded on a deep breath and I practically growled the words that came out next. "I'll bury you in the back with nothing more than my bare hands and I promise that no one will notice you're gone. Now *walk away.*"

Obviously, he wasn't so drunk that he didn't recognize the truth behind my words because he glared at me for a few seconds before he called me a name under his breath and then walked back to his chortling friends. I swiped a hand down my face and took another deep breath before I turned around.

Anna glanced over her shoulder and gave me a blinding smile. Then she threw herself in my arms.

In my arms.

I caught her easily and instinctively, wrapped my arms around her back and took a fleeting, selfish moment to hold her against me. Anna was flush to my chest, and her arms were latched around my neck, which meant her heeled feet dangled off the floor.

"You came," she whispered into my ear and I pinched my eyes shut. *Always,* I wanted to whisper back, but carefully set her down instead, giving her an affectionate smile when she had to hold onto my arms to stay steady. How much of this would she remember tomorrow?

Her hair was as mussed as I'd seen it, and her cheeks were flush with warmth.

"Had a few drinks, huh?"

She nodded. "My new friend Gretchen made them for me after date number six called me a bitch and walked out."

My head snapped up. "*What?*"

But Anna waved that off and walked unsteadily toward the bar, where the bartender was watching us with a small, mysterious smile on her face. After plunking herself on one of the stools, Anna drained half a glass of water that was waiting for her. Then she licked her lips and grinned at me again.

"Do you want anything while we're here? Gretchen makes an *excellent* Paloma." Her words were slow, not slurred, but definitely not her normal cadence either.

"Uhh, no thanks. I'm ... driving." I was still struggling to process what she'd said about her date. What the fresh hell was wrong with the men on this stupid app?

Anna snapped her fingers. Or tried to and failed, her thumb brushing uselessly off the wrong digit. "That's right. I called you."

I felt my face soften. "You did."

"She's a sweet one," Gretchen said, like Anna wasn't humming in the stool right in front of her. Her eyes were pinned on me, full of warning and understanding. "Thanks for getting her home safe."

Who was this woman?

"No thanks necessary." I pulled out my wallet. "How much for her drinks?"

Anna sat up in her stool. "Oh! I paid. I think. Did I pay, Gretch?"

"You did," she said. "I ran your card before you went over to the jukebox. Why don't you finish that water before you leave, then make sure to drink another one that size before bed, okay? Otherwise you'll be in a world of hurt tomorrow."

Anna saluted her. "Yes, ma'am."

Discreetly, I slipped Gretchen another twenty, just in case Anna forgot to add a tip, and for looking out for her. Gretchen nodded her gratitude and tucked it into her black apron.

I braced my hand on the back of Anna's stool, even though I wanted to run it up her spine and cup her shoulder. I wanted to see how it would feel under the curve of my palm, where my fingers would land on her arm, how the bone would feel underneath both my skin and hers, how they'd fit together. My control was thin, impossibly weak, in a moment when it needed to be iron and steel.

She was drunk.

It was even more apparent when she spun in circles trying to get her arm into her wool coat and I had to gently steer her. But her laughter was loose and easy, and it lightened something in my soul. This was the Anna that had been missing for years. The Anna that I'd first met.

Laughter and light. Happiness.

We said our goodbyes to Gretchen, and Anna gripped my arm as we walked silently outside to my truck. I held the passenger door open for her and she hopped up far more nimbly than I expected her to in what looked like four-inch heels. I cleared my throat when I found myself staring at the bare length of her leg as she curled up in the seat.

When I walked around the hood of the truck, I could feel her eyes heavy on me. For the first time since I received her text, I felt a moment of pause. Of caution seeping into my bones, making my steps slow almost to a stop before I joined her in the truck.

Anna was drunk in my car after a bad date. She was blissed-out happy drunk. She may or may not remember anything that was said or done during our entire exchange.

All of which had the makings of complete innocence, where I'd help her home, make sure she was locked in safely. But on the flip side lay my worst-case scenario—one I'd never spent a single moment entertaining—where a drunk Anna gave me a green light. Gave me the signal I'd been waiting for all these weeks and months and years.

My eyes pinched shut when I wrenched the door open and I didn't open them until I was seated and facing forward.

"Thank you for coming for me. You're the perfect knight in shining man-bun," she said quietly.

I huffed out a laugh and risked a glance at her. She'd pulled her red coat up around her face, and all I could see was her perfectly straight nose and big dark eyes that were heavily lashed and heavily lined.

They were assessing me in a way that did not seem drunk. It was almost a relief when her eyelids fell shut and her breathing evened out as she rested her head against the window.

My cheeks puffed out when I exhaled and started the truck, and

I was in no rush to wake her, if sleeping was what she was doing. All I needed to do was deliver her safely to her mom's house. Tonight, that was my only job.

While I drove to her mom's house in Wash Park, I kept the radio off. Silence allowed me to process, something that I'd always needed to do. Sort and sift through my thoughts without anything to distract me.

Anna didn't stir the entire drive, and as much as I craved moments spent with just her, I was grateful. At a red light, I twisted in my seat and stared, something I couldn't indulge in often. The dim cabin of my truck, the sporadic bursts from oncoming cars sliced her form with varying shades of light, until she looked like an abstract painting brought to life.

A living, breathing piece of art. That's what Anna had always been. She was art to me. Not perfect, but exactly perfect for me.

The house was dark and imposing when I pulled up the driveway, not even a porch light left on, and I carefully slid the gearshift into park.

"Anna," I said quietly, and she didn't so much as stir. I said her name again, hesitant to touch her and ruin her peaceful sleep. Still nothing.

My head dropped back onto the headrest and I closed my eyes. What if I just left the truck running and we slept there? If I allowed myself this small shared space with her, where I could know she was fine, know she was taken care of and watched over.

I almost laughed at my own ludicrous thoughts when Anna stirred, blinking slowly first at the inside of the truck, at the house, then back at me.

"Oh." Blink, blink. She yawned, covering her mouth with one of her small hands. "That was quick."

I gave her a small smile. "Feeling okay?"

She stretched her arms and settled back in the seat, clearly in no hurry. "Sleepy. I feel sleepy."

"You're not seeing two of me?"

Her mouth stretched into a smile, even as her eyes closed again. "Can you imagine? Two of you? The female population of Denver would spontaneously combust."

Hope and embarrassment tangled dangerously with better judgment. She was drunk, and commenting on my physical appearance didn't really mean anything.

"We wouldn't want that," I murmured. She nestled her face into the bench of the truck and some hair slipped over her face. I almost lifted my hand to brush it away, but I stopped. Barely.

My fingers curled uselessly into my palm and they rested on my lap like they weren't one step away from shaking.

"Why have you never asked me out?"

For a moment, I wondered whether I was having a hallucination. Whether I'd imagined her asking it, because her voice was so soft, so innocent. There was no accusation. Just naked, unfiltered curiosity.

My eyes found hers and I worked very hard to keep breathing.

"What?" I managed to croak out.

That smile again. Slow and spreading like ivy, until it lifted her face, made her eyes crinkle in on the edges. "Why have you never asked me out?"

Had someone said something to her?

No. I dismissed that immediately. If Anna had the slightest inkling of how I felt, she wouldn't even be asking, because she'd probably be intimidated by the sheer, overwhelming, crushing intensity of what I felt for her. While I struggled and stumbled through my thoughts, her smile faded and her eyelids started to flutter.

"You should go in and get to bed," I told her gently.

"Can you help me unlock the door?" she said, a slur finally present in her words.

"Of course."

"I might need help walking too. But I won't make you carry me. That would be embarrassing."

And it would kill me, I thought. Just the idea of pulling her up into my arms, cradling her next to my heart, the single most important organ in my body, the one that beat viciously for her, was almost too much to bear when she was like this.

A porch light went on and Anna sat up. "Nope, *that's* embarrassing."

I couldn't disagree. I scratched the side of my jaw while she pushed her keys back in her purse. "I feel like I'm in high school."

In the passenger seat, she swayed a little and I wondered if I should still help her to the door.

But Anna was one step ahead, leaning down to slip off her high heels. "Now I won't fall flat on my face."

"I wouldn't have let that happen," I admitted quietly.

Her eyes met mine, suddenly lucid and completely terrifying. "You still didn't answer my question."

With a heavy swallow that felt impossible to complete, I forced myself to not look away from her. I forced myself to not take the easy way out, to not allow this small, tequila-induced window pass me by. I forced myself to open my mouth and make a promise that I knew I would never back out on.

"If you remember this conversation tomorrow, I promise, I'll answer your question."

For a moment, she didn't speak, only stared at me from across the bench of my truck. Her mouth was relaxed, and for the slowest, fastest, most selfish second, I glanced down at her lips.

It was something I'd never allowed myself to do before, allow a moment where my notice might be caught. If I leaned forward now, she'd taste like tequila, and I knew she'd kiss me back.

But this ... this wasn't the time. And I think she knew it, even if she didn't understand what kind of mountain lay beneath the tip of the iceberg that she was starting to unearth.

"You will?" Her voice was tiny, the thread of hope, the backbone of vulnerability so vivid that I swallowed again.

"I promise," I vowed.

She nodded and started to open the door. Before her bare feet touched the cold ground, she looked at me over her shoulder. "I should probably admit to you that I have no freaking idea if I'm the type of person who forgets things when I'm drinking."

I smiled at her honesty and in response, she positively beamed at me. Then she hopped down and walked quickly to the front door, which was opened for her immediately.

It took a second for me to throw the truck in reverse, because suddenly there was a guillotine hanging perilously over my head. Sleep would be slow in coming, unless I did some drinking of my own. But I knew that I wouldn't drink a single drop, not if there was the slightest chance she'd wake up tomorrow and collect on my promise.

In the space of only a few heartbeats, my strongest hope and my single greatest fear was the sunrise. It couldn't come fast enough for me, and I knew without a doubt, it would still come too soon.

CHAPTER TWENTY-FIVE

ANNA

Of course, I remembered asking Tristan.

There was never really a chance that I wouldn't remember. At an unholy hour, my eyes popped open to a headache that wasn't as bad as the one I deserved to wake up with. Probably all the water that various people had forced on me; Gretchen, and my mom once I was safely ensconced in the kitchen.

There'd been no sermon from her, only relief that I'd been smart enough to call Tristan for a ride home, and a tight hug that I leaned shamelessly into before she watched me pick my way carefully up the stairs to my room.

I'd slept like the dead for about five hours before I woke, the headache minor, but the question booming like a bass drum.

Maybe tequila didn't make my clothes fall off, but it did erase the filter separating my brain and mouth. But there was no way I could've not asked him. He was just sitting there, watching me so carefully, so much about him that felt barely restrained, so tightly and violently bound behind those brown eyes, that I couldn't stop myself from trying to figure out why he looked at me that way and hadn't done anything about it.

There.

That was the piece that I either hadn't been able to see, or refused to acknowledge.

Tristan looked at me one way, but treated me in another. And in a way that felt desperate and selfish, I wanted to know why.

I laid in bed until my room slowly brightened with the rising sun. When it was a more manageable hour, I rolled over and leaned up on my elbow before draining the water and taking the Advil that Mom had had the foresight to give me.

When that was done, I picked up my phone and scrolled carefully to Tristan's name before starting a new message. Every word felt important, weighted in significance, because I had a feeling that he'd be waiting to hear from me. My heartbeat sped up when I thought of how he looked at me after he promised to give me an answer, on that one flimsy condition.

And for a moment, no more than the space of one breath, he'd looked at my mouth. With the tips of my fingers, I traced my lips and exhaled shakily.

Me: Thank you for getting me home safely last night.

Almost instantly, the three dots appeared, and I found my stomach flipping, my lips curving against the pads of my fingers.

Tristan: No thanks necessary. I'll always come if you need something like that.

In my throat, my breath caught, and right along with it, I felt a light burst of wings and the swooping sensation in my stomach that I normally reserved for roller coasters or driving up a winding mountain road before you peaked at the top.

Butterflies.

More than anything, I wished he was in front of me, just so that I could see his face when I told him I remembered.

This was the feeling of butterflies. Of what Gretchen said last night. Someone who made you want to be around them more than you ever wanted to meet someone new.

It was addictive and terrifying. I could hear the blood whooshing in my ears, and my smile was so wide that I couldn't believe that it hadn't split my face. My thumbs flew across the screen and I chewed on the inside of my cheek.

Me: I remember.
Me: Asking you, I mean. I remember asking you the question.

When he didn't start typing right away, I sat up and set my phone down on the nightstand and forced myself to take a few deep breaths. Reality broke through the butterflies, because I still didn't know what the answer to the question was, but *come on* ... his response was loaded with a bit more subtext than anything he'd ever communicated to me before.

My phone buzzed and I took another deep breath before I turned it over.

Tristan: I thought you might. If you'd like to talk today, I'll be at my shop for a few hours this afternoon, or I can come to your place, if you'd prefer that.

I kept chewing on my cheek while I tried to discern anything from his response, but failed. Face-to-face was good, right? It probably meant that he wasn't just going to tell me that he equated me to a cute puppy. He was also willing to come here, which meant he was willing to forgo his own comfort level for whatever he needed to tell me.

245

That might be bad.

I sat up straighter at that thought.

Bad.

In my head, I'd already equated him telling me he didn't want to ask me for some reason that couldn't be overcome as bad.

Because I wanted Tristan to ask me out. Sometime in the last few weeks, he'd become somewhat of my prototype for the kind of man that I could imagine in my life, in my future. And I didn't need to wait for him to ask me out. It was twenty-seventeen, for shit's sake. The asking out could be done by me.

If that was the case, if I decided to take the leap for the both of us, I wanted him to be comfortable. And his shop would achieve that even more than his own home. Definitely more than my mother's house.

Me: I can be at the shop at 1. Sound good?

Tristan: Sounds good.

There was no cliché *it's a date* response to clear things up for me. But I couldn't help but smile as I went about my morning, showering and eating a quiet breakfast over the kitchen sink. The stretching sense of anticipation felt like something weightless had been suspended in my stomach, buoying my heart in a way that was entirely foreign.

Because of Tristan.

"Who'd have thunk it?" I whispered as I went about cleaning up the kitchen.

My mom was gone at church and lunch with friends, so I cleaned the kitchen and downstairs bathrooms, mopping floors and scrubbing mirrors until they shone, my music playing from the built-in speakers mounted in the ceiling. It hit me as I wiped some sweat from my forehead that I missed it. I missed taking care of my own house.

My home with Marcus may have felt like a cage sometimes, but I'd been in charge of keeping it up. And while I hadn't missed that house since I left, I missed the sense of responsibility that had come with it. I thought about that as I took my time showering, blowing out my hair and then taking the flat iron to it until it shone a glossy black.

Maybe it was time to find my own place. Once the divorce was final, I'd feel comfortable making that sort of large purchase, whether I touched Dad's settlement or not. That still hadn't been decided in my head.

With my hair done, I stood in front of my closet and settled on black skinny jeans and boots, an army green top that made me feel pretty. I'd be early, but I had a feeling that Tristan would already be there, working on something beautiful.

I slipped my arms into my coat and left a note for my mom that I didn't know when I'd be home and started the twenty-minute drive with the same fluttering sense of expectation that hadn't abated all morning. Tristan's truck was the only vehicle at the shop, and I briefly glanced in the rear-view mirror to make sure my mascara hadn't flaked.

"Oh my word, Anna," I whispered harshly at myself. Like he'd care. Tristan was the last person to judge whether my makeup was perfect or not. I got out of the car and tightened my coat around me at the blast of cold air. The smell of snow was in the air, and I walked quickly to the heavy metal door, knocking quietly before turning the handle.

Tristan was at the main work bench, safety glasses on and a small sander pressed against the wood he was manipulating. Whatever he was working on wasn't for Millie, but it was beautiful. The curved lines looked like they'd eventually be the back of a chair and his large hands moved with skill and precision. I stood quietly so as not to disturb him, and smiled when he frowned at something he saw in the wood.

When he lifted his hand, the sander turned off and I cleared my throat. He almost dropped it, giving me as close to a rueful grin as Tristan was capable.

"Sorry," I said. "I knocked, but I should've known you wouldn't hear it."

He didn't say anything right away, just nodded and set the sander aside before unplugging it. His long hair was pulled back tightly, and a piece caught in the arms of the glasses when he pulled them off his nose, which made him grimace.

"Long hair problems," I teased, and he laughed under his breath.

"Yeah, I guess." He ran a hand over the top of his head. "Sometimes I dream about buzzing it all off."

I tilted my head and gave him an appraising look. Tristan without the long hair. What would that be like?

His sharp cheekbones and straight, proud nose would stand out more. And his eyes would seem bigger. His beard darker and more dangerous.

"I think you could pull it off."

Tristan stared at me and then lifted an eyebrow. "Yeah?"

"Only if you wanted to save a lot of money on shampoo." I shrugged lightly. "But long hair works for you, so don't break out the clippers too fast."

He caught his smile before it was full and nodded. "Okay." When I knit my fingers together, he caught the motion, then gestured to two stools. "Take a seat?"

It felt so formal. All of this felt different than I thought it would, and I found myself hesitating.

"Please," he said.

"I don't know why this makes me so nervous all of a sudden," I admitted in a rush.

Tristan looked pained for a beat, like my honesty hurt him. Maybe it did. Maybe he was preparing to say something that would hurt me. Maybe he knew I had a right to be nervous. Maybe... okay, stop, I thought firmly. All the maybes in the world wouldn't replace the truth. And he was the only one who could give it to me.

"Are you going to make me ask the question again?" I asked, half-joking, half-serious. Because as much as I'd been looking forward to this conversation, I hadn't really agonized over what I might say to the things *he* might say.

Tristan pulled in a slow breath and scratched his jaw before he looked past me. Okay, this was torture. The slow popping of all the fluttery feelings was painful and awkward, because just a few hours earlier, I felt so *good* in the knowledge that I wanted to go out with Tristan.

And now? Now we were just staring at each other while I waited for him to find the words as to why he hadn't. Or maybe not.

"I'm sorry I'm making you nervous," he said finally, eyes steady on me once he started speaking. "Will you please sit with me?"

"That makes me *more* nervous for some reason."

Inexplicably, that made his lips curve into a mysterious half-smile. "Anna, the irony of this entire exchange is that you've made me this kind of nervous for years."

My eyes narrowed and I shifted, trying to ignore the way my stomach flipped dangerously. "What?"

Tristan licked his lips and mirrored the way I squared my shoulders. "That's not how I should've started."

I didn't say anything, but his nerves were showing, so I slowly took a seat on the stool closest to me even though I very much wanted to stay standing. *What does that mean?* I wanted to ask, but I stayed quiet, allowed him time to process.

He visibly reset, taking the seat opposite of me and letting out a deep, slow breath with his hands clasped in between his open legs. The plaid shirt he was wearing bunched around his biceps when he squeezed his hands together.

When he spoke, it was quiet, and slow. His words deliberate. "I have wanted to ask you out, Anna. It was never from a lack of desire that I didn't."

The flutters were back, and I felt my entire body relax at the careful way he spoke. No words would be wasted from Tristan, nothing would come out of his mouth that didn't hold weight. Didn't I already know that about him?

I risked a tentative smile. "I'm glad to hear that."

He licked his lips, and I knew there was still something missing from this picture. One I couldn't fully see. I peered at him, willing the words to come, because I just wanted to *know*.

"But it wasn't that simple for me," he said, holding my eyes like he was begging me to understand something that he hadn't spoken aloud yet. "Asking you out wasn't just wanting a single date from you."

My tentative smile grew at his caution, the sweet way he spoke. I wanted to make this easier on him, and the relief at knowing I hadn't been imagining all these moments loosened my tongue. "Are you trying to say that you like me, Tristan?"

The answering smile I imagined didn't come, though his face did soften and warm deliciously. His eyes swept my face, and I fought a shiver.

Carefully, he reached forward and took one of my hands in his, let his rough, calloused palm slide across mine. My eyelids fell shut at the contact, and when I opened them again, his mouth was the first thing I saw.

"Not exactly," he said with a smile barely lifting the edges of his lips. The tips of his fingers traced the line of my wrist. "I'm ... I'm trying to say that I'm in love with you."

I was so busy watching the way his lips moved over the words that the full weight of them didn't hit me until the beat of silence that followed.

My eyes snapped to his and I blinked. My lips fell open and I struggled to pull in a solid breath, enough to expand my lungs. "Wh-what?"

Blood rushed loudly into my ears as his fingers tightened around mine, an anchor to where we were sitting. The lights around us were brighter, like someone had just yanked a bag off my head, dropped me into a room that I didn't recognize.

Tristan stared into my face, color high on his cheeks when I didn't say anything.

My heart was racing, because this was bigger, this was *more* than anything I expected him to say.

I shook my head. "Tristan, I..."

When my voice trailed off, it was because I didn't even know what words I wanted to form. What words I was capable of. In all the maybes I'd considered, this hadn't been in the top hundred contenders.

My free hand came up and rubbed at my chest, and he watched the movement with his lips rolled up between his teeth.

"I don't understand," I finally whispered. "When?"

"You needed time, Anna." He held my eyes, even though I blinked rapidly at his oddly phrased statement. "After you left him, I felt like you needed time to figure out what you wanted. Before you could..."

I held up my hand, and he stared at the way my fingers were shaking. My mind raced wildly at his words. "Wait. Tristan, I'm still trying to catch up to the first part."

Misery was etched into his forehead, his eyes. "I'm trying to explain, and I know I'm not doing a good job of it."

I swallowed back any words that I wanted to say, tried to rein in the racing thoughts that made my slowly chugging brain feel like it was coated in sticky tar. "It's okay. I'm just ... I'm trying to understand."

Sitting there staring at him, the way he was watching me with such careful, wary eyes, I knew my reaction must be absolutely terrifying to him. All I could manage was to squeeze his fingers back, and his entire frame relaxed when I did. But even that felt half-hearted, felt weak because I was still so wildly disoriented.

"Believe me, I did want to ask you out," he said. "When you asked me that last night, it took everything in me not to tell you how I feel. It's always taken everything in me to hold that back."

"Why would you?" I asked, the pinch in my chest growing tighter and tighter. "We've spent all this time together." My jaw dropped and a yawning sense of horror had me pulling my hand out of his.

"Tristan, I made you listen to all my terrible dating stories. And I didn't *know*."

His chin dropped slightly and he made a self-deprecating sound that made my stomach roll, imagining what that must have been like for him.

"That wasn't easy, no."

"Then why?"

None of this made sense.

"I thought it was more important to be your friend, Anna."

"Until when?" I asked, unable to stop myself. This all felt impossible. It felt so much bigger than anything I imagined was waiting for me here, when my biggest worry was whether my mascara flaked. It was almost enough to make me let out a hysterical laugh.

His eyes held mine, intense and focused and heavy with meaning. "I needed to know that you had time to heal, or maybe even not that, that you were ready for something real. Something serious."

"I've had time, Tristan," I said when I couldn't stop myself, and some unnamed energy zipped through me, rendering me unable to stay quiet anymore. "I saw the way you looked at me." That energy, frantic and frenetic, made me reach out and grab his hand with mine. "I saw it, and I knew how it made me feel and it doesn't make any sense right now why none of this ever came up."

He didn't speak, his eyes trained on where my fingers wrapped around his. The choppy breaths he let out made his broad frame almost tremble and he shook his head.

"Anna," he begged quietly. "Because of what I feel when you say that, when you touch my hand, it's so much and so big that I feel like you won't be ready to hear it and you won't *know that* until it leaves my mouth. And once it does," he stopped and raised his head to look at me. I lost my breath at what I saw, something cold and hot and prickly and massive covering my entire being. It was good, and bad, and big, and scary, and wonderful. "Once it does, I can't ever take it back."

"Take what back?" I whispered.

"I Googled how long it takes someone to get over a divorce," he said on a rush. "I felt ridiculous doing it, but the thought of making anything worse for you, harder for you, that's why I didn't say anything. It was better to be your friend, Anna."

My mouth popped opened at the thought of Tristan Googling something like that. But immediately on the heels of that was sadness, poking tiny holes in anything that could possibly seem humorous in this situation.

"Better than what?" I said. "Better than being *honest* with me?"

To his credit, he didn't drop my stare, he met it, but I saw the slow climb of heat in his face. It probably matched my own.

"You weren't ready for it." So steady. His voice was so steady and even, placating, and that did not help. I didn't want to be placated, I wanted to be talked to like an equal.

I stood, my hand falling from his when I did. Nerves zipped and bounced around my body, impossible to contain. "How could you know whether I was ready without *talking* to me? I've been sitting here, analyzing all our interactions, wondering whether I was imagining all this in my head, and..."

I felt so stupid.

A stupid little girl who went on awful dates because she was blind to what had been right under her nose for so many years. And he was giving me the answers that he'd practiced, probably thought about a hundred times, questions that I didn't realize I was supposed to be asking until right now.

"It felt like there was nothing to say until you were ready for something more serious, Anna. He gave you nothing for so long, and I didn't want to give you too much. Not when you were just figuring how to move on."

"This is not about Marcus," I said firmly. "This is about you, and me."

Emotions clogged my throat, but I swallowed them down.

"You didn't even try to say anything, Tristan. 'Anna, I like you. I have feelings for you, and I'd really like to take you out to dinner?'"

I threw my hands up. "That's all it would have had to be, and you didn't *even try* to talk to me about any of it."

Tristan stood, only a few inches between us. His eyes were wild, and my heart raced to match. Before he opened his mouth, I felt like there were hands on my back, ready to push me off a cliff that I wasn't aware of just seconds before.

His hands reached out and gripped my upper arms and I gasped at the rough contact, something I'd never had from him. Then, his forehead pressed against mine and I felt the burn of sudden tears at the back of my throat. When he spoke, his voice was tortured and tight, and I shut my eyes against the onslaught of what it made me feel.

"Because there was no way for me to have that conversation with you without telling you that I have been in love with you for the past six years, Anna. And if all you needed from me was casual, something to be left in the dark of a shared night, something that wouldn't leave a bed or would only give us a handful of hours together, it would have *killed* me. It would have ripped out a piece of me that I'd never get back, and I've already given you more of myself than I've ever given anyone. I couldn't do that to you, and I couldn't do it to me either, not when you've been everything that I've wanted for so long."

If his voice made me feel, his words ... oh his words cracked a jagged split down the middle of my body. A tear fell down my cheek as I pulled back to stare at him. His hands hovered in the air where my arms had been, and with pain-filled eyes, he watched that tear drip off my chin.

Six years?

Six years?

Any shock I felt was replaced with something much bigger, something there wasn't a name for. The entire time I'd known him?

Every interaction, for *years*, and this is what he'd had hiding inside of him?

"I..." I shook my head frantically. Nothing made sense. His

words didn't. My head didn't. My heart ... my heart felt like it was frozen in my chest. I pressed my fisted hand against it, desperate to make it beat again. "That's *impossible*."

"I know it sounds crazy," he said slowly. Tristan's entire being was held still, held carefully so close to me, like he knew how dangerous it would be to touch me too quickly, push me too far. "It's felt impossible to me too a few times over the years."

"Oh God," I whispered, every interaction I could remember flitting through my head like I was shuffling a deck of cards. The images too blurry to focus on, moving too quickly for me to try and stop it. If I had, I would have lost them all in a messy burst.

This, this was too much. I wanted to scream. I wanted to cry. I wanted ... I wanted him to grab me and hold me and make it make sense.

"When you first said it," I said on a choked whisper, "I thought you meant ... m-meant since I left Marcus."

Slowly, Tristan shook his head. "No. Not since you left Marcus."

I couldn't breathe. Violent gasps of air were coming out of my mouth. I needed air.

"I have to go," I whispered, barely seeing him.

Tristan gripped the sides of his head. "Anna, wait."

"Six years," I repeated, feeling a sob crawl up my throat. Six years where I was miserable and trapped and stuck somewhere voluntarily. "Six *years*, Tristan."

"What do you need?" he asked frantically.

In some dark corner of my mind, I knew I was being irrational. Knew that I wasn't handling this well, that my panic was misplaced and barely understandable, but everything about this entire conversation made me feel recklessly out of control.

What did I need?

I needed to understand why suddenly, all those years spent wasting away with Marcus, all those years that I'd wasted with my own inaction, felt even more pathetic now. And he'd had to sit back and watch it.

What must he have thought of me?

The sob broke free and he looked like I'd shot him. He stepped forward like he wanted to wrap his arms around me. I may have let him. I felt like I was one breath away from flying into a million tiny pieces.

I willed myself to think, to not lash out because I was so fucking confused by what had happened since I walked through the door.

Tristan was in love with me.

Correction: Tristan had been in love with me *for years*.

Panic had my throat closing up and I tried to breathe through it.

"I ... I need to think about all of this." I searched his eyes. "Just ... it's a lot. It's not what I expected."

"I know," he said in a low, rough voice.

I backed up a few steps, one hand covering my mouth.

Then I turned and fled.

I made it to my car, cold and blessedly quiet, and the tears began in earnest. I didn't stop them, didn't even want to, because the release felt like the only thing keeping me sane in a moment that made absolutely no sense. After a few minutes, I sniffled and scrubbed furiously at my face, drying it with my hands. In my cold and quiet car, I stared at Tristan's shop, trying to make sense of what he'd just told me.

The moments that I had, they were nothing compared to the ones he'd apparently been shoring up.

A pinprick. A drop. Insignificant in comparison.

But they hadn't been insignificant to *me*. Those moments, my moments, were precious and important. They'd revealed things about myself, about him, about what we could be. And I'd held on to them because I'd been operating under some misguided assumption.

For all that time. All these months. The wasted time, the mixed signals and the missed opportunities.

And just like that, my hand was on the door handle, because confusion turned to frustration and I needed answers. No longer was I willing to run and hide from the things that were happening to me. That was Anna before, and that's not who I was anymore.

CHAPTER TWENTY-SIX

TRISTAN

You just lost her.

It was all I could think as the door slammed shut behind her. *You just lost her.* I couldn't even sit down. I was frozen, absently wondering what would happen when she drove away. Would my legs finally decide they could give out? Force me to rest on a seat that seemed far to flimsy to hold me up? Run after her car and hope she saw me in the rear-view mirror?

There wasn't a single sound in the shop, except the ragged sounds of my breathing. My eyes were dry, and my mouth seemed incapable of closing because that would mean I had no chance of pulling the words back in, reframing them into something less ... something less terrifying, less intense, less, less, less.

Just *less.*

I swiped a hand over my mouth and let it hang there. How had I messed that up so completely? It wasn't supposed to happen that way? Was it?

I'd thought all morning about what I'd say to her if she remembered.

Anna, I've wanted to ask you out for a long time. That's always how it started in my head, but making my feelings *less* felt like I was trying to shove an ocean into a gallon jug. Impossible and ill-advised. Messy. An inevitable failure that would only serve to make things worse.

A laugh burst from my lungs, raw and desperate. Yeah. I'd certainly managed that.

But the words were supposed to come. They were supposed to be earnest and sincere, and she would have had a moment of shock, but ... but then, she was supposed to, what?

What?

Fall into my arms?

I closed my eyes and let myself sink against the work table, just as the door shoved open with a sharp pop that had me standing up straight.

She came back. She came back.

And she was *pissed.*

"You need to start from the beginning," Anna said, her hair wild around her face, and her face pale and streaked with dried tears. And still, she was the most magnificent thing I'd ever seen. "You need to make me understand this, because I *don't* understand this."

"Anna," I said miserably.

Her eyes filled again. "No, Tristan, I'm serious. You need to tell me how you came to this decision about what I was ready for and what I wasn't. I just spent years somewhere miserable and lonely, where my feelings were never considered. Years in the dark about all these things that you felt for me, and I don't understand how you'd possibly know what I was ready for."

The anger I felt just moments before, directed at myself, burned bright and hot, looking for an outlet other than myself. This wasn't how it was supposed to happen. It wasn't.

But she kept going, and I ached to reach out for her, because the pain in her words sliced me clean through.

"Grief doesn't fit into a neat box, you know?" She speared her hands through her hair and stared at me. "You can look up a million articles and books and stupid motivational quotes about moving on, and it doesn't mean the same thing to people. Someone can be ready the next day. Maybe it's the next year. That's not for *you* to decide, no matter what Google article you read. It's for no one to decide except the person who's in the situation. I knew my marriage was over for at least two years before I walked out that door. Did you know that? And I was the coward who stayed anyway. I was the one who started grieving the loss of it while my ring was still heavy on my finger. I was *ready* to walk out the door when I finally did."

"You're not a coward," I said fiercely. "Don't ever say that about yourself."

"And how do *you* know? How could you *possibly* know that about me? That's what I don't understand."

In my silence, she shook her head. I took a deep breath and tried not to lose my tenuous grip on the lid that held everything in, everything that had been shoved down for the past six years, now clawing desperately to get out.

My insides felt like they were shredded into bloody ribbons for all I'd done to keep my feelings for her repressed, keep them to myself.

She pointed a finger at me and it was shaking wildly. "If I had walked out that door and the next day woke up ready to find my soul mate, that's my decision."

"Are you?" I snapped out and she blinked in surprise. I took a step closer to her. "Are you?"

"I ... I," she stammered and backed up against the wall behind us.

"Are you telling me that what I said didn't scare the shit out of you?"

"Of *course,* it scared me, Tristan." Her eyes were huge in her face, begging something of me, something I couldn't define. But she wasn't running. She'd come back. And I knew that if I made my feelings less, if I pushed them into a smaller box, they'd never have a chance to find their home in her. That's what I wanted. All I could do was pray that she'd feel the same. "Don't you get it though? When I was sitting out in my car, it was like someone fired off a gun and I was miles behind in a race that I didn't even know I was supposed to be running. You're so far ahead of me—"

"I was trying to do what was best," I interrupted loudly. "You needed time, Anna."

"And what's best for me is not someone making that decision for me. You should have talked to me first. You should have asked me. You never even gave me the *chance* to catch up to where you are. I deserved that chance. That choice." She lifted her chin, and she was so fierce in that moment that I wanted to fall to my knees in front of her. When she spoke again, it was a whisper. "What I need is honesty, Tristan. I need to know why I've been standing in front of you all this time, without any clue of what's been in your head, when I've been desperately trying to figure that out. And to find this out? Yes, it's scary, Tristan."

She pressed a fist to her heart, and I clenched my teeth together so tightly that my jaw almost cracked. "Anna, I'm so sorry."

"Don't be sorry," she begged. "Be honest with me. I can handle it, even if it scares me. Because more than anything might scare me, what I need from you is your truth."

Kneeling like a supplicant wasn't what she needed. Even though every word from her mouth slayed me, humbled me, weakened and strengthened me, made me love her even more than I had an hour ago, Anna needed an equal right now.

I dropped my chin and tried to breathe the words to life, and all I could do for a moment was shake my head and curse my uselessness. My complete ineptness now that I was in front of her and she was begging me for this. For the feelings that I'd let define me for so long.

"Tristan, please," she whispered, tears choking her voice. "I just don't understand how this has been happening for years, and I had no clue. I wasn't even an option. I wasn't available. I don't understand how you could've loved me that long, held on for so long when I never even... Oh Tristan, I had no idea, and I just need to understand it." Anna took a hesitant step toward me, and just that, just that half a step closer to me, what I needed to say flooded me in an overwhelming wave.

"It was like loving a ghost, Anna." I took a step of my own, and she mirrored it, backing up against the wall again at my raw spoken words. Carefully, slowly, I lifted a hand and it trembled visibly before I cupped the side of her face and felt the silk of her hair against my fingers. "I could see you. I could hear your voice and your laugh and see all the things that made me fall in love with you. But I couldn't touch you. I didn't know what it felt like to pull you into my arms and tuck you against my heart. I didn't know. It was almost like you didn't even really exist some days, because I didn't have any of those memories to keep me sane. Everything that I wondered about had never happened."

A tear slid down her cheek and instead of brushing it away with my other hand, I braced it on the wall next to her head and let myself stand flush against her. She let out a quiet sob, a small exhale and I watched her face for signs that I should back off, but she held my eyes steadily, leaned her face into my palm.

If she let me, I'd stand like that forever. I dropped my forehead against hers again, like I'd done earlier, and one of her hands came up to encircle my wrist. Not stopping me, not pulling me back, just ... holding me there.

And we fit.

"I can't explain it to you, Anna. Because it doesn't make any more sense to you than it does to me. If I could explain it away, maybe I would've been able to move on, instead of live in this agonizing half-life that I've been in for so many years without knowing if you'd ever be able to feel something for me in return."

"All this time," she whispered, closing her eyes as more tears fell. One slipped against my fingers and I brushed my thumb to absorb it into my skin, another piece of her that I'd never felt.

"All this time. I didn't know you were married when I fell in love with you. I swear, I didn't."

Anna nodded while she processed that and her eyes closed briefly again. It felt like my soul was falling from my mouth with every word I offered her, the parts of me that no one had ever known, the parts of me that I always saved for her.

"It was the way you spoke to me, the way you understood me, the way you made me feel. The way you spoke to others, the way you treated them, the way you smiled and laughed and were so strong, when others couldn't possibly have stayed strong for all those years."

The slippery smoothness of her hair against my fingers was the best thing I'd ever felt. Her breath against my skin while she let me say the things I wanted was even better than that. Each new sensation topped the one before it.

She sniffed, and I kept talking, knowing that my feelings were safe with her, that I could trust her with them. Finally.

"The moments that made me fall for you were small. And through all these years, I've experienced a thousand more—even if they were from a distance—that told me that you were it for me. That even though you were his, I was right to love you."

Another tear slipped down her cheek, and she watched me quietly, her face so close to mine.

"When I had a hard day, I'd sit on this old chair on my deck and wish you were there with me. Wish you could tell me about yours, if it was good or bad or stressful, because you always make me smile, Anna. You're one of the only people who ever make me *want* to laugh, who lighten the world around me just by being there. And it was so lonely because you weren't there with me. But at least I knew that the thought of you, the real you—not the version of you that stayed with him—and the way you made me feel, that belonged only to me."

She sniffed and shook her head where it was still pressed to mine. The movement made her nose brush up against mine and we both froze. Her breath left her opened mouth shakily, and I inhaled, my chest expanding until I felt it brush hers.

All it would take was a lift of her chin, a dip of mine.

"Tristan," she whispered.

"If I kiss you right now," I told her, careful not to let my lips touch hers in even the smallest increment, "I'll never get my heart back, Anna. You've already had it for so long."

She tightened her hand around my wrist, and I wondered if she could feel my pulse hammering under the skin.

"You are breaking *my* heart right now."

I exhaled and briefly closed my eyes, somehow holding myself back from sinking into her fully, from wrapping my arm around her back and pressing up the length of her spine. "I'm sorry."

Anna smiled through her tears and tentatively brought her hand up to touch the side of my face. "Don't be sorry."

I shook my head. That was impossible. I was sorry for so many things. Wished that I could do so many things differently, even if I was still standing here with her in my arms.

Her fingers delicately traced my cheekbone, the edge of where my beard started. "Now what?"

I felt my own eyes burn as I looked down at her, and I lifted my forehead off hers. My thumb smoothed along her skin, her perfect, smooth skin. "When I kiss you, Anna, when I touch you, *really* touch you, it will be because you're ready to give me your heart. When you're mine."

This close, I could see the way the deep brown of her eyes faded to the black of her irises. She blinked, a conscious effort to clear her tears.

"The way you're mine?" she said tentatively. Testing out the words on her tongue. Like she was tasting them, not sure if they were right for her yet.

I nodded slowly, let my gaze drift greedily over her face. "I've always been yours. The entire time. You just didn't know it."

The way she peered up at me while I spoke, I felt hope pour warmly into the wounds left behind when she'd run. She licked her lips, not in a seductive way, so I kept my eyes on hers and slowly pulled back. She tightened her grip on my wrist and carefully turned my face using her other hand. My heart hammered as she lifted up on her tiptoes and pressed a soft kiss onto my cheek.

She didn't linger, she didn't try for more, but I felt that kiss, the simple touch of her lips like a balm to my weary, exhausted soul.

Anna kept her hand on my face and wouldn't let me look away. "You are such a good man, Tristan." I tried to look away in embarrassment, because it felt like a brush-off, but she wouldn't let me. "I just need some time. To think about all of this. To sort through it. Is that okay?"

I nodded, taking my hand off her face to smooth her hair down. Under my palm, it was smooth and cold. "That's okay."

"Thank you," she said feelingly. Then she slipped away from the wall and gave me one last smile over her shoulder before she walked out the door.

This time my legs did give out, and I sank heavily onto the stool behind me.

Now, all I could do was wait.

I should have been good at it by now, but it only felt impossible.

CHAPTER TWENTY-SEVEN

TRISTAN

Waiting was a peculiar sort of torture. Every hour that passed, the waiting took on a different shape and form, a living, changing entity that I couldn't hold in my hands, but I could feel move through me all the same.

The first day, I felt naked and vulnerable. Like my truth about Anna, the truth that I'd held close to me for so long was now out in the world made it more fragile, more breakable.

By day two, I woke knowing it was the opposite. It was stronger. The words hit the air, and it fueled them like someone had thrown gasoline onto an already burning fire.

By day three, I was sick of pacing my house, sick of pretending like I was sleeping peacefully, sick of feeling useless in my own skin, so I threw myself into work, the force of which took me by surprise. With every worn edge, every flame licking across a raw surface and making it burn and char into something newer and stronger, I found a peace in my feelings for Anna that I'd never felt before.

By day four, I learned that I could spend hours of the day pretending like I wasn't staring at my phone and imagining what it would be like to text her, call her, check on her, simply to hear her voice again.

By day five, I'd spent so many hours at work that my hands were raw and splintered. My arms ached and my back was sore, but my shop was filled with finished items, each one beautiful and unique and stamped with Anna's name within each piece of wood. Each fiber that I'd transformed felt like something that I'd created only for her.

By day six, my heart was calling her name, desperate to know what she felt, missing her with a fierceness that took my breath away if I dwelled on it too long.

I had to stare in the mirror and remind myself, over and over, out loud and with a determination that I wasn't sure I believed yet, that I could be patient.

I woke on day seven, drank my coffee and watched the snow fall over Denver, watched it coat the ground until it no longer resembled what it had been just hours before. The yellow dry grass was now a solid blanket of white, the rising sun making it glimmer to the point that it hurt to look at.

Maybe now I was past the point of counting days, adding to a tally that didn't prove anything other than the passage of time. It didn't matter if I'd loved her for years, or weeks, or hours. All that mattered was that this was the time that I *proved* my love for Anna. It wasn't in the words I spoke to her, it wasn't measured in days and weeks spent pining for her, it wasn't a figment of my imagination or because it was safer to love someone who wasn't free.

It was real. And this ... this test, this torture, this waiting, I could withstand it

For her, I could wait.

CHAPTER TWENTY-EIGHT

ANNA

It was my favorite kind of snow. Fluffy, large puffs of white that stood out against the black sky, flakes so big that they almost didn't seem real. I used to think they were magical, when I was a kid.

Now, it felt like a new beginning. Real enough, nothing magical or unreal about my days, but every single minute that passed felt like I was one step closer to a door opening fully. Wide enough that I could pass through it. Not just pass, but run.

In the corner of my family room, of my newly rented town-house, I sat in a large navy-blue velvet chair and sipped hot choco-late while the snow fell. The TV was dark, and in the corner oppo-site of me was a small white Christmas tree, only decorated so far by white lights. Unopened boxes of ornaments were stacked next to the ivory couch, and as much as I loved everything I'd picked out, I couldn't bring myself to move from my spot underneath the blan-ket covering my legs. Music played softly, my favorite instrumental Christmas album, one that was only piano.

A perfect December night. The kind I used to dream about enjoying.

The hot chocolate wasn't so hot when I took another sip and let my head rest on the side of the chair, but there was nothing about the moment that could be ruined. I had my own space, and even three days after moving in, I couldn't—didn't want to—let go of the overwhelming sense of peace that it had brought me.

My eyes landed on the tree and I sighed deeply, feeling the smile spread across my face. It stayed there as I looked back out the window and wondered, yet again, what Tristan was doing.

Somewhere out there, probably at his house, he loved me.

He *loved* me.

It still seemed impossible. Almost as unbelievable and extraordinary as the snow that was falling from the sky. But as each day passed, eight of them since I walked out of his shop, I felt more and more settled in the knowledge of it. The truth of it. It was creeping slowly across my heart the same way my smile had over my face, unconscious, unforced and real.

I missed him.

Me: I'm watching it snow from my new townhouse, and thinking about you.

Me: Thank you for giving me this time. X

Tristan: You're welcome.

Tristan: Don't forget to text if accidental explosions are on the line.

Me: :) Noted.

Smiling, I set my phone back down on the table, and almost immediately, it buzzed again.

Rory: DID YOU TEXT HIM YET, YOU BITCH? YOU ARE KILLING ME. He was here a couple hours ago with giant puppy dog eyes and I had to fight not to burst into tears every time I saw him look at your picture.

I smiled but didn't laugh, because the thought of Tristan with puppy dog eyes made my stomach twist uncomfortably.

Me: Calm down. I texted him that I was thinking about him a couple minutes ago and thanked him for giving me time.

Rory: THAT'S IT?
Me: *eye roll* Isn't that better than nothing? He deserves me to be completely SURE, Rory. I'm going to treat his feelings with the respect they deserve, and I think that's what he wants me to do, even if it takes a few days.

Rory: I hate it when you're rational.

Me: Did he really have puppy dog eyes?

Rory: Oh no, I'm not telling you SHIT. Text him yourself and ask. Tell him how badly you messed up your first adventure in living alone yesterday. I'll never forgive you if that grease doesn't come out of my pants. I GOT THOSE IN ITALY.

Now I laughed. There'd been a slight leak in my kitchen sink, and instead of calling the landlord, I wanted to see if I could fix it myself. I had a hot pink tool kit that Garrett bought me, and isn't that what YouTube tutorials are for?

Well, a few gallons of water on the kitchen floor later, and a surprise visit from Rory where I roped her into helping me, I had to cave and make the call anyway.

There was a brisk knock on my front door, and I set my phone down before peering down into the parking lot. Garrett's black BMW was parked next to mine, and I threw the blanket off my lap with a groan.

"I was warm under a blanket, you ass," I said as I pulled open the door.

One arm was clutching two brown paper bags, and the other gripped a bag I recognized from Mom's basement.

"I brought Chinese," he told me as he walked past me. "You can beat me up after we eat."

"What do I owe the pleasure?"

He humphed as he set the food down on the large kitchen island. "Mom thinks you must be lonely. She guilted me into getting you food and bringing you some of the Christmas decorations she forgot to send with you when you moved out."

"Forgot?" I said under my breath.

"I know. Highly unlikely, as she has the memory of an elephant."

While I rummaged through the divine smelling takeout boxes, I snickered. "I'm going to tell her you called her that. She'll love it."

Garrett raised his middle finger while he opened up his Pad Thai. We ate in silence, and occasionally, his gaze would travel around the large family room that connected to the kitchen by way of an arched-in dining room that still sat empty.

"You need furniture."

"I've been here for three days. Besides, there's no rushing perfection." My eyes landed on my sole Christmas decoration. "Like my tree?"

He snorted. "No. I hate it. At least it's not like, pink or something."

"I really hope you give me more credit than that."

His hazel eyes zeroed in on me, unblinking and surprisingly serious. "I give you a lot of credit, little sister."

I finished chewing and then wiped my mouth with one of the napkins tucked into the bag. "I know you do."

Garrett was quiet after that, as was I. But it wasn't uncomfortable. Just me and my big brother, standing up in the kitchen and eating Chinese. A lump of emotion stuck in my throat as I stared at him.

"Did you come to check on me?" I asked quietly.

When he sighed and looked into the other room, I bit back my smile. He set down his chopsticks. "Maybe."

I moved next to him and laid my head on his shoulder. "I'm happy. You have nothing to worry about."

"Happy ... like, happy being single?"

"Oh my *gosh*, you are as subtle as a hurricane, Garrett." I shoved him and went back to my food. I couldn't help but tease him a little. "So, are you more worried about me or Tristan?"

My statement hit right on target, even if it wasn't my intended target. I thought he'd laugh, wrap me in a brotherly hug and say, *Of course I'm worried about you. You're my sister.* But that's not what he did. Garrett shook his head and got a distant look in his eye.

"Of anyone I know, Tristan is the last person who would ever need me to worry about him."

Questions sprang up like bubbles, my curiosity unleashed like someone had popped the cork off a champagne bottle. "Tell me about him," I found myself saying.

Garrett raised his eyebrows. "You haven't gotten to know him yourself the last few months?"

My face heated, but I didn't take it back, didn't wave it off. "Yeah. I mean, I know him. More now, of course, than I used to. But from your perspective, I'd like to hear about him."

For a moment, he looked at the ceiling. "I was not mentally prepared to step into some romantic drama starring my sister. I'm not sure if I can do this."

"Oh yes you can. Want to know why? I kept talking myself out of liking this guy because of what you told me the week I left Marcus."

His eyebrows shot up. "Oh no, this is not my fault. I just told you not to aim his direction if you wanted a one-night stand. And why did I do that?"

"Because you knew how he felt," I murmured guiltily.

"Because I knew how he felt. It wasn't my story to tell, and I think you know that."

"I do, I do." I glanced at him. "So you're going to talk about him now, right? Everything's laid out there, no more secrets that I need to learn." Garrett groaned dramatically. I slugged him in the shoulder and went to toss my empty carton in the garbage canister next to the island. "I have beer."

"Sold."

We cleaned up the counter and I put the leftovers in the fridge, grabbing a beer for Garrett and more hot chocolate for me. When I took my mug out of the microwave and blew on the steaming surface, he rolled his eyes. Sniffing haughtily, I reached next to the fridge and pulled out a bottle of Irish cream, pouring a liberal amount into the mug.

"Better," he said around the mouth of the bottle.

I took my seat in the blue chair and Garrett sprawled on the couch.

After wrapping the blanket around my legs, I gave him a stern look. "Talk."

My brother looked so miserable, I almost told him to forget it. But this ... this was important. The last handful of days, while they felt long to me, I couldn't even imagine what they'd felt like to Tristan. I owed it to him to figure out what I felt.

Was I attracted to Tristan? Not even a question

Did I like Tristan? Yes, absolutely. I liked Tristan a lot. Butterflies, heart-eyes, tummy flips, the whole shebang, when I thought about him.

Was I ready to say that his love for me was a weight I could carry, accept responsibility for within a relationship that would be emotionally uneven? I wasn't sure yet.

"I met Cole first," he started. "He was my real estate agent, and lived a couple streets over. He moved into his place around the same time that Michael and Tristan moved into theirs, so Cole introduced us about a month later. From the very beginning, Tristan was quiet. Reserved. But not an asshole, you know? Marcus was a quiet asshole because you knew he just wasn't paying attention to you, but Tristan was like," he paused and searched for the right word. When he found it, he smiled. "He was the observer. Always paying attention to what was going on around him. If something made the rest of us laugh, Tristan would maybe give a small smile, you know? Always just a bit ... separate, I guess. But always paying attention."

It was the Tristan I knew, too. The one I'd seen over the years. The one that I remembered meeting, liking almost instantly.

"Separate on purpose?"

Garrett nodded slowly. "Yeah, I think he prefers it that way. He hates being the center of attention. Michael is so different. He's the extrovert, the one who always makes people laugh. I guess it was the same when they were growing up. Their dad left when Tristan couldn't have been more than six or seven, from what I've heard. He came around occasionally, but not for long. Tristan stepped up to help his mom a lot, and then went right to work for his uncle after high school. Same as Michael."

I wrapped my arms around my legs and set my chin on the top of my knees while I tried to picture a younger Tristan, helping around the house, trying to fill the absence left behind from his father. I missed mine with an ache that would probably never really go away, and he had to try and take the place of his for completely different reasons.

An absence of choice on the part of the man who should be featured most prominently in your childhood. No wonder he'd answered me the way he did when I asked if he was like his father.

"Tristan is one of the hardest workers I know," Garrett continued. "When he does decide to string together enough words to make a complete sentence, he can give some damn good advice. He's loyal to the people he cares about. He'd give the shirt off his back if someone needed it. His hair is awful and I wish I could hack it off while he's sleeping."

I burst out laughing. "It's not awful. It fits him perfectly."

Garrett sighed. "Yeah. I guess."

"You love him," I mused. "You love all your friends."

He was quiet, head resting against the back of the couch, even closed his eyes for a couple seconds before he answered. "I do. And Tristan is honestly one of the best guys that I've ever known. Even though there were times that I thought he was certifiable for not figuring out how to move on from you, I never doubted the sincerity of what he felt. Never doubted his intentions toward you." Then he dropped his chin and looked at me. "Because the thing about Tristan is that once he makes up his mind about something—about someone—that's that. He'll never waver. Never turn his back."

There was a spot behind my breast bone that felt warm and melty, and I wanted to rub at it, but didn't want to move. "How long have you known?"

"Honestly? I feel stupid about it now, but I didn't even realize until Rory pointed it out pretty early in our relationship."

I smiled. "Really?"

"Really," he admitted easily. "Tristan doesn't exactly spew his emotions everywhere, if you hadn't noticed. And he was very, very good at keeping what he felt for you under wraps. Rory and Kat picked it up before any of the guys did, I think."

There were two different parts of me when it came to Tristan. One that was ready, so ready, to learn more about him. To soak up any pieces that I could. And the other part wanted to keep him a secret, just for a bit longer, until I could decide that *he* should be the one to tell me all these things, show me all these things.

"Were you mad at him when you found out?"

Garrett didn't even have to pause before shaking his head. "No.

I wasn't mad. I knew him well enough at that point, and had been around the two of you in enough situations to know that he'd never push you. He'd never disrespect you or make you feel uncomfortable."

I closed my eyes against the sudden wave of sadness that I felt for Tristan. The years he sat back, undoubtedly aware that I was miserable, but still doing nothing because he had so much integrity, so much respect for my decision to stay with Marcus.

I swallowed my emotions down as Garrett kept talking. "I did have one *That's my sister and I'll beat your ass if you do anything to hurt her* talk with him though."

"What?" I narrowed my eyes at him. "When?"

"Not too long after Dad died. Maybe I was feeling a bit more protective than usual."

"Garrett," I said, unbearably touched.

That was waved off. "You had that whole thing in the will, and I know I didn't handle it too well. I could've gone easier on you, supported your decisions more. I guess I wanted to make sure that Tristan wouldn't complicate the situation for you."

"He wouldn't have." As soon as I said the words, I knew how true they were. Even if he'd known about the caveat in my dad's will, even if he'd known the extent of how miserable I'd been, even over a year ago, he never would have been the person to push me in a direction I didn't want to go in. Tristan would never have used his own feelings to try and manipulate the path I was taking, certainly not to make things easier for himself.

And in the moment that he finally admitted how he felt to me, I'd basically accused him of exactly that.

Shame had me closing my eyes. Not because I'd had such a strong reaction to him, that was only human when confronted by feelings as strong as his were for me. But because I'd lost the ability to take a deep breath and think about what my situation—stretching back so many years—must have been like for him. And then to have that barrier suddenly lifted, he was probably as confused as

I'd been in a lot of ways.

If he'd told me eleven weeks ago how he felt, I would've slammed the door in his face. Figuratively, of course. But the words would've fallen on deaf ears. Even though it wasn't that long ago, I wouldn't have been ready. Not even remotely.

"Anna, I can't tell you what to do when it comes to Tristan. I'm not going to push him on you, because you already know he's a great guy. The best kind of guy." My brother's eyes were so kind and so warm that I almost burst into tears. "But that doesn't mean *you'll* think he's perfect for you. If you don't? He'll be okay eventually. You're not indebted to him because of how he feels. You only need to pursue a relationship with Tristan if that's what you want."

I knew he wasn't wrong, and it was something that I'd thought about since I walked out of his shop, until my head and heart and gut all tangled together. Was I ready to fully bear the weight of Tristan's feelings for me? Let him fully bear the weight of what I was still working through? Some days I thought I was.

Those were the days I reached for my phone with his name on my mind, ready to hear his voice say my name. Some days, it felt like a burden that was too precious to take on, a responsibility that was too great when I was still dealing with issues outside of him.

I stood, as did Garrett, and he wrapped me in a tight hug. When he dropped a kiss on the top of my head, my eyes stung with tears.

"It's nice when you're not being such pain in the ass," I told him.

He laughed. "I'm glad you think so."

"Give Rory a hug for me."

Before he walked out the door, he grinned. "Oh, I'll give her more than that."

"Garrett," I whined. The sound of his retreating laughter was drowned out once the door slammed shut behind him. Shaking my head, I made my way back to my chair.

I took another sip of my drink, the Irish cream warming my belly. The music from the speakers paused briefly before restarting, and again, I watched the snow. The flakes were smaller now, swirling in the air to unseen gusts of wind. Tomorrow, it was supposed to be sunny and in the fifties. Welcome to Colorado in the winter. Christmas was just around the corner, and shortly after that, I'd flip the calendar over.

A new year.

If everything went the way it was supposed to, I'd be Anna Calder again before that happened. Any day now, actually.

Officially divorced. Officially free.

On a whim, and not really thinking through what would happen if he ignored me, patronized me, or just didn't give me the answer I was seeking, I sent a text to Marcus.

Me: Why did you stay? I never thought to ask.
Me: I'm not asking to change anything that happens from here on out. I'm just curious.

Not expecting him to answer, I set my phone down and snuggled further under the blanket, worrying the soft edges with my fingers. My phone buzzed and I took a deep breath before picking it up.

Marcus: I've thought about that a lot the last few months. I think it felt easier than trying to start over, because there was no guarantee that that would be any better.
Marcus: Why did you?

It was the most honesty I'd gotten from him in years. And I didn't really feel much of anything when I read his answer again. My thumb traced the edge of my cell phone case and I realized it was because it didn't really matter why Marcus hadn't left. Getting an answer from him might clear up some confusion I had about the past, but it wouldn't alter my steps moving forward. And that was all I really needed to focus on.

Me: Pretty much the same.

It was the truth. I could've blamed his affair. I could've said that until that moment, I was clinging tightly to our vows, but my inaction for all those years was as much about me, as it was about him. But going into all of that wouldn't matter to him. I'd asked, and he'd answered, which was more than I expected, as anti-climactic as the exchange may have turned out to be.

As I set my phone down again, I knew that there wouldn't be another text from him, wouldn't be another that I sent. The next exchange would be our names traced in ink on legal papers, and that would be that. The final piece set into place, another cog in the wheel of what I was trying to build. Necessary to set it into motion, something I'd never be able to erase about my past, something that would always shape a part of who I was in the future.

And while the snow kept falling, I smiled, because I knew that there was one person who wouldn't ever want to change that part of my past, because it brought me into his life.

Now I just had to decide what I was ready to do with that.

CHAPTER TWENTY-NINE

TRISTAN

Christmas came with little fanfare, other than a few random texts from various friends and family that I only heard from on holidays. Michael, Brooke, the twins and I had done dinner at my mom's the night before, as was our tradition. Michael, if he knew what had happened with Anna, never asked me about it. Neither did Brooke. And for that I was grateful.

I woke late that day, did some reading while the radio played quietly in the background. There were no decorations at my house, because it felt unnecessary for just me to enjoy. Especially since I was rarely home. But it seemed I was forced to be that particular day.

Michael and Brooke wanted to celebrate with the twins. My mom was at my uncle's house, and then with friends like she did every year. My uncle, the jerk, had forbidden me to work on Christmas Eve and Christmas Day, which felt like a jail sentence since I still hadn't heard from Anna, aside from that one text exchange.

Stores were closed, even if I wanted to go wander around. And I didn't feel like I had the energy to go skiing, even though the snow we'd gotten over the past few days would've been perfect for it.

I convinced myself that I could spend the entire day at home and keep my mind off of the fact that it had been nine days, almost ten, since I'd seen her. Heard her voice.

And I was doing all right until around lunch time, when there was a timid knock on the front door. My heart leapt and I forced myself to walk slowly to see who it was.

Through the windows next to the door, I saw Cole's wife Julia peek her head around and give me a friendly wave. Disappointment sliced through me and the force of it was so strong that for a moment, I struggled to breathe. But I fixed my face into a more pleasant expression and opened the door regardless.

"Merry Christmas," she said warmly, holding up a small gift bag. "I come bearing gifts."

"Come on in. It's cold out there."

She stomped the snow off her boots on the porch before she did. "Thanks, I promise I won't intrude for long."

Julia was someone that I didn't spend much time with, certainly not just the two of us. As Brooke's sister, and Cole's wife, you'd think I would have had double the reason, but they were so busy with work and their foster son who they were close to being able to adopt that it was hard for them to get out socially.

Not only that, but the first time I met Julia, I wasn't exactly friendly, so I still felt a certain level of unease around her, even though I knew she'd forgiven me for it. All I'd known of her was that she'd been gone for years, and my friend still loved her. When she came back to Denver, my worry about Cole had made me suspicious of her. Wary of her intentions. But she'd more than proven herself.

"Merry Christmas to you too," I said belatedly, as she unwound the red scarf she had wrapped over the top of her brownish blonde hair, in lieu of a hat.

"Cole asked if I could bring that over before we go to my parents for lunch. He's feeding Marcus and didn't want to relinquish his job."

I smiled, even though their admittedly adorable foster son's name being the same as Anna's ex still gave me pause. That thought was immediately followed by another, that we didn't have to deal with the asshole Marcus anymore, and now that name would only have good associations, the child that Cole and Julia had been waiting for the past eight years.

When I didn't immediately look in the bag, she gave me an expectant smile. "Oh, right, sorry."

There was an abundance of tissue paper sticking out the top of the bag, and she laughed when I stared at it for a beat, unsure of how to go about unwrapping whatever was in there.

"Just pull it out," she said with a patient smile.

I did as she asked, letting the green and red paper fall to the floor when I spied what was in the bottom of the bag. A beautifully frosted small cake and an ornament with little Marcus' picture, alongside a smiling Cole and Julia, framed inside a handprint, presumably Marcus', made with red paint. Very carefully, I pulled it out by the silver ribbon attached to the top and saw the words, Merry Christmas, from the Mallinsons.

I smiled at her, feeling the unwelcome but not unsurprising pinch of emotion in my throat. They'd waited for this for so long, and been through so much to come out the other side. In the picture, Marcus' tawny skin and wide, toothless smile was smooshed in between Cole and Julia's faces, and they all looked so happy that my voice was rough when I spoke.

"Thank you. If I had a tree, it would go right in the front."

She glanced around the room, laughing a little at my complete lack of decorations. "Oh well, maybe next year."

A year away. What would my life look like in a year? When I thought of next year, I couldn't see it, couldn't picture it, couldn't pretend like I was so sure anymore that I might be lucky enough to be sharing it with the person that I'd dreamt of for so long.

I set the bag down on the dining room table and let out a deep breath. I nodded slowly. "Yeah, maybe next year."

Julia watched me, rolling her lips in between her teeth for a moment while she did. "Tristan, can I ask you something? Not ask, I guess. But can I say something?"

Unable to stand, I pulled out one of my dining room chairs and gestured to it. Once she sat, I took my own seat at the head of the table. She placed her gloved hands on the table's surface and gave me a considering look.

"I don't know you very well, and I don't know Anna very well either, but it's almost impossible in this group of friends to not hear things, even with as absent as we've been the last few months." She licked her lips nervously. "And I know that your situation is different than what Cole and I went through. Very different," she clarified instantly when I raised my eyebrows. "But if I may, I might be able to offer you some insight from Anna's perspective."

I sat back and watched her warily, finally nodding when I wasn't exactly sure what to say to that.

"It's true that I've never been in her particular situation," Julia started slowly. When her eyes held mine, they were full of compassion, understanding. "But I do know what it feels like to be ... oh I'm trying to even think of the right word ... *overcome* by the depth of someone else's emotions for you. It's staggering to realize that there's a person out there who cares about you so much that they're willing to wait for you for so long, to put their happiness aside for your own. It's humbling, and honestly, a little terrifying to come to grips with. To figure out how to take this astonishing level of commitment from another person and try to fit yourself into it, especially when you've changed so much."

While I listened, I rolled my neck and struggled not to fidget in my chair. I knew she wasn't wrong, but it was hard to hear some of the words she chose.

Astonishing.

Humbling.

Terrifying.

Staggering.

Julia must have seen what was written over my face because she leaned forward and laid her hand on mine. "I'm not trying to scare you, I promise."

"It's not working," I admitted.

Her answering smile was kind. "What I'm trying to say is that she *will* figure out what she feels. I just wanted to tell you that my opinion—for what it's worth—is that you're doing the exact right thing by giving her space."

It was what I kept reminding myself when another day passed. When the sun rose and set with no indication of her feelings. Hearing it from Julia did help, because if there was anyone that I knew who could most empathize with Anna, it was her. Cole loved her for years, never knowing whether he'd ever see his ex-wife again. Didn't even know where she'd moved. I was the only person in our group of friends who didn't think him insane for it, actually. Probably because his level of devotion to Julia made me feel ... also not insane.

"Thank you, Julia."

She stood and smiled. "No thanks necessary. I should probably get back to my boys, or we're going to be late."

I lifted the bag that was still holding the cake. "And thanks for this, too. It'll probably end up being my lunch."

Julia laughed and slipped her scarf back on. "Oh, don't tell me that. It makes me want to feed you."

I found myself smiling, which felt good. "Don't worry too much. My mom sent me home with enough leftovers yesterday that I'll be set all week."

She sighed. "Good."

When I opened the door for her, I saw that the sun was shining brightly off the snow, and the wind had died down a bit. She smiled again before she walked back across the street. "Merry Christmas."

"Merry Christmas," I told her.

The fresh air felt good against my face and I breathed deeply before making my decision. I grabbed my coat and winter boots from the laundry room and shoved my hands into some gloves. Maybe a walk would do me good. Shake off some of the stagnancy that seemed to be brought on by my quiet day of inaction.

I closed the garage door behind me and took my time walking through the neighborhood. I passed a few families, some people walking their dogs, and everyone was smiling and friendly, holiday cheer like a brand they were all wearing.

My lungs expanded on each deep breath of bright, cold air and I felt my head clear. I wondered what Anna was doing today, whether she was spending time alone like me, or if she was with her family. Garrett and Rory's house was quiet and dark when I walked past it, so it was likely they were together.

But I tried as best as I could to not think about the future. To simply think about what was right in front of me. What was concrete and true. There was nothing for me to worry about at this point, because that wouldn't help. It was enough to recognize that waiting for Anna was hard, but ultimately worth it.

So instead of belaboring what was, I breathed and looked at Christmas lights strung along rooflines and draped over trees. For close to an hour, I walked around, until my stomach rumbled with an unhappy reminder that I hadn't eaten anything before Julia showed up.

But I felt good. Centered. Calm.

Until I turned the corner onto my street and saw Anna's SUV parked in my driveway. I stood perfectly still, because she was nowhere to be seen. All the calm that I'd felt moments earlier was gone. It fled in a rush, overcome by unstoppable hope.

It took everything in me not to sprint the rest of the way.

She must have used the spare key that I never felt like moving after she let herself in the first time, because she walked out of the side garage door that led to the porch, not realizing that I was only yards away. Hands propped up on her hips, she glared at her car.

"Mother effing stupid son of a bitch piece of shit vehicle. I have *always* hated you," she said loud enough that I could hear her on the sidewalk.

My smile was immediate, and I swallowed down a bark of laughter.

For a second, I stood there watching her, and when I felt like I had a slight leash on my emotions, I walked to her. Walked to Anna, who was here, waiting for me.

CHAPTER THIRTY

TRISTAN

"Car trouble?"

She whirled, hand on her chest. Her cheeks were pink, and she wore a white cap pulled down over her black hair. "Holy *crap*, Tristan. Where did you sneak up from?"

I jerked my chin over my shoulder. "I was out for a walk."

Anna took a deep breath and nodded. "It's a beautiful day."

"It is."

Why are you here?

Do you have any idea how much I've missed you?

Those were the things I wanted to say, but instead, I just moved closer to her, but left enough space between us that eventually she'd have to bridge the gap. If she wanted to.

She grimaced adorably and walked down the couple steps of my front porch, then gestured at her SUV. "I, ah, locked my keys in my car."

My lips curved up, and her eyes flicked down at them. "How'd you manage that? Did your car teleport into my driveway?"

Anna exhaled a laugh, tucking a piece of shining hair behind her ear underneath the soft fabric of her hat. If this was my Christmas present, if *she* was my Christmas present, I'd never ask for anything again for the rest of my life.

"No, smartass, I drove here. You didn't answer the door, or your phone, so I was going to leave your Christmas present inside."

For a brief moment, I imagined Anna herself wrapped in a bright red bow, perched on the kitchen counter, waiting for me and I fought the urge to smile like a crazy person. I loved how she looked in red.

I pulled off my gloves and patted my jacket, but found my pockets empty. "Must have left it inside. Sorry about that."

"No, I, ah, I should have called earlier to see if you'd be home." She sucked in a breath, her eyes wide and nervous in her face. My hands itched to cup her cheeks and draw her closer, like I could feel the pull of her, a magnet to every cell of blood that ran through me. "It is a holiday. It was silly to assume."

Why are you here?

Do you have any idea how much I've missed you?

We stood quietly in the snow, my eyes searching her face and hers searching mine before she smiled. "I guess you'll have to help me break into my own car to get your present."

I scratched my jaw and regarded her vehicle. "I suppose that depends on what's waiting for me. Julia already brought me a cake and a homemade ornament, so it better be good if I have to break into a locked vehicle for it."

My teasing made her jaw drop open slightly. Simply being in her presence like this, without a single inkling of what she came here to tell me, had me feeling almost high. Buoyant and effervescent in a way that was completely alien to me.

She straightened her shoulders and lifted her chin. "I suppose you'll have to wait and see." Then her shoulders drooped. "But I had this whole plan once I realized you weren't home. It was very dramatic and meaningful."

"Was it?" I murmured, taking a step closer to her. She did the same, holding my eyes as she took another.

"Very."

I pursed my lips and gave her a thoughtful look. "Will it be less dramatic and meaningful if you just tell me what it is?"

Anna reached out and shoved at my shoulder, smiling widely. "Of course! That's not how Christmas presents are supposed to work. *Telling* the person what it is isn't very fun."

As she was pulling her hand back, I snatched it in my own and she sucked in a quick breath. Her bare fingers were ice cold when I wrapped both hands around them. Slowly, watching her the entire time, I pulled them up to my mouth so I could blow warm air between my fingers, warming hers while I did.

Anna swallowed roughly, color flooding her face beautifully.

"Your hands are freezing," I whispered as I released her. For a moment, her hand hovered in the air before she dropped it.

"My gloves are in the passenger seat by the keys."

Why are you here?

Do you have any idea how much I've missed you?

I felt the words on the tip of my tongue, ready to jump out to her, but something about this small dance we were doing felt too important to rush. This weightless moment of *before*. Before something big. Before something possibly life-altering. Before she might be mine.

Because the way she was looking at me, that's what it felt like. It felt very much like we were existing in a state of anticipation, and neither of us knew how to propel forward into action. Into *after*. After she told me why she was here. After she told me what she'd decided. After, after, after.

"Maybe," Anna said quietly, "maybe I could warm up inside for a while."

Then she held out her hand to me.

Before and after. Concepts that couldn't be touched, couldn't be held. Except in moments like this, where my fingers wove through hers and I saw her eyes fill, felt my own burn at how perfectly they fit together.

I lead us to the house, and the strangest realization crept over me. My heart wasn't on the verge of exploding, wasn't pounding or racing or stuttering.

It was beating in a strong, steady rhythm behind my ribs. Never more sure. Never more certain.

And her fingers squeezed around mine when we reached the front door.

I went to dig my key out of my pocket when I paused. "It's already unlocked, isn't it?"

Anna gave me an embarrassed smile. "Maybe?"

Under my breath, I laughed. I was shaking my head when Anna turned to me and raised her free hand to cup my face. Her thumb traced the groove in my face that appeared only when I really smiled.

"I love it when you smile," she whispered shakily. "It makes me feel like I just earned something precious."

The breath I pulled in was ragged, and Anna heard it, because she dropped her hand to turn the door knob, leading me into my house. She was silent while she shut and locked the door behind us.

Because I was incapable of doing anything, apparently. Except watch her movements, confident and smooth and determined. She turned her back to me and started unbuttoning her coat. Just as she pulled it off her slim shoulders and draped it over the back of one dining room chair, reached up to remove her white hat, I felt the cord snap off my repeated thoughts.

"Anna," I rasped and her movements halted. "Why are you here?"

Do you have any idea how much I've missed you?

Calmly, she set the hat down on the table and turned to me again, her eyes finding mine unerringly. She knew exactly where to look, knew exactly how much I needed to see her face in that moment.

And what I saw there...

I saw my answer.

"I'm here for you," she said simply.

A tear hit my cheek, and Anna tilted her head as she walked to me. Slowly and sweetly, she reached up and swept it away with her thumb.

"I'm here for you," she repeated, taking my face in her hands and then pushing the cap off of my head. My eyes fell closed and I memorized the way her fingers felt over my skin, the way she traced them lightly over my brow bone, the line of my nose, my jaw. The edge of my lips.

My eyes opened and she was closer. Closer. Closer.

I lifted one hand to cup the back of her neck underneath the heavy curtain of her hair and she shivered at the possession in that grip. My thumb lay perfectly at the edge of her jaw and I drew my finger along that hard line of bone under the silk of her skin.

Her chin lifted and the weight of her breath hit my lips. "I am here for you, Tristan. For *you*."

I only spoke once before I kissed her, and it was to whisper her name.

"Anna."

My chin dipped to close the scant sliver of space in between us and I brushed my lips against hers. Just once. Her eyes fell closed and she leaned up to do the same. Her mouth was cool and firm, her top lip fitting between mine while we both breathed into the kiss.

She pulled back to smile at me, and my entire world rocked with the gentle curve of it. Hope exploded, and I wrapped my arms around her waist, drawing her flush against me so I could fit my mouth against her again. Anna whimpered at how tightly I was holding her, and my tongue brushed the edge of her lips.

Let me in.

She did. Her tongue swept against mine, slick and wet, and I fought not to growl into her mouth. Anna lifted up on tiptoe and gripped the back of my neck with a strength that surprised and thrilled me. I sank into her lips, sucking and tasting as our tongues tangled.

This. This kiss. Her lips against mine. Deep and hot and unending. It was the most powerful thing I'd ever felt, and I was stripped bare against it. She could have been wielding bullets and bombs, weapons that might have been dangerous before I experienced this kiss, and I would stand with arms wide open to take every single one of them if it meant that I could still own this kiss.

My armor was gone in her arms, I had no way, no will, no desire to protect myself against her, and we wound around each other, my hands trembling as I dug into her hair, let it wind silky and soft in between my fingers.

Her teeth scraped my bottom lip, and then I did growl. Against mine, her lips curved into a satisfied smile.

I pecked at her top lip, then her bottom lip, then each corner of her mouth. Her hips rocked against mine, and I walked us backward until her back met the wall.

Beneath my hands, she curved into my body like melted metal. Pliable and hot. I wanted to sink into her and never, ever leave.

I heard her sniff when I tilted my head to the side and deepened the kiss yet again. My head pulled back, and I saw a tear leak into her hairline. I kissed it off her skin before it disappeared, and she slid her hands underneath my coat, around my back and fisted my shirt in her small hands.

"Don't cry, my love," I whispered against her skin and she buried her forehead into my neck. "Don't cry."

"I've ... I've never felt..." her voice drifted off and she sniffed again. Her lips pressed against my throat, where my pulse hammered.

"What?" I said, tilting her chin so I could speak against her lips. Soft kisses. A harder press of my mouth against hers, which she met and gave back with sweet suction and slow licks of her tongue against my own.

A tease and a promise, and all I wanted was more.

Her voice was shaky. "This. I've never felt anything like this."

I slid my hand over her cheek and cupped the back of her head, pressing my forehead to hers as I rested my body against her, over her, around her. "Do you have any idea how much I've missed you?"

Instead of answering, she smiled, and her hands started to push my coat off my shoulders. I helped as best I could, but my hands didn't want to leave her body. Ever again. My coat hit the floor by our feet. Her hands smoothed over my chest, my shoulders, my biceps, and I had to close my eyes.

My entire body was on fire, trembling slightly at how out of control I felt.

"You could tell me," she said slowly, her hands stopping only when they reached the space over my heart. I clasped my hands over them and pressed them there. "Or I could tell you something instead."

"Tell me what?"

Desperate for her words, for her thoughts, for what she'd pondered and puzzled for the past two weeks, I held myself over her, her back still pressed against the wall.

That's when my phone buzzed. I ignored it easily, but Anna let out a breathy laugh that I captured with a soft kiss. Then another. She sighed into my mouth.

"Tell me," I said gently. "Whoever it is can wait."

"Even on Christmas?" she teased.

It buzzed again and I growled in frustration. "Even on Christmas. I don't care what day it is. Whoever, whatever it is, it can wait."

My fingers found their way underneath the back of her shirt to trace the bumps on her spine and she arched closer to me, our stomachs pressed tightly together. Anna closed her eyes and tilted her chin back. I nipped the curve of it with my teeth and she whimpered.

"It can wait," she agreed breathily.

This time, the buzzing was louder, angrier and I dropped my head into Anna's shoulder. She laughed as she wrapped her arms around me. "I am going to kill whoever that is."

Anna sighed, her hands moving in slow circles on my back. I wanted to arch into the soothing contact, something I'd only dreamt of from her. "It might be an emergency. Trust me on that."

Her dad. I knew she was thinking about her dad. I blew out a hard breath and straightened, taking a brief moment to look at the picture she made slumped against the wall like she was. Her hair was messy from my hands, her lips slightly swollen and pink, her cheeks flushed and her shirt un-tucked and crooked.

She was perfect.

When I walked to my phone, I heard the sound of her hitting her head against the wall and smiled. When I found where I'd left it on the counter, I saw three missed calls from Michael. As I picked it up, another started coming in and I swiped my thumb angrily to answer it.

"Yeah," I barked.

"Holy crap, dude, answer your phone much?"

"What do you want, Michael?"

"Geez," he muttered. "Merry Christmas to you too."

I closed my eyes and rolled my neck. "You have ten seconds to tell me if there's an emergency or I'm hanging up."

"It *is* an emergency."

"A real emergency or just something you think is one?"

A quiet laugh came from behind me.

Phone pressed to my ear, I turned to face Anna again, where she was still leaning up against the wall watching me. There was heat and promise in her dark, dark eyes, and I had to blink away to pay attention to Michael.

"It's a babysitting emergency."

I exhaled loudly. "I'm hanging up now."

"Tristan, come on, Mom was supposed be doing her friend thing but I guess she woke up with a fever today, and I forgot I promised Brooke I'd take her to a movie on Christmas Day which is like, one of her favorite traditions and aren't my kids so damn cute you just want fourteen of your own? I swear, you won't even know they're there."

Anna had started walking toward me, and I knew she could hear Michael because she was smiling widely. I narrowed my eyes at her. "Michael, no."

"Don't you remember how cute it was when Piper called you Uncle Tristan for the first time? Even your stone heart grew three sizes. Besides, you told me you had nothing to do today."

Nothing to do today. My eyes swept down the length of Anna's body, and she did the same to me. My mouth went dry when she started unbuttoning her shirt. The nimble movement of her fingers had me transfixed, with each sliver of skin she uncovered had my heart skipping into the unsteady rhythm that I'd expected earlier.

"No, Michael," I repeated more firmly.

"You still haven't said why."

"I'm hanging up now."

Anna's shirt fell off her shoulders, and underneath it was a simple ivory camisole. With nothing underneath. I knew from the shadows of her nipples, the curve of her breasts. Against it, the sleek lines of her skin glowed. I disconnected the call and tossed my phone with a loud clatter.

"As I was saying," Anna said like we hadn't been interrupted. I took a step toward her, and she backed away as her hands went to the button of her black pants. "I think I should tell you something instead."

When she pushed her pants down until they rested along the tops of her slender hips, I worked to swallow.

"You are making it difficult for me to pay attention to what you're saying."

Anna's smile was temptation and sex and amusement and I found myself mirroring it.

"I'm sorry."

"No, you're not," I said, working on the buttons of my own shirt. "If we're going to stand here not touching, you better start talking, or I'll find a way to make you," I threatened.

She laughed deep in her throat and my skin tightened in response. "Yeah?"

I hissed in a breath through clenched teeth when she pushed her pants down with slow, teasing motions before kicking them away. My own personal striptease.

"Then you'll have to catch me first."

I narrowed my eyes and her smile grew. I lunged, which she wasn't expecting, because she shrieked in laughter when I caught her by the waist and hoisted her easily into my arms. With one arm under her knees, one around her back, her arms looped around my neck, I carried her down the hallway, her laughter bouncing off the walls, and I realized that I'd never wanted a quiet house at all.

All I'd been waiting for was her to fill it with her happy sounds.

To fill me up with the same.

There was a moment where I paused before carrying her through the doorway and into my bedroom. Should we have talked first? I still didn't know exactly what had happened during the last two weeks, what had made her show up today.

"What is it?" she asked quietly, sliding her fingers slowly against the skin at the back of my neck.

I tried to gather my scattered thoughts in a way that would sound simplified, pared down to what was most important. Briefly, I gave a meaningful look into the room beyond us, only one lamp lighting it. "This changes things."

She smiled in understanding and tilted her chin up to kiss me sweetly. I felt it gather like a ball of light, somewhere deep in the pit of my belly. Just as our tongues touched and I held her even more tightly against my chest, Anna pulled back.

"I want to feel your skin on mine, Tristan." She held my eyes, and I saw the truth in them. "All I want is for you to hold me while

I tell you everything. Can we do that?"

My answer was to take two long strides forward and kick the bedroom door shut behind us, closing out the world, closing out everything except me and the woman I loved.

CHAPTER THIRTY-ONE

ANNA

He carried me like I weighed nothing, and underneath me, I could feel the shifting and bunching of his muscles. Where my inner vixen had come from while he was on the phone with Michael, I had no freaking clue. At that point, I was acting on sheer instinct.

The shift had gone from heavy and emotional to playful when I heard his clipped answers and growls to whatever Michael had asked of him on the phone. His eyes, when he was across the room, felt like slow drags of his fingers over my skin. That's when I started unbuttoning my shirt.

There'd been no second guessing, no questioning, because it was him. The moods we'd already captured in just a few short minutes eclipsed anything I'd ever felt before. Heat—unbearable, incendiary heat—and laughter. Sweet, skin-splitting happiness all mixed in.

This. This is what I'd been missing for so many years.

Before he released me, Tristan nuzzled his mouth to my jaw and breathed in deeply against my skin. Goose bumps popped over my arms, but not because I was cold. There was so much heat coming from his body that I felt like cold would never touch me again. He'd make me impervious to it, just by being near me.

Desperate for the touch of his mouth, I sought his lips with mine, and reveled in his immediate response. His tongue against mine, his lips pressing and moving perfectly with mine. His arm moved, and suddenly my feet were on the ground, but only long enough for him to run his hands up and down my back over my camisole.

Against my bare skin, the rasp of his shirt felt decadent and naughty. Underneath the silk of my top, my breasts felt heavy and tender.

My fingers traced the V of his throat before I leaned in to place a single kiss there. His skin was hot underneath my lips and I lingered, because his scent was perfect; spicy and clean and Tristan. Softly, I allowed my teeth to nip at the edge of his collarbone, and his hands tightened around my hips, fingers digging underneath the edge of my underwear.

"Anna," he whispered and I glanced up at him. It made me feel powerful, the way he looked at me. I felt impossibly free wrapped in the hard circle of his arms.

"Shirt off, please," I said, working my fingers underneath the hem of soft cotton. The pads of my fingers found hard muscle and hot skin and my eyes wanted to devour it as much as my mouth did. "I just want to feel you."

His lips, those talented lips, curved into a half-smile and I found myself grinning. I couldn't help it. Any time I saw his face transform with such slight movements, I felt more joy, more happiness than seemed possible.

Mmm, and then my joy shifted to something darker and lower in my body, a black spark of heat that spread over my entire body, because he did that guy thing where they reach behind their head to yank their shirts off. When he tossed it aside, I let out a deep, contented sigh.

He was *perfect*.

Hard muscle, stacks on either side of his stomach that I drew the tip of my pointer finger between, a deep V on either side of his hips leading down into jeans. This was a *man*. His frame was big and imposing, roped with muscles and veins and ink. Someone who earned his strength with hard work. I wanted to devour every inch of him, so viscerally that I almost felt possessed.

I stepped into him and pressed my nose against the skin directly between his pecs and inhaled greedily, my hands lightly running up and down his arms. He held himself so carefully in check, allowing me to explore, allowing me to touch and look my fill. When my fingers traced along his palms, the length of his long fingers, they curled up against my own.

By the heat in his eyes, I knew that he'd get his turn soon. And more than anything, I wanted to see this man undone. My man undone.

I blinked for a moment, because he'd said something before we came into the room. Something important.

This changes things.

"I had a whole speech prepared," I told him suddenly.

The sudden shift in topic—even though my hands were still on his skin and I hadn't pulled away—played out over his face. First confusion, then sweet, sweet warmth. Affection, followed by heady desire.

"Did you?"

His voice was a rumble, like a bass drum behind my sternum. It made every bone in my body vibrate tightly. I nodded.

Tristan took a step, forcing me backwards. Then another, until the backs of my legs hit the edge of his massive bed. When I sat and looked up at him, he planted his fists on either sides of my hips and gave me a hot, searching kiss, sweeping his tongue into my mouth until I had no choice to bend my back to meet the force of it. Match it and give him the same heat back.

"What was it?" he said against my mouth.

"Wh-what?"

My dazed response elicited a single breath of air, maybe a laugh, I couldn't be sure, because I was practically yanking him down on top of me. I needed more. More kisses. More skin. More of his weight on top of me. Just ... more. More of him.

Against my neck, he spoke again. "Your speech." He bit the tendon on my shoulder and my entire body shivered.

"Oh, umm, it was really..." I gasped when he used his hands to scoop underneath my arms and toss me higher on his bed. My legs fell open and he all but prowled on top of me to fit himself in between them. "It was *really* good."

"Yeah?" He bent his head and nosed up the edge of my camisole so he could kiss my belly button. His tongue dipped inside and I gasped, arching up underneath him.

"Uh-huh." My fingers dug into the muscles of his back and he hissed when I scratched down the length of his spine. My brain couldn't focus on anything except where his mouth trailed, soft, sucking kisses that landed on each hip bone. My hands dug into his hair when his tongue followed the top edge of my underwear. "Tristan," I breathed, not entirely sure what I was pleading for.

He gripped my hands in his as he came up over me, and pinned my arms above my head, kissing me deeply until I was writhing and whimpering. My legs came up around him so I could try and find purchase, find a way to ease what was building and tightening inside of me.

Tristan spoke into my ear, the drag of his lips against the sensitive skin there making my thighs tighten painfully against the roughness of his jeans still around his hips. "I'm sure it's incredible."

I squirmed. "What's incredible?"

Besides his mouth. His hands. His smell. His tongue. And oh, the hard ridge pressing against me when we moved together.

His mouth widened against my cheek, a broad smile that I quickly turned my head to see. His teeth flashed against the dark backdrop of his beard. I yanked my hands out from under his and shoved at his shoulder.

"You're teasing me," I laughed.

Tristan's eyes searched mine before he nodded. "I am."

Then he got right back to it.

I sucked in a breath through gritted teeth when he dragged his nose down the length of my throat, then used his teeth to pull down the straps of my camisole until they were hanging off my shoulders. When I imagined how this would play out—rushed hands, deep kisses, clothes flying—it all made sense.

But this? This drawn out torment, this slow, excruciating unveiling had never made an appearance in my mind. His body above me trembled slightly with each new part of my body that he tasted. I could feel the vibration underneath my hands when I was conscious enough to feel his own reaction beyond what he was doing to me.

Suddenly, I wanted to know what he felt. Focus on Tristan's responses to his hands on my body, his mouth on my skin. I pressed my fingers down the length of his back and arched up when his mouth closed over my breast, still covered in silk. His frame shook under my hands and a sound came from deep within his chest, the kind you can only make when you're not thinking about how you sound or whether anyone can hear you. Pure feeling, unconscious emotion dragged straight from your heart with a yank and a pull.

How was he being so patient? I'd never experienced it like this, intimacy that was meant to draw out the pleasure and extend it beyond what you thought your body could handle before someone snapped, before something broke open in screaming, back-arching relief.

"I- I still haven't told you anything," I stammered when he pulled the camisole up with the tip of one finger and blew lightly over the skin he unveiled. I covered my mouth with my hand and tried not to groan in frustration and sweet, toe-curling pleasure. It was official; Tristan Whitfield would be the death of me. Here lies Anna Calder. Death by foreplay.

He ignored me and kissed down my rib cage, like each curved

bone was precious to him, important to what he was doing. Then he set his chin there and stared up at me. "Right now, I only need to know one thing. Just one, and then I'll give you what you need, take what I do too."

Yes. That, please. Just that.

I nodded frantically. "One thing. Oh, please just tell me, what's the one thing?"

Tristan moved, the muscles in his arms popping deliciously as he held himself over me, bracketing my head with his forearms. His eyes, dark and direct, held my own as I relished in his heavy weight on top of me.

"Are you mine?" he asked slowly, meaningfully. No further explanation as we laid there together, he didn't dip down and kiss me after he said the words. He simply watched my face, saw the way I smiled softly, and his eyes warmed in response.

I smoothed a hand up the side of his neck, dragged my fingers through his beard and traced the line of his lips. I knew what he was asking me. I understood the subtext of those three little words. He wasn't asking me if I was in love with him yet, wasn't expecting me to be in the place that he'd been emotionally for so long.

He was asking me if he could trust what this meant to me, to be here with him like this. He was asking if I was willing to trust the same thing from him. This wasn't just sex, to either of us. To him, and to me, this was a vow for more. It was all the things I'd had to reckon with, before I got in my car and drove here, that I could be sure of what my answer would be at the moment he asked it.

And I was.

Slowly, I pulled his face down to mine and kissed him gently. His eyes pinched shut and he repeated the press of our lips. Neither of us deepened the kiss. When he pulled back, I held his eyes.

"I'm yours, Tristan."

After I said it, everything took on a slow, decadent quality. His kisses felt more lush and wet, the way he moved against me harder and more intentional. The skin over my bones felt tight and sensitive, every brush of his fingers triggering a slow roll of fire that I could feel down to my toes.

My hands searched for the loop of his belt and he pushed down my underwear while I did, using his hands between my legs so deftly, with such skill, that I cried out after only a few moments.

We didn't bother getting under the covers, me because I couldn't imagine possibly needing more heat than what Tristan himself generated, and him because he whispered over and over against my skin that he just wanted to see more and taste more and touch more.

When he finally kicked off his jeans, he was naked underneath, and my camisole was quickly tossed to the floor. For a moment, Tristan pressed his forehead against my chest and just breathed, his hands trembling against my hips and his mouth open against my skin.

"It's like I can't see enough, I can't open my eyes wide enough to see all of you," he whispered, and I tilted my chin up toward the ceiling, struggling to contain the violent heat I felt at those words.

With my heel pressed to the bed, I rolled us over so that I was straddling him. My hands braced on his chest and I sat up straight, my hair brushing down the length of my back. His brow was pinched, almost like he was in pain while he looked at me.

"Is this better?" I asked, moving my hips in slow circles, even though we were still teasing, still delaying the inevitable.

He shook his head and slid a palm up my belly, between my breasts and curved it around the back of my neck. His other hand gripped me tightly, the thumb pressed into the sensitive skin underneath the jut of my hip bone. "You're so beautiful."

I leaned down and kissed him, and he wrapped his arms around my back, clutching me tightly to him. My hands cupped his face and we rolled again so I was on my back under him, Tristan drawing my knee up against his side.

Against my mouth, he whispered, "I love you."

And then he was inside me, one sure, slow thrust and we both groaned. He held that way, and I hugged his neck so tightly that I was afraid he'd think I was in pain.

Tristan began to move, and oh, he could move.

Our kisses were tongue and teeth, messy and deep and searching and full of harsh exhales and whispered expletives when it only took me a few minutes to tense up, the sweet silvery threads of release making me clutch around him and cry his name. Tristan's forehead was tight to mine as he chased his own finish, my name repeating endlessly on his lips when he did.

"Anna, Anna, *Anna*."

As I held him close, never in my life had I felt more safe or cherished or perfect. Tristan slumped against me and gathered me even more tightly to his heart with hard, muscular arms and hands that couldn't stop moving over my skin. I was shaking, and so was he, and it was all I could do not to burst into tears.

He pulled back and held my cheek, emotion making his face tight and wild and impossibly handsome.

"You really should look more relaxed right now," I teased, leaning up to give him a soft kiss. We lingered for a moment and his hand made a soothing line up and down my back.

Tristan exhaled roughly. "I was just trying to figure how we can manage staying in this bed for the next week without anyone noticing."

I laughed and kissed him again. "I think we can figure something out."

CHAPTER THIRTY-TWO

ANNA

"You could give me your speech."

"Now?"

Tristan stretched and groaned, rolling to his side and pulling me so that I was tucked perfectly underneath his chin. My fingers traced lines on his chest and I breathed deeply. I pulled my knee up and laid it over his leg while his hand covered my shoulder.

We fit. It was as simple as that.

I took a deep breath and thought over the words that I'd practiced, in my head and out loud. "Well, it will lose some of the impact given that my Christmas present for you is still locked in the back of my car."

His broad frame shook with silent laughter. "You never told me what it was."

My mouth found the skin over his heart and I hovered there for a moment before pressing a soft kiss to where I could feel the thrumming underneath my lips, steady and sure and strong. Just like him.

"I had this grand idea," I said, briefly looking up and smiling. "I *was* going to attempt to build a bench for your deck. One where we could sit together and talk about our day. Just like you'd imagined we would."

Tristan leaned back so he could see my face better, a bemused smile curling his mouth. "Yeah?"

"It didn't work out so well. Apparently, woodworking is a very tough skill to master."

He laughed out loud, a wide smile splitting his face in two. When would I lose the desire to feel those smiles under my fingertips? Never, I hoped.

"When that didn't work," I continued, "I ordered this massive porch swing made of metal and plastic, with a huge canopy and drink holders and cushions and oh, it's ridiculous and gaudy compared to what you could make. And then, the box was so heavy that I had to pay my neighbor's son and his friend to load it into my car because I couldn't lift it by myself."

He kissed my forehead, and I could feel his wide smile against my skin. "What was your plan for when you got it here?"

I sighed. "I hadn't quite figured that out yet." My arm tucked around his waist, and I couldn't help but marvel at the length of his torso, the shifting muscles underneath me and the way that he was so comfortable in his own skin. We were completely naked, over the covers of his bed, and he showed no sign that he wanted to move anytime soon. "I was too busy practicing what I was going to say to think about the bench, or leaving my car keys on the passenger seat apparently."

Again, he laughed under his breath and I added it to the mental tally of how many times he'd smiled and laughed since I held out my hand to him in the driveway. This was the part I loved the most, seeing this new, warm side of him.

Because he was happy.

Unrehearsed, and nothing like what I'd practiced, the words I hadn't been able to say started to flow.

"I knew that if I came here—came to you—that I had to be all in. It was as much about me and what I'd been through, as it was about what you told me. That's the realization I needed to come to. I believed what you'd told me as soon as you said it, I didn't doubt your feelings, the strength or depth of them. But it was about us being equal parts of this. Not me always feeling behind or like I was wrong for not being at the same place as you, at the same time, knowing that I could match your commitment to what we could be, and know that I meant it with every part of who I am."

Tristan held me tighter, breathed in deeply against the top of my head, but he didn't interrupt me.

"It was waking up one day and knowing that I didn't want to try life without you anymore. What I wanted was a life with you in it. Where I would wake up every day, secure in the knowledge that we were each other's. Not just you being mine, me being yours. But us together." I set my chin on his chest and watched his face. "Does that make sense?"

He swallowed roughly and nodded. "Yeah."

"You've been alone in this for so long, Tristan," I whispered, feeling tears build against my will. "And I don't feel pity for you, or embarrassment for not seeing it earlier, because any earlier and it wouldn't have worked the way it did. Maybe you should've talked to me about it at some point, but you didn't make that decision to be manipulative or selfish, to coerce me into something I wasn't ready for, and you weren't wrong about me needing time."

"I should've respected you enough to be honest with you though," he interrupted. "Maybe it wasn't manipulative, but it certainly wasn't my bravest decision."

Shifting up so I could reach his mouth, I kissed him again. "Any time you choose to love someone, it's brave, because it gives them the power to hurt you. Believe me, I've lived the last handful of years in self-protection mode, because getting hurt was harder than numbing myself to it. And you, choosing every single day to continue risking your heart for something that had no promise of a return is one of the bravest things I can imagine, no matter when you finally told me. Once I trusted in that, once I recognized it and knew that I wanted any piece of you that I could get, I knew that I needed to be here. Needed to risk that you might tell me it was too late."

He shook his head. "You think I would've ever said that?"

I smiled. "I didn't think you would, no."

Tristan rolled so that he was on top of me again and I grinned happily, shifting my thighs against his, loving the feel of his coarse leg hair against my smooth legs. A week in bed sounded like an excellent idea, because already, I missed him. I needed him, wanted him, felt desperate for him.

He kissed me sweetly and I wound my arms around his neck when he tilted his head to deepen it. I made a mewling sound into his mouth when he sucked on my tongue. Then my stomach growled loudly. Mouth still over mine, Tristan laughed.

"Do you need me to feed you?"

I licked my lips, and they touched his in the process, which made him hiss in a breath through gritted teeth. "Maybe. Do you cook?"

"Not well. You?"

Humming contentedly, I arched my back and our stomachs pressed together. "Oh, I can manage a few things all right."

Tristan narrowed his eyes, knowing exactly what I was doing. "Food first." He pressed a hard, fast kiss to my mouth and then smacked my bottom. I squealed and he gave me a smirk so dangerous, so sexy that I had to clench my thighs together. "Then bed again. For the rest of the day."

TRISTAN

Coming in from the garage, I blew warm air in between my cupped hands. After using an old coat hanger trick to unlock her car, Anna's vehicle was moved in next to my truck so that it didn't gather more snow, and also so that my nosy-ass friends who all lived within two streets of me didn't have anything to gawk at this first blissful day that she and I got to experience.

Bliss.

It was a lighter feeling than I expected. Turning the corner from the mudroom into the open kitchen, I felt like I'd lost a hundred pounds of iron from my frame. Especially as I stopped to watch Anna stand in front of the stove top range, where she hummed carols and flipped perfectly golden pancakes on the griddle I didn't remember owning.

A late Christmas meal when you were staying in demanded breakfast for dinner, according to her. The smell of bacon permeated the room, the sweetness of the pancakes was just behind it. She wore my t-shirt and her black hair was tangled, pulled back into a high ponytail. Her legs were bare, as were her feet.

Against the sudden wave of happiness, of peace, I had to close my eyes. The lightness inside of me was almost disorienting in its foreignness.

Anna must have sensed me watching her, because she glanced over her shoulder and smiled. "Ready to eat?"

My eyes tracked slowly down her body, and she blushed furiously in response.

"Pancakes, Tristan. Are you ready to eat *pancakes*?"

"I 'spose," I said and walked over to her. I peeled off my coat and tossed it over the back of the couch. As I stepped behind her and buried my head into her neck, she sighed happily.

"You're going to distract me again. I almost burned the bacon earlier when you did that thing with your hand."

Her breathy voice made me grin wickedly. The hand of which

she spoke slipped underneath the hem of the shirt and I traced the edge of her underwear before sliding my fingers under the silky fabric.

"This?"

Anna's chin lifted and she turned to kiss me, making a sound into my mouth that I could taste on my tongue. "That," she moaned when she broke off the kiss.

"I have *years* of imagining what I'd do to you if I ever got you here, Anna," I whispered, biting her bottom lip. "You better get used to being distracted."

The thing I loved most is that I could see in her eyes that she wasn't intimidated by my honesty. The things that I used to choke on were there with readiness and ease. The things that were impossible to imagine verbalizing rolled easily off my tongue.

Since I really was starving, and I knew she was too, I gave her one last kiss and backed away so she could finish the pancakes. Pulling two plates down from the cupboard, I had a bizarre moment where I wondered if this was really happening. She looked real enough, mussed and disheveled and grinning down at the food she was making for us. The twinge I felt in my thirty-six year old hip from the second round against the wall in the family room felt real enough.

But I couldn't have done anything to deserve this. Nothing that I'd accomplished or given that was remotely at the level of earning her presence in my life.

With graceful movements that belied her experience and love for being in the kitchen, Anna served up two pancakes for each of us, my battered spatula getting more use in the last thirty minutes than it probably had in the last six months. She popped a piece of bacon in her mouth before she looked up at me.

"How many?"

"Four, please."

She raised an eyebrow. "Are you a growing boy?"

I narrowed my eyes and she laughed. When she sat down on

the couch, she tucked a bare leg underneath her and faced me. The pancakes were light and fluffy and I shook my head when I demolished half of one in only a few bites.

"You'll be making these a lot," I told her.

"Oh yeah?"

"Yeah."

Anna finished chewing a bite and gave me a thoughtful look. "Favorite movie?"

I balanced my plate in my lap and reached out to tug her leg so that it was stretched out toward me. My free hand ran up and down her smooth shin. "*Cinderella Man.*"

"Great movie. I think I've only seen it once, though."

I took a bite of bacon and jerked my chin in her direction. "Same question."

"Mmm." Her fingers found mine on her leg and she drew circles over my knuckles. "*Mary Poppins.*"

My eyebrows popped up, not expecting that answer, but loving that she surprised me. "Why?"

"I loved it as a little girl, but when I watched it again in college, I just ... fell in love with it for completely different reasons." Her eyes lit up as she spoke, and I stopped eating to watch everything play over her face. "Mary Poppins is the ultimate hero to me. She's tough and firm and loving, she knows who she is and doesn't apologize for it. And she's selfless. She doesn't want to leave the family, but she does because she knows that she made them better, made them stronger, and left a bit of herself there in the process."

"Maybe we should watch it later," I found myself saying. "New Christmas tradition."

"Yeah?" she asked with a tiny, hopeful smile.

When I nodded slowly, she must have seen the weight of my emotions shift in my face, the set of my shoulders. Anna set her plate to the side and then leaned forward to take mine and set it on the coffee table.

Nimbly, she crawled over my legs and set herself in my lap so that she could smooth her hands over my shoulders and behind my neck. My hands landed naturally on her thighs and I loved the way her skin was under my hands, warm and firm.

She bit her lip and looked around. "And maybe a Christmas tree next year? Right in the corner by the slider."

"You think so?" My hands worked their way up her naked back and she inched closer.

"Mmmhmm. And we can have pancakes and bacon before we watch *Mary Poppins* and *Cinderella Man*."

As I inhaled, I leaned forward and kissed her slowly. She didn't hurry the way our lips met over and over. Didn't move in my lap in a way that would entice or seduce. She was just there, right there with me, feeling exactly what I felt as we talked about a future that suddenly felt clear and vivid and bright and perfect.

I knew she couldn't say yet that she loved me. It was too soon for that. And even if no one believed me when I said that, I meant it. Her being there, her understanding what I felt and not just accepting it, but embracing it, reveling in it, meant more to me than her forcing words simply because she thought I'd want to hear them.

Anna hugged me tightly and her slight frame shivered when I whispered into her ear. "I love you."

The way she lifted her head and looked into my eyes, not shying away from what I'd said, not acting like she was hiding from it or afraid of it, that's why I was okay with her not saying it back. And her smile, her brilliant, sweet smile, was a salve to my heart after so many years of being without her.

"I think you're the best Christmas present I've ever gotten," she said. "The best *anything* I've ever gotten."

I kissed her again, chuckling under my breath. "I'll wrap a red bow around myself next year."

She tilted her head back and laughed loudly. "Now *that* I like the sound of."

While she sat contentedly in my lap, we finished our food. Once she'd set her plate down, she shifted so that she was tucked in between me and the couch, my arm wrapped around her shoulder.

Her fingers picked at the buttons of my shirt before I felt her pull in a deep breath. That, I was learning, was a sign she was about to ask me something.

When she did, her voice was quiet, a soft pleading tone that made me want to scoop her up and never let her go. Though that was the plan anyway. "What other traditions will we have?"

"On Christmas?"

She shook her head. "Every day. Monday morning. Sunday night. Just normal days."

I hummed when I felt the weight of that question hit me square in the chest.

What will our life be like together?

That's what she was asking. That's when I realized that whether I felt like I'd done something to deserve her in my life or not, it didn't matter. Maybe I'd never deserve her, just like she'd never deserve the way I'd loved her all these years. It wasn't a checklist that you could tick off, a list of acts that you could complete to earn enough points. It was love. And none of us truly deserved it, but the right person would always give it freely.

My fingers found the curve of her chin and I gently tilted her face toward me. "Monday mornings, I'll make you your coffee and bring it to you in bed, and it'll get cold on the nightstand while I wake you up."

Her smile was slow and sweet, which was exactly how I saw Monday mornings turning out. "Tuesdays?"

"Tuesdays you'll bring me lunch at work because we won't be able to wait to see each other until we're done."

"We sound *very* desperate to be around each other."

I kissed the tip of her nose. "We are."

"Maybe on Wednesdays I could always make you dinner at my place, and you could stay the night in my too-small bed."

"I don't mind too-small beds, especially if you're in it with me."

"Thursdays, I'll return the favor and make you coffee in the morning, bring it to you while you're in the shower, and it will go cold on the bathroom counter."

"You gonna make sure my back is all scrubbed up?" I murmured against the top of her head, overcome by the pictures running through my mind. Not even the passion behind the words, but the intimacy that was implied. It knocked the breath out of me.

"Of course," she said on a laugh.

"Friday nights we'll cook together, but we're only allowed to wear our underwear."

"That sounds incredibly dangerous," she said with mock sincerity.

"Saturdays you can show me your favorite places to go, and then I'll do the same. We'll sit on the porch swing you bought and talk about the things we saw. Sundays we'll stay under the blankets and watch movies and visit our families and see our friends and maybe find a dog we can take on hikes." As I spoke, my voice deepened, and Anna's eyes filled. "And we'll probably fight sometimes. We'll always make up though. We'll live, Anna. And we'll be happy."

It took her a second to answer, and she swallowed a couple times before she did.

"I've always wanted a dog," she said in a shaky voice.

I smiled. "Yeah?"

Anna nodded. Her hands held the back of my neck and her eyes were serious when they gazed into mine. "And I've always wanted that life. I just *wish* that I'd known sooner that I wanted it with you."

She curled into my arms and I pressed my chin to the top of her head, my eyes closed and my heart full.

"We get to start it now," I said quietly. "And that's all that matters."

CHAPTER THIRTY-THREE

ANNA

It shouldn't have surprised me that on the Monday morning that followed, Tristan woke me up by bringing me coffee while I was still cocooned under the heavy covers of his massive bed. And he was right, it did go cold on the nightstand.

Monday mornings with Tristan were *good*. Multiples good.

It also shouldn't have surprised me that on Tuesday, I brought him lunch and we sat in his shop, discussing the delivery of all his finished items for Millie's house, each one more stunning than the last.

Wednesday, I made him bulgogi, the only Korean dish I'd ever managed to master, and watched him wander around my place as he made sure everything was in good condition. He slept in my too-small bed and neither of us had a single issue with the amount of mattress space we were forced to share.

Thursday, I brought him coffee while he took a shower. It went cold, but his back was completely clean by the time we got out. My skin was pruney, and I conked my skull on the showerhead when he lifted me against the tiles. But we laughed so hard that he almost slipped and fell, so it was worth it.

Each day of that following week played out with an ease that was almost impossible to believe, through the weekend where we stayed in due to lots and lots of snow. It was exactly what we needed, like every day was a different kind of first date, a side of the other person being shown that we very much wanted to discover.

We hadn't shared with our friends yet, mainly because we hadn't seen them. The holidays were busy for everyone, so nothing about it felt like we were keeping a secret, or purposely keeping our relationship under wraps.

Every day, he told me he loved me, and every day, I knew that I was falling in love with him right back.

That was something I realized on a Saturday night, a week after I'd shown up at his place, as we got ready for Kat and Dylan's engagement party at his house. My dress was short, bright pink and fitted, with long sleeves and deep V in the back. He was straightening a dark gray vest over a white dress shirt, the sleeves rolled up to show the ink on his arms. Occasionally, we'd lock eyes in the mirror and he'd give me that smirk.

I knew it well now.

It was the smirk he gave me when he was about ready to throw me back on the bed. Honestly, after seven days with Tristan, it was a miracle I could still walk in a straight line. Or walk at all, actually.

"Tonight is a pretty big deal," I said, ignoring the smirk and adding a bit more blush on my cheeks.

"Yup. I'm happy for them." He lifted his chin and fidgeted with the collar of his shirt.

Quietly, I sucked in a deep breath and saw him notice, saw him narrow his eyes.

"What is it?" he asked.

Damn him and his perceptiveness. I set the blush down and perched my hip on the bathroom counter. "I think, just for tonight, we should wait to tell everyone that we're together."

His hands froze and he gave me an incredulous look. Or incredulous for Tristan. Basically his eyes widened slightly and that was about it. But for him, I knew what it meant.

"Tonight is about Kat and Dylan, and they've been together for so long, I don't want to detract from what the party is about." I slid in front of him, settling myself between him and the counter while he gave me a steady look. My hands smoothed up his chest, stopped when I could feel the comforting thump of his heart under my palms. "Just for tonight. Tomorrow we can shout it from the rooftops."

"You really think they'd be bothered?"

"No," I said, worried he would take this wrong, but it had been weighing on me all day at work. "It's like … the unspoken rule that you don't wear white to someone else's wedding, or get engaged at their reception."

His eyes, warm and golden in the bright bathroom light, searched my face and then softened. "You don't want to be the center of attention tonight."

The sigh that left my mouth couldn't be stopped. "It's not even really that. I just … they should be the center of attention. At least for tonight." Tristan still wasn't sold, or at least, even worse, he might have been disappointed. And that was the very last thing I wanted him to feel in me. I felt myself waffle as I stared at the notch at the base of his throat. Dylan and Kat wouldn't be mad. Would they? Everyone would be happy for us, I knew that like I knew my name.

"You're right," he grumbled.

My eyes lifted. "You're not just saying that to appease me?"

The edge of his thumb pressed deliciously against my hip bone, and I felt the corresponding zip up my spine that he could elicit with one simple touch.

"No." It was all he said, but I was learning with him that that was okay. If it was important to him that I knew more than that, he would've elaborated. Which is why I didn't push for more than that. "But … you'll owe me for my silence."

One of my brows lifted slightly and I arched my hip into his hand. "You think so?"

Tristan lifted me onto the bathroom counter and I opened my legs as far as the short skirt allowed so he could step in between them. This man. I never thought I could feel so wanted. So sexy. Whether I was in pajamas or lingerie or a beautiful dress, he made me feel like the most beautiful woman in the world.

He stepped closer and carefully pulled my hair over one shoulder so he could kiss my neck lightly. Then he dragged his nose up my throat until he could kiss the edge of my jaw. "For hours. You'll owe me for *hours*. Whatever I say goes."

His laugh was husky and slow when I shivered. Diabolical man. "Sounds like an even trade to me."

Tristan's teeth nipped at my bottom lip and I wound my hands around his neck.

"Great." He backed up so quickly that I almost fell off the counter, even though I was achy and wanting. My mouth dropped open slightly. He gestured to the door. "Don't we have to leave?"

"Wh-" I stammered. "Now?"

Tristan lifted his wrist to look at his large watch and then shrugged. "Might be traffic."

For the first time in my entire adult life, I pouted. He tipped his head back and laughed, the deep dimple in the side of his face making one of its very rare appearances.

That small dent in his skin, the deep sound coming from his chest made something in my heart clench, something sweet and profound and absolute. That was when I knew that if I made it another week without falling completely in love with him, it would be a mother effing miracle.

When I realized he was serious about leaving, I sighed and walked out of the bathroom after him. He helped me into my coat before we walked into the garage, and then opened the passenger door for me. As I watched him climb into the truck, neither one of us commented on the massive flaw in my plan to keep this under wraps, given that if anyone saw us drive in together, it would be a pretty damn big clue. But he stayed quiet, resting one large hand on my thigh as he drove, his other wrist resting casually on the top of the steering wheel.

Often while we drove, the radio stayed off, because we were usually talking. Tonight, it was quiet, and that felt okay too.

After about ten minutes, he turned to me when we were stopped at a red light. "I forgot to tell you earlier, but you look beautiful tonight."

I sank further into the seat. Melted, actually. Because of how dark it was outside, Tristan's face was difficult to see, and the hard line of his jaw was in shadows. His lips were too, but I saw his smile all the same. I smiled at him and laid my hand on top of his.

"Thank you," I replied quietly.

He looked forward again, lifted my hand so he could press a kiss to the back of it.

Little did I know that the real torture of the evening wouldn't start until he walked in the door only a few minutes after he dropped me at the front of the bar. An upscale sports bar might have been an odd choice for an engagement party, but Dylan managed the place, and it's where he and Kat met, so it felt appropriate that they closed early one night in honor of the couple, and it was filled with happy, smiling, laughing people when I entered through the large archway into the main dining room.

I saw Kat and Dylan first, and couldn't help but grin at how happy they looked. He was so tall, with dark hair and bright blue eyes. As they stood talking to someone I didn't recognize, he had his arm proudly around Kat's shoulder, laughing at whatever story she was telling. Her arms were waving frantically, her normally messy blonde bob hair sleek and straight down to her shoulders.

When she caught sight of me, she smiled in apology at the person in front of her, and practically skipped in my direction.

"You made it! Oh, you look amazing, Anna." Her eyes were huge in her face when she held my hands. "Like, glowing."

My cheeks heated. Multiple orgasms every single day will do that to a girl, but I simply smiled. "You are too. Now let me see that ring again. I didn't look closely enough when we were at the bar."

I was oohing and aahing over her beautiful, simple ring when I felt the air shift in the room at Tristan's appearance.

That is when the hard part began. Because I seriously, really, massively, one thousand percent underestimated how difficult it would be to be in the same room as him and pretend like I didn't know what his skin tasted like under my lips, or how he looked when he told me he loved me, that the first thing he did every morning was kiss the back of my neck.

How was I supposed to do this?

Look over at him and pretend like I didn't know all of those things?

Somehow, I finished my conversation with Kat before Dylan had to politely interrupt to drag her away for a different conversation. Garrett and Rory took her place, and I managed small talk, but out of the corner of my eye, I saw Tristan next to Michael and Brooke. I could see his profile, but not his eyes. If he'd just ... turn a bit, I'd know more of what he was thinking. Be able to have that small connection, that window into his fascinating brain that I was learning everything about.

"You okay?" Garrett asked.

"Yeah. Sorry. Just ... tired." I smiled at him and then Rory, who looked concerned. "I promise. I'm fine. Just not getting much sleep this week."

Rory nodded. "It can be hard getting used to a new place."

Yup. Sure. That was definitely it.

I took a flute of champagne off a tray from a smiling server and took a sip that was larger than was probably polite. "Mmmhmm."

Over the next thirty minutes, I barely remembered a single conversation, but I must have been managing all right, because no one else asked me if I was all right. Cole and Julia were there, and she showed me sweet pictures of their foster son. Brooke chatted with me about the twins, and Michael proudly told me that they were genius children because of their advanced potty-training skills.

That made me laugh, because now all I could see when I looked at Michael was how different he was from his brother. When Michael and Brooke walked away, I risked another glance at Tristan, and he was standing next to the massive fieldstone fireplace, watching me over the rim of his beer.

His eyes on me were steady and even, no concern whatsoever as to whether anyone noticed. I couldn't look away. One edge of his lips curled up and I found myself smiling back. When Dylan whistled for everyone's attention at the front of the dining room, I blew out a slow breath and tore my gaze away from Tristan.

"Thank you for coming tonight, everyone." He curled his arm around Kat's shoulders, his broad chest dwarfing her frame almost completely. She grinned up at him. "Kat and I appreciate your patience in getting this party planned. It uhh, took longer than I thought to convince her to marry me."

A laugh rippled through the room. Kat blushed prettily and smacked his stomach.

"But now that she has, we couldn't imagine celebrating without all the most important people in our lives." He tilted his pint glass toward a group of people on the opposite side of the room, all of whom bore similar hair and eye color to him. "Our family was able to come, as well as friends and coworkers who've been so important to both of us getting where we are today. I never imagined that making one decision in my life—the decision to move here from Michigan—could've led me to this kind of happiness."

He paused and cleared his throat, and I felt my own tighten up at the emotion in his face. Kat's eyes were shiny as she looked up at him.

"But it did. And no matter what I would've had to go through to get here, I'd do it a million times over if it led me to her."

Embarrassed of her tears, Kat buried her face in his chest, which made everyone laugh again, interspersed with a few sniffles.

Dylan raised his glass for everyone to toast, and they did, all but me. Because I sought out Tristan. He was staring right back at me, no smile on his face now.

He blinked and nodded slowly, and I could practically hear his voice saying the same thing. *No matter what I would've had to go through, I'd do it a million times over if it led me to you.*

That's when it hit me, like someone dropped a brick over my head.

There was a reason it felt impossible. To pretend that I didn't know that he licked his bottom lip when he was concentrating on something. That he refused to pour syrup directly on top of his pancakes, always around the perimeter of the plate so that the pancake didn't get soggy, even though I teased him mercilessly about it. That he hated watching the news, that he loved when I sat scrunched behind him on the couch so I could rub his shoulders.

It felt impossible because I knew what it felt like to be in love with him.

I was in love with him.

The number of days were irrelevant. It could've been hours, and once the curtain dropped, I would have known that it was right and real.

As hard as this was for me tonight, he'd done this over and over and over and over. Stood in the same room and pretended like he was something else to me, that I meant something else to him. Something less. I felt a tear hit my cheek before I knew I was crying, and he saw it, starting toward me in the next heartbeat. Then he stopped, his face tight with pain.

And I didn't care who was watching. I didn't care whether I was stealing the spotlight, or if it was rude. All I cared about was that he knew that he was more important than any of that. I set my glass down and ran to him, throwing my arms around his neck and burying my face into his neck as he lifted me easily, his arms banded tight around my waist.

When I pulled my head back and kissed him full on the mouth, a loud roar erupted around us. Cheers, whistles and catcalls, clinking glasses. Tristan inhaled deeply and then smiled against my lips.

"Couldn't wait, huh?" he asked.

I touched my forehead to his, unable to speak, as he held me.

"Are you okay?" he asked quietly, worry evident in his low voice.

After giving him one more soft kiss, I held his eyes. "I love you, too, Tristan. And no, I couldn't wait to tell you."

He exhaled a heavy breath against my mouth, and I smiled.

Someone yelled, "Finally!" It might have been my brother.

But Tristan was too busy holding me tightly, kissing me deeply, for us to pay any attention. The world might have been falling down around us—and maybe someday it would—but in that moment, he and I were the only thing that could have possibly mattered.

This time when he set me down, he held my hand and we walked through the rest of the night together. Just like I had every intention of doing for the rest of our lives. And as he looked down at me, I knew he did too.

A million times over, Dylan had said. I'd go through anything a million times over, if it led me to him.

EPILOGUE

TRISTAN

Six months later

The first time I saw the cottonwood tree in the back of the property, thick branches stretching out like massive arms, I knew that the swing bench would go right there.

We hadn't even bought the land yet when I realized it. Hadn't designed what would end up being our home.

Now the home was there, a perfect combination of my taste and Anna's. Through the floor-to-ceiling windows flanking a stone fireplace, we could see that tree from where we set the couch. The length of the porch wrapped the entire house, but I wanted the swing in that tree.

It would provide shade in the summer, the breeze would smell like crisp leaves in the fall, and in the winter, I could move the swing to the porch if we wanted, but that tree was meant for a swinging bench that could hold us both.

Anna hadn't seen it yet, didn't know I'd been working on it for the last two weeks. In fact, I took more time obsessing over that bench than I did picking out the ring that I would give her while we sat on it later that day.

No, the ring was easy. I'd picked that out two months after she told me she loved me at Kat and Dylan's party. Earlier that day, I stopped by to visit her mom and ask for her blessing.

She'd teared up in the kitchen, not bothering to wipe her face.

Not the reaction I'd expected. "Are ... are you okay?"

She nodded, reached over to grab my hand. "Yes. It's just moments like this where I miss my husband so much it hurts. I wish he was here. I wish he could see the kind of man that loves our daughter. Could see how happy you've made her.

I took a deep breath and gave her a moment to compose herself. "I wish I could've gotten to know him better. It would have been an honor to ask him this, too."

For a moment, she stared at me, then she smiled through her tears. "Of course, you have my blessing, Tristan."

"Thank you," I said on a heavy exhale. She laughed at my obvious relief. Then I held up a hand. "I'm not sure when I'm going to propose just yet. It's ... it's soon. But I know."

Her smile was small, enigmatic. "Your secret is safe with me."

And all these months, she'd kept her word. When Anna and I decided we wanted to live together, but in a house that was *ours*, brand new to both of us. She kept her word when Millie offered us the opportunity to purchase five acres on the far edge of her property in Boulder. And she kept her word during the whole construction process, which went awfully quickly when your uncle put it as the number one priority of the entire company.

We spent our nights and weekends pitching in, using our own bare hands to build the place where our future would unfold.

Anna never pressured me for an engagement, or even press as to when I thought we'd get married, maybe because the piece of paper wasn't something either of us needed in order to build that future.

The subject of kids came up often, and we'd never done anything to prevent it. There were two rooms that we knew would be used as nurseries in our home, down the hallway from our master suite.

Someday, I'd swing them on this bench too, I thought as I tightened the second eye hook into the tree branch. As I folded the black nylon rope twice over and threaded them into the climbing carabiners attached to the hooks, I wondered what those kids might look like. What Anna would look like pregnant.

A grin spread over my face, satisfaction roared through my chest, because given how much practice we'd had, her getting pregnant couldn't be too far down the road.

Yanking on the ropes one more time to test their weight, I nodded when I stepped back and carefully pulled the blanket off the bench. It was considered a bed swing, even though I wouldn't be covering it with a cushion. The oak backrest arched up into a sharp peak, and I'd carved a design snaking through it that I knew she'd like.

The arms were sturdy, and when Michael and I tested how much weight it could hold at the shop, I knew this was a piece that would withstand the passage of time with me and Anna, no matter how our family grew with us.

For the past six months, we'd used the swing that Anna bought me for Christmas, and it fit us both comfortably, but I wanted something new for this place. Something that was only ours.

I glanced at my watch. Our housewarming party was due to start in about an hour, but Michael promised he'd come early so he could help me lift and hang it.

Brooke and the twins were going to distract Anna while we did, and then she'd send Anna out when Michael sent her a text.

They were the only ones who knew what I planned to do tonight. Everyone else would hear once they arrived.

"Oh my *goodness*," Anna exclaimed from behind me, and I hung my head. "Tristan, where did that come from?"

Or maybe it wouldn't happen that way at all since she got home from the store earlier than I expected her.

I turned and held out my arms. "Surprise."

She clasped her hands to her chest and stared at the bench, still sitting uselessly on the grass.

"It's beautiful," she breathed. Her arms slipped around my waist, and I wrapped my arm over her shoulders, then kissed the top of her head.

"You like it?"

Anna laughed. "Umm, yes. Am I not supposed to be seeing this yet?"

"Nope."

She buried her head in my chest with a groan. "I'm so sorry. I ended up going to a different store that was closer. I wanted to get that non-alcoholic sparkling cider for Rory, since she can't drink. Pregnant women are very picky, you know."

When she looked up at me, my heart turned over behind my ribs. I'd never get used to how beautiful she was, or the fact that she was mine.

"It's okay," I said, and leaned down for a kiss.

Her face lit up with a smile. "We can still sit in it, right?"

"On the ground?

"On the ground."

I cupped the side of her face and kissed her deeply. "If I can't stand back up, it's your fault."

Anna laughed. "Fair enough, old man. But I have a feeling you'll be just fine." With a happy sigh, she slid from my arms and settled herself in the swing, her legs dangling forward onto the grass. When she looked up at me, she gave me a sly smile. "Besides, I think your hips are working adequately. You did that thing this morning in the bathtub and didn't seem to have any mobility issues."

"Is that so?" I murmured. "You almost blacked out, they were working so adequately."

Yes, we'd discovered that the edge of our sunken tub was perfect for Anna to hold onto when I kneeled behind her. Adequately, my ass.

Anna's grin was unrepentant. I laughed as I took a seat next to her. My arm came around her and she snuggled easily into my side.

"This is perfect," she whispered. "Thank you for making it for us."

I took a moment and closed my eyes, committed the moment to memory. The way she smelled—lemongrass and grapefruit from her shampoo. The sound of the breeze through the leaves above us. The warm sun against my face.

When I opened my eyes, the green of the grass was vibrant and green, the sun so bright that I squinted. And in the distance was our home. The welcoming front porch with massive timber beams holding it up. Crisp white siding against dark gray plantation shutters, the bright red door that Anna and I argued over for a ridiculous amount of time.

And in my arms, the comforting weight of her.

"I love you," I said quietly.

Anna lifted her chin to look at me and smiled sweetly. "I love you too."

On a deep sigh, I said, "This isn't happening the way I practiced."

"What's not?"

Without speaking, I pulled away so I could slide out of the swing. Her arm dropped without me to hold it up, and she watched me with a furrowed brow as I moved in front of her, propped on one knee.

My hand dug into my pocket until I found the ring: a princess cut vintage diamond ring.

Anna's dark eyes widened in comprehension before I held it up, before I opened my mouth to speak.

"Oh, Tristan," she said on a shocked whisper. Tears shone glossy in her eyes, and she covered her mouth with one shaking hand.

I held up the ring as the first fat tear slid down her cheek.

"Marry me," I said, my voice rough with my own overwhelming emotion. Another tear fell and she sniffed. "Be my wife. Let me love you—just like this—for the rest of our lives."

She laughed and launched herself into my arms. I wrapped her up tightly, breathed her in as she chanted, "Yes, yes, yes, a million times, yes."

We kissed, through her tears and one of my own. She swept it away with her lips, planting kisses all over my face as I pushed the hair back from her face.

Her hand was trembling as I slid the ring onto the fourth finger of her left hand and then pressed a reverent kiss to the knuckle below it.

With her in my lap, we sat in the grass and kissed, the sun warming us from the bright blue sky overhead. Peace. All I felt was peace.

Her eyes were dry when she pulled back to smile at me. "Maybe it's not how you meant for it to happen, but I think it was perfect."

I smiled back at her, and she traced her thumb along the side of my mouth.

"I think it was perfect, too."

She buried herself against me, and my arms tightened around her.

Nothing that had led to this moment with her was the way I would've planned it, but it happened precisely the way it was supposed to.

As long as it ended with her by my side, then Anna was right, it was perfect.

THE END.

AUTHOR'S NOTE

If you've made it to Tristan and Anna's story, then likely you've been with this group of friends since the beginning. I can't find the right words to convey how much that means to me. There are countless books that you can read, and I don't take it for granted that you've chosen to read mine.

Saying goodbye to the Bachelors on the Ridge is bittersweet for me, and maybe to my readers, it feels the same way.

I shed many tears writing this series, but nothing can compare with the number of tears that came with finishing Tristan. I am genuinely sad to say goodbye to him and Anna, and to this group of friends. But as sad as I am to say goodbye, I feel a profound sense of relief that all of them have found happily-ever-after.

To a lot of people, that would sound crazy, but if you're an author, or a hard-core reader, I know you'll completely understand. I needed Anna to fall in love with Tristan the way he's always been in love with her. And now that she has, I can breathe a little bit easier.

I hope you love them even a fraction as much as I do. If you do, then I've done my job.

Here's to the next adventure.

OTHER BOOKS BY KARLA SORENSEN

The Three Little Words Series

By Your Side
Light Me Up
Tell Them Lies

The Bachelors of the Ridge Series

Dylan
Garrett
Cole
Michael

Hooked: A dark romantic comedy co-written with Whitney
Barbetti

The Bombshell Effect

ACKNOWLEDGEMENTS

I'm not going to lie and say it's not SUPER weird/emotional to think about wrapping up my time with the Bachelors on the Ridge. I've spent two years writing their stories and it's been a roller coaster. Tristan was the one I was dreading, to be perfectly honest, so the people who've helped me get through it deserve more recognition than whatever words I might put down on these pages. If I forgot someone, please forgive me, there always seems to be one or two people whose names come to me riiiiight after the book gets uploaded.

My family, friends, and my boys (the little ones that I birthed and the big one that I'm married to) who granted me space and quiet time to write, who (I think) understand my process by now and don't think me crazy for it.

The beginning stages of this book were frustrating, one of the most frustrating times since I began this author journey, and I realized that I needed to disconnect. Personally, and professionally, I needed a brain reset. I need space to think through this book, space to allow my brain to breathe while I wrote it, and I can't tell you how appreciative I am of the friends who respected that need. Not only respected it, but encouraged it, allowed me to be admittedly selfish while I dug into Tristan and Anna. You know who you are.

Jena Camp and Becca Mysoor- the only eyes to read my first draft, and an alpha reading team that was beyond excellent. I know, without a doubt, this book wouldn't be as good if you two hadn't read for me, if you hadn't given me such thoughtful, in-depth feedback. You encouraged me, and allowed me space to process my thoughts on the story and allowed me to talk about these characters more than I've ever talked about characters before. I love you two so, so much.

Kandi Steiner- I can't even tell you how appreciative I am that you gave me honesty and vulnerability, and how brightly your strength shines through those parts of you. You didn't have to make time for me, or for my book, but you did anyway. I adore you.

Amy Daws- You indulge a lot of my crazy, and I'm just really freaking glad you came into my life. Here's to more beta feedback, video chats, broody heroes who end out our respective series, mental breakdowns on release days, and DEFINITELY more porch-hangs at your house. Why do you live so far away again?

Stephanie Reid- For fitting Tristan into a crazy busy schedule, and as always, giving me feedback that has become completely necessary to my process. NO PRESSURE.

Caitlin Terpstra- Your gifs and excitement to read for me mean everything!! I'm so grateful for you.

Staci Brillhart- I met you shortly before this series kicked off, and one of the biggest things that I've learned from you, from being part of your process, is how deeply you invest yourself into how your characters think and why they think that way and who they are. When I started to plot, you asked me why Tristan loved Anna so much, and my immediate response was BECAUSE I SAID SO IN THE FIRST BOOK IN THE SERIES, OKAY? But that wasn't enough. And from you, I've learned the value of *really* digging into who my characters are. I love you, and I'm grateful that you're in my life.

Alicia Gewinner- For a perfect Saturday spent with an old friend, and for the Bumble stories. May they never get worse for you. You have one of the best hearts of anyone I know.

Braadyn Penrod- For another beautiful set of pictures! You have been a joy to work with and I can't wait to see what the future brings for you! You deserve every piece of success that comes your way.

Evan Zalic and Annie Nguyen- my perfect Tristan and Anna. A year ago, I contemplated shaving his hair and giving him a new heroine because I was like, *shrugs* there's NO WAY I'll find them. But it all turned out great, because you exist and are perfectly gorgeous and take even more gorgeous pictures! Hooray!

Najla Qamber- I just ADORE working with you, and you bring my covers to life perfectly. THANK YOU.

Alexis Durbin, Amanda Yeakel and Ginelle Blanch- For making Tristan clean and error-free and especially Alexis, for ALWAYS making me think about birth control. :)

Ena and Amanda at Enticing Journey for the promo, the amazing bloggers that I've gotten to know the past three years who've supported me, and to the readers who have joined me on this crazy journey, who've loved my characters and made me feel that love in return. I could not do any of this without YOU.

Occasionally, in my previous books, I've thanked a random author who will probably never, ever in a million years read my stuff. I have two that I want to add here; Jen Hatmaker and Rachel Hollis. Jen's book, *Of Mess and Moxie*, came at a perfect time for me, right as I started this book. Her chapter on creating, on the beauty of creating any sort of art, was so affirming and refreshing, and it bolstered me in a way that I can't quite explain. The entire book was providential, and my highlighter got a MAJOR workout. Thank for being approachable in your faith, and honest in your life.

And Rachel Hollis. Hoo boy. If I ever meet you, I'mma hug you so tight, you'll be weirded out. Your 90 Day Challenge changed my life. I do not say that flippantly. I do not say that lightly. Your words of inspiration, encouragement and affirmation were the kind that pinned me to the wall and wouldn't let me look away. It was convicting, and eye-opening, and I hope I never, ever forget the lessons that I learned in the process.

"Consider it pure joy, my brothers, whenever you face trials of many kinds, because you know that the testing of your faith develops perseverance. Perseverance must finish its work so that you may be mature and not lacking anything."
James 1:2-4

ABOUT THE AUTHOR

Karla Sorensen has been an avid reader her entire life, preferring stories with a happily-ever-after over just about any other kind. And considering she has an entire line item in her budget for books, she realized it might just be cheaper to write her own stories. She still keeps her toes in the world of health care marketing, where she made her living pre-babies. Now she stays home, writing and mommy-ing full time (this translates to almost every day being a 'pajama day' at the Sorensen household...don't judge). She lives in West Michigan with her husband, two exceptionally adorable sons, and big, shaggy rescue dog.

Photo credit: Perrywinkle Photography

Find Karla online:
karlasorensen.com
karla@karlasorensen.com
Facebook
Facebook Reader Group

Made in the USA
Middletown, DE
26 March 2019